Other historical fiction books
by
Paul W. Feenstra
Published by Mellester Press

Boundary

The Breath of God (Book 1 in Moana Rangitira series)

For Want of a Shilling (Book 2 in Moana Rangitira series)

Gunpowder Green

Into the Shade

Falls Ende short story eBooks
1. The Oath
2. Courser
3. The King

Falls Ende full length novels.
1. Falls Ende – Primus (eBooks 1,2 & 3)
2. Falls Ende – Secundus
3. Falls Ende – Tertium
4. Falls Ende – Quartus
5. Falls Ende – Quintus

Leonard Hardy Series
A Sinister Consequence
A Questionable Virtue - Coming soon.

First published in 2022 by Mellester Press
Copyright © 2022 Paul W. Feenstra

978-1-99-118240-1 Soft Cover
978-1-99-118241-8 Hard Cover
978-1-99-118242-5 Kindle
978-1-99-118243-2 eBook

Published in New Zealand
A catalogue record of this book is available from the
National Library of New Zealand.
Kei te pātengi raraunga o Te Puna Mātauranga o Aotearoa te
whakarārangi o tēnei pukapuka

With heartfelt thanks.
Jane Petersen
Cover Design by Mea

http://www.paulwfeenstra.com/

A Sinister Consequence © 2022 Paul W. Feenstra
Leonard Hardy © 2017 Paul W. Feenstra

Published by
Mellester Press

A SINISTER CONSEQUENCE

By

PAUL W. FEENSTRA

Acknowledgements

I am grateful for the assistance from many organisations and people whom I hounded and tormented with persistent regularity; without them, this novel would not have been possible. The amount of research required to write a book like this is incalculable. Thankfully the resources exist, and people have been only too willing and kind to offer support and provide me with the information needed to complete this novel.

In particular, I would like to thank Jeff Hathcock, Jude Pickthorne CNS, and Jane Petersen. Histology Services Unit - The University of Otago; Archives Support - Wellington City Council; and Capital & Coast District Health Board - Wellington Hospital and the New Zealand Police.

If we don't know life,
how can we know death.'

- Confucius, 551 BC - 479 BC

A SINISTER CONSEQUENCE

Chapter One

Leonard Hardy's cottage nestled snugly against the lower slopes of Mount Victoria in the small city of Wellington and was surrounded on three sides by thick, green bush. He once had neighbours, an excitable Welsh couple, but their house burned down a year and a half earlier when an unattended oil lamp inexplicably caught fire. After the fire, Mr and Mrs Jones told Leonard they'd decided to move further north, where the wind, rain and cold were less bothersome. They relocated soon afterwards, and as it turned out, Leonard didn't miss them much.

Even though the Welsh were touted as outstanding singers, which according to Gareth Jones, had something to do with his family's mining heritage, his tuneless screeching was always an unpleasant distraction and far removed from the agreeable melodic harmonies Welsh miners were commonly renown. Just because his father was a miner didn't mean Gareth was. As Leonard often remarked, "He's no miner; he's a damn bookkeeper."

Leonard was convinced the closest Gareth ever came to going underground was when he had to retrieve his spectacles after they fell into a post-hole he was digging for a new boundary fence.

Then the Joneses had the gall to complain about the weather - and they claimed to be Welsh! Leonard questioned that assertion and suggested to Gareth over the new fence one day that their vaunted heritage probably lay in the more moderate climate of southern England. That was around the time Gareth refused to talk to him anymore.

But the neighbour's fire had left its mark. The unfortunate incident could easily have destroyed his home, and thankfully, due to his quick reactions, it only scorched the side of a wall. Afterwards, Mae urged him to repaint the entire house instead of just the wall as he'd initially suggested. The whole cottage was now painted cream, with a red roof and matching trim, and it was warm, inviting and looked beautiful.

It wasn't a fancy house like some other grand colonial estates perched on Mount Victoria. Leonard's cottage had been built in England about forty years earlier, in the mid-1840s, then transported to New Zealand by ship and fabricated on site. Leonard presumed the cottage had been assembled on a Saturday when workmen were thinking about furlough and not the finer points of precise craftsmanship. Despite its dubious assembly, previous owners had taken good care of the cottage and kept it well-maintained.

A narrow veranda spanned the south side, facing the street, and the front door was centred perfectly in the middle and bracketed by large sash windows that Leonard always had difficulty opening. A hallway separated the living room on the right from the main bedroom on the left, and the kitchen and a second bedroom were in the rear.

Leonard and Mae purchased the cottage about two years earlier, and they had been thrilled with it. She had lovingly tended to the garden, and in Leonard's opinion, their house was still the finest on the steep street.

As he did most evenings, Leonard sat before a small writing bureau in the living room. A lamp burned reassuringly, its warm yellow glow providing enough light for him to peruse his notes in the comfortably furnished room. A davenport dominated one wall, and a well-worn armchair sat near the open window. A narrow bookcase that rose unsteadily from the floor contained an eclectic assortment of fine books, and a small fireplace was built into the rear wall. A small pewter-framed portrait of Mae sat on the bureau facing him.

The curtains swished and rustled, tugging against the hangers as a mild cooling gust of wind found its way inside, swirled around the room and exited down the hallway. Leonard straightened, arched his back and enjoyed the brief respite from an uncharacteristically warm evening, one of Wellington's little surprises.

Caught by the gust, Leonard's notes began to flutter, and before they scattered on the floor, he held them fast and took the opportunity to read through them one last time. They were the obituary notices he'd written in shorthand – the common language of reporters. To meet his deadline, he would transcribe them the following morning, and they would be published in Wednesday's edition of the *Evening Standard* newspaper. It wasn't required for Leonard to work from home, but being rather particular, he preferred to check his notes before transcription. Then at work, he'd rewrite a sentence here or there or add a literary flourish to an otherwise dull necrology before submitting it for approval. Leonard was good at his job, and the paper's senior staff and publisher appreciated his diligence and accuracy.

In addition to his responsibilities of writing the obituaries,

Leonard also had other duties and often wrote copy or checked the grammar on advertisements submitted by paying customers. The *Evening Standard* also published a short column that listed the dates ships were scheduled to arrive and the dates of their expected departures; this was called 'Shipping Intelligence,' which he also compiled. Occasionally, the editor would find other work for him, but never the prime stories - those were typically assigned to veteran reporters with seniority and experience. Leonard didn't complain; his responsibilities took him away from the office to the docks, the coroner's office, the morgue, or to visit an advertiser. It kept him busy, and that was what he needed to be.

It was getting late, and Leonard was unusually weary. He put his notes in his valise and picked up an empty teacup; Mae always chided him for leaving empty cups and plates in the room, and so out of habit, he took the cup to the kitchen, shut and locked the front door and went to bed.

At precisely 7:00 a.m., Leonard woke. After dressing and before attending to his morning rituals, he lit a fire, placed a pot of water on the stove and patiently waited for it to boil. He didn't feel his usual energetic self this morning and hoped he wasn't becoming ill. A strong coffee would help, or so he hoped.

A regular advertiser with the newspaper, a man who hauled grain and seeds from the docks to his warehouse, had recently given him a large sack of Arabica coffee beans. An accompanying wink suggested no questions should be asked about their provenance. After some trial and error, Leonard perfected the grinding and roasting technique and was now partial to a cup of coffee before beginning his day. As the water approached boiling, he thought about the tasks he had to accomplish and remembered he also needed a haircut.

If asked to describe himself, Leonard would have replied he was of average height and weight, although a raised eyebrow may have prompted him to redefine his weight assessment slightly. He was in his early thirties, with a slight premature thickening of his middle, which added a few pounds to his otherwise unremarkable physique. His hair was fair and thick and, despite constant grooming, always looked untidy. Wellington's persistent winds did little to help in that regard. Mae had always preferred he kept his golden locks short, but he seemed to forget to have them trimmed these days. Unlike many men, Leonard kept his face unfashionably clean-shaven as he couldn't grow a thick full beard, and when he tried, it looked thin and raggedy.

An unexpected knock on the door disturbed that moment of pleasure when he took his first sip. It wasn't the timid knock of a neighbour or the rapid, harried knock of someone needing assistance; it was an authoritative measured rap, an important knock requiring an immediate response. Guiltily, he placed the coffee bag out of sight, buttoned his waistcoat and quickly checked his appearance before walking down the hallway to greet the caller.

The constable at the door was tall and stood confidently with his hands clasped behind his back. His chin was tilted slightly upward, which meant he had to look down his unusually long nose to make eye contact. *Not a welcoming first impression*, Leonard thought, somewhat pleased the Arabica coffee was safely hidden from the constable's inquisitive gaze.

"Mornin', sir. I apologise for the early intrusion, but I'm a wondering if you could spare a moment to assist me with my inquiries?"

The constable's eyes darted everywhere, down the hall, through the open window, and even towards the garden and the unusual assortment of herbs Mae had passionately cultivated.

Leonard leaned to the side and looked inquiringly behind the constable, but he was alone, besides his horse tied to the fence. The movement caused him to feel briefly giddy, and he almost fell. He quickly grabbed the doorframe for stability and, luckily, remained standing. It happened so suddenly, and he doubted the constable even noticed. *Perhaps it was the strong coffee rather than the beginnings of something more serious*, he thought with a naïve measure of hope.

"I'll be happy to help in any way I can," said Leonard with natural curiosity after composing himself. "Er, need I be alarmed?"

"This way, sir." Without hesitation, the constable turned briskly and walked down the short garden path to the road, where he waited for Leonard to catch up.

As Leonard reached the road, he saw Mrs Theodopoulous standing just down the hill, wearing the same grimy threadbare housecoat she always wore. Her dog, as usual, was straining on its leash and sounded like it was choking. She scowled at him. He didn't take it personally - she scowled at everyone.

The constable walked across the road, stopped and pointed at the dense bush that grew along the road's edge. "Right here, sir."

Curiously, Leonard approached the bushes and recoiled at the morbid sight of a body lying on the ground. He assessed the young man appeared to be a few years younger than himself, perhaps in his late twenties and reasonably dressed. Astonishingly, the poor chap had a hole in his head, presumably an entry wound from a bullet. It was a disturbing sight, especially this early in the morning, and it didn't help his queasiness - Leonard was horrified. The body was only thirty feet from his home and accompanied by a distinctly unpleasant odour that smelled like urine. He turned away from the disturbing corpse.

The constable extracted a notebook and a pencil stub from his pocket. "Are you familiar with this man, sir?"

"What happened? Why is he here?" queried Leonard with wide-open eyes. "Was he shot?"

"Was hoping you could tell me that," replied the constable as he inclined his head at Leonard. "You'll notice the man is deceased."

"Apparently so, but why?"

"Sir," sighed the constable, "is this man known to you?"

"Ah, no, I've never laid eyes on him before."

"Name?"

"I told you, I don't know the poor fellow, and I certainly don't know his name."

"The constable closed his eyes briefly. "Your name, sir?"

"Of course - Hardy, Leonard Hardy."

"Mrs Theo..." The constable consulted his notes. "Mrs Theodopoulous was walking with her dog at six this morning when the dog encountered the deceased right here. She hadn't heard any disturbance during the evening, and since the body was found outside your home, it makes sense to expect you'd know something," elaborated the constable.

That explains the smell of dog urine, thought Leonard. "That surprises me."

"What does, the fact that there's a body in front of your home?"

"No, er, yes, but... that Mrs Theodopoulous didn't hear anything. She's got a nose and ears to rival her dog." Leonard looked over his shoulder quickly and saw Mrs Theodopoulous still scowling.

The constable lacked the gift of humour and didn't respond. He cleared his throat. "Ah, Mr Hardy, what time did you hear the gunshot?"

"I didn't hear a gunshot."

"Of course you did - perhaps a memory lapse?"

Leonard thought long and hard. There was no sound he'd heard that could be construed as a firearm being discharged during the evening. "No, there was no gunshot," he reiterated.

"Could you be mistaken, Mr Hardy?"

"I had my windows raised, as you can see," Leonard pointed to his windows, which remained open since the night before. "If there were a loud noise or a disturbance, I would have heard something, don't you agree?"

The constable swivelled his head in the direction Leonard indicated, looked down his nose at the open window, and grunted.

"Have you checked his pockets for identification?" asked Leonard.

"Yes, they contain nothing," said the constable as he scribbled in his notebook.

"No doubt you'll be taking the body to the medical practitioner?"

"Yes, I'm waiting on a dray to arrive."

Leonard gave the matter some thought as the constable completed his notes. "I write the obituaries for the *Evening Standard*, so I will get any further details from the coroner a little later."

The constable looked up, his pencil poised, and smiled

condescendingly. "Very good, sir."

Leonard was uncomfortable being near the body. "If there's nothing else, I, uh, really must go to work...."

"Of course, Mr Hardy. If I have further need, I know where to contact you. I apologise for disturbing your morning. Good day, sir."

Relieved, Leonard turned and gave Mrs Theodopoulous, who was still gawking, a version of his own scowl and returned to his home, somewhat perplexed. This was an unexpected turn of events. There was a murdered man, a body lying in the bushes outside his house. Who would do such a thing and why? He'd visit the medical practitioner to retrieve the coroner's obituary list a little later; perhaps Alex could shed some light on the identity of the poor chap. Leonard put on his jacket, grabbed his hat and valise and walked to work, lost in the perplexities of a homicide and a gunshot he did not hear.

The offices of the *Evening Standard* newspaper were a good twenty-minute stroll from Leonard's home. He walked along Courtenay Place, Manners Street and finally onto Willis Street.

The reporters all worked at their cluttered desks in a large room called the bullpen. In order of seniority, the most experienced sat at the rear, while the junior reporters were positioned tactically in front, where they could be keenly observed and productively managed.

Undaunted and with some excitement, Leonard turned around and told the story to a few reporters, but an unidentified body with a bullet hole through its skull surprisingly attracted no more than a little interest; deaths were commonplace to seasoned reporters.

From his exalted position at the very rear, Mr Pembroke, the

Evening Standard's senior reporter and editor, looked up and over his spectacles and offered some advice. "Mr Hardy, let me tell you, there are only three ways you'll make a story out of this. Either the killer confesses, there's a witness, or, lastly, the victim happens to be a well-known public figure. If you haven't any of those... then you're wasting your bloody time." In concurrence, the other reporters nodded in supplicant agreement.

"Don't you think it's peculiar that a man was killed, I mean murdered, with a bullet right in the middle of his forehead? Somehow he was taken away from the crime scene and then tossed to the side of the road. It suggests that the murder wasn't random, and it probably wasn't an accident, but a carefully thought out plot containing dark elements of mystery and intrigue."

Someone sniggered.

"You may be right, lad, but you don't have anything unless someone comes forward with information." Mr Pembroke sighed and scratched his head through his sparse grey hair with a pencil. "Of course, we'll devote a few lines to it, but unless the post-mortem uncovers useful and valid evidence, and that's probably a long shot, then what do you have? Certainly not a story."

"Hmm, yes, I see your point. Then perhaps I will ask around, and someone may yet come forward."

"Worth a try. Check with the constable in a day or so; he may have some news for you."

"Thank you, Mr Pembroke."

Mr Pembroke grunted. "And now, if you'll allow me some peace, I'd like to finish this feature on the Woman's Temperance Christian Union meeting - now that's real journalism." He held up a sheath of notes to emphasise his point. Everyone laughed. Mr Pembroke was in inordinately good humour this morning.

Leonard looked puzzled.

"You doubt the commitment of these fine women, Mr Hardy?"

"Ah, no, sir."

"Women's rights, prison reform and nutrition. Bear that in mind." He waved his notes like a pennant.

"Yes, sir, and thank you, sir," replied Leonard feeling a little less spirited. Perhaps he was romanticising the unfortunate incident and instead should channel his enthusiasm to more realistic ventures like prisons and food as his superior urged.

"It would behove you to make yourself useful, Mr Hardy."

"Yes, sir." Apparently, Mr Pembroke's good mood was short-lived.

By early afternoon, Leonard had the latest shipping information he needed, and once he'd checked his work, sought approval from Mr Pembroke, and dropped it off at the typesetter's in the adjoining rear building, it was time to leave. As scheduled, he left the *Evening Standard* offices and headed to the northern end of Kent Terrace, where the city morgue was situated.

Chapter Two

$\mathcal{A}$ pervasive odour assaulted Leonard's nostrils as he approached the morgue. It was a smell he could never get used to. Some days, if he was lucky, the wind kept the stink away, but at the height of summer, the warmer than usual temperatures strongly contributed to the fetid rank pungency of rotting garbage.

The morgue was located near Wellington's waste collection site, and the source of the smell was its refuse. Ineffectual incinerators could not handle the volume of accumulated rubbish, so it lay rotting in piles until it was eventually burned. There were rumours that a large incinerator was to be built to cope with the growing need, but predictably there was always the pecuniary argument that slowed actual progress. Mr Pembroke had covered that story for the paper.

Leonard entered the morgue through the unattended rear employee door, as he'd done hundreds of times. It was a small, quiet place, and to respect the dead, he always felt he should act accordingly - with brevity and solemnity, emotions he'd grown somewhat accustomed to. Today, though, was a little different, and he felt vulnerable to a flood of sentiments he could typically suppress.

He felt a chill that preceded an overwhelming feeling of sadness and loss and stopped momentarily to steady himself. He knew he was foolish, and he shrugged, swallowed once and searched for

Alex.

The sound of whistling from one of the rooms was a clue that the venerable Dr Alexander Leyton was performing a post-mortem examination. When Leonard opened the door and entered the room, the whistling stopped. Alex was aggressively removing the top half of a cranium he had just sawed through while his assistant watched, enthralled. Blood cascaded onto the floor as the cadaver's brain lay exposed.

"Ah, Leo, welcome - perfect timing. Come and look here; you'll never see a better example of the mess an aneurysm can make."

Leonard had been subjected to these sights countless times, as Alex enjoyed seeing him in obvious discomfort at the gruesome sight of a partially eviscerated body.

"I'd rather remain here for the moment if it's all the same to you." He swallowed a time or two and stared at a blank wall.

Alex grinned and turned to the corpse, poking around in the deep recesses of the deceased's brain. "Cause of death: a subarachnoid haemorrhage."

The medical practitioner's assistant, William, dutifully recorded Dr Leyton's finding.

"We're finished here, William - clean up, and I'll look over the notes later."

William turned to Leonard and gave a small wave as he began shifting the disfigured body and cleaning up the mess.

Alex walked over to a tub and began washing his hands. "I heard they discovered a body outside your house this morning."

"I had a constable banging on my door at 7:30 a.m. And woe and behold, across the road, there was a poor chap lying in the bushes with a hole in his head."

"The constable believes you aren't being cooperative," said Alex, raising an eyebrow as he dried his hands. "He claims you failed to inform him when you heard the gunshot."

Leonard shook his head in frustration. "The man was murdered somewhere else, Alex, and the body was likely tossed into the bushes later. There was no gunshot; I heard nothing."

"Then it does seem very likely the man was killed elsewhere. Why is the constable being so obstinate?" Alex stepped away as William began mopping the floor.

"Because he's lazy, and it makes the investigation easier for him if the man *was* killed outside my home."

Alex laughed and led Leonard away from the room to his cramped, dark office down the hall.

Dr Alexander Leyton enjoyed his profession. His patients seldom complained, never returned for additional treatment, and other than having an assistant, as was legally required, he was left alone to do his work. Alex was a competent physician and enjoyed pathology.

Outside of regular working hours, Alex devoted all his time to his beautiful wife, Bridgette. They were a wonderful couple; she was truly delightful, and Alex doted on her. Dr and Mrs Leyton enjoyed socializing and hosted frequent get-togethers with close friends. Alex was an excellent host, and an evening of entertainment with the Leytons was well spent.

If there was one thing Alex was sensitive about, it was his pate -

15

he was prematurely bald. If he lacked self-confidence by not having a healthy shock of hair, he more than compensated for it with his affable, gregarious nature.

"Have you had an opportunity to look at the mystery man?"

Alex removed his apron and hung it on a dusty skeleton in the corner. He claimed it was once a sweetheart he used to see on occasion. "I had a cursory look when they brought him in, but I cannot legally examine him until twenty-four hours have passed and the coroner has exhausted all avenues to ascertain his identity and notify the next of kin." Alex removed a small stack of medical reference books that prevented Leonard from sitting down on the only chair.

"There was no identification on the body. I wonder who he is," Leonard mused. "Sad, though, a healthy, young man killed by a bullet to the head...."

"He was not," Alex said, dropping the books on the floor with a thump.

Leonard looked at his friend in surprise.

"He was far from robust - the poor chap looked to be in a torrid state."

"Oh! Then I'm mistaken," Leonard amended.

"Look, Leo, I will likely begin the post-mortem examination on him tomorrow morning. If I find anything interesting, I will not keep it from you." Alex paused a moment as he looked at his friend. His eyes softened, and his smile wavered. "Are you still coming over tomorrow evening? Bridgette is quite eager to see you."

"I don't think so; I have some matters to attend to."

"I see," Alex paused. "We'll be playing Cupid's Box."

16

Leonard couldn't help but smile. "That's your favourite parlour game."

"It is indeed, and we are a gentleman short. If you don't come, we won't be able to play the game as intended, will we?" Alex looked at Leonard with an expectant grin.

Leonard let out an audible sigh. "Very well."

"Good chap, eh." Alex leaned forward and clapped Leonard on the shoulder. "You realize that pretty, little thing, Mary, will be there? And I happen to know with some authority she has more than a casual interest in you."

Leonard turned away.

As was customary when Leonard visited Alex at the morgue, they discussed a few topics of mutual interest and made arrangements for upcoming events of social importance, most of them, Leonard habitually declined to attend.

Finally, Alex handed over the coroner's reports for the obituaries. Leonard glanced at them casually before putting them in his valise.

"I can inform Bridgette to expect you tomorrow evening, then?" Alex said when Leonard stood to leave.

"Yes, I'll be there, don't worry. I'm only attending to ensure you don't misbehave."

They said their goodbyes, and Leonard exited the building. The wind had changed direction, and the unpleasant refuse odour was virtually undetectable. Not trusting Wellington's fickle weather, Leonard rushed away to his next errand.

He was always greeted warmly at the markets, and the Chinese vendors at their stalls plied him with fresh vegetables and fruit in season. They often refused to take his money and engaged him in small talk, which was conducted in halting English and, worse Chinese - as Leonard knew only a few words of Mandarin, including a simple sentence or two of greeting. He stayed with the sellers for a while, but the onset of a headache prompted him to leave.

He picked up his gifts and valise and wearily trudged home.

Leonard reached for his Macassar oil, applied a liberal amount to his scalp and worked it through his hair. Then, using a rag, he patted his head to absorb the excess oil and carefully styled his hair with a brush. Again, he'd forgotten to have it trimmed – *tommorow*, he reminded himself. Satisfied, he looked in the mirror and decided he was more or less presentable, then washed his hands to remove the oil. He felt tired this evening and still suffered from the effects of a lingering headache that diminished his interest in socializing, but he wouldn't renege on the promise he'd made to Alex. He eased into his coat, looked in the mirror one last time, and hurriedly left the house - he was going to be a little late. Rather than utilize the convenience of notoriously slow public transport and take a tram, he reluctantly decided to take a faster Hansom cab.

He patiently waited for a cab at the bottom of his street. It wasn't a long wait as there were abundant cabs, all competing for fares. As the closest cab pulled up, Leonard carefully assessed the driver, who sat high at the rear of the coach, to ensure the man wasn't intoxicated. For a good reason, the driving habits of cabbies and coachmen were of some concern to him. It was a regular occurrence for cabbies to suffer from inebriation, and in such a state, it was not uncommon for them to fall from their high perch as they rounded a corner. This left the horse in charge of the driverless conveyance, and the animal was unlikely to obey a barrage of panicked verbal commands from an agitated passenger or pedestrian. This wasn't a desirable scenario for a gentleman on his way out for an evening socializing with friends.

Not entirely convinced of the driver's sobriety, Leonard, nevertheless took the risk, opened the door and slid into the two-man bench seat. The hatch on the roof squeaked open, and the cabbie waited for an address. Within moments the black, painted Hansom cab clip-clopped towards the suburb of Newtown at a moderate and safe speed.

Bridgette greeted him at the door with a warm hug and a fashionable peck on each cheek, while Alex shook his hand and gave him a friendly pat on the shoulder. Once inside, Leonard greeted the other three guests cordially. He knew them all well, except for Mary, whom he'd only met a few times. It was no secret that Bridgette and Alex had deviously schemed to play matchmakers.

Mary and Bridgette were distantly related. Mary, a recent immigrant from England, had few friends in her newly adopted country and only one relative on her mother's side, an ageing and frail aunt who resided in Upper Hutt, a northern community twenty miles away. Mary currently lived in the Leytons guest room as a boarder, an arrangement that pleased everyone. Bridgette and Alex had decided that Mary was a suitable match for Leonard and that the two would make a handsome couple - a sentiment Leonard was somewhat ambivalent about.

The Leytons' house wasn't ostentatious, but it certainly was adequate, and everyone managed to squeeze into the living room and sit comfortably after extra chairs were brought in. Refreshments were immediately offered, and an assortment of *hors d'oeuvres* graced a small table. It was no surprise for Leonard to find himself seated beside Mary, and she immediately struck up a pleasant conversation. It would have been rude not to engage with her, so he listened politely as she recounted an anecdote about a French farmer who insisted Napoléon Bonaparte had been reincarnated as a rooster. It was a delightful story, and to his surprise, he enjoyed Mary's company and laughed heartedly at her wit.

The other two guests were both unmarried. Jonathan, a tall and lean man, was a solicitor and a junior partner in one of Wellington's most prestigious law firms, mainly specializing in criminal law. Meredith was a midwife. Jonathan had met Meredith at the Leytons a few months earlier and was now calling on her regularly. Meredith was a widow; her husband had succumbed to a malady and sadly passed away at sea during their voyage to New Zealand four years earlier. It seemed to Leonard that Jonathan and Meredith were quite enamoured with each other and appeared happy; he was pleased for them.

Bridgette stood, clapped her hands once for attention, and reminded everyone it was time to play. Once a week, she invited her friends to her home for an informal evening of fun, laughter and parlour games. This week's game was Cupid's Box. Bridgette held a small wooden box and, with mock ceremony and as the rules required, passed it to the nearest person on her right, Alex. The game was his favourite.

"I give you my Cupid's Box, which contains three cards. On each card is a single short phrase; whom do you love, whom do you kiss, and whom do you dismiss," she said.

Alex now held the box and opened it. Without looking, he randomly pulled out one of the three cards and read aloud the single question written on it. "Whom do you love?"

Bridgette theatrically looked around the room and then pointed, "Mary!"

Everyone laughed, and Alex repeated what Bridgette had said earlier. "I give you my Cupid's Box, which contains three phrases - to love, to kiss, and to dismiss," and then handed the box to Mary.

Without looking, Mary pulled out a card from the box and asked Alex, "Whom do you love?"

Alex rose from his chair and made a show of looking at everyone in the room. He raised his hand, swept it dramatically from one person to another and stopped. "Jonathan!"

Naturally, there was more laughter.

Mary turned to Leonard and said, "I give you my Cupid's Box, which contains three phrases, to love, to kiss, and to dismiss." She stood.

Leonard pretended to push his sleeves higher up his arms as he rummaged in the box. He looked up so all could see he wasn't cheating and pulled a card, holding it firmly to his chest so no one could see what was written on it. He waited.

"Leonard!" Bridgette cried impatiently.

Grinning, Leonard looked down and slowly read the phrase on the card." Whom do you kiss?" According to the rules, Mary had to make a decision.

The room erupted with laughter. The girls were clapping; Alex was bent over, enjoying the anticipation of watching Mary receive an awkward kiss, while Jonathan was beaming in delight. They were all savouring the moment. Mary had a twinkle in her eye as she slowly looked around the room. Everybody waited expectantly: whom would she select? Gradually, Mary's arm pointed from one person to the next, paused momentarily and then continued on and stopped. "Leonard!"

Alex wasn't surprised and burst out laughing. Jonathan was stamping his feet with glee, and Meredith blushed while Bridgette smiled and observed Leonard. Leonard felt his face flush and couldn't look Mary in the eye. He swallowed uncomfortably.

"C'mon on, old boy," encouraged Alex and burst out laughing again.

Mary remained standing and waited. She didn't look at Leonard, but a small smile played on her face, and Leonard had to oblige - such were the game's rules. He slowly rose to hoots of merriment and moved closer to Mary, who hadn't moved. He leaned forward as Mary turned her head towards him, raised his hands and gently held her shoulders as he tilted his head down. Mary held his eyes; she didn't look away as her mouth opened, and they kissed. The room fell silent. It was a long kiss.

"Oooohhhh," cried Alex. "You saucy devil, Leo, I didn't know you had it in you; well done."

Leonard sat down, unsure about what had just happened. It wasn't the quick peck everyone expected, and his heart was beating furiously. He turned to face Mary, who also sat down. She returned his look, and her eyes continued to shine.

Slightly out of breath, Leonard turned to Meredith. "I give you my Cupid's Box, which contains three phrases - to love, to kiss, and to dismiss." He stood.

Meredith quickly grabbed a card, hoping for another kiss question. It wasn't to be. "Whom do you dismiss?"

"Noooo," they all cried in unison.

This was easy; Leonard waved his arm over the room and pointed at Alex. Being dismissed meant that Alex had to fill his glass with whatever he was drinking and empty it in one gulp. He did this with gusto.

And so the game was played, everyone had fun, and the evening progressed smoothly. Jonathan and Meredith said farewell and departed early while Mary was helping Bridgette in the kitchen.

Alex casually brushed away cigar ash that had fallen onto his trousers, placed the cigar on an ashtray, and leaned in. "I performed a post-mortem on your mystery man this morning, Leo."

Leonard looked up from the cake he was eating. "I'd forgotten all about that."

Alex looked thoughtful. "I believe that if the bullet in his skull hadn't killed him, then the *Atropa belladonna* I found in his stomach eventually would have - and sooner than later, I may add."

"Isn't that a common weed called deadly nightshade?"

"Yes, or simply belladonna. It's poison, Leo - someone wanted that man dead."

"That's astounding. I almost feel sorry for him. I wonder what he'd done to deserve that?"

"His liver and kidneys were not healthy, which is unusual for a young man," Alex remarked.

"Are you sure it was belladonna? Could you be mistaken?"

"I had a case earlier this year where a young girl died, you remember that?"

"Yes, the Martin girl, I recall."

"She had been eating belladonna for a while; she thought they were cherries...."

"And the case of this chap has, uh, similarities?"

Alex nodded. "I'm going to make some enquiries with a colleague at the hospital."

"Why? Didn't you just say he'd been poisoned and shot?"

"I found some peculiarities - some inconsistencies when I dissected his thalamus."

Leonard gave a quizzical look.

"Part of the brain."

"Oh, is it relevant?"

"It might be. I don't know for certain just yet. Oh yes, he also had a mild contusion around an ankle."

"What would cause such an injury?"

Alex shrugged.

"I knew there was something odd about that murder, I told you so." Leonard scratched his head. "But we're no closer to discovering who he was, are we?"

"No, we are not, my friend."

"Well, that's a job for the police, and they're better equipped to investigate the murder than I," said Leonard.

Alex laughed. "And you're no longer interested in playing at sleuth?"

"No, I don't think so. If the police discover anything of interest that points to his identity or who the killer is, then the paper will assign an accomplished reporter to cover the story. There's no room for me, sadly."

Bridgette and Mary returned with the tea.

"Why the glum expression?" asked Bridgette as she rotated the teapot to help draw the tea.

Even though there were empty seats, Mary continued to sit

beside Leonard.

"Leo is disappointed he can't investigate that murder I told you about."

"That's not true," Leonard said defensively. "I made a decision earlier, and it isn't worth the time and effort."

Alex laughed. "If the situation changes and more information comes to bear, you'll think differently."

"I don't feel I have the energy at the moment. I've been a little out of sorts the last couple of days."

"Are you poorly?" asked Mary, surprising him with a look of worry.

"It's probably the weather - it has been unseasonably hot, and you may have caught a chill in a draught," offered Alex.

"You need to rest, Leonard. You've had a trying year, and you really should take better care of yourself," suggested Bridgette as she poured the tea through a strainer.

"I've felt better," Leonard said as he turned back to Mary. "And I will return home and rest once I've finished my tea."

All three of them stood on the step and said goodnight to Leonard. Then Alex and Bridgette returned inside, leaving Mary alone with him. Leonard felt awkward. Neither spoke.

"Thank you for your friendship, Mary. I enjoyed this evening very much," Leonard finally said. "I'm sorry I'm not good company, it's just...."

"I understand, Leonard," she said quietly. "I enjoyed the evening too."

They stood facing each other. Leonard felt uncomfortable. "Good night, Mary," he gave her a smile and turned and walked away, down the steps and onto the street where he'd catch a cab home. He looked over his shoulder - Mary was still there.

Clouds partially obscured the moon as he ambled slowly down the hill to Adelaide Road. He wasn't in any particular hurry. He was thinking of the evening, the fun he'd had, and the laughter they'd all enjoyed. His friends were truly fantastic, genuine and caring. He replayed the kiss with Mary over in his mind. But his thoughts were confused, unsettled and jumbled. It took him a few moments to realize that someone had stepped up and walked beside him.

Chapter Three

Leonard didn't break stride as he turned to look at the man. The stranger faced straight ahead and walked along, ignoring him for the moment. He wore an expensive coat, although it wasn't really cold, and a stylish homburg hat pulled down low over his brow. A full beard and darkness made it difficult to see his features, but Leonard didn't think he was elderly. *Perhaps the gentleman just wants company,* he thought.

"It's a lovely evening, Mr Hardy."

"Are we acquainted?" asked Leonard.

"In a manner of speaking, yes, we are."

Leonard remained quiet while he tried to place the man. Realising he'd never seen him before, he stopped. "Then you have me at a disadvantage, sir. Please identify yourself!"

The stranger stopped one pace ahead but didn't turn around.

"Do you intend to see me come to harm? If so, sir, can I suggest another time when I'm feeling better so that I might defend myself?"

"No, Mr Hardy, we do not wish to see you come to any grief, far from it." The stranger took a step to the side, faced Leonard, and extended his hand. "My name is Winston Crumb."

Unsure, Leonard held back. "Crumb, as in biscuit?"

"Yes, and same spelling."

"I find your approach and manner quite unsettling, Mr Crumb. Would not it be better to approach me in a more civilised and less threatening way?"

"Of course, Mr Hardy, I apologise. Perhaps we could talk

27

briefly?" Mr Crumb raised his arm, inviting Leonard forward.

"I'm about to catch a cab, Mr Crumb, so you don't have much time." Leonard waved to a Hansom cab that conveniently loitered nearby.

"Then let us share the ride and the fare," offered the dapper stranger. "That will give us some privacy during our discourse."

Again, Leonard looked closely at the driver before cautiously following Mr Crumb into the cab. As soon as he was seated, the stranger continued.

"Mr Hardy, please let me be frank." Mr Crumb adjusted his position on the narrow seat so he could easily see Leonard's face from the glow of a tiny oil lamp. "You seem to have found yourself in a rather precarious position, and we feel compelled to give you a warning: you are placing yourself in considerable danger."

"Excuse me, sir, the only danger I find myself in is riding in a cab with a driver who may be intoxicated and a stranger who knows more about me than he should!" Leonard was becoming angry.

"Please, Mr Hardy, calm down. May I address you familiarly as Leonard?"

"No, sir, you may not!" Leonard looked away from Mr Crumb and out of the window.

There was a moment of silence as Leonard placated himself.

Mr Crumb spoke again. "Mr Hardy, you had the distasteful experience of encountering a body outside your home a day or so ago."

Leonard's head whipped around to stare at the stranger.

"We have learned that your persistence in determining the victim's identity and the reason for his untimely death may lead to complications that could have severe, if not fatal, consequences for you."

"Is this some sort of threat, Mr Crumb?"

Crumb placed his hand on Leonard's arm. "No, no, please do not misunderstand me. We have reliable information, and we know with some certainty that any further inquiries you and your esteemed friend, Dr Leyton, are pursuing may result in an unfortunate accident for either one or both of you."

Leonard made to interrupt, but Mr Crumb held up his hand. "Wait, please. We don't want to see you or the good doctor succumb to any misfortune and urge you to stop this folly. Please take our warning seriously."

"Come now, Mr Crumb - I'm a lowly copywriter for a newspaper. I have no authority, no power and keep my employment purely at the pleasure of the newspaper's publisher. I pose no threat to anyone. Why would anyone want to..?"

Mr Crumb tapped his fingernails on the window as he considered his response. "I'm not at liberty to divulge all we know, but I can tell you that events you cannot control were put in motion some time ago. The recent murder and your admirable natural curiosity that prompted you to pursue this has brought you under the attention of a… let's say, an undesirable element."

The cab pulled over at the bottom of Leonard's street, and the driver waited patiently.

"If what you told me is true, why can't you share any details?"

Winston Crumb sighed. "Because we have not identified who those people are, Mr Hardy. Please accept my word on this."

Leonard was silent as he considered the warning. "Who are you? You keep saying *we*."

"We, Mr Hardy, are known as Patrons of New Zealand."

"I've never heard of you."

"And it's likely you never will again. I believe this is where you depart, Mr Hardy. I do hope you feel better soon. Good evening."

Leonard opened the door and alighted onto the street. He turned back to Winston Crumb, who remained inside and held his gaze. "You and your people may rest easy, Mr Crumb. I have already decided not to pursue this matter any further." He closed the door firmly and walked away.

His head spun. To be accosted on the street by a stranger and told he was in danger? Ridiculous! *What in heaven's name is going on?* He turned back to the cab, but it was already making its way down Courtenay Place. He buried his hands in his pockets and began walking the short distance up Marjoribanks Street towards home.

He wasn't feeling well. The walk up the hill was a struggle, and as soon as he arrived, he threw off his clothes and collapsed on the bed.

His dreams were disturbing – vague nightmares consisting of images and voices. When he woke, it was still dark, and he was thirsty. His mouth felt like cardboard. He stumbled to the kitchen and drank a glass of water, then returned to bed, where he tossed and turned. He was hot, couldn't sleep and wished morning would come. The encounter with Mr Crumb repeated itself over and over in his mind, and it was disturbing.

When the sun rose, Leonard slowly sat up. He must have dozed for a while and felt unwell and exhausted. He felt miserable as he sat on the edge of the bed with his head in his hands. With a concerted effort, he stood, pulled on a robe, and went to the kitchen to light the stove and make coffee. While the water was heating, he went to his writing bureau and composed two notes, placed them in envelopes, and then addressed and sealed them. He padded back to the kitchen and prepared his coffee - a little stronger this morning. The coffee helped.

Once dressed, he grabbed the two envelopes, slowly walked down the road and waited for a cab. He paid the driver and asked him to deliver each envelope to its addressee. The first note was to Mr Pembroke at the *Evening Standard,* informing him he was ill and wouldn't be at work that day, and the other to Alex, letting him know he was unwell and asking to speak with him urgently at home.

It seemed like an age before he finally crawled back to bed and fell into a fitful sleep.

A timid knock on the door woke him, and he sat up with a start. He knew it wasn't Alex - his knock sounded more like a *rat-a-tat-tat.*

"Oh, Leonard, you look dreadful," said Bridgette as she pushed past. "Go back to bed. I brought some chicken soup and some chlorodyne, orders from Alex."

"Well, hello, Bridgette," he said in surprise, still holding the door open long after she passed.

"Are you back in bed?" He heard her voice from the kitchen, along with the sound of clanging pots.

"Just about," he grunted as he pulled the sheet over.

"Good. I'm pleased the stove is still lit!"

Bridgette walked in and sat on the bed. "You poor boy, you really are sick, aren't you?" She felt his forehead with the back of her hand. "You have an elevated temperature," she patted his leg. "I'm heating some soup for you."

"Thank you." Leonard looked at her with watery eyes. "Where's Alex? I need to see him, Bridgette, it's urgent."

"Oh, don't fuss - he'll visit later, he couldn't leave the morgue. Apparently, there's a kafuffle, and everyone's in a panic, and he asked me to come and attend to you." Bridgette stood, turned to the mirror, and pinned down some wayward strands of hair.

"What's going on down there?"

"Something about William not showing up this morning. Do you think green suits me, Leo?"

"Is he sick as well?"

"No, nothing like that. It seems they can't find him... Oh dear, the soup!" With a swish of skirts, Bridgette exited the room.

Leonard shuddered with apprehension.

"You really need to clear these boxes of junk from the kitchen, Leo!" shouted Bridgette.

Mr Winston Crumb's ominous warning resonated through Leonard's mind.

Bridgette carried a tray into the bedroom. "Eat the soup before it gets cold." She stopped, noticing Leonard's worried expression. "Leo, what's wrong?"

Leonard closed his mouth. "Uh, nothing, Bridgette. I was just thinking."

She frowned, placed the tray on his lap, and then produced a bottle which she began vigorously shaking.

"When will Alex be here?"

"Later, Leo, I'm not sure when. Now you must have some of this, Alex said so."

Leonard refocused. "That had better not be chlorodyne. I don't care what Alex says, I refuse to drink that putrid stuff - it's poison. Put that bottle away, Bridgette."

She gave him a sympathetic look and placed the medicine on the dresser, and handed him a spoon so he could eat the soup. She returned to the mirror and continued to fix her hair. "Mary enjoyed your kiss last night, Leo," she said with a smile he couldn't see.

"Bridgette, you will not draw me into a conversation about kissing."

"I know you did too...."

"Bridgette!"

Satisfied her hair was again as it should, she began folding the clothes that were scattered on the floor and placed them neatly on a chair. "You really need a good woman here."

"I have a...." He stopped and looked down.

"I'm sorry, Leonard, that was very insensitive. We all care and worry about you. You know this, don't you?"

He nodded, unable to speak.

She returned to the bed and sat down. "Come; finish your soup and sleep. Alex will be here in an hour or so, and you don't need me here to needle you."

They sat in silence as Leonard finished eating. She removed the tray, arranged his pillows and kissed him on the head before departing quietly. He drifted off into a troubled sleep.

Leonard sat up with a start. The room was dark. It was evening, and he felt the presence of someone in the house. *How long had he been asleep*? He eased the sheet off and quietly slid out of bed. Fumbling around, he found his robe and slipped it on. He paused a moment and listened but couldn't hear anything. Then he heard it - a creak. Winston Crumb's words echoed in his head. *The cause of his untimely death may lead to complications that could have severe, if not fatal, consequences for you.* Was there a villain in the house? He had no weapons. He felt around with his foot until he found his shoes. He carefully picked up the left one, as the right shoe already had enough scuff marks, and held it firmly by the toe. He crept around the door and paused, the shoe held high and back, ready to strike. He heard the creak again; it came from the living room across the hallway. He took another step and saw a shadow move. His heart began pounding in his chest.

"Leo?"

"I heard a noise, I...."

"You're awake?"

Leonard immediately relaxed and felt relieved. He dropped the shoe. "Let me light the lamp, Alex. How did you get in?"

Once the lamp was lit, Alex saw the shoe and grinned. Leonard stood in the middle of the floor in his robe, with his hair standing at oblique, impossible angles. He was a sight. "Bridgette left the door unlocked so I wouldn't wake you if you were sleeping. More importantly, how are you feeling?"

"Miserable, but we must talk, Alex. Something happened last night on the way home from your place."

Leonard told of his odd meeting with Winston Crumb.

"What do you think, Alex?"

Alex stirred his coffee and watched the dark liquid spiralling in his cup. It was like a mini whirlpool. "Patrons of New Zealand?" He took the spoon out of the cup and sipped the steaming brew. "Your Mr Crumb sounds like an oddball."

"But he says we are both in danger if we pry further into the mystery man's death."

"I also have my profession to consider, and I have a deontological obligation to the coroner's court, Leo. I have to do my job," Alex replied earnestly.

"Well, I have no moral or legal obligation to investigate anything. I want no part in this," he replied.

"And never a wiser word was spoken."

Both men remained silent for a heartbeat or two as they enjoyed Leonard's finest Arabica coffee. "Can you ask your friend at the docks to get me some of those beans?"

"And what of William? Is his disappearance part of Crumb's unhinged assertions?" asked Leonard, ignoring the request.

"I wish there was a rational explanation for his absence today, but I can't possibly think of one. I can only hope he arrives at work tomorrow with a plausible excuse."

"And if he doesn't?" inquired Leonard.

Alex shrugged. "I don't know."

"Do you think they could come after me? After all, it's not like I've actually done anything…"

"They know where you live," laughed Alex.

Leonard's watery eyes opened wide. "That's it! I knew something was bothering me about last night, but I couldn't put my finger on it."

Alex looked up from his cup. "About what?"

"The cabbie - he never asked for an address, and I didn't give him one. We both got in, and Mr Crumb began talking almost immediately. The cabbie knew where to go. And as I now recall, the cab wasn't very far from where Mr Crumb and I were talking on the street."

"So you're saying the cabbie is part of this? Oh, come now, Leo, that's a little far-fetched."

"They knew of the body that was discovered outside my home!"

"You've been unwell, tired, and probably a little overwhelmed by meeting Mr Crumb and still under the effect of that rather passionate kiss with Mary. Perhaps you just forgot you told him."

Leonard glowered at his friend. "And how did Mr Crumb know I'd be walking down the street from your home? He was waiting for me, Alex. I think I was followed, and I'd wager you were too."

"I think that's highly unlikely."

"When have you ever known me to be forgetful, Alex?" Leonard didn't think it appropriate to mention his forgetfulness about getting haircuts.

"Never."

"It's a conspiracy!" Leonard said. "But I'm not concerned because I have no interest in the case of the man who was killed twice - shot and poisoned!"

"I think you need to go back to bed," suggested Alex, "and you do need to take some medication."

"Not the poison Bridgette tried to give me. I've got something around here I can take."

"Good, see that you do," said Alex, rising. "I must go home, I'm exhausted. I hope you feel better tomorrow, Leo."

"Yes, and I'll try to get you some of those coffee beans."

Leonard remained in bed all the next day. Mary came to visit and brought more soup. She fussed over him and, to his delight, even made coffee. He didn't remember her leaving, but when he woke late in the afternoon, he noticed she'd cleaned the house for him.

Alex also visited. He brought his doctor's bag, which made Leonard nervous - his patients were usually dead. He gave Leonard a thorough examination and pronounced him alive – only just; then, to Leonard's chagrin, he double-checked to make sure.

The bad news was that William had failed to make an appearance, and the police were now involved. Alex still scoffed at the notion it had anything to do with the mysterious Mr Crumb and had not mentioned his warnings or the peculiar encounter with Leonard to the police.

Leonard slept well the following night, and in the morning, he felt remarkably better. He noticed Mary had done a thorough cleaning, and the kitchen was tidy and organised, more than it had been in some time. He found a note she had left for him. With care he unfolded the paper and read it several times. It made him laugh. How very characteristic of her. In a neat hand, she had written, 'Everything is better with a smile.'

While cleaning, Mary had found some boxes and, unsure where they belonged, placed them on the kitchen table for him to sort through. Leonard began looking through the contents while he waited for the water to boil.

He remembered now – this was an assortment of herbs Mae collected and dispensed. Taken for various maladies and ailments, these herbs all had peculiar curative properties and were a good alternative to western medication, provided the correct herb and dosage was prescribed for the appropriate condition. He recalled she had previously given him a herb called Echinacea when he was ill. He smiled; he could still remember its Chinese name, *Zi Zhui Ju.*

He pulled a few jars out of the box and looked at the labels. Her handwriting brought back a flood of memories and emotions. He still missed her so much. She'd told him that some jars were made of clay to prevent sunlight from ageing the medicine and weakening its effectiveness. Others were made of brown-coloured glass, and some were clear. Each vessel had a small label affixed. Written precisely in her fluid handwriting, there were the English and Latin labels and then, in Chinese characters, the Chinese name. Mae had begun to teach him how to speak and read Chinese but never finished.

There was forsythia, mulberry leaf, chrysanthemum, perilla leaf, liquorice and belladonna. He stopped and stared as the water boiled furiously on the stove. Without taking his eyes off the jar containing belladonna, he took a couple of sidesteps to the stove and removed the pot.

"Belladonna," he kept saying the name over and over. "Belladonna." Why would Mae have poison? She wasn't a killer; she wouldn't even allow him to kill insects when they found their way into the house. At her insistence, he had to remove and relocate them safely outside. No, Mae wasn't a murderer; she was a healer trained in Chinese herbal medicine. He picked up the bottle and studied the label. Underneath the written word *belladonna* was the Latin name *Atropa belladonna,* and then the Chinese characters. He would show Alex the jar when he arrived later. He rummaged through a few boxes and eventually found the Echinacea jar, but it was empty and needed refilling. He took a deep breath. He had avoided visiting Uncle Jun and his dear wife Ming, but he knew he could postpone it no longer. Uncle Jun's shop was where Mae had obtained the bulk of her herbs and remedies. He made up his mind and would call on them on Saturday.

It was dark when Leonard woke. He felt so much better after sleeping and lay in bed, listening to the calming, peaceful sounds of the evening. Where was Alex? He'd never come to see him.

"Alex? Alex, are you here?" he shouted. There was no response. Leonard climbed out of bed and walked to the living room, hoping Alex had snuck in again, and he wasn't there.

Chapter Four

Leonard sat at his desk at the *Evening Standard* and re-read the document he'd just written.

> *Sudden Death*
>
> *Michael Lawrence Taylor died suddenly at his residence on Grant Road at half-past 7 o'clock on Tuesday evening. The cause of death will, in all probability, be determined upon by a Coroner's jury. It appears the deceased returned home shortly after 6 o'clock complaining of being attacked by pains inside the head. From a chemist, a tincture was obtained with the object of allaying the pain. This, however, had little effect, and death ensued at the hour named. The services of a medical gentleman do not seem to have been solicited. The deceased was about 40 years of age, a widower, and possessed two dwelling houses in Adelaide Road. No suspicious circumstances surround the occurrence.*
>
> *The inquest will be held at the Metropolitan Hotel on Molesworth Street Wednesday next at 10 a.m.*

He was distracted and couldn't focus. He re-read the notice. He'd last seen Mr Taylor at the morgue with his head sawn in half and his blood draining on the floor. His thoughts returned to Alex; no one had seen him, and William still hadn't been found. He began to feel genuine concern for both their safety.

Leonard's life revolved around death. Death provided him with income, and his best friend dissected dead people. Was it a preoccupation, some morbid need to surround himself with the dying and deceased? Was death the cause of his own sadness and misery? His dear Mae had been taken from him, and how he's suffered since. The enduring pain was all but unbearable.

No doubt someone was suffering as a result of Mr Taylor's death. Yet he, Leonard Hardy, gave little thought to Mr Taylor's relatives and loved ones who now grieved, but instead, he dwelled selfishly on his own misery and sense of loss.

Should he continue to allow Mae's death to dominate his own existence? Would it disrespect and devalue his memory of her, and would it diminish the love he felt if his grieving for her were to end? But surely memories are lasting, and couldn't he remember and honour her and press on with his life without the agony of endless sorrow? And of Mr Taylor and a hundred others like him, who mourn for them? Does everyone who loses a loved one endure the same feelings? But grief was a solitary avocation, Leonard reasoned, and when we experience bereavement, we withdraw into ourselves, often without a care or thought for the feelings of others.

Yet those who die do not know it – being dead is not an event experienced by the living. So grief and sorrow are selfish. We mourn for our loss, not theirs. *A petulant wont to evoke sympathy from others?* he wondered. How many times had he accepted condolences when Mae died? How differently people treated him before she died and now. The benefits of grief were numerous, and he had allowed himself to wallow in the advertency of commiserations. In pity. Was it time to let go and wake up each morning joyous? If Mae truly loved him, she would want nothing more than to see him embrace life and love again.

Leonard again read the document he held. Would he write one of these for William as he had done for Mae? He placed the obituary back on his desk, stared blankly at the wall, and strangely thought of Mary's kiss and his guilt at having enjoyed it.

"Mr Hardy?"

Leonard pulled guiltily away from the wall and his dark thoughts and looked at the youth.

"Mr Beaumont requests the pleasure of your company immediately, sir."

"Did he say why?"

"No, sir."

Leonard was puzzled. *Why would the publisher want to see me?*

"Very well." Leonard rose from the chair and sighed. "In his office?"

The youth nodded and walked away.

He knocked once and waited. He couldn't see through the frosted office windows.

"Enter!" came the muted reply.

Leonard entered and was surprised to find the constable with the long nose sitting comfortably on one of Mr Beaumont's fine leather chairs.

"Please sit, Mr Hardy."

Leonard nodded in greeting to the constable and sat as he was told. The constable returned to reading notes from his pocketbook.

"Are you feeling better?" asked Mr Beaumont.

"Yes, very much, sir, thank you."

Beaumont nodded. "You still look a little drawn."

The constable cleared his throat, a reminder to discuss the business at hand.

"I believe you've met Constable Hastings. I will let him continue."

Leonard shifted his position so he could better see the constable. He was curious and a little apprehensive.

"When was the last time you saw Dr Leyton?"

In the blink of an eye, Leonard's apprehension turned to fear, and he turned to Mr Beaumont in question. Beaumont kept his expression neutral.

Leonard swallowed. "Two days ago. I was unwell and at home, and Alex came to check on me and gave me an examination. Why is this relevant, constable?"

"Did you see Dr Leyton yesterday at all?"

"No, he was supposed to visit me later in the day, but he never arrived. Has something happened; is this why you're asking these questions?"

Constable Hastings flicked back a page or two in his pocketbook and tapped the page with his pencil. "Unfortunately, Dr Leyton met with a tragic accident late yesterday afternoon on Riddiford Street near the hospital. We believe he was struck by a carriage and is now deceased."

Leonard groaned aloud. He raised his hands to his head and

rocked in the chair. Mr Beaumont came round the desk.

Hastings' eyes narrowed as he watched Leonard's reaction.

"How did this happen?" asked Mr Beaumont, who was also acquainted with Alex.

"We suspect the coachman may have been intoxicated, although there were no witnesses."

"So why did you come here to question me?" spluttered Leonard. "If you knew the cause of death, why come here?"

Mr Beaumont poured a glass of water for Leonard.

Leonard turned and looked at the constable.

"As there were no witnesses, I'm attempting to ascertain his movements – the direction he was walking, where he was going..."

"And where was he going?" Leonard asked.

"I now believe he had departed the hospital after visiting with an associate and was probably on his way to call on you."

"Is his death suspicious?" Leonard asked as he wiped his nose on a handkerchief.

"I'm not at liberty to comment on that, sir," replied Constable Hastings sternly. He paused a moment as he considered his next question. "Are you aware of anyone who has a grievance against Dr Leyton?" He raised an eyebrow in question.

"No, I don't. Alex was liked by everyone."

Mr Beaumont returned to his seat. He listened patiently and remained quiet.

Leonard's head spun. ...Alex? Dead? He felt nauseated and couldn't think. He shook his head slowly from side to side in disbelief. Poor Bridgette. "And what of the disappearance of Alex's assistant, William? Is Alex's death in any way connected?" Leonard asked.

"Difficult to say, sir. What motive could there possibly be to connect the two gentlemen, other than they work together? It seems that Dr Leyton's death may be purely the result of an unfortunate accident." The constable made eye contact with Leonard. "Certainly, there have been two linked deaths. The unknown gentleman who was shot in the bushes outside your home, and yesterday, your friend, Dr Leyton." Hastings' gaze didn't waver. "And further, the mystery of his assistant who is missing. People around you are dying, Mr Hardy. I caution you to take care." Constable Hastings inclined his head.

Leonard looked down at the floor at his feet. His best friend was dead. Was this really happening? His world was being turned upside down. "I don't know what to say," Leonard said, just above a whisper.

"I apologise for being the bearer of bad tidings. Gentlemen." The constable rose and walked to the door.

"Wait!" Leonard had a moment of clarity.

Constable Hastings stopped.

"Did Alex have any documents or paperwork with him?"

Constable Hastings retrieved his notebook from his pocket and flipped a few pages. "Ah, here it is. I have the inventory of his possessions." Hastings looked up and smiled. "Items found in his possession were one billfold, one packet of pipe tobacco, one pipe, one box of matches, a set of keys and a pencil. Nothing more, Mr Hardy." Hastings turned to leave again.

Leonard thought a moment. He knew what Alex always carried with him. "What about a portmanteau?"

The constable shook his head.

"If there were no witnesses, how can you suggest the coachman was intoxicated? Was he detained?"

"A coach was in the vicinity and seen around the same time driving erratically in a dangerous and reckless manner. An assumption was made that it was that coach which struck Dr Leyton."

"So you actually don't know who killed Alex, and the suspect remains at large?"

Constable Hastings flicked his eyes to Mr Beaumont, "That is correct, Mr Hardy."

"Then it may not have been an accident at all?"

"Is there something you're not telling me? Mr Hardy, if you have information about his death, then you have..."

"Constable," Mr Beaumont interrupted, "if Mr Hardy has any information, I'm sure he will pass it on to you. Thank you for coming by." The constable was dismissed.

Constable Hastings paused and gave Leonard a long unfaltering look before he opened the office door and departed without another word.

Leonard was in shock. He sat unmoving.

"I think it may be best if you went home, Leonard."

For reasons obvious to Leonard, he declined the offer of a cab, choosing instead to walk. His heart was heavy. The news of Alex's death rekindled recent painful emotions and threatened to boil over in frustration, sadness and loss. Feelings only a short time ago he felt he could master. He walked alone with his valise and his introspection. Passers-by were ignored, he greeted no one, and by the time he approached the morgue, he was perturbed. He stopped and faced the building, ignoring the smell of refuse, and stared at it reflectively. He could walk past and go home or go inside and experience a quiet moment to grieve. Because he was a frequent visitor, Alex had shown him how to enter the building using the employee entrance, a non-descript door surrounded by crates and rubbish inside a small, enclosed yard.

Leonard walked briskly into the yard, opened the door and confidently entered the building. He could hear voices from another room. Without pausing, he turned right and headed towards Alex's small office. It wasn't locked and probably never was. He stepped inside and glanced around the small room. As expected, Alex's apron hung irreverently from the lower jaw of the skeleton. Leonard smiled in honour of Alex's vivacious personality, a fond memory. He didn't know why he came here, and he didn't know what he sought. Although the thought of discovery was unnerving, and what would he offer as an excuse if challenged? He didn't care. It just made him feel closer to his dear, departed friend to be here.

Memories came to mind of the good times they'd shared ... laughter, lots of laughter... Despair threatened to overwhelm him, and he shook his head defiantly, refusing to succumb to the emotional storm that threatened his consciousness. "Not now, not here," he mouthed quietly.

He eased behind the desk, sat on Alex's chair and looked around the room at the clutter. Notes galore. Reference papers, journals, and medical books. He even saw a bone. Without touching anything, he methodically scanned the items scattered over the small desk and felt reassured by the familiarity of his friend's possessions.

The desk was messy like someone else had already rummaged through it. He began at the left side and worked his way towards the right. Most notes were related to appointments and had references to specific injuries. He stopped when he saw a piece of paper with his name written on it, but it wasn't written in English, and Leonard knew precisely what it was. With a furtive and pointless glance around the room, he quickly placed the paper in his pocket and continued looking. There was nothing more of interest, and he decided he should leave before he risked discovery. He exited the building with his heart pounding and thankfully didn't encounter anyone.

Leonard slowly walked home and mulled over the strange interview at the newspaper with the constable. There was an unsettling malevolency to Constable Hastings, and it frightened him. It was almost like the man harboured a deep-seated loathing for him as if it were personal, and he took perverse pleasure in seeing his reaction to the news of Alex's death.

And of Alex? Was it just an accident, or was he murdered? Was this part of Mr Crumb's warning, and was he behind his death? And what was Alex doing at the hospital? He mentioned he wanted to check on something about the mystery corpse. Was that why he went there?

By the time Leonard trudged up the hill, he was tired and emotionally spent. He needed to see Bridgette soonest.

An envelope had been pushed under the door and lay on the floor in his hallway. Leonard picked it up and saw that it was from Mary. Once inside and at his writing bureau, he opened the envelope and was immediately enveloped with her fragrance. Altogether, not unpleasant. He began to read.

Dearest Leo,

I apologise for the quintessence of this missive as you have been recently indisposed, but circumstances prevail that require your presence here this evening. I find myself overcome by a profound sadness and appeal to your generous nature and friendly disposition to attend to Bridgette in her time of need and despair. It would suit Bridgette to share in fellowship, and as her closest friends, we can make this torrid time less wretched and share together in geniality and memories.

It is my pleasure to receive you at 6:00 p.m.

Ever your friend,

Mary Worthington

He felt Bridgette's loss and would do whatever he could to help ease her sorrow.

He ate a quick dinner, washed up, and left the house.

It was too far to walk from Marjoribanks Street to Newtown, and Leonard reluctantly decided to use a cab instead of the slower tram. It wasn't a long wait, and as customary, he spoke briefly to the driver. Something about the cabbie was familiar, but he couldn't identify what it was. After a few words, he judged the cabbie to be sober, gave him the address to Bridgette's, and they set off.

At the path leading to Bridgette's home, he paused and took a deep breath, steeling himself for what lay ahead. He walked up the steps, knocked and waited. Mary came to the door and welcomed him warmly with a generous hug followed by two pecks, one on each cheek. No doubt a habit picked up from Bridgette. For some odd reason, Leonard didn't object or feel uncomfortable; he enjoyed her affections. Mary's eyes were red, and she'd apparently been weeping. She led him into the living room where Bridgette sat, dabbing her eyes, looked up at him and immediately burst into tears again. She stood to greet him, and Leonard walked over and held her tightly. Once he'd pried himself free, he greeted Jonathan, who sat stoically, and Meredith, who sniffed away into a delicate and colourful foulard.

It was difficult at first; everyone was quiet and melancholic, and then Mary began telling a story about Alex that changed the mood. Soon everyone was talking. They spoke about the good times they shared, and each recounted an anecdote, a memorable time they had with him. The atmosphere changed from despair and sadness to amusement and laughter. Alex had that effect on them, even in death. Jonathan had just finished telling a tale, and Leonard was laughing so hard he needed to wipe his eyes. He put his hand in his pocket for a handkerchief and found the note he acquired from Alex's office. With curiosity, he unfolded it and studied it carefully.

"What is that?" Mary asked.

"It's a note from Alex's office. I was there today, and I saw this note on his desk and took it," he smiled sheepishly.

"Leonard, you can't do that!" admonished Bridgette.

Everyone turned and waited for him to explain his actions.

"It doesn't look like a note," Mary stated. The unfolded paper contained a series of pen strokes, half circles, dots and angled lines.

Leonard held the note so that everyone could see. "It's shorthand; it's how reporters write quickly when they wish to record word-for-word what a person is saying."

"Yes, a similar form of swift writing is used in the courts," volunteered Jonathan.

"Except the medical profession isn't exactly supportive of doctors using this method to write," said Leonard. "Too many opportunities for errors and misdiagnosing."

"Why did you take the note, Leonard, and what does it say?" Bridgette asked.

Leonard raised the note again, pointed to the symbols, and explained the message. "The first characters say 'Leo,' which is underlined, and the second set says '*Atropa belladonna*' and the other words…" Leonard had to look closely, "It looks like the next words are 'shaking palsy', and there are two question marks after it. Then the word 'stomach' and it looks like he's written 'died,' each underlined."

"What is the relevance of this note?" Jonathan asked.

"Well, that comes back to why I took it."

Bridgette and Mary knew about the discovery of the body outside his home, while Jonathan and Meredith did not. Leonard went on to explain how Alex found belladonna inside the stomach of the mystery man and then the strange meeting with Winston Crumb and being warned away. Leonard explained everything he knew from the beginning.

Jonathan looked thoughtful, "I've heard of the group 'Patrons of New Zealand.'"

"You have?" Leonard exclaimed.

"Yes, it was a year or so ago. It was a minor criminal case, as I recall. A witness claimed to have overheard a conversation between two men, and I remember it quite clearly because the group appeared to be xenophobic."

"What's that?" Bridgette asked.

"Where someone has an intense dislike for foreigners," replied Jonathan.

"Oh dear," said Mary, "that includes all of us, doesn't it? None of us were born in New Zealand."

"I think you'll find that in this case, it's also a racially inspired dislike."

"Race?" asked Leonard.

Jonathan nodded, "You have all heard of the organisations called the Anti-Asiatic League, Anti-Chinese League or the Anti-Chinese Association."

"Don't forget the White New Zealand League," added Leonard.

"These organisations are quite the trend these days, and they all have an aversion for Orientals entering the country. In fact, I've heard rumours the government is considering imposing a 'Coolie Tax' to limit the number of Chinese immigrants entering New Zealand, or something like that. Many people dislike them taking work away from New Zealanders."

Leonard was riveted and sat quietly listening.

"And what of this Patrons group?" Bridgette asked.

"While all the anti-Chinese groups are very public and open about their activities, I think the Patrons of New Zealand are more clandestine. They operate behind closed doors but ultimately, I believe, share the same harsh sentiments as the others."

"I think that's disgusting," Meredith finally contributed. "Such behaviour and hatred are unchristian." Jonathan patted her hand in support.

"Then why would this Mr Crumb, from the Patrons of New Zealand, warn Leonard and Alex away from investigating that man's death? And why is belladonna involved, and what does that have to do with it?" Mary asked.

"Alex found belladonna in the body."

"I presume that's a poison?" Jonathan asked.

"It's also known as deadly nightshade," answered Leonard. "He told me if the gunshot didn't kill the man, then the poison probably would have. He suspected that two separate people were trying to kill the poor fellow or one very determined person. At first, they tried to poison him, which didn't work, so they used a gun. I just don't know what the reference to shaking palsy is," Leonard said.

"Oh, that's easy," said Mary, "shaking palsy is an illness, and these days it's called Parkinson's disease. We've had a few patients who've suffered from it, isn't that correct, Bridgette?"

Bridgette nodded.

"Parkinson's disease, that's an affliction that affects the elderly, is it not?"

"Not always, although most are aged," Mary stated.

Leonard scratched the back of his head.

"I wonder what your mystery man did to incur the wrath of a person, or persons unknown, to want to kill him?" Jonathan asked reflectively. He stood and walked to the window and looked out. "Leonard, do you believe this group, Patrons of New Zealand, is behind this?" He turned around and faced his friends. "The disappearance of Alex's assistant, Alex's death, and the murder of the man outside your home? Are they all connected in some wicked plot?"

This was the question Leonard had been asking himself. He gave himself a few moments to collect his thoughts, then looked up at Jonathan. "I think they are nothing more than unexplained random coincidences and a series of unconnected events that we could easily convince ourselves are related but probably are not."

Jonathan had everyone's attention. He stroked his beard and came to a conclusion. "I'm not so sure, Leonard." He tried to pace the floor in the living room, but it was too small; he returned to his previous position with his back to the window. "I have an old client whom I shall call on. I hope he can provide me with some information on this suspicious group, Patrons of New Zealand. We at least know with some certainty they exist."

"Don't you go upsetting that lot," Meredith said, "I don't want you coming to any harm."

"Of course, dear," Jonathan replied as he left the window and sat beside her.

"Have the police provided you with any information?" Leonard asked Bridgette.

"Only that the carriage that struck Alex has not been identified, and they are doing their best to resolve the matter," she replied bitterly and began weeping again.

Chapter Five

Overnight rain had turned the streets of Wellington to mud. It was nothing like the devastation of a heavy winter's downpour, but of concern, a few small puddles of dirty water now collected in deep ruts, a good reason to be wary of a passing coach or cab. Leonard stepped around or leapt nimbly over puddles and navigated his route so he could walk on dry, firmer ground. He kept an eye on approaching wagons and ensured he wasn't near any standing water as he was convinced coachmen took particular delight and aimed to shower pedestrians with filthy water as they passed.

As customary and weather permitting, Leonard always enjoyed a stroll on Saturday mornings. Today he had chosen to visit Mae's uncle, who lived with his wife above a small shop they owned on Frederick Street. They were a delightful couple, and he'd always enjoyed accompanying Mae when she called on them. This would be the first time he would visit them since she had passed.

He walked down Kent Terrace and planned to cross Tory Street, then head towards Frederick Street to avoid the abhorrent Haining Street. A most unpleasant, narrow thoroughfare where criminals loitered on corners, brazenly hustling the virtuous and chaste, or for that matter, even surreptitiously each other. Brawls were common, theft rampant, and many who called this area home thrived in the culture of lawlessness and need. Opium dens, teashops that overtly sold more than char, and women of immoral character and habits plied their trade with jaded expressions and lost hope. One street south lay Frederick Street, perhaps not much better but undoubtedly safer.

As he approached the neighbourhood, a few bystanders gave him wide-eyed suspicious stares, and even a small, speckled dog took interest, sniffed him and moved dejectedly on. Above him, through an open window, he heard a quarrel, the accused being flayed with a host of profanities. Further along, a middle-aged woman hung out a window and beat a dusty rug, uncaring of those who passed beneath her, the debris scattered, borne on the wind like winter snow.

As Leonard walked closer to his destination, the buildings began to change. No longer predominantly residential, they became businesses with a few shops scattered amongst them. He passed furniture makers, coachbuilders, locksmiths and blacksmiths. A few places sold fruit and vegetables and a variety of imported goods and Oriental spices. Some sold alcoholic spirits. There were more people in this area, and most chose to ignore him. Leonard was neither big nor small, he walked with purpose, a gentleman intent on reaching his objective. He didn't dilly-dally, stare at people or loiter; he was just another individual briskly going about his lawful business. Which was why he was surprised when a man stepped in front of him and barred his way.

"Can I helps ya?" asked the unkempt man.

Leonard had to quickly stop, or he would have collided with him. "Thank you, but no." He sidestepped to walk around him, but again the man moved and stood in his way.

"You'll be need'n sumthin, or ya wouldn't be here, now would ya?" He gave a knowing wink. "You want'n some ladies or remedies? I can help ya, I can." He smiled, showing a mouthful of decaying teeth. "Ah, I knows what you're after. You'd be wanting Chinese molasses."

Leonard recoiled; the man's breath was rancid. "Thank you, but no, I'm in no need of anything, and if you kindly move, I'll be on my way." He smiled.

A few curious people stopped to watch, but no one offered assistance.

"You gots money, then? I bets you ave, haven't ya? A gentlemans like you don't comes here unless you want somethin." He laughed. "How much ya got?"

Leonard took another step to the side, but the detestable man prevented him from continuing.

"I will not ask you again, move aside, sir!" This time Leonard raised his voice and extended his arm to push the man away but had his arm batted down.

"Are you tryings to assault me? Yes, I think you are. You might be a robber."

Things were becoming a little complicated.

Leonard turned to walk back from where he'd come, but the man grabbed his coat. He couldn't step farther into the street because a Hansom cab approached, and he was trapped.

His heart racing, he tried to think of a way out of this predicament. He didn't hear the cab stop.

The cabbie leapt down from his high seat carrying a horsewhip that he brandished with expert confidence.

"Give me your money, mister!" the robber snarled as he held a fistful of Leonard's coat.

The cabbie stomped up to the aggressive stranger and loomed

threateningly over him, "Get out of here, or I'll lay this whip alongside your head, I will. Leave the gentleman alone!"

Needing no encouragement, the would-be robber released Leonard's coat, held his hat firmly on his head and, in fear, ran in the other direction. Some bystanders laughed.

"Sorry about that, sir. Are you all right?" asked the cabbie.

"Yes, thank you, I'm fine. I'm pleased you stopped when you did," Leonard replied earnestly.

"Very well, if you don't require a cab, then I'll be on my way. Good day, sir."

"Yes, again, thank you." Leonard watched the cabbie climb back onto his high seat and urge his horse to move on. As the Hansom cab passed, the cabbie doffed his hat. Leonard immediately recognised him. It was the same driver who delivered him to Bridgette's late yesterday afternoon. An extraordinary coincidence, or was it?

Leonard was a little shaken by the encounter, especially as it happened during daylight and not in the evening, as one would typically expect. He knew the man's intention was to waylay and rob him, of that he had no doubt whatsoever, and fortunately, the familiar cabbie had come to his rescue. He walked on, contemplating the strange events.

Frederick Street was just around the corner, and with dawning realisation, Leonard suddenly came to a halt. The cabbie! He was the same person who drove the cab with Mr Crumb. Of course, how could he have not seen that earlier! He glanced around to see if he was still close, but there were no cabs nearby; one had passed a few seconds earlier with a fare and headed down Tory Street, but no empty cabs were waiting. Had that cab been following him? This was very odd.

Haining Street was ahead of him and easily distinguishable by the rabble who lingered on the corner. A man lay in a yard, incoherently blethering in an opium-fuelled fantasy, his opium pipe discarded on the ground at his side. Leonard ignored him and turned right.

Known locally as Tong Yan Gaai, or Chinese People's Street, Frederick Street was almost wholly inhabited by the Chinese. Even mid-morning, the animated sounds of gambling dens, the upward pitched shriek of triumph or the downward howl of anguish drifted onto the street outside. A small Oriental girl tugged his sleeve and confidently held her hand out for money. She stared at him hopefully with large innocent eyes. Leonard reached into his pocket, fished out a halfpenny, and placed it in her hand. It wasn't enough, and her expression suggested he could afford more. He shook his head and moved on, intrigued by the activity, the people, and as always, the hurly-burly of Chinese culture.

A hand-painted sign hung at a precarious angle above an open shop front. Prominent Chinese characters with English written beneath advertised, *Chen Jun Qiang, Purveyor of Medicaments and Chinese Herbal Remedies.*

Leonard cautiously entered the shop and took in the familiar disarray. Along one entire wall were row upon row of small wooden drawers stacked almost from floor to ceiling. The opposite wall contained glass jars on shelves full of unidentified dried matter. Some floated in liquid, preserved like aged relics. Hemp sacks were stacked randomly, some with their contents open for inspection or purchase. The smell was a medley of a thousand ingredients blended into a singular complex and distinctive odour; it wasn't unpleasant, just unusual.

The countertop displayed bowls of mysterious powdered substances, colourful and potent. Part of the counter was cleared and wiped clean, and a large mortar and pestle sat waiting to be used beside a worn abacus. Behind the counter, Chen Jun Qiang was on a step stool and reaching high for a drawer; he extracted a dried tubular root, closed the drawer, climbed down, expertly cut a small portion, and crushed it with the pestle. He added a small handful of herbs and tipped the contents into a small glass bottle. The satisfied customer, a portly Oriental, handed some money to Mr Chen, bowed his head twice and gave Leonard a suspicious look on his way out.

Chen Jun Qiang looked up and recognised Leonard immediately. "Leo!"

Early gold discoveries brought Chen Jun Qiang, 'Jun,' his wife Ming and their young family to New Zealand in the 1860s. Most Chinese gold miners came to New Zealand alone, their wives not permitted to join them, but Jun had no intention of returning to his homeland. Before restrictions were devised to discourage Chinese immigration, he brought his family with him. With moderate success in gold mining, Jun and family slowly travelled up the southern island and eventually settled in Wellington. With pockets bulging with gold, he bought property on Frederick Street and fulfilled his life-long dream of establishing a business in *Zhongyao Xue*, or Chinese herbal medicine, that he was formally trained in. His five grown children now lived locally with their young families.

Jun grinned as he threaded his way around merchandise towards Leonard. It was difficult to guess Jun's age; Mae estimated he was between sixty and eighty, but he moved and acted like a man half that age.

"Oh Leo, Leo, Leo, is good to see you," cried Jun in his high-pitched sing-song voice. "Why you no come to see me before?" He barrelled around some sacks and embraced Leonard warmly.

"Is wonderful to see you, Uncle Jun, and yes, it has been some time."

Jun separated himself from Leonard, stepped back and held him at arm's length as he looked him over. "You no look so good."

"I've been ill, but I'm feeling much better now, thank you."

Jun frowned and shook his head. He turned quickly and shouted over his shoulder in rapid-fire Chinese. Immediately a female voice responded. Within seconds Ming threw back the curtain that separated the shop from their private area in the rear and, with her arms spread, ran to Leonard. After a lengthy hug, the tiny woman rattled off more Chinese. Ming spoke only a few words of English, and Jun translated. "She say you are bad boy for not coming to see her. Why you no come?"

Before Leonard could answer, Ming led him by the elbow through the shop, out back and pushed him to a chair. "Tea?" she asked. One of the few English words she knew, although from experience, he knew it wasn't a question.

"Yes, please."

Jun sat opposite Leonard at a small table, looking thoughtful as Ming boiled water.

"Is because of Mae-Ling?" Jun said.

"Pardon me," replied Leonard, taken back by the directness of the statement.

"You know." Jun smiled.

Leonard looked across the table at the old man. He was tiny, diminutive and frail. His cheeks were hollow, his teeth were gone, and wisps of grey hair poked out from beneath the traditional *jin* cap he wore. Yet his clear eyes radiated energy and spirit, and his skin glowed in vitality and health. He stared intently and knowingly with the wisdom of experience and the patience of age.

With certainty, Leonard knew that he had to tell the truth. If he didn't, he may as well leave and turn his back on these warm and generous people.

He returned Uncle Jun's scrutiny and nodded slowly. "Yes, it is." He swallowed and, unable to maintain eye contact, looked down.

"Is sad what happen to her, but her death will kill you if you not make peace." Jun leaned slightly closer and inclined his head. "We have saying, 'Saddest thing in world is death of heart.'"

Ming placed a cup of tea in front of them and sat silently at the table. The pale green liquid steamed.

Leonard looked up and met Jun's eyes. "Every day, I am reminded of her death. Every time I catch a cab, cross the road or hear the sound of a coach, I think of her." His mouth was suddenly dry, and he reached for the tea and took a sip.

Jun translated quickly for Ming. She nodded in sympathy, and her eyes glistened.

"I think of the agony and pain she felt. I feel heartbroken that I cannot be with her, to talk and tell her how much I love her." Leonard paused briefly. "If I had been with her that horrible day, it might never have happened, and she could still be alive. Coming here to see you, it, er… reminded me of her. That is why I never came."

Jun sat back in his chair and crossed his bony legs. Ming's eyes darted from Leonard's face to Jun's and back again. She spoke quickly to Jun.

"But you come, you are here today."

Leonard shrugged. He took another sip of tea and enjoyed the refreshing mild flavour.

"Do you feel different about her after she dead than before?" asked Jun. The tone of his voice suggested this was more than a simple question.

Leonard paused so he could answer the question honestly. "No, I loved her the same." It dawned on him the point Jun was making.

"Mae-Ling knew you love her, but her painful death is very, very sad," said Jun. "How could you know stupid cab will knock her to ground and run over her? You don't know this will happen. What could you do? No, Leo, you sad for wrong reason."

"Wrong reason?" he questioned. "Then tell me the right reason, Uncle Jun?"

Jun smacked his gums and pointed his finger. "You sorry for yourself."

Ming reached across the table and placed her hand on Leonard's.

Leonard took a cleansing breath and held his emotions in check. He knew Jun was right.

A noise in the shop alerted Jun to a customer. He unfolded his legs and stood and, without a word, parted the curtain and shuffled into the shop. Leonard thought about the conversation. Ming was still watching him closely. She spoke softly to him, but he didn't understand her. It didn't matter, it was obvious, and he knew she supported and cared for him. He gave her a smile.

"Hungry?" she asked. Another English word she knew.

She retracted her arm and began stoking the fire that was positioned near the rear entrance of Jun's shop. She placed on it a curved pot with a rounded base, called a *wok*, and waited for it to heat. Within minutes, the smell of cooking food had him salivating. His thoughts returned to what Jun had said, and it was true. He was feeling sorry for himself and had come to the same conclusion at work.

Leonard took in the storeroom they sat in. It was clean and organised, although crates and sacks were stacked high against the walls. Part of the space was used as a kitchen; the table where he sat and the fire were cleverly positioned so that Jun and Ming could go about their daily lives and never leave the shop unattended. The heat from the fire kept the harmful dampness from his wares during winter and kept the rooms upstairs warm on cold winter nights. The open doors at both ends of the shop allowed a breeze to keep the premises cool during summer.

Jun returned and smiled when he saw the food sizzling away. Leonard felt relaxed, almost relieved like a great burden had been lifted from his shoulders. It wasn't so much what Jun had asked that made him feel different. It was his own response to the questions that gave him some insight and helped him to better understand his own emotions. He smiled; it was like he was home again with family.

Suddenly, Leonard remembered one of the reasons he wanted to visit Jun and Ming. "Uncle Jun, do you sell this?" He handed over the empty small glass Echinacea jar he'd taken from home.

"*Zi Zhui Ju!*" said Jun, nodding. "For you?"

"Yes."

Ming and Jun conversed briefly, and he showed her the jar. She pointed at Leonard and shook her head while Jun laughed. Finally, Jun responded. "She say you sick. No look good. Yes, I have for you, but you must balance fire and wind, and I give you something better to help you. First, we eat."

Ming had finished cooking and placed a steaming dish on the table. She handed a bowl and chopsticks to each of them, which Leonard could use expertly without fear of embarrassment, and they ate.

Once their midday meal was over, Leonard patted his stomach, indicating he could eat no more. "My belly is full," he said. Then he remembered the belladonna Alex had found in the stomach of the mystery man. "Uncle Jun, do you know of the poisonous plant belladonna?"

Jun looked at him quizzically.

"Bell-a-donna, deadly nightshade," Leonard repeated slowly.

"Ah, yes, yes," replied Jun. He turned to Ming, "*Dian Qie Cao*! But, Leonard, is not just poison, is medicine." He nodded his head, seeking affirmation.

"Medicine? For what?"

"Pain, uh, swelling, many thing."

Leonard was thinking. Of course, the note from Alex's office! "Would you use belladonna for shaking palsy, Parkinson's disease?"

Jun thought momentarily, "Ah, yes, but careful to give with other medicine. Wind and fire need balance, remember I tell you this, and also health of patient. Good for liver and kidney." Jun smiled, and then his face creased into a frown. "You have this sickness?"

"No, no. Not me." Leonard was trying to remember what else Alex had said about the mystery man.

"Do you give belladonna to many people?"

67

Jun shook his head. "No, not much. Many weeks ago, young white man, very, very sick, he have this Parkinson you speak of. I give to him."

"But you didn't want to poison him?"

Jun explained to Ming, and they both laughed. "Not poison, good for sick man. If I want to poison man, I use other plant, is quick, much better and very strong."

"This man, what did he look like, can you recall?"

"He younger than you, very sick, skin white. Dark hair."

It sounded like the same person, the mystery man and Leonard was encouraged. "Do you know who it was, the man's name? Please, say yes," Leonard asked excitedly.

Jun spoke to Ming, and she shook her head in response. "No name, Leonard. But maybe get for you?" smiled Jun. "You want name?"

"And anything else you can find out about him. This is very important."

Jun was staring at Leonard. "Why you need? Did this man do wrong to you?" He kept his eyes firmly fixed on him.

Leonard was trying to decide how much to tell the old man, and he came to a decision. "If you make any enquiries about the young man who was sick, you must be careful."

Jun laughed, "Who must I be careful of, what man is this you are frighten from?"

"No, it's not a man, I think it's an organisation called Patrons of New Zealand."

Jun immediately sat back, and his smile vanished. "Leo, you listen. These man of Patron, they are very bad man. They have many important friend, and I know this. You are good boy, keep away from them."

"You've heard of them?"

Jun nodded.

"Perhaps you shouldn't ask about the young man. I don't want to see you hurt."

Jun laughed, he laughed hard, and it ended with a fit of coughing. Ming looked up sharply with a look of worry.

"Leo, we not frighten of Patron people. You, I am worry for. I give information you want, but you must tell me why you need, yes? You can do on Saturday. We want to see you again and talk more." Jun pointed a skinny finger at Leonard. "You be careful, look over shoulder." Jun translated to Ming, who was watching. She nodded, her face serious.

Leonard rubbed his chin. Uncle Jun and Ming were uneasy, and they obviously felt the Patrons of New Zealand was a threat to him but not to themselves. This was growing stranger by the day, he thought.

"I will be careful, I promise. Thank you both for your advice."

"You wait, stay here." Jun rose from his chair with the empty Echinacea bottle.

Leonard thought he heard voices in the shop, but Jun said he had no customers when he returned a few minutes later with the bottle full of Echinacea and another bottle containing a mixture of herbs. "You take a little with water in morning and evening. Is good for you, make you healthy." Jun beamed.

Leonard reached into his pocket for some coins, but Uncle Jun shook his head, "No money!"

It was time to go; Leonard thanked them both, said his goodbyes and hugged the elderly couple. He promised to return on Saturday, and with his medication in his pocket, he walked blinking into the bright sunlight of Frederick Street.

His head and thoughts were in turmoil; he'd learned so much today. He felt more at peace than he had in some time. Uncle Jun's perspectives were refreshing, and he began to feel better about himself and the sadness that had consumed and dominated his life since the death of Mae.

There was more to Uncle Jun than met the eye; Leonard knew this with almost certainty. The ageing diminutive Chinaman was connected, not with criminal activities because Jun was honest and principled, and deeply involved with the Chinese community. Mae had suggested once that Uncle Jun was an influential and respected leader. Others sought his counsel and wisdom, and it was a fool who underestimated him. *That is worth remembering,* he thought. Leonard began his walk down Frederick Street, and as Uncle Jun suggested, he looked carefully around. Feeling secure, he retraced his steps towards home.

Not far behind, two young Oriental men discretely followed. Leonard No one spared them a second glance, nor did they attract any unwanted attention, and anyone who did recognise them kept their distance – they weren't to be trifled with. Little did Leonard know they'd been given precise instructions to ensure he made it home safely.

Ahead, a handful of men stood on the corner of Tory and Frederick streets and were handing out leaflets. As Leonard walked past, one was thrust at him. Out of politeness, he accepted it and slowed to quickly glance at it. It was an advertisement for a meeting hosted by the White New Zealand League. At the top of the page was written their precept. Leonard read carefully:

WHITE NEW ZEALAND LEAGUE
Your obligations to New Zealand are great.
Your inheritance is a white New Zealand.
Keep it so for your children's children,
and your empire.
Of relevance to our future and continuance.
Meeting at The Thistle Inn
Wednesday, half-past five.

Citizens of the future are the children of today.

In distaste, Leonard crumpled the leaflet and looked to toss it, but a sudden change of heart gave him cause to reflect. IHe instead, he put the leaflet in his pocket. Lost in thought, he never heard the Hansom cab careen around the corner onto Tory Street, its wheels squirting mud and dousing him as it passed.

Chapter Six

In solemnity, most stood in groups comprised of people they knew. Leonard could see Mr Beaumont and the coroner, Mr Aiken, along with a couple of city councillors looking dignified and doleful . Near them were a doctor and a couple of tearful nurses from Wellington Hospital. A slightly larger group stood on the peripherals and appeared to be mostly curious onlookers or old colleagues who'd come to pay their respects. At the front, Bridgette, Mary, Meredith and Jonathan stood beside Leonard, each dressed appropriately in black and fighting with their emotions at the open grave. None of Alex's family was in attendance as they all lived in England.

Reverend Hartwell finished another lengthy prayer, and everyone expectantly raised their heads, fervently hoping it was the last. Like a dear old friend, the reverend began a colourful, descriptive monologue listing many of Alex's tributes and qualities. While a stranger could be forgiven for thinking the good reverend was well acquainted with Alex, truth be told, they'd never actually met. Leonard regretted providing the minister with detailed background on Alex and felt it demeaned the service, although he did suspect the reverend's oration was more for the benefit of a few notable mourners he wished to impress.

As the reverend intoned, Leonard began looking closely at the people who had gathered at the Bolton Street Cemetery to say farewell to Alex. Most he knew and recognised, although a few were unfamiliar. Leonard was puzzled at the appearance of one man in particular. *What business did Constable Hastings have at the funeral,* he wondered?

The constable was in uniform and casually standing behind the councillors. He seemed less interested in the service and more focused on watching closely those who had come to mourn. He looked arrogantly down his nose as his head swivelled from one face to the next as he studied each person carefully.

In a moment of abstract thought, Leonard wondered how the constable's perception of the world would alter if his nose was smaller.

Mary tugged on his arm. He looked down and was surprised to see he held her hand; he couldn't for the life of him remember if she had taken it or he'd grabbed hers. It mattered not, he felt comfortable, even at the risk of offending some people's sense of propriety. She clutched a handkerchief she'd used to dab her eyes and tilted her head to whisper to him. "Who is that gentlemen behind you? He has been observing us for some time now."

Leonard looked over his shoulder. He was startled - standing alone in the shadow of a tree, a few yards back, was Winston Crumb. "That's Mr Crumb," he whispered to her excitedly with raised eyebrows.

She quickly risked another look.

Leonard shifted his position slightly and leaned over to tell Jonathan, who stood at his side. "See that man under the tree behind us, that's Winston Crumb, in the flesh."

Jonathan turned and saw the man.

"Do you recognise him?" whispered Leonard.

Jonathan shook his head and looked at Leonard questioningly.

Leonard again turned to look. Seeing he was attracting

unwarranted attention, Mr Crumb slowly walked away, scattering three foraging magpies in his path. He wondered if Constable Hastings had seen Mr Crumb, but he too was leaving. Both men walked away in opposite directions.

Reverend Hartwell reluctantly finished the service and waited in anticipation of compliments that were sure to come. As befitting the occasion, he looked dignified as the wind tugged at his vestments. He graciously acknowledged the offerings, as one by one, assorted people approached him with awkward, polite smiles and thanked him for his eloquent liturgy.

The dignitaries, the two councillors, the coroner, and the newspaper's editor had not approached the reverend; instead, they were gathered around Bridgette and Leonard, the two people who knew Alex best and offered their heartfelt sympathies and condolences. Leonard was only half listening to Councillor Knight, who was making a passionate statement about regulating cabs in the city and was thinking back to the unexpected appearance of Winston Crumb and Constable Hastings. Reverend Hartwell, who'd ambled over in search of affirmations, interrupted his musings.

Jonathan was warming to the discussion and had casually suggested to Councilman McKay and an attentive coroner about introducing a city by-law when Meredith gave him a furtive glance. Her meaning was clear. Poor Bridgette was overcome, and they needed to leave and take her away.

They all sat in Jonathan's sunny living room in Thorndon, a short distance from the cemetery. No one spoke; they were all emotionally drained and wearied, as it had been a difficult afternoon.

Mary sat beside Bridgette, providing solace while Meredith decided it was time for tea. Jonathan went to help, leaving Leonard alone with his thoughts.

Although not gifted with a desire to make a career in law or medicine like Jonathan and Alex, Leonard felt his talents lie in other areas. He was a thinker. Few that knew him would dispute the assertion that Leonard had a logical mind, and his ability at deductive or inductive reasoning was remarkable. So, it was to this natural faculty he now turned.

As customary, when deep in thought, he stretched out in the chair, crossed his legs and surreptitiously wiggled his toes. He turned his mind to the first unusual incident, the mystery man found dead outside his home. He reasoned that if the man had been discovered at a different location, then many events that happened since would not have happened at all, so therefore the dead man was crucial. Obvious but important.

If the body hadn't been found where it had, would Alex still be alive? Using the same logic, he first needed to know what Alex was doing on Adelaide Road near the hospital and to whom he spoke. Or was Alex's death merely the result of an unfortunate accident? Were Alex's activities linked to the mystery man? The answers could help determine why Alex had become a target. Systematically, Leonard analysed each premise and prioritised a small mental list.

"Your tea is cold, Leonard," admonished Meredith.

Leonard sat upright and glanced around the room; everyone was staring at him. "I've been thinking …."

"Yes, we gathered that," Jonathan quipped.

"This is significant, and I want you all to listen."

"Go on," encouraged Mary, speaking for everyone

"I've changed my mind; I no longer believe that all these things that have happened since that body was discovered outside my home are just a random series of events. I think they're all connected."

"So Alex's death wasn't by chance?" asked Jonathan.

Leonard turned to Bridgette. "I have no facts to support that theory, but I can't eliminate it either. If I were to guess, then you are right."

"Oh, Leo," Bridgette cried.

"Let him continue, Bridgette, I'm in agreement with him," said Jonathan insensitively.

Meredith turned to glare at him but said nothing.

"Things are happening around us, occurrences that we are completely unaware of. Take Mr Crumb, who we all saw today, and by his own admission, a representative of the secretive organisation, Patrons of New Zealand. But as soon as he saw our interest in him at the funeral, he departed. Why was he there?" Leonard looked around the room, and no one had an answer. "An unidentified body is discovered outside my home, William disappears, and Alex has a fatal accident, which amounts to two deaths. And possibly a third because I suspect William is also deceased, making it three. It is implausible that those incidents could be just an arbitrary series of coincidences." He shook his head. "Of course, I'm warned by Mr Crumb not to pursue any interest in the mystery man who died, or something bad could happen to me. And if I did, then I would be the fourth casualty." Leonard paused to take a sip of his cold tea. "I went to see Uncle Jun on Saturday. I hadn't seen him in a while. He told me to be careful of the Patrons of New Zealand group," Leonard paused briefly, "and he may even know the identity of our mystery man."

"What, really?" asked Jonathan. "How is that possible?"

"Alex discovered what he thought was poison in the mystery man's body and believed it was belladonna. As Uncle Jun told me, belladonna is used as a medicine to treat various disorders. Someone fitting the description of the mystery man came to him about two months ago seeking medication to treat an ailment, and Uncle Jun gave him belladonna."

"Oh, for heaven's sake, Leonard," Bridgette said, "that's too much of a coincidence."

"Perhaps, but since Uncle Jun is the main supplier of Chinese herbal medicine in Wellington, it's only logical the mystery man would go to him."

"Yes, I suppose so," Bridgette conceded.

"But you said the mystery man wasn't Oriental. Why would a European go to a Chinese apothecary?" asked Mary.

"I'm not sure that's even relevant," Leonard replied, "but I will ask him that question on Saturday when he tells me the name of our mystery man."

"And what about the constable?" asked Mary.

"I'd have to believe he was there on police business," Leonard offered. "Well, that's it then, easy. You've figured it all out, Leo," said Jonathan grinning.

"No, I haven't. The mystery man died before William disappeared and before Alex died. Others are involved."

"Who, the Patrons of New Zealand?" asked Bridgette.

"Oh yes," interrupted Jonathan, "and speaking of... I asked an old client about them. Strangely, when I said Patrons of New Zealand, he refused to talk anymore. Wouldn't say a word. No amount of prompting would loosen his tongue," said Jonathan. "The poor chap was visibly flustered."

"He obviously knew of them, the pompous bampot!" Mary stated with a measure of disgust.

"I'm going to find out who murdered Alex. As we've been warned not to investigate, I understand if you have no appetite to help. But I will need your assistance." Leonard looked to each of his friends in turn.

"If Alex was indeed murdered, then I want to know who the culprit is. I'm with you, Leonard," offered Jonathan.

Mary, Bridgette and Meredith all readily agreed.

Leonard fished in his jacket pocket and pulled out the brochure handed to him on Saturday. He passed it to Jonathan.

"I want to go to that meeting early tomorrow evening; I don't think I should go alone, and it will be safer with the two of us. Can you come with me?"

"Of course," replied Jonathan as he read the advertisement.

"Why do you want to go to that meeting, Leonard?" Bridgette asked.

"Because I believe the White New Zealand League and the Patrons of New Zealand are similar, as Jonathan said. He thinks they are xenophobic organisations. I want to understand what they're all about. Can't do any harm to pay them a visit, can it?"

She nodded in understanding and then blew her nose.

"Do either of you know the doctor Alex saw at the hospital the day he died?"

Bridgette and Mary turned to each other in question. Mary shrugged. "I think it was Dr Schrader. Alex mentioned his name to me and asked me what I thought of him as a physician," Bridgette replied.

"What did you tell him?"

Mary began to laugh, "That he's a detestable little man."

"But a fine doctor," Bridgette offered, she couldn't help but frown a little.

"That's settled then. Can either of you arrange for me to visit Dr Schrader later this week after I finish work?"

"I can, and I will go with you," Mary offered.

Leonard wasn't satisfied, not yet. There was one thread he wanted to explore, and he would do so alone and keep this information to himself.

The suburb in Wellington known as Mount Cook borders the southern end of Taranaki Street, not far from Haining Street, and extends to the growing community of Newtown a little further south. It isn't a mountain as its name suggests; it was a hill, and much of it had been levelled to accommodate the military barracks built years earlier. The 'Depot' as it was known, had recently housed the 'Armed Constabulary' and was now the home of the newly formed 'New Zealand Constabulary,' New Zealand's newest police force. A street dissects the depot, and some years earlier, large gates were used to keep people out or, depending on your perspective, thought Leonard, to keep people in. Due to the number of complaints by locals who wanted access to the other side, the gates are now left open and thankfully have never been closed since. Buckle Street has become a busy public thoroughfare.

Leonard walked up the gentle slope of Buckle Street and saw his destination near the top. He finally entered the building and looked around. Typically, it was institutionally dull; a few grimy out-of-date posters graced the walls, which depicted unflattering descriptions of individuals sought by the police for questioning. One section of the wall was devoted to recruitment and detailed the benefits of working for the close-knit brotherhood of the constabulary. At the rear, a large wooden bench ran the room's length, and Leonard took a seat while waiting for the gentleman before him to conclude his business. On the left, a sign near a door clearly indicated a urinal for public use. Leonard was debating if he should avail himself to the facility when the constable at the front desk hailed him.

"Next!"

Leonard walked to the counter.

"How can I be of assistance, sir?" asked the constable without looking up. He was busy writing in a log book.

"I'm looking for Constable Hastings. Is he currently available?"

With a heavy sigh, the constable finished his log entry, retrieved a clipboard from a hook, and ran a stubby finger down a column, "Hastings, Hastings, let me see, Hastings, ah yes, here he is."

Leonard smiled benevolently.

"No, sir, I'm afraid he isn't scheduled to work until a little later." He replaced the clipboard and continued writing. "You can wait, or is it something I can help ya with?"

"What time is he scheduled to begin his shift?"

"Soon, I think." He looked up at Leonard. "Are you sure I can't help ya?"

"No, thank you very much."

"Very well, have a nice afternoon, sir." Leonard was dismissed. The constable continued with another log entry. "Next!" There were no other people in the room.   Leonard walked outside into the warm late afternoon sun and was deciding if he should wait or return another time.

"Well, if it isn't Mr Hardy his self!"

Leonard turned to the voice, "Constable Hastings! I was hoping I could find you."

"And find me you did, is your lucky day." The constable stood waiting and looked down the considerable vast expanse of his nose at Leonard.

"May I encroach on your valuable time and ask you a question or two? Perhaps we could go somewhere a little more private?"

The policeman waited a moment and then came to a decision. "This way."

Leonard followed him to the side of the building, where a table and wooden benches were arranged beneath the shade of a large tree. Hastings indicated for Leonard to sit, which he did, while the constable remained standing. "Now then, what can I do for you?"

"Have you ascertained the identity of the man found outside my home?"

"No one has come forward, and we've been unable to positively establish who he is."

"I see." Leonard thought carefully and rubbed his chin. "And have you been able to locate the coach that struck Alex Leyton?"

"No, sir, not at this time. May I ask why you seek this information?"

Leonard ignored the question and continued. "And what about the assistant medical practitioner? I understand he is missing too. Do you have any information on his whereabouts?"

"Mr Hardy, are these questions related to your work at the *Evening Standard*?"

Looking up at the constable was proving to be an effort. "No, not exactly. I'm here because I want answers, and I believe you can provide me with them."

A vein on the constable's neck began pulsing rapidly. Hastings took a step back and turned away as he considered how to deal with Leonard's impertinence.

Something Mary had asked made Leonard question himself. He rose from his seat.

"I have another query. Why were you at Alex's funeral service?"

Constable Hasting immediately spun and faced Leonard. His jaw was firmly clenched. Leonard knew he'd struck a nerve, but why?

"Constable?" Leonard pushed while he felt he had the upper hand.

"I'm not at liberty to discuss any details around an ongoing investigation with you, Mr Hardy." The constable's cool façade was returning.

"Nonsense," Leonard shot back without pausing. "Your presence at the funeral was not related to any police work, was it, constable? Nor was your visit to the *Evening Standard* to question me!" Leonard took two steps and stood directly in front of the larger man. He stared him down, or somewhat up at him, under the shadow of his nose.

The vein pulsed rapidly.

"Constable Hastings, I expect an honest answer." Leonard had the edge and knew it. He wouldn't give the constable any leeway and maintain the pressure on him. "Your actions are not consistent with the duties of a constable going about his lawful business; you are acting in accord with others, and to what purpose, Mr Hastings?"

Leonard could see the constable was on the verge of losing control. "Answer me!" he shouted.

Constable Hastings lost all measure of restraint and discipline and stepped forward, thrusting a finger into Leonard's chest. "Your kind make me puke. You're so righteous and uppity!" Hastings continued to jab with his finger and forced Leonard to take a step backwards. "If I'd had my way, then I'd a let 'em get to ya I would have. But no, they said no! Ha, and you came so close you did, nearly joined your interfering mate!" Flecks of spittle formed at the side of the constable's mouth. His face was bright red and his anger palpable as he continued to prod Leonard. "All I gots to say to ya... Bollocks to you and your coolie loving kind. Next time..."

"Constable Hastings! What in goodness name is going on here?" The voice of authority echoed around the buildings.

Hasting's head whipped around and saw his commanding officer. Immediately the constable's hands dropped to his sides, and he turned to the officer and froze. His eyes stared vacantly into the distance. "Sir, we was having a chat, sir!"

Leonard's heart was threatening to leap from his chest. He wasn't a brave man and took all his willpower not to turn and flee while Hastings unleashed his tirade at him. But he was satisfied and sought answers from the constable; provoking him had worked.

"What were you doing to this man, Constable Hastings?" The officer didn't wait for a response and glared at Leonard. "Is everything in order, sir?"

"It's, as the constable said, nothing more than an emotional exchange of ideas. I am well, and thank you for your concern," offered Leonard. He saw no purpose in further angering Constable Hastings.

The officer studied Leonard carefully and then turned to Hastings. "Are you on duty?"

"Ah, yes, sir. Just now."

"Is this police business?" asked the officer warily.

"No ... not exactly, sir."

"Then what are you standing about here for, be off with you!"

"Yes, sir." Constable Hastings double-timed it to the building without looking at Leonard.

"I apologise for his unacceptable behaviour, sir."

"Everything is at it should be," replied Leonard, somewhat relieved to see the constable disappear.

"Then I bid you good day." The officer turned and followed after Constable Hastings while Leonard let out the breath that he'd been holding.

His hands shook. The constable frightened him. Not only was the man much larger and physically intimidating, but it was also what he said. Leonard decided to return to the building and take advantage of the convenience.

Jonathan laughed, "You did what, to the constable?

"I deliberately provoked him, made him angry and then he lost all vestige of sensibility."

Both men sat at a table near the window of the Thistle Inn, a public hotel near the northern end of Lambton Quay where the White New Zealand League meeting was to be held. They were early, and Leonard, with the aid of beer, recalled his encounter with Constable Hastings to Jonathan.

"Leonard, you surprise me at times, you really do." He shook his head.

85

"I surprise myself."

"So, what conclusions can you make?"

"Actually, quite a few. He said a great deal more than he intended." Leonard scooted his chair closer to Jonathan. "There is definitely a link to racism and the Chinese. As he said, and I quote him, 'Bollocks to you and your coolie loving kind'. Certainly, he made his own position clear, and he has no affinity for the Chinese and sees them as socially inferior."

"You sound like a lawyer."

Leonard smirked, "More insults."

Jonathan laughed, "What else?"

"What frightens me is when he said, 'If I'd of had my way, then I would have let them get you, they said no, and you came close and nearly joined your friend.' This is what is really troubling me, Jonathan. Someone is telling Hastings what to do, and he suggests another entity wants to see me come to harm. He claims I nearly died!" Leonard rubbed his face. "Truthfully, I find this very unnerving." He looked up at Jonathan, "I'm frightened, I really am, and I have no idea how I can protect myself because I don't know whom I'm in danger from. And why? For what reason, what have I done?" He took a healthy swallow of beer and looked around the room. It was rapidly filling with people and those already seated seemed to have been drinking for some time.

Jonathan stared into his beer, lost in thought; he finally looked up. "Leonard, as a lawyer, we are trained in conflict resolution, often through positioning and litigation. Do you follow?"

Leonard nodded.

"But some alternative and successful methods of resolving disputes are through mediation and the practice of collaborative law.

You find a solution to satisfy both sides. To make that work, I try to find and focus on the other parties' interests and their position. Are you still with me?"

"Yes, continue," said Leonard, listening intently.

"Rather than investigate and look into the deaths and backtrack, how about looking to see who gains. Out there somewhere," Jonathan spread his arms wide, almost knocking the beer from the table, "a person or persons is benefitting from all these deaths. Shift the mindset a little; perhaps it will open up new avenues to explore."

Leonard was quiet as he mulled over Jonathan's words. They appealed to his sense of logic and reasoning. He nodded in agreement. "That's good, I like that, and it gives me a different perspective. I'll give it some thought when I return home."

Chapter Seven

*A*ll the tables and chairs were occupied. Mostly men filled the room, and those unable to be seated stood elbow to elbow at the room's rear against the windows. It was difficult for Leonard and Jonathan to talk privately without being overheard; instead, they drank their beer and quietly surveyed the occupants. Most of the men inside the Thistle Inn appeared to be workingmen, labourers, many from the nearby docks and the harbour reclamation project. Surprisingly a few Māori mingled amongst the attendees. A dozen or so roughnecks, loud and boisterous, made their presence felt with their ribald banter and derisive comments. They were tolerated and ignored.

At the other end of the room, two tables had been dragged together, and three men sat down with a sheaf of papers, a couple of jugs of beer and an air of self-importance. Their hats had been removed and placed on the tables beside them.

One of the three stood and clinked loudly on a glass with a large knife; the banter and talk petered immediately. Oblivious of the proceedings about to begin, one man at the rear of the room, evidently challenged with insobriety, persisted unabated with his discussion. All heads turned to the drunk in amusement as he continued, unaware of the attention he drew.

"Thank you, Tom!" shouted one of the men seated at the table in front. "Perhaps you can tell us what finally happened to your neighbour's wife after our meeting?"

The room exploded in laughter.

Finally mindful of what was happening, Tom stopped mid-sentence and sheepishly looked around the room, wobbled a little and grinned.

"Would someone find Tom a chair before he falls and injures himself?"

Once order had been restored and Tom seated, the man clinked his glass a few more times. The barroom in the Thistle Inn was deathly quiet.

"I call this White New Zealand League meeting to order!"

"Hear, hear!" cried an unknown voice from the room's rear - he was ignored.   "We have lots to discuss on our agenda this evening, and we'll try to keep this meeting brief so you can go home to your families. I will let our chairman, Mr Ernest O'Rourke, take the floor." He swept his arm down in a dramatic gesture to the man seated beside him in the middle.

A few clapped in appreciation, and some cheered. One man yelled, "Go Ernie!" as Mr O'Rourke slid his chair back and rose.

He was reasonably well dressed and carried himself with the confidence of a man used to speaking in front of an audience. Leonard noticed his hands and shoulders were large, a man familiar with the ardours of hard physical labour.

"Some of yer may not be aware, but we've extended an invitation to our Premier, Mr John Hall, to becomes our patron. We feels we has a like-minded vision fer New Zealand and one that's free from the yellow Oriental scourge that's invading our fine country." He held up his hand to forestall the applause he knew was coming. "We'll have ter wait for his official response, so notting can be confirmed… or celebrated just yet." He received raucous cheers and applause.

Jonathan and Leonard exchanged glances. Near the front, Leonard saw Mr Pembroke, the *Evening Standard*'s editor and senior reporter, studiously taking notes. He wasn't surprised to see him there; it was expected that the newspaper covered meetings such as these.

"We're all deeply concerned and worried," continued Mr O'Rourke, "Tis a shame it is that dis fair country is being invaded." He shook his head to emphasise the gravity of the situation. "Our jobs are being taken, and hard-working men like you have lost work to the Oriental plague. Yes, even our women are in danger!" He paused to allow the upwelling of anger to rise within the Thistle Inn. Men shouted; some raised their fists and pumped them in the air in support. Mr O'Rourke waited for the clamour to diminish.

"Unchecked, the Orientals enter the country without family, without women, and what do they want?" He repeated himself, louder with gusto. "They want our jobs, our livelihood and yes, my brothers, our fine lasses!" Again the swelling of vocal support was astounding.

"But not anymore! With yer help, we'll end it!" exclaimed Mr O'Rourke. He paused to take a healthy swig of his beer.

"Whatcha goin' to do, Ernie?" yelled a voice.

Mr O'Rourke pointed to the man who yelled. "Good question me 'ol mate. Lets me tell yer." With slow deliberation, Ernest O'Rourke turned his head around the room. He looked into their tired eyes and rough, weather-beaten faces, and they returned his look with belief and hope.

Mr O'Rourke raised a finger and held it aloft. "We're goin ter petition the government to charge a levy on each Oriental immigrant...."

Someone tapped Leonard on the shoulder. He turned and saw with surprise a man standing behind him.

So as not to disturb the meeting, the man bent down to whisper in his ear. "Sorry to bother you, sir, but am goin' to have to ask you to leave."

"Leave? Why? Leonard looked puzzled.

"This way, sir." The man pointed to the nearest door.

Leonard leaned towards Jonathan and explained what the man had said, then looked up at the man. "Perhaps you can tell me the reason?"

"I've been polite up till now. It's time to leave, sir."

A few heads began to turn and watch. Mr O'Rourke continued.

"Tell me why we must leave? We're not going anywhere unless you tell us."

The man pointed to Jonathan. "He can stay, but you must go now if you please. We can do this the hard way if you'd prefer?"

"If I've done something in error, then allow me the courtesy of knowing so I can make amends, but don't evict me without providing a reason," Leonard appealed, his voice becoming louder. More heads turned, and even Mr O'Rourke glanced his way disapprovingly.

The man reached in and grasped his arm. Leonard shook it free, "Unhand me!"

Mr O'Rourke stopped and turned to face Leonard, as did every other person in the barroom, including Mr Pembroke. The bar fell silent.

Jonathan leaned forward, "Perhaps we should leave Leonard, this really, er, isn't good."

Leonard reluctantly slid his chair back and stood; he turned and faced the man. "Why?"

"You know the reason, now get out!" All sense of civility was gone.

The man again tried to grab his arm and steer him to the exit, but Leonard shook it free and began threading his way around tables towards the nearest door. He was seething. Hostile glances and unfriendly faces followed him the entire way. He turned back, looked over his shoulder, and saw Mr Pembroke shaking his head sadly.

Jonathan quickly stood and followed.

Once outside, Leonard was furious. He stomped backwards and forward, clenching and unclenching his fists. "I've never felt so humiliated in my life, Jonathan. Why on earth would they single me out? I've not given them any reason to act this way."

Jonathan looked at his friend with sympathy as he watched him pace to and fro. "I believe there can only be one explanation, Leo."

Leonard stopped, "Because I was married to a Chinese woman? Is that the reason?"

"I believe it is; what else could it be?"

"What business is it of others to decide how I choose to live my life or whom I will take as my wife? Answer me that, Jonathan?"

"Now isn't the time to enter into a philosophical discussion on human frailties, Leonard. Take a moment and compose yourself before you do yourself harm."

"Is prejudicial, that's what it is." Leonard seethed.

"I agree, but your anger isn't helping things, is it?"

"Perhaps." Leonard looked at the ground, his fury dissipating quickly. He shook his head slowly from side to side. He knew Jonathan was right. He looked up at him. "Then how did they know that?"

Jonathan shrugged. "I don't know. Look, we should probably leave and go home."

Leonard risked a look back at the Thistle Inn. "Let's remove ourselves from this place."

"A wonderful suggestion."

They said goodbye, and each went their separate way.

It was just nightfall, and the people he passed paid him no untoward attention. Occasionally he stopped and looked behind, but he wasn't accosted, confronted, or threatened; it was just an everyday stroll like he had done hundreds of times.

Had Leonard been conversant in the art of spy-craft, he may have thought differently. He had no knowledge or training in surveillance and thus failed to see the two men who'd been following him across town. When Leonard reached Marjoribanks Street, he paused momentarily for one last look. The two men who had been shadowing him casually strolled past, deep in conversation, and nothing about their demeanour seemed suspicious or dubious. While cautioned to be careful and observant, Leonard had no idea what to look for. Privately he imagined seeing enormous, swarthy men with squinty eyes and the glint of steel from partially concealed weapons flitting from door to door. However, the only men he saw who fit that dark, complexioned appearance were a couple of Italian and Greek men. One walked with his mother, the other with his daughter. They greeted him amicably, and he saw no weapons, and it was unlikely he would be set upon by an elderly widow dressed from head to toe in black carrying a cabbage or a six-year-old girl with a rag-doll.

Leonard continued on and politely greeted an Oriental peddler hawking miscellaneous items from a small handcart at the corner of his street and then trudged up Marjoribanks Street towards home. The hawker observed him all the way to his gate.

Once home, Leonard retired to his armchair near the open window and relished the pleasant, cooling breeze as the moon slowly began its ascent over the distant western hills. He thought of his marriage and the beautiful and intelligent woman who once shared his life. What would Mae have said about what happened earlier at the Thistle Inn? She had always been outspoken and an advocate for those less fortunate, and he knew with absolute certainty that had she been there with him, she would have made her feelings known and rebuked the White New Zealand League and their bigoted, racist views.

He smiled as he thought back to how they'd met. It was at the markets. He had seen her there several times and always stopped briefly to chat. Her English was impeccable and precise, as was everything about her. He'd been enamoured at first sight of her even then.

One day, as he arrived at the markets, a well-dressed gentleman was hurling abuse at one of the Chinese market gardeners who didn't understand English. Mae had quickly interceded and stepped in to defend the poor man. The abusive gentleman was surprised to see her and was convinced she was a woman of suspect and immoral character and insisted she accompany him elsewhere. Much to the horror of gawking spectators, he seized her arm to lead her forcibly away. That only angered her more, and understandably she resisted. The man quickly lashed out to strike her face.

Luckily, she saw the swinging arm, twisted her body, and was struck across the shoulder. So enraged was the man that he prepared to assault her again when Leonard approached. It was the first time in his life that he had deliberately exposed himself to violence, and he had done so without thinking. Thankfully the gentleman wasn't tall - he was short and very round with an enormous girth and by all appearances, not in the best of physical condition. He challenged the man and didn't concede, and even when the man threatened him with a physical beating, Leonard defiantly held his ground. Realising he would achieve nothing, the man eventually stalked away, seething in frustration.

Still feeling brave and chivalrous, he accompanied Mae safely back to Chen Jun Qiang's, on Frederick Street, where she lived. From that day forward, they'd become virtually inseparable and saw each other almost daily. A year later, they were married. They saw the gentleman one other time, and again, he foolishly demanded that Mae accompany him. On Leonard's insistence, Mae reported the incident to the police and thankfully never saw him again.

Leonard looked up, and bathed in the yellow comforting glow of the lamp was a picture of Mae staring back at him. Her flawless skin, her dark eyes, and beautiful jet-black, straight hair was truly perfection. He closed his eyes and slowly inhaled through his nose, a long deep and unhurried breath; he could smell her, he could feel her presence, and if he reached out, he was sure he would touch her. But his hands felt nothing but air; she wasn't here in the room with him as she once had been, she was dead. His arms dropped dejectedly onto his thighs and he lifted his head. Mae still stared at him, her unchanging expression a reminder of what once was.

He inhaled again, a cleansing breath, and slowly his mind refocused to the present and reality. Mae wasn't coming back; she never would. He wanted to say goodbye to her, but no words came to him that were meaningful and sincere. He just lacked the courage to let her go.

With a conscious effort, Leonard shifted his thoughts to the events over the last couple of weeks. None of it made any sense and he failed to see a logical path and a solution. While it seemed highly unlikely that the White New Zealand League was directly linked to Alex's murder and William's disappearance, their fundamental tenets and opinions may follow a close parallel to the Patrons of New Zealand organisation. The only connection to them, and Alex's death, was himself, and that was where the path ended.

Was the volatile Constable Hastings associated with these xenophobic groups? Winston Crumb, Uncle Jun and the constable had warned him of danger, but as yet there had been no incidents that remotely suggested he'd been under any threat of harm. All was well and as it should be. Was it just an exaggeration… and why would anyone want to hurt him? An answer wasn't forthcoming. He hoped tomorrow's visit with the doctor at the hospital would provide some additional revelations.

Eager to begin his day, Leonard departed for work a little earlier than usual. On reaching Courtenay Place, he noticed a small group of onlookers staring at something laying on the street. Curiously, Leonard made his way through the few spectators and asked what the commotion was about.

"Is a body, mate," offered an informed man. "Was stabbed by a knife, most likely. If ya look you can see the blood trail." The man pointed back towards Leonard's street.

Leonard watched with some distaste and cautiously moved around the perimeter to gain a better and unobstructed view. A constable was diligently writing notes, and another was ensuring no one could approach the scene of the grisly slaying. Covered by canvas, the body was being hoisted onto the coroner's dray that arrived earlier.

"Does anyone know who it is?" asked Leonard to another bystander.

The man shook his head and moved off. Leonard watched curiously for a short while before he continued, somewhat perturbed, on his way to work.

Another death. Was it connected somehow to him? He couldn't fathom how it could be related and put the incident down to the effects of hard times and a robbery gone awry.

If Leonard had glanced over his shoulder he would have seen an unidentified man walking only a handful of steps behind. ,The stranger followed him all the way to his work.

The morning proved to be otherwise uneventful; all the reporters were out, and Leonard completed all his duties efficiently and gave no more thought to what he'd seen earlier. He found himself excited at the prospect of seeing Mary later in the afternoon and he began checking the clock frequently.

One by one, with their assignments completed, reporters drifted in and the bullpen began to fill. Mr Pembroke arrived, and much to Leonard's relief, other than his normal, gruff greeting, he made no mention of the previous late afternoon's embarrassing incident at the Thistle Inn.

Finally, it was time to leave. Leonard grabbed his things and hurriedly exited the building and looked for a cab, as the trams were especially slow at this time of day. After carefully scrutinising the driver, Leonard was soon heading to Wellington Hospital, in Newtown, to meet with Mary and a doctor, Lawrence Schrader.

The Hansom cab turned into the hospital driveway that curved around a decorative garden and stopped directly in front of the arches at the main entrance. After paying the driver's tariff, Leonard turned to the entrance and saw Mary waiting for him. He stopped and stared; he'd never seen her in uniform before and he was momentarily struck by her beauty. Certainly, a nurse's uniform wasn't designed to emphasise her figure or highlight her femininity, but it affected him all the same. He knew the bonnet she wore had practical uses and wasn't intended to showcase the latest fashion trends in hairstyling; nonetheless along with the high neckline of her uniform, it framed her face and drew attention to her cheeks, long neck and classic facial lines. Perhaps it was the way she stood. Her hands were clasped in front of her, and the vivid white of the apron only accentuated her narrow waist and flare of her skirts. She was smiling at him and for the briefest of moments he was captivated. It took him a moment to clear his head.

"Leonard, what is wrong?"

"Uh, Mary, ah, nothing, I, um... I have never seen you in uniform before. You look, uh ...splendid," he replied as he climbed the few steps to where she waited. He inwardly cringed, and couldn't believe he told her she looked splendid.

"Thank you, Leonard, that is sweet of you to say. I've never had anyone tell me I looked splendid in uniform before." She grinned and her eyes shone.

Leonard chastised himself under his breath.

"Is everything in order? You seem flustered."

"Yes, all is well." He leaned over and gave her a quick peck on the cheek. "And thank you for arranging for me to meet with Dr Schrader. As a ward sister, it may be helpful if you are able to attend and sit in with me?"

"Yes, my work shift is over and I have the time if you'd like me to."

"Yes, I would," he said quietly.

"Then let's go and find the doctor, shall we?" Mary wasn't thrilled about attending the meeting with Schrader but decided she would say nothing to Leonard, and assist him any way she could.

A hospital porter opened the door for them both.

Leonard knocked twice on the door and waited. He turned and gave Mary a warm smile.

"Yes?" came the reply.

Leonard politely opened the door for Mary who entered first. Dr Schrader sat behind a desk in a cluttered office not that dissimilar to Alex's. The difference being the chairs did not have a stack of medical reference books on them.

The doctor slid his chair back and stood; he wore a black suit, typical sombre attire for a physician, and extended his hand. "Lawrence Schrader - and you must be Mr Hardy?" Dr Schrader was not tall, in fact, he was tiny and round. He had a remarkable girth as was evidenced when he stood. His waistcoat appeared to defy the laws of physics and was stretched to breaking point and beyond. *It must be uncomfortable for him to wear*, thought Leonard.

The doctor's eyes were small and shifted lecherously to Mary. He made no attempt to disguise his interest in her, and then realising he had another guest, reluctantly focused on Leonard.

Leonard shook his hand and noticed the weak, limp grip. "Yes, thank you for seeing me, doctor. I'm Leonard Hardy, and of course, you are familiar with Ward Sister Worthington."

The doctor inclined his head at Mary, offering her an obscene smile, then waved them both to chairs. "Then how can I be of assistance?" He smiled again and looked at each of them in question as he sat. A handkerchief mysteriously appeared and Dr Schrader patted his head. Devoid of hair, it shone with brilliance.

Leonard extracted a notebook and pencil from his jacket. By using shorthand, he would transcribe Dr Schrader's replies so he could reference them later. "A dear friend of ours, Dr Alex Leyton, the medical practitioner for the coroner, met with a tragic accident and as a result he was killed."

"Yes, I was devastated to hear of the news, a splendid chap. I'm sorry for your loss."

Mary gave a playful look to Leonard at the use of the word 'splendid.' It didn't go unnoticed by him.

"Thank you. Alex, uh, Dr Leyton was working on a case and he died shortly after visiting with you. Do you recall the nature of that meeting, doctor?"

"Yes, it was a routine consultation between colleagues, discussing a patient, nothing out of the ordinary."

"I'd wonder if you could clarify a couple of points for me." Without waiting for an answer, Leonard continued. "Firstly, was that patient afflicted with Parkinson's disease?"

"I never examined him and cannot determine if he suffered

from that malady, but from Dr Leyton's detailed post-mortem notes, then I believe he may have been."

· Leonard transcribed the doctor's replies into his notebook.

He nodded. "How do you think Dr Leyton arrived at that conclusion?"

"If my memory serves me correctly, he initially believed the patient was being poisoned by Atropa belladonna. He also discovered some irregularities in the thalamus, which is part of the brain. When he described to me what he'd found, I confirmed with him that it was likely the patient was suffering from Parkinson's disease. It has been known that belladonna may have curative benefits that could help sufferers with the effects of Parkinson's disease."

"Then as far as you're aware the patient wasn't being poisoned?"

"No, I don't believe he was. Although, at first, Dr Leyton believed so."

"Yes, that's what I thought, too." Leonard extracted the note he'd taken from Alex's office and glanced at it again. "Was there anything that you thought was peculiar about the post-mortem results? Had Alex performed a thorough examination?"

"Other than the man was too young to be suffering from Parkinson's disease, he was unremarkable. Dr Leyton was extremely thorough and that's supported by his discovery of belladonna and rice in the stomach."

"Rice!" exclaimed Leonard.

"Yes," a look of anxiousness passed over Schrader's face, but he recovered quickly.

"Isn't that unusual for a Caucasian male to have just rice in his stomach, doctor? If the patient was Oriental then his stomach contents would have been unsurprising, but not for a European."

"Perhaps," Schrader said dismissively and didn't elaborate.

Leonard scratched his head. "Were there any other oddities about the patient you are aware of?"

The doctor shook his head.

"What about the mark on one of his lower legs?"

Schrader looked puzzled and didn't respond.

"You don't recall, doctor? Dr Leyton said he had some contusions near his ankle."

"Oh, yes, of course," remarked Schrader finally remembering. "He had some peculiar superficial abrasions with mild contusions above his ankle. I'm unable to expand further on that as I never saw the patient."

"Dr Leyton believed he knew who the deceased was. What did he tell you?"

"There's not much to say really. Dr Leyton felt he had some relevant information that would assist in determining the identity of the deceased. That is all."

"And he never told you who he thought the patient was?"

Dr Schrader shook his head. "No, and it wasn't relevant to our consultation."

"Would he have written that information in his notes?"

"If he had that information, then possibly, I expect so."

"Then you would have read the notes from his examination?"

Schrader looked uncomfortable and wiped his brow. "Oh good heavens no, our meeting was informal., Dr Leyton didn't bring his notes with him."

Leonard thought a moment and flicked back a few pages of the transcription in his notebook. He found what he was looking for and underlined the words. He cleared his throat. "Dr Schrader, are you certain you didn't read Dr Leyton's notes on this particular case?"

"Yes, I am certain." Schrader looked uneasy. "And now if you'll excuse me, I have my scheduled rounds to attend too." Dr Schrader rose from behind his desk with some difficulty. The meeting was over. He enjoyed another healthy long look at Mary.

"Thank you very much for your help, doctor. I've taken enough of your valuable time."

Dr Schrader took extremely short steps, perhaps necessitated by very short legs, towards the door and opened it for Mary and Leonard.

"Good day, doctor."

Dr Schrader smiled graciously in response as he watched them depart. Slowly his expression changed as he ogled the disappearing form of Mary.

"He is a very disturbing man," she whispered once out of earshot. She had unconsciously grabbed Leonard's elbow as they walked away.

They walked back through the corridors towards the main entrance and outside into the garden.

"Was he helpful?" Mary asked.

"That was very useful. Thank you for arranging that, Mary. I think I have more questions now than answers. One thing I have learned, the man is evasive and a liar."

"I find him unsettling." she shuddered.

"Yes, a very peculiar man, indeed."

Mary looked up at Leonard expectantly. "Leonard, my shift is over and if you'd care to wait, I can change into my normal clothes, we can go home and you can share with me your thoughts."

"Yes, that would be a wonderful idea," Leonard replied as he scratched his chin.

Leonard was seated alone at his customary place on the sofa at Bridgette and Mary's home, while Mary was making tea in the kitchen for them both. He sat silently and stared at a fixed point on the wall as he pondered all he had learned earlier in the afternoon. The ticking of a clock marked the silence. The measured, mechanical strikes of the second hand grew oppressively louder, the clamour competing with ideas, thoughts and notions that swirled in a vague abstract turmoil that interrupted his orderly ruminations.

"Well, tell me then," said Mary as she carried a tray into the room, "I'm beside myself with curiosity."

Leonard shook his head to clear his mind. "Something is going on, Mary. I don't know what it is, or why, or who is behind it. The more I learn the more perplexed I become." He sighed and extracted the note he'd taken from Alex's office and looked at it again. Something about the note wasn't correct - it bothered him.

Mary poured the tea into both cups and waited patiently.

He showed her the note and explained some basic principles of shorthand writing. He went over each of the words Alex had written. He stopped at the word '*Died.*'

"What's wrong?"

"This word," Leonard pointed to the paper. "I said '*Died*' but I read the word incorrectly, it's actually '*Diet.*' The shorthand pencil stroke is similar for both words. That supports what Dr Schrader said about the rice."

"You're right, Leo. It does seem odd that a European man would just have rice in his stomach."

"Yes, unless he was Oriental, then presumably it would be

105

normal."

"What about the marks on his ankle? The doctor said, 'abrasions and contusions,' that's also an unusual thing to have."

Leonard shook his head. "Perhaps more baffling, Mary, is the fact that when Alex was struck by that wagon he was without his post-mortem report."

Mary sat primly on the edge of the settee with her teacup and saucer on her lap, and watched him intently. "Are you sure? Dr Schrader said Alex didn't bring his report to the meeting."

"He lied, Mary. He said earlier in our meeting that he read, and I quote, 'In his detailed notes', and later he denied Alex brought them."

"Perhaps Alex never showed them to him but had them with him?"

"I specifically asked Constable Hastings what items Alex had with him when he was killed. He consulted an inventory and the post-mortem report certainly wasn't one of them."

"Then he is hiding something from you? You've said yourself that you don't trust the man."

Leonard raised his eyebrows. "Or did someone take them?"

Mary quickly looked at him in surprise.

"That may well have been the reason he was killed?"

"Oh, Leonard, do you really believe that?"

"Based on the information we have, then it makes logical sense and there are no other rational explanations."

Mary sipped her tea contemplatively and then turned back to him. "All the information you have leads directly in some peculiar way to Dr Schrader and Orientals."

"Yes." He raised the teacup to his lips, took a tentative sip of the scalding drink and placed it back on the table. "That's what I've come to realise too. That makes my visit to Uncle Jun tomorrow that much more interesting."

"Can I come with you?"

Leonard looked at her in surprise. In the past the thought of bringing a woman with him to visit Uncle Jun and Ming would have been incomprehensible. However, he also had serious misgivings about the safety of the neighbourhood and the colourful people who frequented the area. He'd not forgotten the man who accosted him last week and wondered how it would be if accompanied by a woman.

"Mary, I would welcome your company on a Saturday morning stroll. Frederick Street is an unsavoury area and I even found myself in considerable peril last week. I think it would be irresponsible of me to allow you come with me."

"But your wife, Mae, she walked there alone..."

"I could never forgive myself if something happened to you, Mary."

She looked down into her cup and thought a moment before lifting her head. "I understand, Leonard." She offered him a warm smile.

Chapter Eight

How many times had he been warned? The mysterious Mr
Crumb had warned him, and so had Constable Hastings and even
Uncle Jun. Yet, despite their well-meaning cautions, he had not
encountered anything remotely perilous. Was the *accoster* last
week near Frederick Street more than a random confrontation by an
opportunist? He had ventured into a neighbourhood where illegal
activity was prevalent; therefore, an assault and robbery could be
expected, so it was unlikely he had been singled out to be attacked.
The unforgettable incident at the Thistle Inn was nothing more
than it appeared, and while certainly humiliated, at no time had he
felt threatened. Although on the walk home, he was sure he'd been
followed but never endangered.

Then why did those people feel the need to issue him with
warnings to exercise mindfulness? Admittedly, he and Alex had
both been warned, and Alex was now dead. Why? Because Alex had
information that would lead to the identity of the body found outside
his home? Then, if he himself was still alive, those responsible for
Alex's death obviously felt he didn't pose a threat. When the time
came that he did have information, that view may likely change.
Leonard shuddered. The thought of being stalked by an assassin
was alarming, if not terrifying.

It was Saturday morning, and Leonard retraced his route back
to Uncle Jun's shop on Frederick Street. He was using the time to
think and arrive at reasonable and intelligent illations to help solve

the mystery around Alex's death. Still, it was proving to be more than a little complicated and immensely frustrating.

Leonard deliberately tried to focus on the logical aspects of why he was being followed. Someone wanted to know where he was going, or they would assail him at a suitable location. What other possible explanations could there be?

A Hansom cab passed by very close, and as a precaution, he stepped to the side to avoid being struck. He watched the cab as it moved away, and then it occurred to him - the cab driver! Leonard stopped walking. Last Saturday, the familiar cab driver had been coincidentally and conveniently close when the man had confronted him, and the cabbie had willingly stepped in to avert any trouble - surely that wasn't by chance. Leonard nodded; another reason he was being followed was that someone was protecting him! He thought of his walk to work yesterday and the body near the bottom of the street with the fatal knife wounds. Was that a result of someone safeguarding him? He needed to be more vigilant, more cautious and more cunning.

Whoever was behind the murders had the advantage. They had resources and knowledge and remained cloaked in secrecy. Leonard picked up his stride - he felt he had an adversary and was being challenged - he walked with renewed purpose.

The first indication he was approaching Chinatown and the famed Haining and Frederick street area was the number of people he saw loitering and doing nothing - malingerers casting shifty and furtive glances around them. Many were desperate; he could see it in their body language and demeanour. They were unkempt and sullied and watched him with undisguised envy. He knew they would, at any opportunity, descend on him and feast on his lucre as they would on any gentleman silly enough to allow them the opportunity.

Two slovenly youths stepped out behind a doorway and blocked Leonard's path. Both sneered, lips curled in feral aggression, revealing decaying teeth and unwelcome attentions. Dirt and grime stained unshaven sallow faces, and their cloth caps were pulled low over greasy brows. Leonard had seen this type before, working-class lads, labourers who've succumbed to the torpid pleasures of opium-induced fantasies.

They lifted their heads and, with reddened eyes, made eye contact, their stares meant to intimidate and unnerve. Void of hope, the soulless youths challenged him with aggressive body postures, thumbs hooked into worn vests, legs slightly spread and with a disposition to match their wretchedness, they waited confidently as he approached.

A week earlier, a man in almost the exact location had accosted him, and while Leonard may not have been gifted with the physical prowess to defend against men used to confrontation, he felt he had the acumen and was capable of adapting and learning fast.

He maintained his pace and collided heavily with the first scrawny youth, shouldering him backwards into his accomplice. While Leonard would argue vehemently that he didn't outweigh the larrikins by a great deal, he used his slight weight advantage to its fullest. Without a backward glance, Leonard walked on, petrified they would pursue him.

A few bystanders of equally dubious character laughed at the two youths who went sprawling, but then a warning shout ceased all mirth. Fearful they would come bounding after him, Leonard looked over his shoulder in wide-eyed fright. Two Oriental men had appeared from nowhere and were pummelling the two young rogues who lay on the ground. A few well-placed kicks ended the altercation, and Leonard hurried off. Part of him wanted to go back and question the Orientals as to why they assaulted the two young men. Still, his instinctive need for self-preservation far exceeded the desire to satisfy curiosity.

He was genuinely relieved when he turned onto Frederick Street; the throng of weekend shoppers made him feel more at ease. He approached Uncle Jun's shop and entered with a final look over his shoulder. He removed his hat and wiped his brow with a sleeve, his heart racing.

Behind the counter stood a man, someone who Leonard did not recognise. The man looked up at Leonard with suspicion.

"*Ni hau*," Leonard said respectfully.

The man grunted, not acknowledging the greeting.

Leonard walked to the counter. "Is Mr Chen here? Jun?"

The man shook his head and turned to walk away.

"Where are Jun and Ming? They are expecting me!"

The man raised an arm and pointed outside, "You go! Go now!"

Taking the man by surprise, and before he could prevent him, Leonard quickly walked to the rear of the shop and pulled the curtain aside. He expected to see Ming cooking food; instead, a woman with an infant sat in Ming's regular place. "Where are they?" Leonard asked. The baby began to cry. "Forgive me, I'm just looking for Mr Chen," said Leonard quietly.

"You go!" repeated the man, who'd quickly caught up, his anger evident.

Dejectedly, Leonard walked from the shop and stood outside.

He looked around, hoping to see the happy faces of Jun and Ming. Strangers pushed passed, ignoring him. He knew no other merchants here, and there wasn't anyone else he could turn to for help or ask about them. Where were they?

Rather than venture back the way he'd come and risk encountering further trouble, Leonard chose to walk down Taranaki Street and take the longer and safer route home. He was vigilant and kept a watchful eye around him. Periodically he'd stop, quickly look behind and scan the streets looking for anyone following. He looked up at the cabbies as they drove past and at pedestrians as they unhurriedly ambled by. Everything seemed as it should, and Leonard began to feel at ease, and slowly he began to relax. He turned the corner onto Courtenay Place and stopped – and slowly edged back, peeked around the corner up Taranaki Street, and saw a burly man running towards him. Leonard recognised the fellow; he'd seen him leave one of Frederick Street's tearooms but hadn't given the man a second thought. Now he was running down towards Courtenay Place, towards where he stood. Was he being pursued? An idea came to mind.

Leonard forced himself to walk normally. He slowly crossed the road and made his way down Tory Street, turned right in the direction of the morgue and resisted all temptation to look behind. He walked into the yard, went around the stacked crates, and entered the building through the staff entrance. He waited nervously for a brief time, then walked down a corridor and left the building through the main entrance; luckily, he encountered no one inside. Once outside the morgue, he risked a look around the side of the building and back towards the yard. Near the yard's entrance, the same man stood waiting. *He was being pursued.* He tried to see the man's face, but the distance was too great.

Leonard was fearful for the second time that day. He cautiously moved away from the morgue and walked unseen towards home, half expecting to be struck on the back of the head and dragged into the bushes. Relief set in when he finally arrived home and immediately locked the door. He took a moment to collect himself and noticed his hands shaking – he was petrified. With coffee foremost on his mind, he stoked the fire and set the water to boil.

Leonard took his first sip of the strong brew and was interrupted by a loud rap on the door. He almost dropped his cup. He froze. Again, the fist pounded, and it wasn't the timid knock of a woman; this was the rap of a man demanding that the door be opened. It wasn't like the knock of the constable, this was different, and he was terrified. A thousand thoughts flooded through his head, and only one made sense - there was nowhere to run or hide. He placed the cup on the writing bureau and walked tentatively to the door. He jumped when the fist hammered on the door again. His heart was pounding and threatened to leap out of his chest. He took a deep breath, threw caution to the wind and bravely flung open the door.

"Are you going to let me in or just stand there gawping like a carp?" said Mr Pembroke.

Leonard was mute.

"Well?"

Leonard closed his mouth and waited for his heart to stop thumping. He swallowed. "Mr... Mr uh, Pembroke."

"Are you alright, lad?" The *Evening Standard's* most senior reporter frowned. "You look poorly."

Leonard looked past the diminutive Mr Pembroke and out onto

the street. He saw no sign of the burly man. He swallowed. "Mr Pembroke, what are… what a pleasant surprise, sir. Please, come in." He stepped back and allowed his guest to enter and, before shutting the door, cast another quick glance down the street. "Would you like a coffee? I've just made some." He showed Mr Pembroke to the living room and took his hat.

"Aye, that would be fine, lad."

Leonard returned a minute later with a steaming cup and handed it to the elderly man.

"Uh, have you a…?" Mr Pembroke inclined his head. "You know… helps the sinuses," he smiled.

"Scotch?" asked Leonard.

"Well, since you ask, why not, eh?"

Leonard retrieved his only bottle of Scotch whiskey and allowed Mr Pembroke the pleasure of self-medication. The reporter poured a healthy dollop into his coffee and took an exploratory sip. "Good coffee, that."

"Yes, thank you, sir. I have a friend who provides me with the beans. And what brings you this way? I didn't expect company this afternoon, and I, er, only just returned home."

Mr Pembroke looked around the room. He'd never been here before, and he could see the room had been tastefully furnished - *a woman's deft hand*, he thought. The bookshelf contained an assortment of fine reading material, a few reference books and, of course, one or two obligatory classics. An open book sat on the table, and Pembroke picked it up, squinted and moved it away from his eyes slightly to better read the title. "*Die Penderyn,*" he said and put it back down.

"It's about a Welsh folk hero who was executed for wounding a soldier," offered Leonard.

"Bloody Welsh," muttered Pembroke, seemingly unimpressed. He continued surveying the room with the practised eye of a reporter looking for a story.

The writing bureau was functional, not cluttered, and a framed photograph of Mae held centre position. Pembroke had met her a few times and was intrigued. She was stunningly beautiful, and Leonard had undoubtedly been a lucky man. More so, she was clever, an intelligent, astute woman and popular amongst her people. Satisfied with his perusal, Mr Pembroke sat back on the armchair, crossed a leg, looked to Leonard and sighed disapprovingly.

"What on God's green bloody earth were you doing at that meeting the other night, Leonard?" He paused and saw Leonard formulating a reply, then quickly raised his hand to forestall him. "You of all people should know they're a dangerous lot - damn hotheads!" Pembroke scratched his long combed-out sideburns known affectionately as Piccadilly weepers. "If you wanted to fire 'em up, then you did exactly that. It was bloody reckless, it was. You're a smart lad; you got something up here," Pembroke tapped his head for emphasis, "But I do wonder at times." He took another sip of coffee, then, with a wink, reached for the bottle, poured another good measure into the cup, and sat back again. He raised his eyebrows in question, expecting an answer.

"I wanted to understand the nature of the White New Zealand League."

Pembroke unfolded his legs painfully and leaned forward, "Do you think I was born under a cabbage tree, lad? That excuse may work on others, not me. I'm a little long in the tooth to be that gullible. Tell me, what's going on? Out with it, I want the truth, now."

The whiskey bottle on the table had been almost full, and it was now half empty. Mr Pembroke's coat hung haphazardly over the back of the spare armchair, and he sat listening, occasionally interrupting Leonard with a question or two but patiently waiting for Leonard to detail the recent events.

"And so you thought I was the man who had followed you from Frederick Street?"

"Yes, I was petrified."

"That's an interesting and complex series of events." Pembroke's fingers drummed on the armrest as he considered. "This chap, Winston Crumb, I wouldn't waste too much energy looking for him. Wellington's only a small town, so eventually, he'll turn up."

Leonard shrugged.

"And Constable Hastings... I've met him several times and found him to be a rather unpleasant fellow. His behaviour with you has been questionable to say the least. Again you were foolish to provoke him. However, it got results," remarked Pembroke. His fingers continued to tap as he thought.

"Why did you come here today, sir?" asked Leonard.

Mr Pembroke looked up and met Leonard's eyes. "You're a smart lad, even likeable. You work hard, care about others, and I have never heard an unpleasant or unkind word said about you. The death of your wife was tragic, and we at the *Evening Standard* have all seen the change in you. Then after the death of your friend, Dr Leyton... I feared you'd spiral into the depths of melancholic hell, and who would do your job? That's why I'm here. Damn sinuses have been playing up recently, must be the weather." Pembroke reached down and refilled his cup.

"That's very kind of you."

"No, it's not, it's a bloody obligation, and I have better things to do with my time." Pembroke revealed a hint of a rare smile as he brought the cup to his lips.

"Now that you're here, then surely you are also at risk?" Leonard stood. "People are dying, Mr Pembroke, people I know and care for. The police... what can I say to them that they'll believe – absolutely nothing! Based on what has already happened, I can only presume you are also in jeopardy, and frankly, that doesn't sit well with me!"

"Are you finished squawking? You sound like a bloody politician." Unbidden, Pembroke reached down and poured some whiskey into Leonard's cup. "Start with this, it works wonders on sinuses." Pembroke turned to the photograph on the bureau. "To Mae! Cheers!" Without waiting, he hoisted the cup and drained the contents.

Leonard did the same, "Cheers!" Then grimaced as he sat back down.

"Now then, we have considerable resources at our disposal. If you are so determined to find those responsible for the death of your friend Dr Leyton, then may I suggest looking closer, perhaps even at Dr Schrader? Also, I suggest looking into the Chinese gangs; I think they call them tongs or triads, and if there is Chinese involvement, then you can safely assume the tongs will be involved. If we collaborate, our inquiries may even drive them out from hiding, eh? And I'm most curious to learn what you've learned about this group, Patrons of New Zealand. Although I wouldn't waste my time chasing them, stick to the Chinese and let me know what you discover. Who knows, it may even make a good story - we'll shake the bloody tree, eh? Wellington is small, lad, there's not a lot that goes on that I don't get to hear about." Mr Pembroke gave his Piccadilly weepers a scratch. We'll put the word out and cast our net far and wide." Pembroke leaned forward taciturnly. "People love to talk, Leonard, and given the opportunity, they won't shut up." Pembroke winked, nodded to reinforce his point, and sat back, pleased with himself.

Leonard remembered the body on Courtenay Place. "Did you hear about the body found just down the street?"

"Yes, I heard. Apparently, a Chinese vagrant was involved in some gang dispute. Nothing more than a tiff between Orientals. Why? Do you think it's related?"

"While death is commonplace, murders are relatively infrequent, yet another murder close to where I live … yes, there's a possibility it's related."

"I haven't heard anything to suggest otherwise, but that doesn't mean it isn't. I'll keep an eye on it for you." Mr Pembroke rose to his feet. "And now I must go; if I don't return home soon, I'll have to listen to Mrs Pembroke grouse for the rest of the evening, and I don't wish that on anyone."

Leonard retrieved Mr Pembroke's hat and saw him to the door.

"I would take the cautions about your safety seriously, so don't take unnecessary risks. Even though I think you're correct and someone is protecting you, do be careful. This whole business, it's uh … It's very perplexing," Pembroke turned to walk away and then paused. "Oh yes, can you get me some of those coffee beans?"

"I'll do my best. Thank you, sir and good day."

"Try moving your home to a place where there isn't a bloody hill," grumbled Mr Pembroke as he took his leave.

The next few days at work kept Leonard busy; he had obituaries to create, shipping intelligence reports to finish, and a few advertisements he needed to write. Mr Pembroke kept his distance and acted as if he'd never come to see him. *Perhaps it's for the best,* Leonard thought.

Bailey & Sons, Grain and Seed Merchants, had a warehouse on Taranaki Street, not far from Frederick Street in Chinatown. Ships brought grain and seed into the Wellington, and Mr Bailey and his small army of workers loaded their wagons at the docks and transported the goods to his warehouses from where it was stored and sold.

Mr Bailey had purchased considerable and ongoing advertising space in the *Evening Standard,* and Leonard needed to visit him and have his advertising copy approved before the week's end. As he would be in the vicinity, he decided, once his business was concluded with Mr Bailey, he would detour to Frederick Street and see if Uncle Jun had since returned. *It couldn't do any harm*, he thought.

An agreeable man, Mr Bailey, or just 'Bailey' to his friends, was quick to laugh and quip. He was an exuberant, informal, hardworking businessman of immense proportions, with a never-ending supply of anecdotes to suit any occasion. Sadly, his two sons, both in their late teens, were not gifted with such a pleasing disposition and often trailed morosely behind their father until he reluctantly sent them on their way with a task or two to perform. Thankfully there was no sign of the two malcontents as Leonard entered the warehouse in search of Mr Bailey, Sr.

From the warehouse's deep recesses, the booming laughter

indicated Mr Bailey wasn't far away. Moments later, the big man identified the *Evening Standard's* representative.

"Leo, you've finally takin' me up on m'offer to come an work for me!" Mr Bailey grinned from ear to ear as he approached. "We'll trim some of that puppy fat off ya in no time at all."

Leonard was used to the needling and didn't expect less from the man.

Mr Bailey stopped, placed his huge hands on his hips and looked Leonard up and down. "Seems to me you may have shed a pound or two already!" He held out a beefy hand and shook Leonard's hand vigorously.

Leonard tried hard not to wince.

"Good to see you, Leo." The smile was warm and sincere.

"And it's always a pleasure to see you too, Bailey. I always enjoy coming down for a visit," replied Leonard with equal warmth.

"You must come and have dinner with us again, and soon."

"Thank you, I'd enjoy that."

Bailey's eyes never stopped moving; he knew exactly what was happening at any given time with all his workers and some people even suggested he could tell you exactly how many grains of wheat he had in storage.

Two labourers entered the warehouse and looked around uncertainly.

"The leak is on the far right-hand corner, Mr Wilson. Need it seen to right away, if you please. And a pint or two is on me if you fix it before it rains!"

The labourers immediately rushed off, and Bailey returned his attention back to Leonard. "We got a roof leak."

Leonard nodded in response.

"This is a busy time for us, Leo. We've got ships lined up with grain and seed ready to be off-loaded, and we have to get the stuff away from the docks quickly. Am hoping the advertisement in the *Standard* will help sell our stock. We're bursting at the seams."

"Mr Beaumont is confident the advertisement will increase sales, Bailey. I know you've got plenty to do, but I need your approval on the advertisement before it goes to the typesetters and printing." Leonard unfolded a copy of the advertisement and let Bailey read it a few times. As he waited, Leonard noticed a Hansom cab had pulled up outside.

Bailey repeatedly stabbed with a gnarled finger at the paper. "Who took out the words *Excellent* and *Best in the colony*?"

"Mr Beaumont thought it a mite presumptuous; he overruled me, editor's prerogative." Leonard shrugged.

"Bollocks, I like what you wrote, Leo. Put them words back, and I'll be satisfied."

"Very well," Leonard replied with a smile.

"And when will it be in the paper?"

"On Saturday."

Bailey nodded as a wagon stacked with sacks of seeds pulled up behind the Hansom cab. "Rangi, see to that load that's just arrived!"

"Righto!" yelled an unseen voice. Seconds later, a man trotted past and headed outside.

Bailey smiled, "He's a good worker, that one."

"I will make the changes as you've outlined, Bailey, and inform Mr Beaumont of your request."

"It's not a request, not if he wants my business. If he gives you any quarrel, tell him to come and see me." Bailey grinned. "Leo, how you off for coffee?" Without waiting for an answer, "Dingo?

Dingo? Where the hell are ya?"

"Comin'!" came a reply.

"Fill a small sack of that coffee for Leo, will ya!"

Within a minute or two, a scruffy middle-aged man appeared with a five-pound sack of coffee beans. "Sorry about the sack, is all I have." He handed it over with a toothless grin and walked away.

Leonard looked at the sack and grinned. 'Walnuts' was written in large, stencilled letters, just like the sack he had at home. "Thank you very much, Bailey, it's wonderful coffee."

"Just don't go tellin' people where you got 'em," he winked.

Another wagon, loaded with more seed, was pulling up outside. "I better get these wagons unloaded, Leo. Thank you for coming by." He was already heading out to the street and shouting instructions to the driver.

Leonard tucked the sack under his arm, walked out through the large doors of the warehouse and into the late afternoon sunlight on Taranaki Street. The Hansom cab was still parked where he'd seen it earlier, and the driver was petting the horse. The cabbie turned around at the sound of approaching footsteps, and Leonard immediately recognised him. It was the same familiar cabbie who'd been with Mr Crumb and chased the man away last weekend.

"Pleasant day, Mr Hardy." The cabbie touched his fingers to his hat.

"You!" was all Leonard could think of to say.

"A moment of your time, sir?"

Before the cabbie could speak further, Leonard began with the questions. "What is your business with me, and... and... this Mr Crumb, who is he? Why are you following me? And who are you, your name if you please, sir?" demanded Leonard, clearly flustered.

The cabbie's smile vanished. "You can call me Mr Smith, but I am not here to answer your questions. I am here at the request of Mr Crumb, who extends his greetings to you," Cabbie Smith smiled. "However, he is somewhat perturbed, Mr Hardy." The cabbie stepped away from the horse and closer to Leonard. "It appears to him you've not heeded his advice, and you persist in interfering in matters you've no understanding of. You continue to put yourself in harm's way and pose a considerable risk to your safety and that of your friends. Mr Crumb is finding it extremely difficult to ensure your welfare if you gets my meaning, sir."

Leonard was agitated and having difficulty holding the sack of coffee as his anger increased. He repositioned the bag under his other arm. "How dare you accost me in the street and threaten me! By what right do you have, tell me, I insist, what do you want with me?" Leonard yelled.

A few passers-by gave Leonard a questioning look as they cautiously detoured around him.

"Is the coffee proving to be a burden? Then perhaps I can offer you a ride home so we can chat a little more?"

"I'm not going home! And damn it, answer my questions!"

Leonard hesitated for a heartbeat or two as the realisation dawned on him. He took a half step closer to the cabbie. He was furious, his anger plain. "You've been inside my home!" It wasn't a question; it was an accusation, and it struck a nerve with the self-assured cab driver.

The cabbie was caught off guard. He swallowed and raised both hands, palms out to appease. "Now hold on a minute, Mr Hardy."

"No, you hold on!" yelled Leonard. "There is no way you could ever know what this sack contains unless you've been inside my home!"

A few people stopped to stare.

"How dare you! I will go to the police and file a complaint against your illegal activities. Have you no honour or modicum of respect?" Leonard shook his head in bafflement. "And you appear quite unremorseful about entering a man's home without cause or permission. What is it you sought? Tell me!" he bellowed.

The cabbie suddenly looked alarmed and nimbly leapt onto his perch at the rear of the cab, flailing his whip at the horse. Within seconds, the startled animal was trotting down the road as the imposing figure of Bailey ran up.

"What was all that about?"

Leonard dropped the coffee sack on the ground at his feet and placed both hands on his thighs for support. He could hardly speak and shook his head. "I wish I knew," he finally gasped.

"I heard yellin', thought there was a problem."

"There was Bailey, a big one."

"Are you in some kind of trouble, Leo? I'm always available if you need someone to talk to." Bailey's face showed genuine concern. "Are you in debt to the cabbie? Is it money?" he said with gravity.

"No, no, I do not owe anyone money, thank you, Bailey. I've done nothing wrong, but it's a long story, and you needn't be burdened with my tale of woe. In fact, it's best you don't know."

Bailey watched the cab fast disappearing down the street. He'd seen the cabbie a few times and remember him again if need be, but he wasn't entirely convinced of Leonard's tepid explanation. "As long everything is well, I suppose."

Leonard straightened. "Thank you, Bailey, I'm pleased you ran up when you did. If you hadn't, I believe I would have throttled the man."

"Might have been better to allow me that privilege," smiled Bailey. He patted Leonard's shoulder, "I'll be getting back to work then. Remember, if you need me, I'm always willin' to help you."

"Thank you again." Leonard hoisted the beans under his arm and walked slowly up Taranaki Street with his mind in turmoil.

The situation was becoming unmanageable, his own reactions were uncharacteristic, and his fear was turning into aggression, emotions he felt unfamiliar and uncomfortable with. These people, Mr Crumb and his lackeys had entered his home; they'd searched with impunity and disregard through his possessions, and to what end?

Leonard paused and leaned against the wall, suddenly feeling drained and spent of energy. He knew he needed to restore order to his mind, realign his priorities, and refocus. Above all, not let emotions drive his decision-making. With grim resolve, he pushed off the wall, repositioned his coffee under the other arm and walked. He fervently hoped Uncle Jun and Ming would be in their shop.

Bailey watched as Leonard made his way towards Frederick Street. He knew if Leonard was heading to Chinatown, it wasn't a good sign. He called Rangi over.

"Go up the street and see where Leo goes - there's something going on, and I don't like it. Don't let him see you, and don't be away long, there's work for you here."

Bailey watched Rangi run off and shook his head in wonder. Leo was the last person he'd expect to get into trouble in Chinatown. With wagons to unload, Bailey went back to business.

There were plenty of people about; most appeared to be returning home from work. A few couples strolled casually on the footpath, and Leonard forced himself to slow down and relax. But he couldn't forget what he'd learned. He was still livid and upset at the cab driver and the discovery that the driver and perhaps others had been in his home looking through his possessions, private things that no stranger had the right to see! Not that he had anything to hide besides a few Arabica coffee beans, but just knowing that men had been inside his house rummaging around was unsettling, and he felt violated.

He turned onto Frederick Street and was surprised at the number of people coming and going. Many seemed to be visiting the gambling houses, a few seemed intent on entering the opium dens, while others ate from Chinese vendors selling street-side food. He had no reason to suspect that Rangi was only a few feet behind him.

Without pausing, Leonard turned into Uncle Jun's shop and looked for the familiar face but saw no one. "Hello?" He waited and heard no response, so he walked towards the curtain at the rear of the shop and cautiously peeked around. The same unknown man he encountered before had just risen from a table where he, his wife and a child had been eating. They looked frightened.

The man saw Leonard's face as the curtain moved aside. "You, go! No wan you here!" he yelled.

Leonard released the curtain and waited until the man appeared. Leonard spoke slowly. "I need to speak to Jun and Ming, do you understand?"

The man looked at Leonard blankly. "Jun and Ming," Leonard repeated.

Again the man raised an arm, ready to continue, but Leonard was still angry and lacking patience. "No!" He cut the man off. "Jun and Ming, you tell them Leonard needs to talk." Leonard could see the comprehension in the man's eyes. "You tell them, Leonard must talk."

"You go," replied the man automatically after a moment's pause.

Leonard shook his head in frustration, juggled the coffee beans to his other arm and walked out of the shop. He looked around, just as he'd done previously, hoping to see Uncle Jun and Ming, but all he saw were unrecognisable faces, just strangers. He didn't see Rangi.

Discouraged, Leonard walked away. He didn't check if he was being followed, he didn't care, he just strolled away feeling alone and sad. He missed Mae so much.

Rangi watched Leonard until he disappeared, then hastened back to Mr Bailey and told him what he saw.

Chapter Nine

𝔗t was quiet inside the *Evening Standard's* bullpen, as almost everyone had gone home for the day. Leonard was clearing his workspace prior to leaving, and Mr Pembroke, who had just returned, sat in the rear, sighing and fussing over a new story he was writing. Along one wall near the large windows, stacks of newspapers, all previous editions of the *Evening Standard,* lay in orderly piles along a wide shelf that ran the entire length of the dark wood panelled room. Along most of the rear wall were smaller shelves that held neatly labelled ring-binder folders. Some were labelled according to year, others by alphabetic letters. Beside them, another bookshelf contained an assortment of reference books, dictionaries and a set of well-used encyclopaedias. Against the front wall, a series of small filing cabinets were tucked into the corner; they contained the *Evening Standard's* card indexing system. Also pinned to the wall beside the calendar overlooking Leonard's desk were a few notices, clippings, and an assortment of comic illustrations - a gallery displaying the satirical humour of those who dwelled in the creative space.

It had been a long hard day. Mr Beaumont had approved all of Leonard's work, and as requested, he delivered his *copy* to the typesetters before the deadline. As Mr Bailey demanded, Mr Beaumont had reluctantly allowed the wording for the Bailey and Sons advertisement to be changed. It was of some concern to the publisher to keep his clients happy, particularly Mr Bailey, who could be notoriously difficult at times. The man knew exactly what he wanted and, in the past, had made life onerous for some *Evening Standard* employees, but Leonard had a good relationship with him, and Mr Beaumont was content and relieved to allow Leonard the responsibility to deal with him.

"Leonard, a moment of your time?"

Leonard turned, surprised at Mr Pembroke's summons. He walked curiously up the narrow aisle between the desks and waited for him to finish writing. After a few moments, the senior reporter waved him silently to a chair, removed his spectacles, breathed on them a few times, and gave them a thorough vigorous rubbing as Leonard watched.

He held them to the light and once satisfied they were clean, placed them carefully on his desk and twisted in his chair to observe Leonard; he grimaced with the move. He placed a finger between the high collar of his shirt and neck and slid it around to ease the discomfort.

"That's better. Mrs Pembroke insists on buying bloody shirts that are a size too small, and I swear she does it deliberately to make my life miserable."

Leonard had never met Mrs Pembroke, and if he believed everything Mr Pembroke said, then surely his own life would be in mortal danger if he were ever alone with her. He smiled sympathetically in reply.

Able to once again breathe, Pembroke continued. "Your Mr Crumb doesn't exist, Leonard."

Leonard looked surprised.

"I called on a few contacts and had them dig around -- City Council records, even ship passenger arrival lists and a few clubs and organisations, and nothing. Not even remotely close."

"But that's not possible, I know he's real, I met the man. Even my friend Jonathan McGready saw him at Alex's funeral."

"Of course you did. But your Mr Crumb doesn't wish to be found."

"Then he gave me a false name!"

"Obviously." Mr Pembroke studied Leonard carefully.

"He's doing a good job of it, and it's infuriating. Perhaps I can describe him to you?"

"That isn't necessary."

"Then how will you know his appearance? You may recognise him."

Mr Pembroke paused. "You really are insistent."

"Sir, you may even have seen him."

"Ah, very well then, although I'm not sure that will help. But, ah, go ahead, I'd be disappointed in you if you gave up now." He placed his finger between his shirt and neck again and eased his discomfort. "You've seen Mr Crumb, and I want you to describe him to me in every detail you can recall," requested Mr Pembroke with little obviously fake enthusiasm.

Leonard stood and walked to the window and looked out. "He was tall, approximately six foot."

Mr Pembroke retrieved his spectacles, hooked them securely over his ears, positioned them in precisely the correct location on his nose and wrote as Leonard recounted every feature.

"He had a dark and full, well-trimmed beard, but I suspect his hair was black."

"Age?"

Leonard placed his hands on the shelf and leaned forward to better see down onto the street below. "Perhaps mid-forties, or a year or two younger."

"Weight?"

"That is difficult, Mr Pembroke." Leonard walked away from the window and paced the room. "He wore a coat, but he didn't carry excess weight. He may have even been muscular without being abundant."

"For God's sake, Leonard, stop your pacing and sit down. You're making me nervous, and I get enough of that at home."

Leonard sat promptly.

"Now, tell me more about the clothes he was wearing."

"A homburg hat and the long coat- it was tan in colour."

"Awfully warm to be wearing a coat."

"That's what I thought too."

"Shoes?"

"Yes, he wore them."

Mr Pembroke looked up with a scowl and saw Leonard grinning.

"I didn't notice his shoes, sir," Leonard replied quickly.

With deliberate slowness, Mr Pembroke removed his spectacles. "Leonard, let me give you some advice. Whenever you meet someone for the first time, always check their footwear. You can tell a lot about a man by the shoes or boots he wears. A poor man cannot afford good shoes or wears his best shoes at inappropriate times, and a gentleman wears the right shoes for the occasion. Clean and polished shoes indicate an uncluttered and orderly mind, while dirty or scuffed shoes can reveal a slovenly and slothful character."

"Thank you, I'll remember that." Leonard unobtrusively slid his feet farther under his chair to hide them from his superior.

"See you do." Mr Pembroke settled back in his chair, replaced his eyewear and rubbed his chin as he read over his notes. "Now then, we have a good description of a gentleman with no name."

"Where do gentlemen like this work, where do they go for entertainment, and where do they live? Because I don't know," Leonard questioned.

"Bloody nonsense, of course you do. Will you find men like this in Chinatown?"

Leonard shook his head.

"Yes, I agree, very unlikely. But there are places where gentlemen enjoy spending their leisure time, and I suggest you visit those places. Be patient, and do not go alone, go with friends, the more the better, and you'll feel safer considering the threats made against you. Wellington isn't large, and a man like this cannot hide. He will make an appearance. If you make an effort, you will be rewarded. That is a fundamental principle of good investigative reporting, Leonard."

Leonard reflected on Mr Pembroke's words. They made sense.

"I think I will do exactly that, sir."

"Very good. Meanwhile, I will continue with my inquiries to locate the elusive man you describe, but now I must go home. Mrs Pembroke has guests for dinner, and if I am late, I'll suffer at her displeasure for quite some time." Mr Pembroke scratched his head and then patted the loose grey strands he dislodged back in place.

"My intuition tells me I should begin my search near the public hotels."

Pembroke removed his spectacles, placed them in the breast pocket of his jacket and rose from behind his desk. He meticulously folded the notes he'd written, also put them in his pocket and gathered his case. "Follow your instincts, Mr Hardy."

"Oh, before you leave, I have something for you." Leonard

stood, rushed back to his desk, picked up a sack of coffee beans, half of which he'd restocked his own supply, and handed them to Mr Pembroke. "Perhaps you and Mrs Pembroke will enjoy a fine Arabica coffee?"

"Thank you, Leonard, although it will take more than coffee beans to satisfy Mrs Pembroke," he grumbled. "But I will enjoy them. Thank you kindly... need I ask from where you obtained them?"

"No, sir, better you didn't."

Mr Pembroke mumbled something unintelligibly and shuffled out the door. "Good evening."

"Good evening, sir."

"And Mr Hardy?"

"Yes, sir?"

"There's a bloody good cobbler further down Willis Street who'll raise your shoes to a brilliant sheen," he said over his shoulder as he left.

Leonard smirked and looked down at his scuffed boots. He sat back down and quietly pondered Mr Pembroke's suggestions.

A short while later, Leonard departed work and exited the rear of the building through the printer's door, a habit he'd begun recently in light of revelations he was being followed. He huffed and puffed his way up Boulcott Street and onto Wellington Terrace, then stood behind a tree and waited a short time to see if anyone pursued him. Deciding it was safe, he began a leisurely stroll towards Bowen Street and eventually onto Lambton Quay. He looked carefully at every person he encountered. He looked at clothes and hats, studied faces and even cabbies as they passed. At one time he saw a man who, from a distance, resembled Mr Crumb and followed him to a public hotel. But on closer inspection the man bore no similarities.

Eventually, Leonard arrived home footsore and grumpy; he collapsed in his chair and considered all that had happened. Within a relatively short time, he'd lost his wife, his best friend, Uncle Jun, and Ming had disappeared, and now his own life was threatened. He thought back to the morning he answered the door to Constable Hastings. Could this have been avoided if he hadn't answered the door? He should blame Constable Hastings for this mess.

Leonard abruptly sat up. "Constable Hastings!" he said aloud. He immediately found a pencil and paper, sat at his bureau, and began basic calculations. No matter how many ways he worked the numbers, it didn't make sense; something was wrong, and someone was not telling the truth. Again, he conservatively performed some elementary arithmetic and reached the same conclusion. He leaned back in his chair and thought. Of course, he needed to speak with the objectionable Mrs Theodopoulous; she'd confirm his suspicion.

The thought of engaging Mrs Theodopoulous in any friendly conversation was a little daunting, but he needed confirmation. He looked at his pocket watch and decided it was still early enough to visit her.

He knocked twice, and immediately the incessant yapping of her small dog broke the silence. Within moments, he could hear floorboards creak as someone walked slowly to the door. It squeaked open a few inches, enough for the dog to put his face through the gap at the bottom. He sniffed a couple of times and continued with his shrill, high-pitched bark. The stale smell of boiled cabbage and dog oozed through the partially open door, followed by a bleary eye, which blinked and assessed the smiling, friendly face of her late afternoon caller.

"Mrs Theodopoulous, please forgive the intrusion at this time. Do you remember me? I'm Leonard Hardy." He pointed up the street to his house, but it was unlikely she saw further than his shoulder. The dog manically continued yapping. "I wonder if you could answer a question or two for me. It's about the body you discovered a short while ago!" Leonard shouted above the noise. He looked down at the dog and thought unkind things.

The door generously opened an inch or two more and revealed another eye and a downturned scowling mouth; both eyes stared at him for a moment. Then the door was quickly closed, and Leonard could hear a few muffled words, then reopened wider. Mrs Theodopoulous now held her quiet, darling pet in her arms. The dog looked at him with undisguised contempt, a look he returned. He shifted his gaze back to her and smiled. She wore the same dirty housecoat over a shapeless dress. Her wispy hair was mostly held beneath a stained bonnet.

"What you want?"

The pungent smell of garlic immediately assaulted him - her breath was potent. Leonard quickly tried to mask his reaction; *a wince and smile could be similar*, he thought and hoped she hadn't noticed. He felt the need for urgency. "Can you tell me the exact time you discovered the body?"

She looked at him suspiciously. "Why?"

"Please, Mrs Theodopoulous," Leonard appealed.

She thought a moment, "It was six o'clocks."

"Six o'clock, are you sure?"

She raised a bushy eyebrow, "I knows this."

Her reply left no doubt in Leonard's mind. "How did you inform the police?

She looked at him like he was a cretin. "I goes down heel and yells for help, what else? What you's expect me to do's, runs to police?" She unfolded an arm wrapped around her dog and waved it down the hill. "Wagon stops, man tells me he goes to police to tell thems."

Leonard felt very brave by resisting the urge to flee. The garlic odour was life-threatening, and he unconsciously shuffled a half step backwards. "How much time was it before the police, Constable Hastings, arrived here?"

"Not longs. Why you want to know this?"

"How long, how much time? One hour, three-quarters of an hour...?"

She thought briefly and looked down at her dog and scratched its head. "It was half an hours."

"Half an hour!" Leonard confirmed.

She sighed, "That was whats I said, yes."

"Are you sure? It's important to me."

She gave him another sour look, and this time it was her turn to bark, "Half hours!"

Leonard realised he'd over-extended his welcome. "Thank you, Mrs Theodopoulous. I really must be going, and you've been very kind."

She scowled, stepped back, and closed the door, which cued the dog to begin barking again. Leonard quickly turned his back on her door and decided not to run home.

Even Bridgette, who'd not adjusted well to the passing of Alex, laughed. Jonathan and Meredith were beside themselves, and Mary held a lace handkerchief to her eyes. They all sat in Bridgette's lounge, and Leonard had just finished recounting his earlier visit to Mrs Theodopoulous. Needless to say, Leonard had exaggerated his encounter with the woman slightly, but it had helped to liven the mood a little – noticeable in his absence, Alex was missed.

The three women began discussing cooking aromas while Jonathan leaned toward Leonard. "Are you serious in suggesting Constable Hastings lied?"

"I don't know if he's lied, but according to my theory, and supported by Mrs Theodopoulous, it just isn't conceivable the Constable arrived where the body was found within the actual time frame."

Jonathan looked puzzled.

"It's confounding." Leonard shook his head. "Look, from what I can gather, Mrs Theodopoulous discovered the body at six o'clock, walked to the bottom of the street, and yelled for a passing wagon to stop. The driver said he would inform the police. How far away is it from Marjoribanks Street to the Mount Cook depot?"

Jonathan reflected a moment. "Just short of a mile?"

"Yes, that's what I thought too. From the time the body was discovered to when Constable Hastings arrived was half an hour. That means she doddled down Marjoribanks Street, yells at a passing wagon and then explained to the wagon driver in broken English what's happened. The wagon then drives almost a mile to Mount Cook, and the driver reports the body to the police, and they assign a constable who then makes his way back to Marjoribanks Street - all in half an hour! I'm sorry, I find that implausible. It just isn't possible."

"Yes, as you put it that way, then I agree," Jonathan said.

The women were all listening, having exhausted the topics of vile cooking smells, disagreeable house odours and dirty pets.

"Did he have a horse?" Mary asked.

"Yes. I saw it. But even then, he would likely have had to saddle and bridle it, which takes time."

"So Constable Hastings hasn't exactly lied, has he? What you're unable to determine is how the constable arrived at the body so quickly," stated Jonathan, forever the lawyer.

Leonard nodded. "Something isn't right. That man irks me to no end."

"Then the only course of action is to return to the Mount Cook depot and ask them for the log entry times for when the body was first reported. Their paperwork should also indicate who was assigned and when the constable was dispatched."

"That's what I thought too, and that means returning there and risking an encounter with Hastings again."

"When has that stopped you, Leo? I've never known you to avoid a confrontation, you pride yourself on your wit," said Meredith.

"I never said I was brave," Leonard smirked.

"A physical confrontation is what I believe he's referring to, not a quarrel," said Mary quickly in defence.

"The man is intimidating," replied Leonard. He looked at Mary, surprised at her comment and speaking for him. "Do you know what else is peculiar about that body?"

All heads turned.

"Constable Hastings insisted that I must have heard a gunshot. It was like he wanted me to have heard one."

"If you heard a shot, that would suggest the victim was killed outside your home. Makes for an open and shut case, doesn't it?" replied Jonathan.

"Did the constable carry a weapon?" asked Bridgette.

"Yes, he did, a revolver. Why?" Leonard asked.

"I think he shot the man."

"Are you serious?" exclaimed Jonathan.

"Yes, and I also think he was behind the death of Alex." Bridgette burst into tears.

Mary went to console her as Leonard sought to find a logical explanation to disprove her assertion. The room fell quiet.

The mood in Bridgette's living room had sobered considerably. No longer were the friends having a light-hearted discussion. Bridgette's statement was very discerning, and based on what little information Leonard had, he could find no reason to dispute her claim.

Arriving at the same conclusion, Jonathan contributed. "Leo, I know you, and before you begin a relentless pursuit on this new angle, you must first establish and prove your theory about the timeline."

"I can't believe a policeman would do such a thing. It's ridiculous, and you should all know better than to begin making accusations like that," said Meredith. Her father once was a policeman, and she always defended the constabulary.

"Not all policemen are honest," said Bridgette between blowing her nose and wiping her eyes.

Jonathan wisely refused to be drawn into the argument and reached for Meredith's hand. Leonard was lost in thought and considering the possibilities of a corrupt policeman, but the motive eluded him. He tried to link Constable Hastings to the disappearance of Uncle Jun and Ming but couldn't connect them. Were Mr Crumb and Constable Hastings associated? Leonard still had more questions than answers.

Sensing what he was thinking about, Mary broke the silence. "Leo, I am not working tomorrow. Why don't we spend the afternoon together and visit the Mount Cook depot? Perhaps if you escorted me, there might be less likelihood of any altercation, and you can obtain some answers from the police."

Leonard turned to look at her and nodded slowly. "Very well, Mary. I would enjoy the pleasure of your company tomorrow." He looked around the room and saw Meredith with her lower lip extended, she was pouting, Jonathan looked apprehensive, and Bridgette was still upset. He wanted to lift their spirits. "I have an idea. Tomorrow evening why don't we all go into town and visit a few places, have a dance and a few drinks and dinner?"

"Brilliant, old boy! We haven't done that in a while," smiled Jonathan, hoping to perk up Meredith.

"I don't know," said Bridgette, "it may be a little soon."

"It will be good for you," Mary replied. "You need to get out."

"I forgot to add," said Leonard sheepishly, "Mr Pembroke suggested I needed to visit places where Mr Crumb may visit, so we can use the time to enjoy ourselves and keep an eye open for him at the same time."

Mary gave Leonard a playful elbow in the ribs for his duplicity, and reluctantly Meredith and Bridgette finally agreed, while Jonathan and Mary required no prompting. It was decided and plans finalised.

Chapter Ten

Mary's arm was linked around Leonard's elbow as they waited patiently in line at the Mount Cook Police Depot. Three people stood before them. A man with a bandage around his head was being attended to at the counter, a gentleman reading a newspaper was next in line, and an anxious-looking elderly couple was immediately before them. The line wasn't moving quickly, and Leonard and Mary were resigned to a long wait. Mary had never been here before and was curious about the public notices affixed to the wall. She separated herself from Leonard and walked to the wall to satisfy her inquisitiveness, as he rehearsed in his mind the questions he would ask once it was his turn.

"Next!" yelled the constable behind the counter. As the man with the head injury walked out of the building, the gentleman with the newspaper folded it and stepped forward to the counter.

Leonard couldn't help but overhear the elderly couple talking amongst themselves about the nature of their visit. They seemed like agreeable people and were a little distraught. Within a few moments, he determined someone had savagely killed their cat and left the dead animal on their doorstep. He felt sympathy for them, as he strongly objected to people who treated animals cruelly. He turned his attention back to Mary as she studied the notices pinned to the wall and couldn't help but admire her. He immediately felt guilty, leaving him confused and a little sad. He could rationalise his feelings and understood why he thought as he did, except his logical mind wasn't communicating with his heart. He had to accept Mae was no longer alive. With a resigned sigh, he turned to the front and the couple before him talking about the cat they loved so much.

"Next!" repeated the constable as the gentleman strode from the waiting room.

Mary returned, reattached herself to Leonard and commented on how many people, mostly men, were at large and sought for questioning by the police. "No women on the wall," she said, baiting him.

Leonard knew what she was doing and grinned. He lowered his head to talk quietly to her. "I think you'll find many crimes perpetrated by women aren't reported to the police."

"Is that so? I had no idea," she replied, "and how do you know this?" She looked up at him innocently and playfully batted her eyelids for effect.

"Well, it's logical, isn't it?"

"Is it? I'm not sure I follow your reasoning. Could you explain?" she asked.

Leonard had dug himself a hole and needed to find a way out. Mary knew it and laughed; the uplifting sound instantly changed his mood.

"Next!"

Leonard was saved. He raised his eyebrows and grinned,. sShe had a way of making him feel relaxed and at ease, even when she was toying with him. at Mary.They waited while the old couple shuffled away and then approached the counter. The same constable Leonard had spoken to on his previous visit was bent over and writing in his log. "Afternoon, how can I be of assistance?" he asked politely without looking up.

"I seek some information about a recently reported murder where a body was found on Marjoribanks Street."

The constable finished writing and looked up, his weather-beaten face devoid of expression. "What information do you require, sir?"

"I'd like to know when the police were first notified of the body's discovery and when the constable was first dispatched to the crime scene?"

Calling on years of experience, the mature constable didn't immediately react and studied the measure of Leonard's character carefully. "And who might you be, sir?"

Leonard fumbled in his jacket and extracted his business card, and handed it to the constable, who began to read it carefully. "*Evening Standard*, eh?" He turned it over to see if any information was written on the card's rear.

Leonard smiled confidently. "Newspaper business." As if that justified the enquiry.

"I see," said the constable. He rubbed his stubbly chin and looked perplexed. "I thought you was familiar, and you were here a few days ago."

"Yes, I asked to see Constable Hastings, if you recall."

The constable nodded. "Ah, yes, I do remember now."

All log entries were written onto sheets of paper attached to a clipboard. At the end of each day, the completed sheets were transferred to a large folder. The duty constable hung the clipboard that contained that day's entries onto the appropriate hook on the wall beside him and looked at Leonard. "What date was that body discovered then?"

Leonard shared the details, looked down at Mary, and smiled

as the constable began his search. He was quickly discovering he enjoyed her company more and more.

The constable pulled a large ring-binder folder, similar to those used at the *Evening Standard*, from a shelf and placed it reverently on the counter. He opened it and, with practised ease, licked his fingers and turned back the pages seeking to match the date Leonard had given him. "Here we go. This is the day." He ran his finger down a column, turned the page and repeated his search. He stopped, turned the page back, re-licked his fingers and began his search again.

Leonard and Mary watched curiously.

"I'm unable to provide you with that information, sir."

"Excuse me?" asked Leonard.

"The information you want ain't here, hasn't been entered into the log."

"Don't you find that peculiar? Shouldn't that information be entered into your records as normal procedure?"

The constable scratched his head with the end of a pencil. "Yes, sir. Normally it would, but... nothing's been written down. Here, look." The constable spun the ring-binder around for Leonard and Mary to see. He pointed to the date column. "Here's the previous day's entries, and the last entry is here. The next day, the day you said the body was discovered, starts here." Again he ran his finger down the column, turned the page and stopped at the beginning of the following day's entries. "There are no entries for the discovery of a body or when a constable was dispatched."

"I find this rather disturbing that your records are inaccurate," said Leonard trying hard to remain calm. He could feel Mary beside him as she stroked his arm. She knew he was becoming distressed and agitated.

The constable looked uncomfortable. "Perhaps I can have someone look at this, sir. If you care to take a seat, then I'll be right back." He pointed to the bench seat at the rear of the room, picked up the binder and Leonard's business card, and exited through a door.

As suggested, they sat down on the seat and waited.

"What's all that about? They must be diligent in their record keeping, surely?" Mary asked.

"Yes, they should, Mary. Something is going on, and it feels a little fabricated and altogether very convenient," Leonard hissed.

"But we saw the entries; there were none about the body. So what does that mean?" She placed her hand on his arm. "Are they withholding information?"

Leonard had been staring at the floor; he turned and looked at her. "I don't know, Mary. This is very unsettling."

They waited for an age, and thank goodness no one else was behind them in line. Finally, the door opened, and the constable reappeared. "Mr Hardy!"

"What did you discover?" Leonard asked once again at the counter.

The binder was closed, and the constable had both hands resting on top. "The mystery has been solved, sir." He smiled politely at Leonard, then Mary. "Sorry 'bout the wait." He took a deep breath. "On the morning in question, Constable Hastings was travelling on his way home after completing his scheduled work shift. He was waved down by a passing wagon and was informed about the discovery of a body. This is why there ain't a log entry, sir." He tapped the binder with a hand. "He proceeded to investigate the matter and begin a preliminary investigation when he was technically off the clock, as it were."

Leonard thought a moment. "Where was Constable Hastings when he was waved down, do you know?"

"I believes he was in the vicinity of Courtenay Place and Tory Street."

That was only a few hundred yards from where the body was discovered, thought Leonard.

Mary leaned forward, "Excuse me, constable," she flashed one of her disarming smiles. What time did Constable Hastings finish his shift that day?"

"On that day, I believe it was six o'clock, Miss." The constable turned to Leonard and then Mary. "Will that be all?"

"One last question. What was the outcome of the investigation? Was the identity of the body ever discovered?" Leonard queried.

"As you are aware, sir, that information is publicly available through the coroner's office."

Mary flashed another smile. "You've been so kind and helpful, constable, we just thought you could tell us and save having to go downtown."

The constable couldn't refuse. "I'm told the body has not been identified, and the report indicates the man died as a result of a gunshot to the head at the location he was discovered, Miss."

"But that's not possible!" Leonard stated. Mary pulled on his arm.

"Before we leave, constable, who completed the police investigation?" Mary asked.

"Constable Hastings, Miss."

"Thank you very much for your effort and time, constable."

The constable smiled, "Good afternoon." He did not return

Leonard's business card.

Leonard was seething as Mary led him from the waiting room. "What he said is untrue, Mary. The man wasn't killed outside my home! Constable Hastings is up to something."

"I know, Leonard, but showing your anger to the constable will do you no favours. I also think there is something odd about the timeline. His explanation seemed a little trite."

"What is going on with this? I can't believe what is happening. There has to be a connection between the unidentified body, Alex, and Constable Hastings. You know, I think Bridgette may have been correct with what she said last evening."

"That the constable killed the unidentified man?" Mary asked.

"Yes. It's the only explanation."

"Come, Leonard, let's go home."

Mary and Leonard sat together in her home in Newtown while they waited for Jonathan, Meredith, and Bridgette to arrive from work. They'd been discussing their visit to the police and what they had discovered. Leonard was still visibly upset, and Mary had been doing her best to calm and relax him.

"You said earlier that the constable's explanation was trite; what did you mean by that?" Leonard asked.

"I think the explanation given by the constable was not articulated with belief."

"You believe he lied?"

The pitch of Leonard's voice rose, and Mary again tried to mollify him. She patted his arm and spoke calmly. "I don't know, Leonard. It seems likely he told us what he'd been instructed to say. I just find it so convenient that Constable Hastings happened to be in the area when the body was discovered. Was it just a coincidence?"

Leonard remained quiet as he considered possibilities. "Let's say Bridgette is correct when she said the constable killed that man."

"Yes," Mary nodded in agreement.

"Then the reason the constable may have been in the area is because he placed the body outside my house."

"But we were told that Constable Hastings was on his way home," Mary reminded him.

Leonard stood and spun to face Mary. "So where does Constable Hastings live? That is the question, and I know how to retrieve that information," he grinned.

Laughter alerted them that Jonathan, Meredith and Bridgette had all arrived. While Bridgette freshened up, Leonard told the others of their afternoon's visit to the police depot.

It was quickly decided to first visit the Thistle Inn in Thorndon. As it was the furthest away, they would work their way back towards the town's centre as the evening progressed. Leonard was unperturbed about returning to the Thistle Inn and was stubbornly adamant that his expulsion had nothing to do with the Inn itself and was only the result of the White New Zealand League organisers who held the meeting that late afternoon. They waited patiently for a tram to appear that would take them close to their destination. Even Bridgette was buoyant, and both Mary and Meredith kept a close eye on her, staying at her side while Jonathan and Leonard discussed their search for Mr Winston Crumb.

A clanging bell announced the arrival of a horse-drawn tram. It soon clattered over the tracks and slowly took them across town, leaving them at the northern part of Lambton Quay, a stone's throw from their first port of call.

They entered the Thistle Inn and were greeted by the rowdy commotion of a well-frequented public barroom. The boisterous patrons were mostly labourers and dockworkers, and it soon became apparent the Inn wasn't the best of choices to entertain three beautiful gentlewomen on a Saturday evening. After a quick perusal and receiving some desultory inappropriate comments, Leonard quickly suggested they leave. Certainly, Mr Crumb was not in attendance.

The Shepherds Arms was relatively close but required an uphill walk along Tinakori Road. The ladies were not amused at the thought of trudging to a neighbourhood hotel only to discover it had a similar clientele to the Thistle Inn. Instead, they decided to visit the Hotel St. George, conveniently located close to the centre of town. This option appealed to everyone, and before long, they were seated in more pleasant surroundings and enjoying a beverage.

Leonard didn't lose focus and kept a watchful eye on everyone he encountered. Mary, he noticed, was also looking for Mr Crumb and paying attention to the male clientele. It stirred some unfamiliar and unpleasant emotions. She didn't see him watching her, and he studied her carefully. Her light brown hair was styled in the pompadour design currently in vogue and was fashioned to rise upwards in the central part of her head, leaving curls to fall elegantly and hang at the sides. It exposed her long feminine neck, and Leonard could see creamy, soft, white skin. With the memory of Mae haunting him, he felt ashamed and, with flushed cheeks, turned away.

Jonathan and Meredith were heavily engaged with Bridgette and discussing the appropriateness of dancing and how close partners should stand facing each other. This was a topic with which Leonard preferred not to concern himself.

The lounge where they sat was pleasantly furnished, although relatively small, and the chairs were upholstered in red velvet. Thick drapes hung from the walls, and a quartet of musicians played unobtrusively in the background. Meredith and Jonathan went to the dance floor, much to the delight of the musicians, while Mary kept Bridgette entertained. Leonard decided to have a quick walk around.

Most patrons were couples of mixed ages; a larger group sat together and celebrated a birthday, their banter and joviality a good indication the celebrations had been going on for some time. Two Oriental men sat at a table drinking and ignored Leonard as he walked by, but there was no sign of anyone matching the description of Mr Crumb. He returned to the table and watched Meredith and Jonathan on the dance floor as he decided what locale to visit next.

The Royal Oak Hotel was a grand establishment and very centrally located, only a five-minute walk from the Hotel St. George. It was perhaps the most popular of all the hotels in Wellington, and with high tariffs, it ensured its preferred patrons remained tactfully select. Leonard did not need to encourage the others to leave the St George; the promise of fine dining, notably the well-known chicken dish and exquisite refreshments of the Royal Oak Hotel, were motivation for the group to empty their glasses and all but hasten for the door.

The streets were dark, and plenty of people were out and about enjoying a lovely Wellington Saturday evening. They could hear enthusiastic applause from the nearby Opera House, where a musical production was being staged. A boot-making establishment and a confectionary shop were open and doing a brisk trade, and Hansom cabs hunted in the streets patrolling for fares. Gas lamps provided street lighting to assist the trams that rumbled and clattered up busy Cuba Street, and Leonard used the light to ensure no one was following them or hiding in a darkened doorway ready to leap out.

Their destination was just ahead at the corner of Manners and Cuba Streets, the grand Royal Oak Hotel. Mary had never been inside the hotel and was excited to finally visit, whereas the others had been on many previous occasions and knew what to expect. The doorman greeted them cordially with a friendly smile as they entered the building, and once inside, they headed immediately to the dining room on the first floor.

Once seated and enjoying the opulence of arguably one of the colony's finest establishments, the conversation returned to a lighter tone. Bridgette was showing positive signs of relaxing, and it was obvious to them all she appeared to be enjoying herself. In particular, she was taken by the beautiful, small flower arrangement that featured as the table's centrepiece. Candlesticks illuminated all the tables and highlighted the bold colours of the specially chosen blossoms. In addition, and to supplement the warm ambience of the dining room, a couple of large chandeliers hung majestically from the ornate high ceiling.

As usual, a friendly debate ensued about menu selection as Leonard and Jonathan advocated choosing the Royal Oak's signature chicken dish, Bridgette selected pork, Meredith insisted on lamb, and Mary finally sided with Leonard and also ordered chicken.

Leonard positioned himself at the table so he could easily see the dining room's other patrons, which left his back exposed to the staircase that rose impressively from the ground floor. The dining room was almost at capacity, and only a couple of tables remained unoccupied. Again, Leonard began to survey the clientele, and one particular gentleman caught his attention. Still, on closer inspection, he realised he recognised the well-groomed owner of a haberdashery shop on Willis Street. Leonard politely nodded in greeting when the man looked up and then turned to the newly arrived guests who sat at the table beside them. Again, there was no resemblance to Mr Crumb; the elderly gentlemen and their wives were far from circumspect and flashed their jewellery and status garishly. One of the women saw Leonard watching and gave him a self-assured smile, which he reciprocated, then turned his attention back to his friends. The *sommelier* had arrived and was waiting patiently for someone to decide on which wine to choose. On Leonard's suggestion, an exquisite Provence rosé was selected, and even the dour *sommelier* was grudgingly impressed.

Leonard knew finding Mr Crumb wouldn't be easy. His initial idea of visiting different places seemed to make logical sense at the time, but in practice, it largely and really depended on luck. If Leonard was to be blatantly honest, he now felt Mr Pembroke had sent him on a wild goose chase and it was a waste of time. Mr Crumb may have eaten here earlier in the evening or even now be seated at the Hotel St. George, and their paths may have crossed numerous times. However, he was enjoying the evening regardless until he saw Bridgette, Meredith, and Jonathan look up, their faces displaying concern at something behind him. At the same time, like an ominous warning, his own business card flew down and landed on the table before him.

He shifted in his seat and turned. Standing directly behind him was Constable Hastings.

"What's the meaning of this?" Leonard said with annoyance. As he'd witnessed before, when the constable was angry, a vein throbbed on the side of his neck.

Hastings carefully looked from face to face. He began with Bridgette, then Meredith, Jonathan, and paused at Mary. "Your name, Miss?"

Jonathan rose quickly. "How dare you intrude on our privacy. You have overstepped your authority and have no legal justification to demand anything from us. I shall report your unprofessional behaviour to your superiors and see you reprimanded." He stood a little straighter. "I happen to be a solicitor, you know."

Hastings took a step toward Jonathan, reached out and pushed him back down to his chair. "I don't know you, sir, but I've had enough o' you already. Shut it!"

Leonard took the time to quickly glance around the room. To his surprise, the two Oriental men at the Hotel St. George were now standing on the stairwell watching intently and ignoring the pleas from the doorman to leave. All conversation in the dining room abruptly ceased, and everyone stared at Constable Hastings. The *maître d'* was frozen in indecision.

Satisfied Jonathan wouldn't be a problem, Hastings turned back to Leonard and Mary. He bent down so both could hear and placed a hand on Leonard's shoulder, preventing him from standing or moving and squeezed. His face, mere inches away and so close, his elongated nose threatened to collide with Mary's pompadour.

Leonard could smell onions.

He spoke quietly. "You were asking 'bout me today and caused me some embarrassment. Need I remind you both that interfering in police business and in matters that do not concern you could have a rather severe and unpleasant consequences. Coming to the depot and requesting information about me is..." he turned from Leonard to Mary, and then back again, "unacceptable. I've already warned you once, and I've been ordered not to harm you, but so help me, God, my patience is wearing very thin." He licked his lips. "Do you hear me, Mr Hardy?" he shouted.

Leonard resisted the urge to cringe at the bellow; he looked Hastings directly in the eye and didn't flinch or show fear.

The dining room was deathly quiet.

"We won't be having a similar chat again. Enjoy your dinner." He strode off in anger.

Leonard placed his napkin on the table. As he slowly stood, the sound of his chair scraping along the highly polished wood floor broke the silence. "It was you who killed him, wasn't it?" he shouted at the back of the departing constable. "You murdered the man and left him in the bushes!" His hands shook in fear as he provoked Hastings with his outburst.

The entire room heard, people gasped, and everyone turned to the constable, who, in rage, spun aggressively at the accusation. His flailing arm caught an unsuspecting waiter in the ribs. Fresh from the kitchen, he carried four bowls of scalding hot French onion soup on a beautiful silver platter. Upended by the constable, the bowls flew from the tray and arced, trailing steaming liquid towards a couple enjoying a quiet and peaceful meal near the window.

Seeing the danger, one of the dining couple, the gentleman

closest to the waiter, reacted in panic. He leapt from his chair, turning the table over in haste to avoid the scalding soup, but it was too late. The lady screamed in pain as the scalding liquid soaked through her shawl and onto her back. Cutlery, flowers, and candlesticks scattered and landed on the floor with a clatter. One candlestick came to rest by the floor-length drapes. Constable Hastings paused and glowered with indifference at the turmoil he caused and then, with undisguised loathing, turned to stare at his accuser. With a feral snarl, he lurched forward and stomped towards Leonard - his violent intentions obvious. One of the two Orientals on the stairway yelled something unintelligibly, and both men pushed past the helpless doorman and ran at the manic policeman. Bravely and somewhat foolishly, Leonard stood his ground, and before he could lay a hand on him, the two Oriental men caught Hastings and pulled him quickly away. The *maître d'*, galvanised into action, immediately rushed for the injured diners as the two Oriental men dragged the struggling constable down the stairs.

Leonard was momentarily stunned; he couldn't believe what he'd seen. He shook his head and cleared the fog. "Mary, Bridgette, Meredith, can you help those two people."

In the ensuing chaos, no one saw the flickering candle lick at the drapes. Encouraged by the draught, the tiny insignificant flame danced around the curtain, searching for fuel. It found it, tasted it, and wanted more. The table hid the lit candle on its side, forgotten and unseen. Amidst the noise and pandemonium, not a soul spared a thought for the decorative *bougie* that lay on the floor, and so ignored, the drape caught fire.

The *maître d'* was attempting to restore order and pleading with his guests to return to their tables. Waiters began to clean the slippery floor when flames shot upwards from behind the table as Bridgette, Mary and Meredith attended to the couple who were scalded. They were fortunate; their clothes had prevented serious injury, but it was painful nonetheless.

Leonard saw the flames first. "Fire!" he yelled, and lunged forward, searching for water, a bucket of sand, anything, but it was too late. The fire had now taken hold. Newly ignited wallpaper fed the flames, and they raced up the walls casting eerie, orange incandescent shapes throughout the Royal Oak's beautiful dining room. Dark, acrid smoke lay trapped, rolling beneath the ornate ceiling.

Others took up the cry. Everyone was yelling, and in panic, nearly thirty guests attempted to leave simultaneously; they all headed en-masse for the stairs.

"Jonathan!" yelled Leonard. "We must leave, grab the girls!"

The two injured diners were helped to their feet and, understanding the urgency, were escorted to the stairs. Leonard tried to keep everyone together, but Jonathan was slow to react; he seemed stupefied by the flames.

The main staircase at the Royal Oak Hotel was thoughtfully wide and magnificent; patrons drained down the stairs quickly, and thankfully no one was injured during their pell-mell exit. In only moments, the fire had established itself and now threatened to engulf the entire room as the *maître d'* shepherded his kitchen staff to safety down the rear stairs. A few brave souls attempted to fight the fire but soon gave up. Leonard, Jonathan and the women were the last diners to leave. The *maître d'* checked to ensure no one was left in the dining room or the kitchen before he finally retreated to safety.

In pandemonium, panicked hhotel guests, crying and shouting, poured onto Cuba Street from the main door, some in nightclothes. Others clutched cases and personal belongings protectively as they sought shelter from the raging fire. Bells were rung, pealing their warning and alerting all to the danger of fire feared by all. Flames danced out of shattered windows, and dark smoke belched upwards. Brave men issued orders and took command, but the fire grew. Two constables arrived and immediately began pushing onlookers back to create room for the fire brigade, who had only just arrived in their wagon.

Stable hands began leading wide-eyed skittish horses from the nearby stables, taking them up the street to safety. People lent a hand where they could, but many became a nuisance and hindered organised collaborative efforts.

"There's nothing you can do, Leonard," Mary consoled.

Leonard shook his head in disbelief - he was in shock.

"It wasn't your fault. You didn't cause the fire. That despicable man... it was him, he was the cause, and I hope he pays for what he's done," she said.

Bridgette and Meredith were both weeping, and Jonathan, again focused, held them protectively. The group stood safely on Manners Street and watched flames and sparks soar high into the night sky as the hotel continued to burn. Some enterprising locals began a bucket brigade and were dousing neighbouring buildings with bucket after bucket of water.

Leonard had seen enough; there was nothing they could do. "I think we should leave," he suggested.

They walked up Cuba Street away from the carnage, passing spectators who flocked to the scene and eventually caught a tram to

Newtown. No one spoke, each lost in the thoughts of the destruction they'd witnessed.

They all sat in Bridgette's home and clutched a glass of brandy - it wasn't their first.

"I smell like smoke, it's everywhere," stated Meredith.

Jonathan smelled his jacket, and Bridgette began to laugh, and soon they all joined in. It wasn't funny, and they knew it, but it released some of the tension and worry they all felt.

"Were those two Oriental men attacking Hastings or helping him?" asked Leonard suddenly.

"It looked to me like they were assisting him," said Mary. "They made no effort to hurt him."

"I concur, it appeared to me that way also," said Jonathan.

"Yes, that's what I thought," said Leonard.

"Look, Leo, we witnessed something terrible this evening, and in the interests of your safety, returning home wouldn't be prudent. I strongly suspect that disturbed policeman, Hastings, will want recourse. Returning home places you in an unenviable position of considerable adversity," advised Jonathan.

"That's settled then. Mary, you shall sleep with me tonight, and Leo shall take your bed," Bridgette offered.

Leonard felt strangely relieved. "Are you sure? I'd hate to be an imposition."

Mary leaned over and held Leonard's arm. "Of course not, don't be silly. Jonathan's right you know, returning home isn't a good idea."

Leonard feared a reprisal from the volatile constable and saw sense in Jonathan's suggestion. From the reaction of Hastings at the

Royal Oak, he would've been killed if he'd come within reach. There was no question in Leonard's mind - he knew Constable Hastings would seek revenge.

"Judging from his reaction, I'd say you struck a nerve, Leo." Jonathan leaned in. "What on earth prompted you to stand up and accuse the man of murder in a crowded dining room?"

"I'm not sure, really. I was rather upset that someone could enter the dining room, walk up and intimidate and threaten us with no regard and total impunity. I'd hoped the accusation would touch a nerve, a parting shot." Leonard paused. "I'm just sorry I did. The result of my actions has been devastating."

"Can Leo be held accountable?" Meredith asked.

"No, he is not culpable. Nor can he be responsible for the actions of others. If anything, you could challenge the wisdom and timing of Leo's open accusation, however, legally, he did not cause the blaze, nor is he responsible for the destruction it caused," Jonathan stated.

Leonard felt reassured, and although he'd already arrived at the same conclusion, it felt good to hear Jonathan's reaffirmation.

"What do you think will happen to Hastings?" Leonard asked Jonathan.

"I would presume the constabulary would like to have a chat with the man and, dare I say it, even press charges. I'd hazard a guess that his visit to the Royal Oak was not within the bounds of his duties as a constable, even if he was in uniform. I think there is certainly a strong case to charge him, at the very least, with negligence and inappropriate conduct."

"A drawing of his likeness may yet end up pinned on the depot wall," Mary suggested with a grin.

"Just negligence and inappropriate conduct, is that all?"

Leonard asked.

"What other crime did he commit at the Royal Oak Hotel?"

"Yes, I suppose," Leonard acceded. "So, if I understand correctly, Constable Hastings fled the scene because of the public accusation I made."

"And the questions about that public accusation he will be forced to answer," replied Jonathan. "Leo, if what you accused him of was false, he had no reason to flee. His actions could be interpreted as an admission of guilt."

"I guess Hastings isn't too happy right now."

Jonathan cleared his throat and looked serious, a look he had little difficulty achieving. "I'm going to use every available resource at my disposal to assist you, Leo. What happened this evening is only the tip of the proverbial iceberg. It's plainly evident to me that Constable Hastings, those he leads, and is subservient to, have wronged and mocked our fine judicial system in the process of executing their illegal activities, and believe me when I say..." Jonathan wagged a finger. "They shall all face the consequences of their actions."

Everyone was watching Jonathan closely, he didn't usually make impassioned monologues, and they were surprised at his reaction and overt support.

"While normally I am honoured and privileged to provide legal counsel, in this instance, I shall use my influence and endeavour to bring the full potency of the law to bear."

Meredith clapped in appreciation, and soon the others joined in. Jonathan's face turned scarlet, and he downed, in a single swallow, almost the entire contents of his glass. He grimaced as the brandy burned its way down.

"Well spoken, Jonathan," offered Meredith.

Bridgette was weeping again.

Jonathan's little speech was just what Leonard needed. As a sign of friendship and respect, he held out his hand. Awkwardly, Jonathan took the proffered hand, and they shook.

Mary's scent enveloped him as he lay in her bed. He breathed her in, and as he relaxed and let the evening's horrors dissipate, her presence pervaded all his senses. It wasn't unpleasant or even disturbing; it was calming and helped him fall asleep.

She slowly leaned over him; her long coal-black silky hair hung down and tickled his chest. Her porcelain white, unblemished skin glowed in vitality and health, and with her hand, she reached for him and gently cupped his face, her thumb tenderly stroking his cheek. Her eyes crinkled as she lovingly smiled down at him. He groaned in pleasure and tried to touch her, but she moved away each time, and before he could protest, she gently placed a finger over his lips to hush him. She spoke soothingly, and with reassurance, he heard her say that she loved him. He had nothing to fear, her love was real and everlasting, but her body was not. Mae slowly withdrew, waved and whispered – "Goodbye, Leonard."

He woke with a start, blinking in uncertainty. The unfamiliar bed and room confused him at first, and then he remembered where he was. His heart raced, and he took a deep breath, forcing himself to relax. After a minute or two, he felt better. He lay back down, thinking about his unusual dream, and eventually returned to a restless sleep.

Bridgette had already left for work at the hospital, and Mary was up and about when Leonard woke. They spent the day indoors and talked about the previous evening and the fire. He was curious as to the extent of the damage, but wisely they both decided not to head outside to enquire or even take a stroll in fear of Constable Hastings and his people. Mary decided Leonard should continue to stay at her home until they knew with some certainty that Constable Hastings posed no immediate threat. Relieved, Leonard agreed.

Chapter Eleven

Due to the massive fire that destroyed many buildings in central Wellington, the tram that Leonard caught was unable to continue all the way down Cuba Street. Leonard leapt off when the tram screeched to a halt and, like other commuters on a sunny Monday morning, stared in disbelief at the carnage spread out before them. Knowing he had played a role in the cause of the fire was upsetting. It was sobering. The fire had torn through so many buildings; it was devastating and difficult to comprehend the true extent of the damage. Men swarmed over remains like ants and picked through the embers salvaging anything they could, but little was left that had any actual use or value. A few disconsolate people, business owners, he guessed, stared in hopelessness, their lives forever changed. Workers with blackened faces and dirty clothes were already shovelling debris and burned remains into wagons to be carted away. Regardless of the facts and the reprehensible actions of Constable Hastings, Leonard still felt he contributed to the depredation. He wiped his eyes, looked over his shoulder for any suspicious characters, and with some apprehension, headed to work.

A messenger greeted him when he walked into the building and politely informed him that Mr Beaumont immediately requested his presence in his office. This was it, the moment he'd dreaded; he knew it must come to this, and Leonard knocked on Mr Beaumont's door with trepidation.

"Come!" shouted the muted voice of Mr Beaumont.

Leonard steeled himself and, with a big breath, opened the door and entered. Mr Beaumont sat at his desk; his jacket and waistcoat hung from a hook on a nearby stand, his shirtsleeves were rolled up, and his suspenders stood out boldly in contrast with his white, wrinkled shirt. Opposite him sat Mr Pembroke looking dishevelled and tired. It looked like they'd been here a while. Both men appeared perturbed as they looked at him. He tensed.

"Good morning, sir," Leonard nodded respectfully at his employer, then turned and greeted Mr Pembroke, "Good morning."

Mr Beaumont indicated Leonard should sit, waved him to a chair and then regarded him as if undecided what to say. Coming to a decision, he looked him in the eye. "It is our duty, no, it's our honour to report the news accurately and with impartiality to our readers," began the publisher in a mild neutral tone. "It was never the intention of this newspaper to have its employees create news and become the centre of attention in a manner such as this." He paused briefly. "Wellington has never experienced this kind of destruction, Mr Hardy." Mr Beaumont reached for a sheet of paper on his desk and held it up. "The fire destroyed thirty buildings that covered ten acres of land. We can be thankful there was no loss of life." He paused as he glanced at the document. "Do you want me to read to you the list of businesses that were ruined?"

"No, sir, I've seen the result," Leonard answered meekly.

"How about the estimated loss of advertising revenue?"

Leonard thought it wise to keep his mouth shut.

The diminutive Mr Pembroke was studying Leonard carefully and chose to remain silent.

Mr Beaumont dropped the sheet and rose from his chair, walked to the window and stood with hands on hips as he looked out. From his vantage point, he could see the charred remains of buildings in the distance. The ticking clock, the only sound in the room, added to the tenseness. Leonard was near breaking point and noticed his hands shook slightly.

Mr Beaumont walked from the window, stopped behind his chair, placed both hands on the back, and leaned forward slightly. "If there is one thing I've garnered from all my years as a reporter, an editor and a publisher - there are always two sides to a story." He paused for effect. "I've heard varying accounts of what occurred. I've tried to make sense of what precisely happened on Saturday evening, and so far, I have a little hope and believe you're not complicit," he raised an arm and swept it the breadth of the window, indicating what lay beyond, "and this may not be entirely your fault. As difficult as it has been not to pass judgement... I want to hear in your own words, and kindly explain what really took place." He turned to the clock. "At nine, the police will pay us a visit, and they are quite eager and enthusiastic to question you. It seems you haven't been at home for the last two evenings and have been difficult to locate. They actually believed you'd absconded."

Mr Beaumont returned to his chair and sat. A notepad and pencil had magically appeared in Mr Pembroke's hand.

"If you haven't already guessed, Leonard, I had to drag Mr Pembroke from his home at an unreasonable hour this morning, and we have been here since, discussing the mess you now find yourself in."

"I apologise to you both," replied Leonard earnestly, "I will explain."

Mr Beaumont's tone lightened, "Leonard, Mr Pembroke has already shared with me some information about a series of peculiar events you're involved in, and I am deeply troubled by what I've learned. We both have many questions, so I implore you to be thorough. Spare no detail. Begin, if you please."

Leonard thought back to the morning Constable Hastings first knocked on his door.

As requested, he began his story. Slightly hesitant and embarrassed at first, it took a while before he relaxed and then he was gushing.

Except for the ticking clock, the room was again quiet, and Mr Beaumont still sat at his desk, his head propped up by a hand cupped beneath his chin. Mr Pembroke removed his spectacles and gave them a compulsive rub; he'd been busy scratching away on his notepad and finally gave up as Leonard recounted his tale.

"I can't honestly say I approve of your decision to provoke Constable Hastings in the manner you did, Leonard, however, from what you've said, the responsibility falls squarely on his lap," Beaumont stated.

"Surely Leonard had no bloody idea the constable would react as he did or that a waiter would come barrelling out of the kitchen carrying soup," offered Mr Pembroke caustically. "In my opinion, you've assumed the burden of blame for this fire when you have no sound reason to." Pembroke pointed to Leonard. "I think you need to put those thoughts of guilt behind you and harden up, lad." Pembroke raised an eyebrow.

They were both correct, Leonard knew. He nodded, but it didn't change the fact that many people's livelihoods would forever be affected by the damage caused by that fire.

"This doctor at the hospital, uh, what's his name, Scholler?" questioned the publisher.

"Dr Schrader," replied Leonard.

Beaumont lifted his head and repositioned his suspenders. "Is he the same gentleman we were going to do that story on?"

Mr Pembroke nodded, and Leonard turned in curiosity from one to the other. *A story?*

"Yes, I recall now. Your Dr Schrader was allegedly involved in some inappropriate behaviour with nurses. Some complained, but the surgeon superintendent and the matron decided the nurses were promiscuous and allowed themselves to be put in a compromising situation. Therefore Dr Schrader was absolved of any wrongdoing. The nurses in question were punished. We were going to do a story but couldn't verify information. When it comes to matters regarding lewd or inappropriate behaviour, it appears people would rather not discuss or see it brought to public attention. Isn't proper. At the time, Mr Pembroke was insistent we publish, but I decided not to pursue the story as it would offend many, bring the hospital into disrepute, and no one would come forward to support the claims against Schrader in fear of negative publicity. In my opinion, he is an untrustworthy and crafty man. It wouldn't surprise me if he were linked to your story somehow." Mr Beaumont stated.

"With the death of Dr Leyton, you mean?"

"Yes."

"I completely agree," offered Mr Pembroke.

"Let's dig around a little, find out all we can on Dr Schrader." Mr Beaumont demanded. "And this fellow Crumb, what do you know of him?"

With an arm of his spectacles, Mr Pembroke scratched his scalp, dislodging a few valuable grey hairs in the process as they dropped over his brow. "Nothing, the man's an enigma. I don't believe it's his name at all. I've already checked council records and passenger lists; he doesn't bloody exist and is a waste of time to continue searching."

"Let me look into that," replied the publisher, "I have an idea."

Leonard was puzzled; Mr Beaumont was helping and supporting him. He wasn't going to be dismissed as he'd expected. In fact, they were assisting him.

Mr Pembroke must have seen Leonard's perplexed expression. "You alright, lad?"

"Yes, sir, I, er, am well, considering."

"I have a question," stated Mr Pembroke, who referred to his notes. "How did you come to make the acquaintance of, ah, Uncle Jun and his wife?"

Leonard thought for a moment. "Mae was being accosted at the markets by a man who mistakenly assumed she was a, um, a prost–er, streetwalker and assaulted her. I escorted her home as she was living with Uncle Jun and Ming at the time."

"And her relationship with them, were they family?"

"Jun is not technically a relative, sir. They provided assistance to Mae when she arrived first in Wellington. I understand Jun and Ming assumed guardianship roles as her family were lost to her in China."

"I see." Mr Pembroke diligently scratched a few more notes. "It's the Orientals that I am concerned about, Leonard." He tapped his pencil against his notepad. "The bloody Orientals."

Leonard swallowed, that's what he feared as well.

"Now then, before the police arrive," Mr Beaumont turned back to the clock, "tell me how you intend to remain unharmed?"

"My friends have kindly allowed me to spend a few nights at

their home. I haven't thought much beyond that."

"Very well," said Beaumont. "Now listen carefully. Mr Pembroke and I believe this incident has the potential for quite a story. We'd like to chronicle all that's transpired and conclude with a satisfactory outcome. Do you know what that means?"

Leonard turned to Mr Pembroke, hoping for a clue. He remained impassive. "No, not really, sir."

"We want to solve this mystery and tie up all the loose ends. After some discussion and thought, we believe you've stumbled into the subversive workings of the underground. Gangs and crime, Leonard. Against my better judgement, Mr Pembroke has asked that you assist him in any way you can. If you are unable to perform your normal duties, then let me know, and I'll assign another as a temporary replacement until you can resume. I was reluctant to agree, firstly because I anticipated your incarceration, and secondly because you've been foolish and impetuous. After Mr Pembroke's glowing endorsement of you and hearing your version of the incident, I've changed my mind." Mr Beaumont stood and leaned forward on his desk. "The *Evening Standard* will run your story and bring to public attention the failings of government and police to curtail organised crime. I now understand you're nothing more than an innocent victim in this, Leonard."

"We have to prove it first," chimed in Mr Pembroke dryly.

A knock on the door prevented further discourse. "Yes?"

The door opened, and Mr Beaumont's secretary, a sizeable matronly woman, entered. "You have two policemen here to see you and Mr Hardy, sir." She turned and gave Leonard a disapproving frown. "I've put them in our meeting room."

"Thank you, we'll be there momentarily."

With an air of superiority, she returned to her desk and left a smell of camphor in her wake. Moths thought Leonard.

"Don't worry, Leonard, the police aren't the brightest of individuals," advised Mr Beaumont as he eased himself slowly from his chair.

"And a pity they didn't accept women; Mrs Pembroke would have made a fine constable," offered Mr Pembroke.

Leonard felt his stomach tie up in knots.

The two policemen stood by the window and looked out across Wellington, their focus on the black blot where businesses once thrived and flourished. They turned expectantly as Mr Beaumont, Leonard, and lastly, Mr Pembroke entered the seldom-used meeting room. Leonard noticed the stale, musty smell.

"Inspector Gibbard, it's a pleasure to see you again, I hope you've improved your batting average since we last met?" jibed Mr Beaumont as he held out his hand and smiled waggishly.

"I'm fairly positive my batting statistics would improve considerably if you'd bowl where a skilled batsman could strike at it," replied the Inspector, returning the smile and shaking the publisher's hand. "This is Constable Yates; he is assisting me."

As Mr Beaumont shook the hand of Constable Yates, Gibbard was appraising Leonard.

"And you must be Mr Hardy." Inspector Gibbard didn't smile or offer a hand.

"And this is my esteemed colleague, Mr Pembroke, whom you've met," introduced Mr Beaumont.

Once all the introductions were made and everyone seated, Constable Yates extracted a notebook, and Inspector Gibbard immediately attempted to take charge.

"I'd prefer to question Mr Hardy without your presence, gentlemen."

Leonard's hands were clammy and shook slightly with nerves. His mouth was dry.

"Of course, Thomas," replied Mr Beaumont, using the familiar name of the Inspector to keep things informal. "However, as Mr Hardy is in my employ and performing duties as required of him during the unfortunate incident, then I believe our presence will aid you with your inquiries," he looked at the Inspector and again offered a warm smile. He made no further reference to the recreational game of cricket they both enjoyed.

The Inspector stroked his rather sizeable whiskers that prospered on his pockmarked face as he considered Mr Beaumont's request. The whiskers followed the contours of his heavy jaw and ended with a flourish at the corners of his lipless mouth.

Someone once told Leonard, '*never trust a man with no lips*,' and Inspector Thomas Gibbard appeared to fit this description. He wondered if the Inspector was as cold and calculating as his appearance suggested. He shifted his gaze to the junior constable taking notes. He'd seen him before, around Wellington, and by all accounts, he had a friendly, outgoing disposition, although Constable Yates was not having much luck in emulating his senior officer by growing whiskers. Yates' attempt was a rather sad affair, making his youthful face appear patchy and unkempt. If Leonard was correct in his assessment of Yates, he seemed nervous and out of sorts. Like me, he thought.

"Very well, for the time being, I agree. Now then, Mr Hardy, you have some explaining to do, and I have questions." He looked at

Leonard, his lipless mouth like a gash on a coconut.

Mr Pembroke, as usual, remained quiet; his ever-present notepad sat on his lap with his pencil poised.

"Go ahead, Leonard, answer all questions frankly and honestly," encouraged Mr Beaumont nodding his head.

To Leonard, it was apparent what Mr Beaumont was attempting to do. He was trying to project to the Inspector that he was in charge, that he controlled the interview.

"How are you acquainted with Constable William Hastings?"

"I first met Constable Hastings when he knocked on my door after a body was discovered outside my home."

"And was this the body you were referring to when you shouted...?" the Inspector turned to Constable Yates.

"Oh, one moment." Yates flicked a few pages of his notes and cleared his throat. "*It was you who killed him, wasn't it? You murdered the man and left him in the bushes.*"

"Yes, that was exactly what I said."

"Hmmm, now why would you say that?" Gibbard asked, his eyes boring into Leonard. Before he could reply, Gibbard continued. "You see, in the preliminary investigation and report submitted by Constable Hastings and supported by the Coroner's inquiry, it states quite clearly the cause of death was a gunshot wound to the head. The conclusion being, the deceased was killed outside your home." Gibbard inclined his head in question. "It's doubtful Constable Hastings was the murderer; he'd been assigned elsewhere on another task." Gibbard shook his head disapprovingly. "Are you a drinking man, Mr Hardy? Do you indulge in a tipple?"

"Ah, yes, I do drink socially on occasion, but I am a man of moderate habits," replied Leonard, puzzled at the question.

"Constable Hastings challenges that assertion." Gibbard again turned over his shoulder to Yates. "Please read to Mr Hardy the portion of the report about Mr Hardy's condition on the morning the body was discovered."

"Yes, sir. One moment." Again, Yates flicked through his copious notes. "Found it," he looked up and smiled at his achievement. "Ah, *'Mr Hardy appeared to be in an advanced state of intoxication and stumbled, nearly falling after he opened the door...'* Do you want me to read more, sir?"

Gibbard ignored Yates. "So your judgement was severely impaired. In other words, you were inebriated, Mr Hardy. Had you been partaking in the consumption of alcoholic beverages on Saturday evening?"

"That is untrue. I object strongly to your accusation that I am intemperate. If I recall, I was unwell and dizzy and..."

"I can vouch for that and have a message from Mr Hardy stating he was poorly," interrupted Mr Beaumont. "He was absent from work for the next few days. That's a preposterous allegation, Thomas."

"Please answer my question, Mr Hardy. Had you been consuming alcoholic beverages on Saturday evening?"

"Yes."

"More than one?"

"Look, what does this have to do with the bloody fire, for God's sake?" Mr Pembroke spoke up.

Leonard was thinking much the same.

"He's allowed to indulge, and the man has never arrived at work soused! I'd know -- we work in the same damn room!"

Gibbard turned to Mr Pembroke, studied him carefully for a

heartbeat or two, then turned back to Leonard.

"Well?"

Leonard paused. "Yes, two if I recall."

Inspector Gibbard rose from his chair and approached the window; he rubbed the small of his back.

"After you accused Constable Hastings at the Royal Oak Hotel, what exactly did he do?" Gibbard didn't face Leonard and continued looking out the window.

"Constable Hastings asked me if I heard a gunshot, I told him I had not. There…"

"Please answer the question Mr Hardy," repeated the Inspector tersely.

Leonard turned to Mr Pembroke for support - he shrugged. "After I made the accusation, Constable Hastings, who was quickly walking away from me, turned rapidly. That was when he collided with the waiter. I distinctly remember the constable pausing for a moment before he came at me."

"What happened to the waiter and the serving tray he carried?"

"It flew upwards from his hands. Hastings' arm hit the waiter beneath the tray, in the chest, causing the soup to spill up and out."

"Where were you in relation to the waiter and the constable?"

"Other side of the room, perhaps five or six yards away."

"Then what happened?" Inspector Gibbard returned to his seat.

"I can't be sure, as I was concerned for my own safety, but I believe the gentleman sitting closest to the waiter stood up quickly to avoid being scalded and upturned the table."

"Did the constable make any effort to go to their assistance?"

"No."

"Could you see the candlestick that landed behind the overturned table from where you stood?"

"No, I could not. The table hid the candlestick from my view. It wasn't until the flames exceeded the height of the table that the fire was visible to me."

"Do you believe the constable could see the candlestick from where he stood?"

Leonard considered the question for a moment. "I'm unable to answer that."

"I see." Gibbard paused and thought about the next question.

"I do recall there were two Oriental men on the stairs; the doorman was agitated as he did not want to grant them access to the dining room. They rushed to the constable and took him away."

The Inspector's head shot up. "What Oriental men? Against his will? Did Constable Hastings struggle?"

"There were two men, but I don't know what they were doing. It was rather peculiar. They leapt forward and pulled the constable back, and he struggled, but it seemed more in anger and frustration that he was prevented from reaching me."

"Are you familiar with them, and can you describe their appearance and mannerisms?" Gibbard leaned closer on his chair. His interest piqued.

Leonard knew at this time that the Inspector had not previously been aware of the two Orientals; their involvement was a surprise. He turned his head slightly and looked at Mr Pembroke. As if reading his mind and knowing what he was thinking, the veteran reporter nodded imperceptibly.

"No, I don't believe I'd ever seen them before. I can't describe them; I was rather flustered at the time. But I do recall seeing them at the St. George when we were there earlier." He risked another surreptitious glance at Mr Pembroke and saw the hint of a smile. It also dawned on him that the police had yet to talk with Constable Hastings; they had not found him.

"Constable Hastings is still at large, isn't he?" Leonard suddenly asked.

Inspector Gibbard was caught off balance.

"Mr Hardy has concerns for his safety, Inspector. If the man still has his liberty, then he poses a risk to Mr Hardy and potentially even his companions. Is this not so?" said Mr Pembroke, looking grave. He knew what Leonard was thinking and immediately added his support.

"We are currently pursuing numerous leads and expect to question Constable Hastings within a short time."

"So then, Mr Hardy is correct, and you have yet to locate him?" asked Mr Beaumont, teaming up and applying more pressure.

"Yes, at present, he is unaccounted for."

"Can you tell me where Constable Hastings makes his home, his residential address? If I am to keep a watchful eye for him, as I believe he presents some danger to me, then I can avoid that area."

Inspector Gibbard laughed. "Come now, Mr Hardy, do you expect me to believe that?" he raised his eyebrows in question.

"Dear Thomas, we're amongst acquaintances, you can share that information," pushed Mr Beaumont, offering a syrupy heart-warming smile, "It is in the best interests of Mr Hardy to avoid any contact with the man, is it not?"

"My advice to you all is to let trained professionals do the policing, and I promise not to contribute to your newspaper, John." The Inspector waited for a response from Mr Beaumont, who reluctantly nodded in agreement. "Now, Mr Hardy, can you recall any further details about those Orientals - their age, distinguishing features, or perhaps even clothing?

Leonard shook his head.

Inspector Gibbard continued asking Leonard routine questions for a short while, but it was obvious he had nothing more substantial to ask.

Gibbard turned to the young constable, "Anything I have omitted?"

"No, sir," replied Yates.

"And what of me, am I to be held responsible for the incident?" Leonard asked.

Inspector Gibbard regarded Leonard closely. "I don't believe I have sufficient evidence to recommend legal proceedings against you, Mr Hardy. I do, however, reserve the right to question you again if the need arises."

Leonard nodded sullenly, he felt a little annoyed at the Inspector for his choice of words. He could have simply replied with a 'No'. He was considering a retort when he felt Mr Pembroke's cautionary hand on his arm.

Inspector Gibbard rose from his chair. "Then, gentlemen, thank you for your time and cooperation."

"Inspector, one moment if you please," asked Mr Pembroke.

Gibbard retrieved his hat and turned to the senior reporter.

"Do you believe Mr Hardy is in a precarious situation? I mean, after all, that bloody fool Hastings has made his feelings and intentions well known."

"I seriously doubt Mr Hardy need worry himself over Constable Hastings; the man has quite enough to concern himself with."

"Thank you. I believe Mr Hardy can feel reassured by your

informed perspective, Inspector. It certainly would be disconcerting if Hastings attempts any form of retaliation on Mr Hardy since the police are aware of his intentions. Especially if they did nothing to ensure the safety of a critical witness in the event it all came down to a trial.

The Inspector saw how he'd been manoeuvred. "What are you suggesting, Mr Pembroke?"

"Perhaps you could provide Mr Hardy with a minder when he is most vulnerable during his journey to and from work?"

Gibbard pinched his nose with his free hand. He sighed heavily. "Perhaps we could provide an escort during those times when he is most exposed and vulnerable. At least until such time, we can confirm Constable Hastings poses no immediate threat to Mr Hardy."

"Brilliant idea, Mr Gibbard, well done," offered Mr Pembroke in praise.

Leonard fought to control a smile. Mr Pembroke never ceased to amaze him.

Gibbard was fiddling with his hat as he debated Mr Pembroke's request. Finally arriving at a decision, he turned to Constable Yates. "Mr Yates, please remain behind and arrange with Mr Hardy suitable times and a schedule so that you may accompany him to and from home and work." He looked back to the newspapermen. "I have a meeting scheduled with the commissioner; he is somewhat desirous to resolve all issues related to the fire. So I must take your leave, good morning, gentlemen."

Mr Beaumont stood and walked the Inspector to the door. They began a discussion about the unorthodox bowling technique of a player in their club. Slowly, Mr Pembroke eased himself from his chair so he could return to his duties.

Mr Beaumont turned over his shoulder to Leonard. "I shall look forward to seeing the 'Shipping Intelligence' report before the deadline Mr Hardy."

"Yes, sir!" replied Leonard.

Constable Yates waited until only Leonard remained in the room, then leaned forward complicity and quietly asked, "Do you really fear retaliation by Constable Hastings?"

Leonard liked Yates and didn't want to be deceitful to the man, but he was reluctant to divulge anything to him that hadn't already been previously discussed. He didn't believe Hastings would be so foolish to him harm over just an accusation, and if their paths were to cross, then the worst he'd expect from the long-nosed constable would be a threat or two. Leonard believed the reason Mr Pembroke wanted a minder for him was not because of Hastings but because of the unknown Orientals.

"I believe Constable Hastings is certainly unbalanced and unpredictable and based on his recent behaviour, he certainly poses a danger," Leonard replied shrewdly.

Yates nodded slowly. "Yes, you're probably right."

Leonard made arrangements with Constable Yates regarding his schedule and walked him to the door. "Then I shall see you at half-past five this afternoon, Constable."

Inside the bullpen, Mr Pembroke was working away quietly; he didn't acknowledge Leonard or their meeting. A few other reporters worked at their desks. One or two gave Leonard a curious look, and some, thought Leonard, were probably surprised to actually see him. No doubt they had expected to see Inspector Gibbard lead him away in chains, yelling and screaming like a broken man. The sound of Mr Pembroke clearing his throat was a subtle reminder that work needed to be done.

Chapter Twelve

The delectable smell of roasting lamb greeted Leonard as he arrived at Bridgette and Mary's home. There weren't many dishes he enjoyed more than roast lamb, potatoes, vegetables and gravy, and then to complete the experience, a sweet dessert. He believed food was one of life's pleasures - to be savoured and enjoyed. The thought of the meal Mary was preparing made him salivate, a harsh reminder he'd neglected to eat during the day and was ravenous. Work at the *Evening Standard* had kept him busy all day, and while Mr Beaumont had indicated the newspaper would devote time and resources to helping Leonard solve the mystery, it didn't mean he could overlook his workload. As a result, and to meet his deadline, he'd missed out on luncheon. His stomach rumbled in anticipation of dinner.

Mae had never particularly enjoyed a roast dinner; she felt western foods were too heavy for her, instead preferring more traditional and lighter Chinese dishes, but she had made an effort and learned how to cook the lamb the way he loved it. During winter, he'd often arrive home from work and find Mae standing proudly before a roast lamb dinner she'd lovingly cooked for him. Stimulated by the aroma, the familiar feeling of loss and emptiness washed over him. He shrugged it off.

Mary greeted Leonard excitedly at the door, took his hat, jacket and valise and immediately began peppering him with questions about his day. She knew, as did their friends that Leonard would have to account for what happened on Saturday night, and she was keen to learn what had transpired as a result. It was no surprise that the police sought to question him, but the news of the young constable accompanying Leonard while he travelled to and from work was pleasant and reassuring. He shared all his news excitedly and, in turn, listened to Mary recount her day, how everyone at the hospital had spoken of nothing but the fire. She had not mentioned to her fellow nurses that she had been there and witnessed the entire event.

Bridgette sat morosely with them while they ate and chatted; she picked at her food listlessly and talked even less, then lethargically departed for the hospital soon after they finished eating. Her despair was of grave concern to Mary and only seemed to worsen. There appeared to be little Mary could do to brighten Bridgette's mood; usually bubbly and vivacious, Bridgette was emotionally overwhelmed.

The dinner mess had all been cleared away, and Mary sat beside Leonard on the settee. "I'm worried about her, Leonard, she's becoming worse, and I just don't know what I can do to help her."

Leonard knew precisely what was wrong and understood how Bridgette felt. "Time heals Mary. It won't happen overnight, and you must allow her time to reconcile. It's not a matter of forgetting the love she felt for Alex, it's learning how to adjust and continue her life without him." He turned to look at her more closely. "It's a lengthy process, and one I'm still learning to cope with myself." *Actually, more of a battle*, he thought.

"One of the ward sisters at the hospital made a passing comment to me about it today; even they are worried for her." Mary stared into the distance.

Leonard nodded sympathetically and waited a few moments. "Mary, I have a couple of delicate questions I must ask you, so please forgive me if I offend; it's not my intention to fluster or shame you, but I need forthright answers."

She turned to him with a sharp look. "Have I done something?"

"No, not at all. It's about Dr Schrader and something you said when we visited him. Can you tell me why you found him so detestable?"

Mary visibly tensed and placed her hands primly in her lap. It didn't go unnoticed by Leonard.

"Leonard, this is difficult to answer…."

"I understand, Mary, but there is a valid reason, please… trust me."

She fidgeted for a moment. "He looks at the nurses in a way that makes us uncomfortable."

"Is that it, nothing more?"

Mary looked up from her hands and held Leonard's gaze. "Sometimes he touches, as if by accident, but it isn't."

"He's done this to you or to other nurses?"

"I know he's done it to some of the nurses, but it's difficult to know because they do not wish to discuss it."

"Why? If the man has done wrong, then the matron or the surgeon superintendent needs to know of his ill-mannered behaviour."

Mary shook her head. "No, Leonard. Not long before I began working at the hospital, some nurses did complain and reported their grievances to the matron about Dr Schrader and his unwelcome advances. The nurses were accused of promiscuity and punished."

Leonard's eyebrows furrowed. "How do you deal with him?"

"We do our best to avoid him."

Leonard was becoming angry. "Why did you not tell me of this when we visited him, Mary?"

"This is not something you need concern yourself with, and besides, I was with you, and he would not attempt any improper behaviour in your presence."

Leonard remembered seeing the way the doctor looked at Mary during their meeting. "Then Dr Schrader has, uh... molested you?"

Mary remained silent as she wondered how much she should say. She came to a decision. "Yes, he has, and more so recently. Especially after your visit, and now he follows me around."

Leonard shook his head. "What a despicable man!" He was furious. "You can't let this continue, Mary."

"Matron believes any inappropriate behaviour is the result of provocative conduct by nurses and brought on themselves. Dr Schrader is a respected physician and valued member of the hospital staff; he, therefore, knows better and is beyond censure."

"But why doesn't she report it?"

Mary turned to look at Leonard. "Because reporting it would reflect badly on her personally and her ability to manage the nursing staff."

Leonard sought Mary's hand to offer comfort and, to his astonishment, realised he'd unconsciously held it already. "I'm very sorry, Mary. I had no knowledge of this."

She looked up at him and smiled.

He thought momentarily and decided to tell her what Mr Beaumont had said about the doctor. "Mr Beaumont informed me today that the paper had thought about running a story on Dr Schrader and his immoral penchant for touching women. From what I can gather, the man has garnered quite a reputation, but no one was willing to come forward and speak plainly about it. The public doesn't want to read things of such a nature, and Mr Beaumont decided not to continue with it. He also believes Dr Schrader is linked to Alex's death somehow."

"That doesn't surprise me."

"Is there anything you can tell me about him that you find peculiar or strange other than what we've just discussed? If Dr Schrader is involved in Alex's death and has associations with undesirable people, then there must be signs or indicators."

"Oh, Leonard, I don't know." She sighed. "I try to avoid the man, not learn about him." Mary reached into the sleeve of her dress and extracted a small frilly handkerchief. She gently dabbed her eyes.

"There must be something you've observed, surely."

"He's a respected and competent doctor, that I can say. His patients like him, especially the Chinese, and he won't allow other physicians to treat them, so I suppose you could say he's protective."

"Chinese?" Leonard was puzzled.

"Yes, and predominantly with expectant mothers. You should talk to Meredith, she deals mostly with them, and I usually care for those with sickness or injuries."

"You mean Dr Schrader treats all the Chinese patients who come to the hospital?"

"No, not all, but many. As far as expectant mothers go, he really only sees them if there's a complication and they come to the hospital."

"So, some women go to the hospital to give birth?"

"A few, and it's convenient because he speaks the language."

"He does?" Leonard exclaimed. "I find that interesting."

Mary remained quiet and had nothing more to add; the topic of Dr Schrader was upsetting to her, and Leonard felt it was time to change the subject. He reached over and placed an arm protectively over her shoulder, and without hesitation, she nestled into him. His chin rested on top of her head, and he could smell the delicate fragrance of violet scented soap. He felt the warmth of her body, and for the first time in a while, he felt peace. They sat unmoving while Leonard thought. He stretched his legs and wiggled his toes.

The revelation about Dr Schrader was intriguing; there was a link between the doctor and the Chinese and another between Constable Hastings and the Chinese, and the men he had seen follow him were also Chinese. It didn't take a fool to realise the Chinese were involved. While the dead mystery man, Mr Crumb, the doctor, and Hastings were not of Chinese origin, whatever was going on was not just limited to Orientals. So how did they all relate to each other? And Uncle Jun and Ming, they were Chinese too but had disappeared. It was very confusing.

It was a fitful and restless night for Leonard. He tossed and turned in Mary's bed as his thoughts swung from Mary to Mae and back to Mary again. It was always the same; Mae was present in his consciousness, watching over him, guiding him, never disapproving and always with the feeling of love. Then there was Mary, equally as beautiful, soft, feminine and resolute. Her strength came from character, while Mae had gathered her strength through adversity and experience. He knew it wasn't about making a choice between the two, although it sometimes felt like it. He was pragmatic. Mae was no longer living, and Mary was very much alive, yet inexplicably he felt tied to Mae. How could he still have such a strong bond with someone who had passed and yet, simultaneously, want to sever the tie so he could live and love again?

Leonard slowly climbed from his bed and stood at the window as the sun finally rose above the eastern hills. *Was it an acceptance,? hHad he finally admitted Mae was no longer alive, that her presence in his life was nothing more than just memories?* Something in him had changed during the night – was it Mary?

Constable Yates was precisely on time and greeted Leonard with a warm and affable smile. They walked in companionable silence down to Adelaide Road, where they waited for a tram to arrive. "Constable?"

Constable Yates turned to Leonard in question and waited.

"What can you tell me about Constable Hastings? Do you know him well? I'm just curious to learn more about the man."

Yates inhaled deeply and breathed out slowly. "I don't know much about him, Mr Hardy. The same as everyone else, most likely. He came to the constabulary about two years ago. I don't believe he's married, and he keeps to hisself most of the time. I ain't had much to do with him, thank goodness." He leaned towards Leonard. "Never really cared for the man, to be honest with you."

The clanging bell announced the arrival of the tram. Both men climbed aboard and were fortunate to find seating, and they made themselves comfortable.

"Two years, you say?"

"Yes, sir, 'bout that, I reckon." Constable Yates kept his head moving and was attentive to his surroundings. He looked around him constantly.

"Where had he been prior to coming to Wellington?"

"Ah, I believe that would be Peking, Mr Hardy." Yates saw a look of surprise on Leonard's face. "That's in China, sir."

"China! What was he doing there?" Leonard exclaimed.

"Don't know, sir. If I recall, things became heated for foreigners and, like many people, decided it was safer elsewhere."

"Does he speak the language?

Constable Yates laughed, "You'd have to ask him, I wouldn't know. Although having lived there, I expect he does."

Leonard was thinking furiously. "By any chance, Constable, are you aware of any acquaintances he has at Wellington Hospital?"

"Like some of them nurses, you mean? I've seen them, and ah, well...."

"No, Constable Yates," Leonard interrupted sternly, "perhaps like doctors."

"Oh," Yates looked uncomfortable. "Again, that's another question you'd have to ask him."

"I doubt whether I will have that opportunity any time soon. Have you heard any news; are they any closer to discovering his whereabouts?"

Constable Yates didn't answer; he was looking over his shoulder at something on the street.

"Constable?"

"Mr Hardy, last evening when we left your work, two Oriental men were standing near the rear exit of your work on Boulcott Street. I remember them clearly. Now, we just passed two Oriental men whom I'd wager are the same two men." He pointed behind, but

Leonard could see nothing.

"They're probably the same two men who have been following me. What were they doing?"

"Just standing on the side of the road watching the tram. I don't like it, Mr Hardy."

"I am grateful you are here with me, constable."

"We shall see, won't we," remarked Constable Yates without confidence.

The commute to work continued without any further sightings. The constable remained attentive and vigilant and walked Leonard to the premises of the *Evening Standard's* main entrance, where Leonard arranged a time for him to return for the journey home.

The bullpen was busy, many of the reporters were there, and Mr Pembroke had yet to make an appearance this morning. Taking advantage of their absent senior reporter, they took the opportunity to question Leonard about the Royal Oak fire. Rumours were rife, and Leonard discovered that he was supposed to have lit the fire, saved several people from imminent death, threatened a constable, which caused him to run away in fear, was wanted by the police for murder, and that he'd been paid by the Hotel's owners to deliberately set fire to the Royal Oak so that the owner could collect on insurance.

Leonard made the reporters swear to secrecy, then solemnly told them the rumours and speculation were mainly true and part of a grand scheme initiated by the Australians who wished to invade New Zealand. The sound of the door opening ended further conjecture, and like a miracle from Moses himself, the reporters, with heads down, were diligently going about their business as Mr Pembroke shuffled in.

He paused, looked around the room and sniffed. "I can smell languor, a common ailment that festers obscenely amongst gross inactivity."

No one said a word in response, although one unknown person suppressed a laugh. By all outward appearances, the reporters were too engrossed in their work to pay the old man any attention. Mr Pembroke removed his hat and jacket, neatly hung them from a stand behind him and then fussed with his seat cushion. Once pleased with its position, he eventually sat down heavily with a sigh.

"Something amuses you, Mr Keegan?"

"No, sir."

Mr Pembroke began cleaning his spectacles. "Mr Armitage, perhaps later this morning, you can explain your tardiness to me?"

"Yes, sir."

Thankfully, Leonard was spared being singled out. Every morning was the same; Mr Pembroke always called on someone different to account for their actions and often made a variation on his speech about languor. How he knew who was tardy was a mystery and a source of vigorous debate. As yet, no one had determined how the wily, old reporter always managed to stay one step ahead.

Leonard waited for the appropriate time when he and Mr Pembroke were the only ones in the bullpen. He approached the senior reporter carefully.

"Sir?"

The reporter looked up and removed his spectacles. "Mr Hardy." It wasn't a question or statement, just two words.

"I discovered some information I think you should know about."

"Then out with it, lad. Or are you going to keep me in suspense?"

"Prior to his arrival in Wellington, Constable Hastings made his home in Peking. That's in China, sir."

Pembroke looked at Leonard, thrust his head forward and growled. "I know where bloody Peking is." He rubbed his chin. "China, eh?"

"I also have some information about Dr Schrader, sir. Apparently, he treats most Chinese patients at the hospital, including the troublesome maternity cases, and he speaks Chinese."

"Now that is noteworthy, isn't it?

"Very much, and I also verified that Dr Schrader has a habit of inappropriately fondling women."

Pembroke shook his head, and for a brief moment, his eyes flashed in anger. Just as quickly, the look vanished. "The man's a piece of work, he is. How did you come across all this then?"

"From Ward Sister Mary Worthington, sir. She is a friend of mine."

"Don't know her."

One of the reporters came walking into the bullpen out of breath. "Guess what?" And without pausing, he continued. "You'll be pleased to know the police just apprehended Constable Hastings."

Leonard felt relief wash over him.

"Where was he arrested?" asked Mr Pembroke.

"In a rooming house near Chinatown, sir. Seems a local had a dislike for him and dobbed him in."

"Did he surrender easily?" Leonard asked.

"Apparently not. He put up a bit of a struggle, I heard."

"Then I assume they are holding him at the depot?" Pembroke queried.

"I believe so, sir."

Mr Pembroke drummed his fingers on his desk as he considered. "Go over there, see if they will let you can speak with him, find out his take on the fire. And one more thing, Mr Keegan ...."

The reporter looked at Mr Pembroke with his eyebrows raised.

"Confirm if he came from Peking before arriving in New Zealand. Er, that's in China, in case you weren't sure, and also if he speaks the Chinese language. Understood?"

"Yes, sir."

"Be off with you, and don't loiter or visit the Southern Cross Public Hotel, Mr Keegan, I'll know if you have." Pembroke watched Mr Keegan leave and then turned to Leonard. "I swear that man can drink alcohol. Mrs Pembroke could knock back a few when she drank, but he'd challenge her, alright," he chuckled. "Now then, I believe you can sleep in your own bed tonight, Mr Hardy. Certainly, a relief to know Hastings is off the streets."

"Yes, sir, a big relief."

Actually, it was an immense relief. Leonard could return to his routine and life again and not have to look over his shoulder. He'd come to realise he'd been walking around Wellington in a constant state of fear. Now, if he could find the elusive Mr Crumb, that would be one thing less to worry about.

Mr Pembroke strongly urged Leonard to continue with his work and waved him away. The remainder of the morning and afternoon seemed to drag, and he was relieved when it was finally time to leave work and go home. Leonard left the building through the front door and briskly walked down Manners Street towards the blackened ruins of the Royal Oak Hotel. With Constable Hastings now in police custody, he wasn't expecting Constable Yates to make an appearance, so he walked alone.

Workers had been busy, and vast areas of land had already been cleared of charred debris. A couple of enterprising shopkeepers had set up temporary premises and were doing a brisk trade. A few curious onlookers stared at the destruction, pointed at a few things, and eventually moved on. Leonard stopped to stare, shook his head in sympathy and walked up Cuba Street to catch a tram. He didn't see any Oriental men lurking on street corners or following him.

Surprisingly Mary wasn't home, but thankfully he had a key and let himself in. Bridgette must have left a short time ago for work as the oven was still hot. He gathered the few possessions he had brought from home and packed them in a suitcase. Mary had baked a cake the day before, and tempted with the memory of yesterday's dessert, he cut a piece, took it to the living room and relaxed on the settee while he waited for Mary to arrive.

A clattering on the door startled him. He must have dozed off. He walked down the hall and opened the door to find Jonathan. "Jonathan!" Leonard looked around but saw no sign of Meredith.

"Meredith isn't with me, Leonard."

Leonard looked puzzled and stepped back to allow Jonathan to enter. He walked to the sitting room with Jonathan trailing and sat down, rubbing his eyes. "I apologise, I'm a little tired."

Jonathan didn't sit and stood awkwardly, holding his hat in the middle of the living room.

"What's wrong? And why isn't Meredith here?"

Jonathan didn't immediately respond and couldn't meet Leonard's gaze.

"Is this about Mary? Has something happened to her?" Leonard felt his heart begin to race and feared the worst. He stood. "Jonathan, what is going on?"

Jonathan's mouth opened and closed; it was plainly obvious he was struggling to find the words to express himself, while Leonard, with his hair dishevelled, stared open-mouthed at him.

"What has happened to Mary?" Leonard repeated, his heart still pounding. He knew Jonathan well enough to know something terrible had befallen her. Why else would he be standing in the middle of the living room looking so dour?

Jonathan shook his head. "It's not about Mary, Leonard, although I'm unsure what you are referring to." He cast a quick glance around the room.

"Well, what is it then?" Leonard asked, only minutely relieved.

"Uh, you are aware Constable Hastings was taken into custody this morning."

Leonard nodded. "I'd heard, yes."

Jonathan looked down and began fidgeting with his hat. "Mr Hastings has retained the counsel of Hollister, Hollister and Davidson."

Leonard showed mild surprise. "Yes, that's your employer. I admit I'm a little astounded, but why the glum expression?" Leonard stared blankly at Jonathan.

"The senior partner, Kenneth Hollister, QC, will defend Mr Hastings against all charges brought against him by the crown." Jonathan tore his gaze from the hat and turned to Leonard. "He has prohibited me from communicating with you as it represents a conflict of interest."

"What does that mean, prohibited you? What nonsense is this? You're a solicitor, not a barrister, and certainly won't be pleading for Hastings at the bar."

"Leonard, our friendship means the world to me, I value the time we've spent together, however, until the court has adjudicated, then I cannot communicate with you or continue to propagate our friendship."

"We were friends before this, Jonathan. You should just recuse yourself, and I'm sure your law firm can put barriers in place to prevent sensitive information from passing backwards and forwards."

"If it was only that simple... and I'm afraid it isn't. I'm sorry, Leonard, please forgive me. I really must go, as I shouldn't even be here talking to you." Jonathan wiped his brow with a handkerchief. "When this is over, we can have a laugh and continue where we left off, eh?" Jonathan turned to leave, then turned back, puzzled. "Where is Mary? You expressed concern for her."

"Wouldn't that information be deemed a conflict of interest?" said Leonard bitterly.

Jonathan stared guiltily.

"You promised to help, Jonathan. You promised! Now you devalue our friendship by defending a man you know to be at wrong. I've shared personal thoughts with you, and now you'll likely use them to defend the very person who might be implicated in not one but multiple murders. He may even have been responsible for the death of our friend Alex, your friend Jonathan, or have you forgotten? What kind of a man are you?" Leonard shook his head in silent outrage. "I think you should leave."

"Leonard..." appealed Jonathan, "I have no choice in this matter, and what about our friendship?"

"You should have thought of that when you chose to obey your masters." Leonard elbowed past him to the door and opened it. An invitation for Jonathan to depart.

Jonathan slowly exited the house and walked away dejectedly. He didn't turn, look back or say another word. Leonard returned to the living room and rubbed his face with his hands as he sat. He was angry. Jonathan had bent to the will of his employers without showing backbone or mettle. They'll use him to suit their own needs and the needs of Hastings and, in the process, destroy a friendship without a thought of concern, reflected Leonard.

He began pacing the confines of the living room. *"Where was Mary?"* he repeated to himself over and over again. After a while, he realised he wasn't achieving anything and looked for a note or message she may have left, but he couldn't find anything. He searched for any other signs that she had been at home, but he couldn't tell. Bridgette and Mary's bedroom were in turmoil due to his sleeping in her bedroom. Bridgette, usually very orderly and neat, had left the house in a shambles. He began to fear the worst.

He sat back down on the settee and began to think of anything she had said to him, a clue to her whereabouts when a slow but firm rap on the door made him sit upright. It wasn't Jonathan returning; his knock was always harried and quick. He ran to the door and opened it. Standing on the step was a ruddy-faced reverend, breathing hard.

Leonard said nothing and just looked at the poor man who looked like he would collapse; the exertion of walking up the steps appeared to be too much.

"Good evening, I uh, was expecting to find Miss Worthington here," said the Reverend as he wiped his brow with the sleeve of his black jacket. "Perhaps I'm at the wrong residence?" The Reverend extracted a note from his pocket and carefully unfolded it, and read it again. "I believe this is the place." Unused to the physical activity of climbing numerous steps, he was out of breath, and his chest heaved.

"You are at the correct address, however, Miss Worthington isn't available at present. How may I assist you?"

The Reverend looked disappointed. "It's an urgent matter and of some concern."

"Please come inside, and I will get you a drink of water."

Leonard led the grateful Reverend into the living room and fetched him a glass of water; the poor man was in considerable distress. "I'm a close friend of Miss Worthington. My name is Leonard Hardy."

The Reverend drained the glass, looked at Leonard carefully, and then at the cake that sat uneaten on a saucer. "My name is Charles Hamilton, I'm the pastor at Saint James's Church and volunteer my time at the hospital."

Leonard indicated that Reverend Hamilton should sit and urged him to continue.

"Your name is familiar to me, Mr Hardy, Mrs Leyton has favourably mentioned your name as an alternative."

An alternative? An alternative to what? Leonard leaned forward and nodded, eager to learn the reason for the Reverend's visit.

"I'm here on a matter of some urgency. Uh, when will Miss Worthington return?"

"She is expected back very soon. I'm waiting on her now. Please, carry on, sir."

"Yes, of course." The Reverend held out his arm with the glass, "Can I impose on your generosity and have another?"

Leonard rushed back to the kitchen, returned with more water, and then waited as the Reverend emptied the glass. He spilled a few drops that fell onto the large cross that hung from his neck.

"Oh dear, good thing it won't rust, eh," said the Reverend as he wiped the cross dry. "Now, where was I?"

"You were about to tell me about the urgent matter that brought you here."

"Yes, yes, that's right," he smiled benevolently and again studied Leonard carefully. "I'm not sure I've seen you at our Sunday services, they're very good. Certainly worth a visit, good cleansing for the soul."

Leonard returned the smile and inclined his head, a subtle reminder for Reverend Hamilton to proceed.

The Reverend replaced his smile with a serious expression. "I'm afraid that Mrs Leyton has taken a rather severe turn. According to the doctor, she is suffering from extreme melancholia and has had a breakdown of sorts."

Leonard's hand went to his mouth. *Oh no, poor Bridgette, poor dear Bridgette*, he thought.

"She is currently in the care of the hospital and under observation," Reverend Hamilton gave Leonard a knowing look. "But she needs to be home and taken care of. They will keep her under careful supervision for seventy-two hours before they release her, however, if she cannot be cared for in a suitable manner, she will be transferred to a lunatic asylum for treatment."

Leonard was dumbfounded, speechless. He walked to the window and looked out as he composed himself. "And where is that likely to be?" He swallowed dryly.

"I don't know with certainty. Normally those decisions are

made by the doctor, however, I believe she will be sent to Mount View Lunatic Asylum, just down the road near the Basin Reserve."

"A lunatic asylum? Seems extreme, don't you think, Reverend?"

"Melancholia is considered a mental disorder, therefore, it is commonplace to send a patient to such an institution for treatment."

"Would you like another glass of water, Reverend Hamilton?"

The Reverend shook his head and again cast a sideways glance at the cake that looked so inviting.

"Help yourself to the cake, Reverend," Leonard offered, unwilling to let the poor man suffer any longer, and then went to the kitchen to retrieve a glass of water for himself. He needed some time to think.

"How is she at the moment?" Leonard asked once he returned.

Reverend Hamilton licked his fingers. "I'm not a doctor and can't offer any medical opinions, but she was emotionally up and down. Certainly unstable."

"Does she pose a danger to herself?"

The Reverend shrugged, "I can't say."

"Can I see her? I want to visit her tonight. Is this possible, and will they let me?"

"Again, Mr Hardy, I'm a volunteer and cannot speak for the hospital. I came here today as a courtesy to Mrs Leyton, who asked me to notify Ward Sister Worthington or yourself."

"Yes, of course, and thank you. Perhaps you can tell me, whose care is she under, the name of her doctor?"

Reverend Hamilton placed the last piece of cake in his mouth and pulled the note from his pocket, and studied it carefully for a moment. "I believe it's Dr Schrader."

Leonard felt a chill.

"I must be returning, Mr Hardy. I'm sorry I was the bearer of unfortunate news, and I hope Mrs Leyton recovers. She's a fine woman and a magnificent nurse." The Reverend looked pensive. "Is sad about her husband, he was a wonderful chap, a real shame." He rose from the settee.

"Yes, yes... yes, he was," replied Leonard weakly.

"Are you alright, sir?" asked the Reverend as he noticed Leonard had leaned on the wall for support."

Leonard took a deep breath and pulled himself together. "Yes, thank you. I'm just in shock, it has been a trying week."

Reverend Hamilton followed Leonard to the door and said farewell. He walked down the stairs, stopped, and turned. "We have a morning eight o'clock and a four o'clock afternoon service on Sundays, Mr Hardy, I will look forward to seeing you attend. Good evening."

Leonard stood at the open door staring out across the street long after Reverend Hamilton had departed. He thought of poor Bridgette, unable to cope with all that had happened recently. And Mary. Where was Mary?

He sat down and wrote a short note in the event Mary came home.

Chapter Thirteen

𝒜 porter graciously opened Wellington Hospital's large front door for Leonard. After thanking the man, he immediately walked through the reception area and sought directions from the staff at the main desk. He was lucky; an officious and severe-looking woman told him it was still visiting hours - but only just. If he disobeyed and stayed longer, he imagined the woman hunting him down, throwing him over her shoulder and carrying him outside to be tossed on the street. He was on his best behaviour.

He'd never been in the new hospital wards before, only to the administration area when he met with Dr Schrader and was surprised by its modern design. He found the women's ward without difficulty, and another nurse, a ward sister whom he vaguely knew, guided him towards Bridgette's bed. It was plainly obvious the nurses had been kind to her and allocated a bed at the far side of the ward, furthest from the door, where it was quiet and more private.

"Melancholia is a broad term, Mr Hardy. Essentially, Mrs Leyton has been emotionally overwhelmed by recent events, leading to feelings of emptiness, hopelessness, anxiety, worthlessness, and guilt." The nurse raised an eyebrow to reinforce her statement. "In addition, she has been having problems concentrating on her work and remembering details. Frequently patients suffering from these symptoms also have suicidal thoughts." This time her look softened, and she gave him a sympathetic frown.

Leonard nodded in understanding. He'd been affected by similar feelings after the loss of Mae. "How is she now?"

"Resting for the moment. She's exhausted."

It was a typical Nightingale Ward, a large rectangular room that accommodated about thirty beds, fifteen against each wall and facing each other. Two tables with chairs occupied space in the middle of the room, and to add a pleasant, homey touch, each featured a colourful bouquet as a decorative centrepiece. A fireplace against one wall kept the ward warm in the cooler months, and framed pictures were hung from the wall. Visitors sat on bedside chairs and chatted or just rested quietly with female patients in the crowded room. The nurse led him past the occupied beds, but he kept his head down to not intrude on what little privacy these people had. The ward was exceptionally quiet; even their combined footsteps seemed unnaturally loud on the carpet covering the entire floor. Leonard couldn't resist falling into step with the ward sister as they marched in synchronous time. He kept his gaze firmly on Bridgette's bed and felt his stomach tighten into knots as he approached.

Bridgette lay curled on her side in a protective ball, like a small child, looking vulnerable and helpless. The nurse asked Leonard to wait for a moment and then knelt to speak to Bridgette in a soft, gentle voice. At first, Bridgette appeared unresponsive, then, with aid, she sat up and slowly leaned back against the freshly puffed pillows the nurse had arranged.

Her beautiful red hair had been pulled back and secured beneath a head covering. It wasn't flattering, but it was practical, and it made her look different, almost incomplete. The nurse waved him to a chair, took a few steps back and watched.

Perhaps more than any of her friends, he understood how she felt. He knew what it was like to lose a loved one, to experience grief and loss, to wake in the morning with a heavy heart and to go to sleep at night with only memories for comfort and untold words for regret. As a true friend, he wanted to offer her support, give strength and help her recover.

Bridgette's eyes were puffy, red and surrounded by dark circles; her mouth, normally so eager to smile, was downturned, unmoving, and almost lifeless. Even her skin seemed sallow. *Perhaps it's the colour of the walls*, he thought. He reached out and gently took one of her hands. It felt cold, but she responded and squeezed his hand slightly.

"Oh, my dear Bridgette," he whispered. "The pain you suffer through I know all too well. I know where it hurts, and I understand how you feel, but you are not alone, not anymore. I am here for you."

She managed a small smile, and the corners of her mouth twitched upwards, tears formed in her eyes that she tried to blink away. Embarrassed, Leonard looked away briefly and saw the rotund figure of Dr Schrader standing at the ward's entrance; he was talking with a nurse, and she pointed in his direction. They immediately began walking towards him. He remembered his conversation with Mary about the doctor, and he felt his anger moulder.

"I am sorry I did not pay more attention to you. It was wrong of me to be so consumed with trivial things that I neglected to offer you help and support when you needed it the most, but I won't let them send you away, Bridgette. I will come for you, do you hear me?"

She nodded but said nothing.

"Mr Hardy, what a surprise to see you here. Unfortunately, I cannot have you risk upsetting my patients, and as you are not family, I must insist that you leave. Hospital rules." Dr Schrader's waistcoat looked like it would burst like a ripe tomato as he rocked on his heels. His small eyes darted everywhere except at Leonard.

Bridgette muttered something inaudible. Ignoring Dr Schrader and an apologetic-looking nurse, Leonard leaned toward her.

"Where is Mary?" she repeated, only this time louder. The doctor and nurses all heard.

"I don't know, Bridgette. I was hoping you'd have an idea."

Bridgette looked up at him with watery eyes, then turned and stared vacantly at Dr Schrader. He looked uncomfortable and couldn't meet her gaze.

"That's quite enough, it's time to go," said the doctor, interrupting their conversation.

"Mrs Leyton requested that Mr Hardy visit her, Doctor," informed the ward sister.

"He's not family, she's in an advanced state of distress, and I don't need to justify to you how I care for my patients," spat Schrader.

Leonard gave the doctor a long cold stare and turned back to Bridgette. "Dr Schrader wants me to leave, Bridgette. I have no option and must leave now." He leaned over and kissed her on the cheek. "I will have you discharged as soon as I can."

He left her bed and approached the doctor, who stood watching with his arms arrogantly folded across his chest. Leonard stood only inches away and looked down at Schrader's bald palette's glistening and polished sheen. "I'd like to have Mrs Leyton immediately discharged, Doctor."

Schrader finally looked at Leonard with the confidence of authority. "That isn't possible; you have no legal right."

Arguing with the doctor was futile, he realised. "You and I both know my presence here is at her request, and I'm not causing her discomfort or agitation. This is what she needs, support and love from those who care about her, and what she doesn't require is the meddling of a lecherous doctor more intent on satisfying his impure urges and interfering with her recovery." Leonard looked at Schrader with contempt. "Now stand aside; your presence disgusts me." Leonard was livid and hoped the doctor couldn't see his trembling hands.

Dr Schrader unfolded his arms, and his face bloomed scarlet. Leonard was sure he could hear buttons straining on his waistcoat as they threatened to part from the thin fabric that held them fast. Unwilling to become involved in a conflict between the doctor and a visitor, both nurses tentatively stepped back to create some distance. Schrader's mouth opened, but he couldn't find words. All conversation within the ward stopped; patients and visitors alike stopped to stare and listen.

Finally finding courage, Dr Schrader spoke. "Effective immediately, you are denied access to this hospital. Let's hope you suffer no injuries or medical events as you'll be turned away at the door. You're forbidden to return." He raised an arm and pointed to the door. "And if you don't leave this hospital immediately, I will call for a porter and have you forcibly removed. You know where the door is, see you avail yourself to its use." He stepped aside and allowed Leonard to pass. The two nurses escorted him out.

"Where is Mary?" asked the ward sister when they were safely out of earshot.

"I don't know, I'm unable to locate her. Do either of you know where she is?"

They walked a few steps in silence, and the nurses looked at each other in question, then shook their heads. "No," said one, "we haven't seen her."

Leonard frowned. "Please see Bridgette comes to no harm. I do not like or trust that doctor. Meanwhile, I will do my best to get her out of here."

"We all will look out for her, sir. And please find Mary,. Bridgette needs her."

Leonard walked down the corridor, past the front desk and towards the main exit; he stopped, turned back and approached the two women on duty. The severe-looking woman wasn't the friendly, accommodating type, so he spoke to the other.

"Good evening," he smiled warmly, "May I leave a message for a midwife nurse?"

The woman looked sideways at her unfriendly associate, who remained stoic. "Of course, sir."

She fumbled for paper and a pencil while the unfriendly woman strode purposefully towards Dr Schrader, who had just appeared. Leonard quickly scribbled a few lines, folded the paper and addressed it clearly to Midwife Meredith Rosewarne.

"Can you please see that Miss Meredith Rosewarne receives this? It's very important," Leonard requested.

A porter stepped out from behind a door conveniently situated near the front desk and stood motionless with arms folded as he observed. Unaware of Leonard's banishment but sensing something amiss, the porter at the main entrance curiously watched.

"Yes, sir, I'll make sure," replied the woman uneasily.

"Thank you, and enjoy your evening," replied Leonard and rapidly walked away. He looked over his shoulder to see Dr Schrader still watching.

Meredith was his only hope. There was no one else he could

turn to that could help him with Bridgette. He wondered if Jonathan would find a legal issue to preclude Meredith from assisting. He would find out soon enough.

He continued to walk towards Bridgette and Mary's home, where he had left his suitcase, and quietly hoped Mary would be sitting there happily waiting for him. He planned to check for her one last time, then return to his own home on Marjoribanks Street, but now he questioned the wisdom in that. Perhaps he should spend another night in Mary's bed; it was close to the hospital where Bridgette was, and Mary may yet show up.

She didn't.

He caught the tram as he always did from Adelaide Road and headed to work; it was another lovely summer's morning and the day held promise, or so Leonard hoped. Mary had still not appeared, and Bridgette lay in despair at Wellington Hospital under the looming threat of a transfer to Mount View Lunatic Asylum. He wasn't sure what to do and hoped Meredith would reply to his message with a suggestion or two and an offer of assistance.

Through the tram's window, he watched the scenery slowly glide past. The early morning city streets were busy with people like him riding tramcar's, taking cabs, walking to work or going about their business. Everyone was in a rush, except the horses pulling the tram that plodded along in no great hurry. People climbed aboard, some hopped off, all strangers, all coming and going, so he was startled to find Constable Yates suddenly sitting beside him.

"Lovely morning, innit?"

"Good morning, Constable, and what brings you into town this early?"

"People are pinching stuff from the fire, so they wants me to keep a visible presence in the area. Today, I'm a deterrent."

Leonard nodded; he'd previously wondered if theft had been a major concern after the fire, but now he knew. Distractedly, he turned from the constable and resumed his observations through the window.

"But I was actually hoping to find you, Mr Hardy."

Leonard turned back in surprise, "And why is that?"

"We'll be getting off at the same place, let's talk then where we can't be overheard."

Leonard had liked the constable from the outset, he was open, friendly, and took his work seriously. He instinctively trusted him. "Very well."

Once off the tram, Constable Yates took Leonard to the burned-out doorway of a building on Cuba Street, where their conversation was private. Leonard waited patiently as Yates quickly looked around.

"Mr Hardy, I was thinking about when Inspector Gibbard questioned you, and about the answers you gave. I happen to know the inspector believes you, and I do too. But, you see, I can't for the life of me reason what it's all about and what led to all this."

Leonard nodded, curious as to where this was all heading.

"So, I figure there's things you ain't telling. Maybe because you can't prove anything, or perhaps the police won't believe you. But something is going on."

Leonard remained silent.

"Are you with me so far, Mr Hardy?"

"Yes, I am."

"Righto then, so I'm hearing conversation back at the depot, and I'm thinking about them questions you asked me about Hastings." Yates raised one eyebrow as he looked at Leonard. "If you tell me what's going on, then I'll tells you what I know."

"Why?"

"Now, Mr Hardy," Yates laughed, "I think you're a clever man." He tapped his head with a finger. "You have smarts, sir. But, Inspector Gibbard is focusing his investigation on the fire and Hastings' involvement. He isn't looking deeper, and that's what interests me. The inspector doesn't have time to chase wild stories, no, he doesn't. But I have the time, and I can."

Leonard nodded again.

"Like this morning, something is bothering you, I can tell. It must be bad 'cause of the way you're acting, and I think it's all related, I do." Yates swivelled his head and looked around again to make sure there was no one within earshot and listening.

Leonard didn't need much time to think; this was a godsend. "I tell you what, you come to the house in Newtown where I've been a guest for the last few evenings, and I'll explain. Can you be there around four o'clock this afternoon?"

"Righto, I'll be finished work by then," Yates grinned. And Mr Hardy, you'd better hurry to work, or you'll be late."

Today, Leonard was unpunctual.

"Come and see me later this morning, Mr Hardy, and you can elaborate on why you were tardy," instructed Mr Pembroke when Leonard arrived at work.

It was difficult to concentrate. Again and again, he rewrote the obituaries; they didn't make sense, the grammar was incorrect, there were too many words, and he even wrote the wrong name on one of them. It would have created quite a sensation if the paper published an obituary that stated Mr Henry Stout died while giving birth to twins. At one point and in frustration, he was about to stand up and walk around to clear his mind when he saw Mr Pembroke peering over the top of his spectacles, watching him. He didn't say anything to Leonard - he didn't need to. The spectre of Mr Pembroke looming in the background watching him was enough to help him focus, and as the morning progressed, he finally made some headway.

It was nearing luncheon, and Leonard was looking forward to the recess, even if it were for a short time only. He was behind in his work and had some catching up to do, but he could do it if he could free his mind from Bridgette, Mary and even the ever-present Mae.

"Mr Hardy, come with me, please," Mr Pembroke's voice broke the silence in the room. A couple of reporters looked up, surprised at the summons.

Leonard wasn't even sure Mr Pembroke spoke to him until Mr Keegan whispered for him to get a move on.

With some hesitancy, he walked from the bullpen and followed Mr Pembroke to the seldom-used meeting room. Mr Pembroke carried a pencil and his trusty notebook and stopped at the door, waiting for him to catch up.

"Take a big breath, lad," Mr Pembroke said quietly. "Go on, a deep breath, it will help."

Leonard looked at Mr Pembroke with curiosity. Something was going on, of which he knew nothing about, but as instructed, he inhaled, filling his lungs with air and then exhaled slowly, letting his breath slowly escape through his mouth. It felt good, and Mr

Pembroke was correct, it made a difference.

Mr Pembroke opened the door and allowed Leonard to enter into the dank, stale air of the meeting room. Mr Beaumont and a stranger, an officer wearing the uniform of the New Zealand Armed Constabulary, were already seated and sharing a laugh.

"Of course, you know Mr Pembroke, whom you met earlier," said Mr Beaumont. "And this is Leonard Hardy, whom I told you about. Leonard, this is Major Hutton."

The officer stood, smiled at Leonard and shook his hand. "It's a pleasure to finally meet, Mr Hardy, I've heard much about you."

"Thank you, sir," Leonard replied cautiously. He was still a little unsure of what was happening and why he'd been invited to this meeting.

Mr Beaumont looked relaxed, and Mr Pembroke, who was already seated and typically showed no emotion, fussed with his spectacles and opened his notebook to a blank page.

"Leonard, please sit, you're making me nervous," Mr Beaumont urged.

Leonard dutifully obeyed and looked at the Major carefully; he was trying to remember if New Zealand had press gangs and wondered if the purpose of this meeting was to force him into military service. The officer was tall and surprisingly well-groomed, whereas most military men he'd seen always looked worse for wear. This man was a gentleman officer. His hands were smooth, and his hair was styled neatly, almost fashionably. He was more curious than ever about the reason for his summons.

"I'm sure you're intrigued as to the reason for this meeting, Leonard. We won't keep you long as I'm sure you're keen to return to work," Mr Beaumont began. "After our chat a few days ago, you informed me how you'd exhausted all possibilities to locate your elusive Winston Crumb."

Leonard sat up a little straighter and also noticed Mr Pembroke's surprised reaction.

"One resource you failed to check is military records." Mr Beaumont gave Leonard a disapproving look - his meaning clear. *An accomplished reporter would have known to check military records.* Leonard risked a quick sideways glance at Mr Pembroke, who raised his eyebrows in response. He could kick himself; he should have known.

"Major Hutton is a dear family friend, and I imposed on his kind and generous nature to lend a hand. Being a staff officer to Colonel Roberts, who commands the Armed Constabulary, the major has unprecedented access to all sorts of records." Mr Beaumont leaned forward in his chair and focused on Leonard. "A thorough search of those records will reveal there is no Winston Crumb listed, or even a variation on that name."

Leonard felt deflated. *Then what was the point of this meeting,* he wondered? He opened his mouth to speak when Mr Beaumont continued.

"However, Major Hutton has some information you may find very interesting, Leonard. Perhaps the major would like to elaborate." Mr Beaumont nodded his head for the major to continue.

Major Hutton cleared his throat. "To promote morale within the constabulary, officers are often encouraged to be innovative, especially around the festive season. A few enterprising officers created and performed a short play, a theatrical production of a satirical nature that poked some light-hearted fun at the military. All in spirited humour and jest, of course. One of the main characters in this play was named Winston Crumb." The major paused to allow Leonard a moment to digest the revelation.

He didn't know how to respond and wasn't sure if this was good or bad news.

"Winston Crumb is a fictitious name, of that, there's no doubt," continued the major. "The main character in the play, Crumb, was a dapper man who was always one step ahead of the authorities. He couldn't be caught or located and controlled various undesirable criminal elements whom he encouraged to do his bidding to make the military look foolish, hence the satire." Hutton smiled apologetically.

"But this doesn't help me find out who this man is," Leonard interrupted. He shook his head in dismay and looked to the ground at his feet. "And how come you know so much about this play, Major Hutton?"

"I helped write it," replied the major.

Leonard's head shot up.

"From the description given to me by John," the major turned and acknowledged Mr Beaumont, "I believe the man you seek using the name Winston Crumb is the same man who played that character in the play."

"Then you know his name."

"Henrick Mueller, or more accurately, he was Lieutenant Henrick Mueller."

Leonard could have hugged the man; he was elated and bounced up from his chair. "Now, all I need to do is locate his address and...."

"For goodness sake, Leonard, settle down, you'll give me a heart attack. I have his address." Mr Beaumont held up a slip of paper.

Mr Beaumont and Major Hutton were grinning at Leonard's response.

Mr Pembroke showed no outward reaction, then shifted forward in his chair. "What can you tell us about Mr Mueller, Major?" he suddenly asked as Leonard sat.

Major Hutton rose from his seat, self-consciously straightened his tunic and walked to the window. "He resigned his commission several years ago and returned to civilian life. We always felt the lieutenant enjoyed playing the role of Winston Crumb, not because he was fond of melodrama, but because he fancied himself as being Mr Crumb."

Mr Pembroke scratched away in his notebook as the major spoke. Leonard listened, spellbound.

"However, Lieutenant Mueller wasn't popular with his fellow officers and had an intense dislike for the privileged and wealthy. He made his feelings on that quite well known, and it ultimately had a detrimental effect on his military career. A shame, really, in all other respects, he was charming, intelligent, and surprisingly - he actually came from a well-heeled family with substantial business interests. Many of us speculated as to why he chose a career in the military and did not venture into something that aligned with his beliefs."

"Perhaps he now has," Leonard suggested.

"Possibly," said the Major, who returned to his seat. "I haven't heard from him in quite some time, years, in fact."

"Anything else for Major Hutton?" asked Mr Beaumont. I think we've taken enough of his valuable time."

"One more question, sir. Can you recollect if Mr Mueller had a violent disposition?" Leonard asked.

Major Hutton nodded. "Yes, sadly, he was capricious and unrestrained when so provoked."

Everyone was silent for a moment.

"Thank you very much, sir, I appreciate your time and help. I am in your debt," said Leonard.

Everyone but Mr Pembroke stood, and as Mr Beaumont led the Major from the room, Leonard went to follow.

"Where do you think you're going, Mr Hardy?" snapped Mr Pembroke. "Sit."

Leonard had his back to Mr Pembroke and winced.

He obediently returned to his seat while Mr Pembroke made a show of closing his notebook, removing his spectacles, and stowing his pencil behind his ear. He put both elbows on the table, clasped his hands together, and looked at Leonard paternally.

"Now then, I've watched you all morning attempt to do your work. You've stumbled from one task to the next in a state of total confusion, like a woman in a room full of chocolates. You are never tardy, Leonard, but you strolled into work this morning like the weight of the world lay heavily across your shoulders. I think this is a good time for you to explain yourself."

Mr Pembroke may be in advanced years, his face lined with deep crevasses, but his eyes shone with an intensity that spoke of mental acuity and intelligence. Leonard swallowed, and his shoulders slumped.

"I'm in a dilemma, sir."

Leonard talked about how Jonathan's employer prohibited him from communicating with him, Mary's unexplained absence, Bridgette's breakdown and how he had no idea how to take care of her, and his subsequent banishment from the hospital. He finished with Constable Yates' offer to share information.

Mr Pembroke leaned back in his chair and failed in his attempt to cross his legs; he looked apologetically at Leonard. "Age catches up with us all." He shifted position and leaned forward with his arms on the table again. "After Major Hutton's revelation earlier, I think there is certainly a machination worthy of investigation which supports our earlier assessment. Meanwhile, you are bearing the brunt of its effects, which is plainly obvious. I think your friend, Mrs Leyton is your first priority, and I agree, the sooner she is away from the likes of Dr Schrader, the better."

Again, Leonard observed a carefully concealed flash of emotion from Mr Pembroke as he spoke. There was no love lost between the two men.

"You've had some time to evaluate Constable Yates; do you believe him to be trustworthy?"

"Yes, sir. I find him quite astute and remarkably quick-witted, and above all, he seems honest."

"Then I think we can use him, and his presence will be quite advantageous. This is my suggestion to you. Pack a small bag that contains personal effects belonging to Mrs Leyton. Explain everything you've told me to the constable, but you can leave out the bit about knowing Winston Crumb's true identity- we'll keep that up our sleeves for now. Then take Constable Yates to the hospital with you so you can liberate Mrs Leyton. Despite Dr Schrader's orders to banish you, I don't believe you'll encounter any resistance with the constable in tow."

"But where will I...."

Mr Pembroke held up a hand, silencing him. "Once you have

Mrs Leyton and the bag containing her personal belongings, you will take her to my home. Constable Yates can go about his business.

Leonard was astonished - even if Mr Pembroke allowed, he wasn't sure what to say.

"Once a probationer nurse herself, Mrs Pembroke loves nothing more than to care for the sick; she's tried for years to have me succumb to illness, and I've successfully thwarted all her attempts. Having Mrs Leyton as a temporary guest will be good for Mrs Pembroke, who really needs more to do anyway. It will be best if you are also our guest, so Mrs Leyton has a friend with her, and she may not feel quite so alone."

Leonard shook his head. The generosity of Mr Pembroke was astonishing. "Sir, I, I er, I don't know what to say."

"There's nothing to say." Mr Pembroke removed the pencil from behind his ear, tore a page from his notebook, wrote his address, and handed it to Leonard. "It's an easy house to find, I'm sure you'll have no problems."

"Thank you, sir."

"Now, about your friend Miss Worthington, I don't think there is cause for any worry at this time. Give it a week. There is probably a rational explanation for her disappearance, and you're jumping to emotional and unsupported conclusions. Be patient, lad, she'll show up."

Leonard nodded, although he wasn't quite in agreement.

"Tomorrow, and there won't be an issue about tardiness because you'll be arriving here with me, you will begin to research all you can about this mystery. We won't take any action until we know more about Henrick Mueller and what we're up against."

"I have the 'Shipping Intelligence' deadline tomorrow, sir."

"I've already arranged for someone else to do that. In your current state, you'll report having ships leave before they've arrived."

"And what of Jonathan McGready?"

"I wouldn't concern myself with him or his law firm. Look, Leonard, the most serious charge that could be brought against Constable Hastings is probably negligence. Nothing more. By retaining the services of a prominent and respected law firm, I suspect the crown will drop the charge. I anticipate Hastings knows this too. Your friend Jonathan is irrelevant in this."

"Then the constable will be free and back on the street."

"Not quite. Inspector Gibbard is most capable, and I expect he'd like to know more about the activities of Hastings. Your public accusation opens the door for him to look into that. Hastings may be technically out of gaol, but he might not be entirely free."

"But Constable Yates said Inspector Gibbard had no desire to pursue any investigation beyond the fire and Hastings' involvement."

"Quite so, but I know Gibbard, and he wants blood. That is why he is a competent and proficient inspector, and what he tells a junior constable may not be entirely accurate."

Leonard looked at the senior reporter, "I hope so, sir, I really do.

Chapter Fourteen

Constable Yates was finishing the last of Mary's chocolate cake and, by all appearances, had enjoyed every morsel. He was picking a few crumbs from the plate as Leonard told him everything that had happened over the last few weeks. Realising there was nothing more to be had, Yates put the saucer down and washed the vestiges of cake away with a sip of nearly cold tea.

The room was quiet, and Yates sat digesting not only the cake but all he'd been told. Leonard's account was far more intriguing than he expected, and he felt there was much more at stake than a few random and unrelated incidents and pointed this out.

"Mr Hardy, it seems to me that whatever is going on is of some importance to someone. If the dead man found outside your home, Dr Leyton, and his assistant were murdered as you suggest, then they weren't just indiscriminate killings done by chance, were they? I believe money is behind it. If money is involved, some people will do almost anything to protect it and do almost anything to make more of it."

"Money?" repeated Leonard. He hadn't considered this viewpoint before.

"Yes, money. There's enterprise at stake," nodded the constable. "But anyways, sir here's what I have for you." Yates settled back in the settee. "Do you know what a *triad* is?"

"Ah, isn't it a Chinese organisation of some sort?"

Yates laughed, "A triad is a Chinese gang often associated with crime. It appears Constable Hastings has a relationship with several

Orientals suspected of being involved in organised crime, and it could also account for the money he has."

"What money?"

"Wouldn't you say that retaining the law firm of your friend Mr McGready is expensive? I would. Not something a constable could normally afford. Wouldn't you say?"

"Yes, but openly flaunting his wealth by hiring expensive lawyers isn't wise."

"But what is the alternative for him? Having a criminal conviction, even for negligence, would be a problem. Yes, I admit he's taking a risk, but what would you do in his position?"

"But that doesn't necessarily mean the chap is wealthy."

Yates nodded. "We spoke to some of Constable Hastings' neighbours, and as a result, we believe he has in his employ two Oriental servants. Two young Chinese women."

Leonard raised his eyebrows. "That is odd. Is he married?"

"There is no Mrs Hastings."

That didn't surprise Leonard; he couldn't imagine any woman having affection for the man.

"Not only that, but the house he lives in is quite grand, not a home I could afford. The neighbours, in particular a rather meddlesome elderly spinster, say there are unusual comings and goings at strange times. Mostly Orientals." "But what you've told me doesn't prove anything, does it? I'm not a lawyer, but you cannot build a legal case around servants and a large home."

"And that's where we are in agreement, Mr Hardy. This is why I want to help you. I don't think his wealth is easily explained, and strongly suspect the man is involved in criminal activity. I can't prove it – yet, but with your help, I fully intend to."

"Surely you risk the displeasure of your superiors by sharing police information with me? You put your own career at risk."

"All constables have been told that we enforce the law, not only during the hours we work but twenty-four hours a day. Just because we are off-duty doesn't mean we ignore lawbreakers or those who need our help. The information I've shared with you is not secret, it's all easily obtainable. Some conclusions and observations are my own, therefore, I don't feel I'm doing anything harmful to my career or the community. In fact, if my theories are correct, then I will do the community and the constabulary a great service."

"Then you are willing to help?"

"I will do all I can, Mr Hardy."

"Thank you, and you can begin by calling me Leonard or Leo as my friends do."

"My friends call me Tim."

"Wonderful, but now I need to call on you to assist in the matter of helping me enter Wellington Hospital and discharging Bridgette." Leonard stood and retrieved the small case he had packed for her.

"With pleasure. From what you've told me, this Dr Schrader is an odd character, isn't he?"

"I find him disgusting and repulsive," said Leonard as he walked to the door.

The constable paused for a heartbeat, scratched his head and followed.

It was only a ten-minute stroll to the hospital, and both men walked in silence until they approached the arches at the main entrance. "Perhaps our association should appear totally professional to hospital staff, Tim."

The constable smiled in response.

The porter at the door acknowledged the constable and was somewhat uncertain about Leonard however, a sharp look from Constable Yates encouraged him not to intervene, and he wisely allowed Leonard to enter. The same two women were at the reception desk as the day before. On seeing the two men, the severe unfriendly woman immediately made off, and Leonard presumed she went to inform Dr Schrader of his presence. They approached the desk and waited while Constable Yates stood confidently behind and slightly to Leonard's side as he made his request.

"Good afternoon, I'm here to pick up Mrs Leyton," Leonard requested politely.

The woman glanced at the constable and then gave Leonard a nervous smile, "Forgive me, sir, but you are not permitted on these hospital premises." She looked over Leonard's shoulder to the porter by the door, who shrugged in response.

On cue, Constable Yates stepped forward. He extracted his notebook and flicked a page or two as if referring to his notes. Leonard glanced at him at saw the serious deadpan expression on his face.

"To whom am I addressing?" asked the constable. A pencil had magically appeared.

The woman swallowed and looked decidedly uncomfortable. "Mrs MacGuire, Lilly MacGuire."

Slowly the constable repeated her name, licked the tip of the pencil and began writing into his notebook. "Very well, now then, there appears to be some confusion. Mr Hardy is here at the request of Mrs Leyton, who wishes to be discharged. She is a patient, is she not?"

"No, constable, Mrs Leyton was released into the care of Mount View Lunatic Asylum this morning."

"What?" Leonard bellowed. "No!" He dropped the suitcase and ran down the corridor towards the women's ward where he'd been with Bridgette.

"Mr Hardy!" yelled Constable Yates, who ran after him.

Leonard entered the ward and slid to a stop. Dr Schrader was tending to a patient, and the severe woman from reception was talking to him along with another nurse. They all turned and saw him.

There was no need to run through the ward. Bridgette wasn't there, and the bed against the far wall was empty.

Constable Yates pulled up beside Leonard and held his arm securely. "We need to leave, Leonard, now."

Dr Schrader straightened and laughed.

The anger Leonard felt was consuming; he wanted to rush the doctor and beat him senseless. The firm grip on his arm was a sensible reminder to leave, as Constable Yates urged. Realising the futility of the situation, he wisely turned away as Tim released his arm and briskly stalked back to reception. Constable Yates, on the other hand, paused and stared at the Dr for a moment before following after Leonard.

The woman at reception looked frightened as Leonard retrieved Bridgette's suitcase and walked outside. Constable Yates wasn't far behind.

"Oh, that man infuriates me! He knew I'd come back today and deliberately sent Bridgette to the asylum. What possible reason does he have to be so cruel to her?"

"Perhaps it ain't her, it might be you."

"What? Dr Schrader has sent a young woman to a lunatic asylum purely because I offended him yesterday? That's a preposterous notion."

"There's a lot more to this than first meets the eye. Mark my words, Lance Schrader requires careful watching, he does."

"And Mr Pembroke agrees with you; he too believes the doctor is contemptible and behind Alex's death somehow. And it's not Lance, it's Lawrence Schrader."

"No, it's Lance, I'm sure it is." Constable Yates watched Leonard closely for his reaction.

"Why would you say that?" asked Leonard.

Tim looked uncertain. "I've been trying to remember since we left your home, and then when I saw him in the ward, the name Lance Schrader came to me. I'm absolutely certain and took it for granted that was the doctor's Christian name."

"I suppose it's easy to confuse names in your line of work."

Tim shrugged. "It's possible, I suppose." He scratched his head again. "If you're going to the asylum, then I'll come with you, it's on the way home for me."

Leonard and Constable Yates stood at the entrance to Mount View Lunatic Asylum and looked at the carriageway that swept up through trees, the manicured gardens of the pleasure grounds and onto the main building. The golden, late afternoon sun filtered through branches and foliage, casting textured shadows on the yellowed summer grass. It almost looked welcoming and inviting. It was a place where patients were prevented from leaving, but not their lucid minds; for many, their sanity had already departed.

"You know you can't get her out, don't you? You need a doctor to authorise her release."

Leonard didn't respond.

"Leonard? Mr Hardy?"

"It isn't like she's mad or deranged; she's distraught over the death of her husband. She's had difficulty coping, and the fire at the Royal Oak certainly didn't help her. And I didn't see it; instead, I was consumed by Crumb, Hastings, and Schrader.

"And do you think she's crazed?"

Leonard turned away from the golden dappled grass and faced Tim. "Of course not."

"Then, if you think she's sane, I'm sure competent doctors will also think so."

"I hope you're correct." Leonard picked up her case and began walking up the carriageway to the main building. "Shall we?"

"Good afternoon, I'm here about a patient transferred here from Wellington Hospital this morning, Mrs Bridgette Leyton. I believe she's suffering from a little bit of melancholia."

Tim leaned forward slightly and whispered, "Little bit?"

"Are you family?" The clerk asked.

"No, she doesn't have any family here, but I'm a close acquaintance." Leonard smiled at the man.

The clerk opened a large register and ran his finger down the latest entries. "This morning, you say?"

"Yes, that right, from Wellington Hospital." He smiled again.

The clerk found what he was looking for and glanced at Leonard, "Then how may we assist you, sir." Having studied Leonard carefully, he turned his attention to Constable Yates and gave him equal scrutiny.

"I'm here to take Mrs Leyton home."

Tim rolled his eyes.

"According to the documentation, the doctors have yet to determine whether she is capable of managing her affairs and if she either still poses a risk to herself or the community. Mrs Leyton requires the doctors' permission to be discharged." The clerk closed the register emphatically.

"Oh."

The clerk waited.

"In that case, I have some personal items for Mrs Leyton that she will require; may I bring them to her?"

"The suitcase will need to be searched to ensure that no dangerous or prohibited items are brought into this facility."

Leonard looked crestfallen.

"And Mrs Leyton is having an afternoon rest and isn't able to receive guests at present. I suggest you return tomorrow, a little earlier, sir."

"I see. Can you assure me the suitcase will be brought to her?"

"Only if it doesn't contain dangerous or prohibited items," repeated the clerk in an uninterested, bored tone of voice.

"Thank you, you've been most kind and helpful," replied Leonard.

The clerk wasn't listening and had turned away.

"Well then, there's no room for doubt whatsoever, is there?" said Tim.

Again, both men stood at the entranceway to Mount View. Leonard shook his head. "I'll find a way."

Tim looked sympathetically at him. "And I will ask around and see if any constables know another way to free her."

"Thank you for your help, Tim. And now I should go to Mr Pembroke's home. He is expecting me to arrive with Bridgette."

The tram service did not extend to Wellington Terrace, which was where Mr Pembroke lived, and so Leonard reluctantly caught a cab. As usual, he carefully checked the driver's sobriety, and after a fifteen-minute journey across town, he now stood outside the surprisingly large and stately home of Mr and Mrs Pembroke.

The house had almost no front yard and extended almost to the edge of the road. He opened the gate, entered the property and walked up three wide wooden steps onto an expansive porch. A sculptured metal head of a lion was affixed to the centre of the heavy stout door framed on either side by colourful stained-glass windows. Held in the jaws of the lion was a substantial metal ring; Leonard grabbed the ring and swung it down twice. The metallic clunk resonated inside the house, and he could hear movement within moments.

With a click, the door swung noiselessly open and revealed a small, ageing woman. Her grey, almost white hair was pinned on top of her head, which added a little size to her slight frame. She looked at her guest with intelligent sparkling blue eyes and a welcoming smile. Without pausing, she extended a hand, "Leonard, I'm so thrilled to finally meet you. Please come in. I'm Louise Pembroke."

Leonard reached out, clasped her outreached hand, and felt her warmth and strength. "It's a pleasure to meet you, Mrs Pembroke." He was surprised; she wasn't at all the dragon he expected.

"But where is your friend? Frederick told me you'd be bringing a friend with you." She quickly glanced at either side of Leonard, grabbed him by the arm and led him inside.

"Mrs Leyton was admitted to Mount View Lunatic Asylum this morning."

"Oh my, that's not good, is it?" she tut-tutted. "Let me take your jacket, it's a warm evening."

The house was beautiful; colourful rugs lay across dark-stained wooded floors, the high ceiling kept the temperature cool and pleasant, and paintings hung from the walls like a gallery display of fine art. Leonard didn't know where to look first. Distinguished faces peered at him from ornate gilded frames and others, pastoral, quaint villages nestled into elaborate landscapes. Fighting ships, men-o-war under full sail, burst through powerful grey-green waves; it was a kaleidoscope of colour style and timeless elegance.

"Come this way, Leonard." He followed her down a wide hallway with his head swivelling from side to side, and then they turned right into a spacious room with large windows that faced downtown Wellington and the expansive harbour view below.

Forgoing a greeting, Mr Pembroke watched but said nothing, content to let Leonard survey the room. An assortment of small-framed portraits sat on top of a sideboard positioned near one of the large windows. He could see a girl being held by a much younger Mrs Pembroke, and in another portrait, the girl was older, possibly in her mid-teens. They looked like a happy family. A few books were stacked here or there, and he quickly glanced at them, hoping for some personal insights into the Pembroke household. He saw a large volume on English architecture, curiously a book called *Wage Labour and Capital* authored by the German philosopher Karl Marx, and a well-thumbed copy of a thick book called *Venenum Hortus*. He didn't understand Latin very well but knew *Hortus* meant horticulture, so he quickly surmised it was a gardening book of sorts. Mr Pembroke sat enveloped in an oversized leather chair; he held an unlit pipe between his teeth, and he'd been studying Leonard carefully. "You'd do well to spend your time reading that," suggested Mr Pembroke seeing Leonard's interest in the books. "Better than that tripe on the Welshman you were reading."

Leonard pointed to the Latin titled gardening book.

"Oh good heavens, no, that's Mrs Pembroke's book, *Wage Labour and Capital*. Educate you a little, it will."

"Yes, good bedtime reading," Leonard muttered sarcastically under his breath as he turned away to face Mrs Pembroke.

"What was that?"

"Oh, I said, good bedtime reading, sir."

"And where is your friend, Mrs Leyton?"

"Please have a seat, Leonard. Would you like tea or some of that delicious coffee?" Mrs Pembroke asked. Her eyes twinkled.

Leonard grinned, "Coffee if it's no trouble, Mrs Pembroke."

"Well, what have you done with her?" Mr Pembroke asked again irritably as his wife went to the kitchen.

Leonard sunk into a worn leather sofa and was immediately overcome with tiredness.

"Dr Schrader had her transferred to Mount View," he said disconsolately.

Again Leonard saw the familiar spark of ire. Mr Pembroke placed his pipe in an ashtray and turned his head to look out the windows and across Wellington.

"Did you see Schrader?" the old man asked after a few moments without turning his head.

"Yes, sir, he laughed at me."

Again there was silence.

"I trust you went to Mount View."

"I tried, sir. They would not release Bridgette without a doctor's authorisation. And I had to leave the suitcase I packed for her."

Mr Pembroke leaned his elbow on the chair's broad armrest and cupped his chin in his hand as he gave the matter due consideration. Against the rear wall near the door, a grandfather clock rose majestically from the floor. Its fine woodwork and exterior carvings were like a memorial to honour the craftsmen who laboured lovingly to create the intricate and complex machine. Behind glass near the base, a large brass pendulum swung in flawless time. The measured ticking of its mechanism broke the silence. Leonard felt his eyelids grow heavy.

"Am I interrupting something?" said Mrs Pembroke as she carried a serving tray of cups, coffee and biscuits. She placed the tray on the low table near the sofa, sat down and began to pour.

"The both of you don't seem to be very happy." She placed a steaming cup in front of her husband and one in front of Leonard. "It's that doctor, isn't it?" she asked.

Mr Pembroke broke away from his trance and reached for his cup. "The sod had Mrs Leyton committed to Mount View before Leonard could pick her up from the hospital."

"Leonard told me." She sighed and picked up her knitting. "I don't know why that man hasn't been held accountable for his actions."

"Then you are familiar with him, Mrs Pembroke?"

"No, dear, only what Frederick has told me." She gave her husband a quick look.

Leonard nodded.

"We need to find a doctor willing to discharge Mrs Leyton. That's the bloody problem."

"Freddy, please," warned Mrs Pembroke.

"She doesn't like my language, says it's too coarse," said Mr Pembroke leaning towards Leonard.

Leonard hid his smile behind his cup. The coffee was helping, and he felt more alert.

"Frederick has told me about the events that have befallen you, Leonard. I hope you don't object?"

"Not at all, Mrs Pembroke."

"And you have a friend whom you are unable to contact at the moment?"

"Yes, a Miss Worthington, she is also a nurse at Wellington Hospital."

"Then she may know of a doctor at the hospital willing to help."

"Leonard doesn't seem to be very good at holding onto women these days. He lost her as well," said Mr Pembroke dryly.

Leonard took a sip from his cup. *Never a truer word spoken.* "I confess, Mary Worthington's disappearance has me very concerned, and I believe she may have fallen victim to foul play."

"As I told you already, I think you are worrying needlessly; she will show and have a rational explanation," said Mr Pembroke.

"I hope so, sir. I really do."

"Give it a few days more, Leonard," Mrs Pembroke added kindly.

"Mr Pembroke, Constable Yates said something rather peculiar earlier; he referred to Dr Schrader as Lance Schrader and not Lawrence, which is his Christian name. He seemed insistent that Lance was correct. Does the name Lance Schrader mean anything to you?"

He put the cup to his lips and took a sip, then carefully set it down on the table. "It does, but I cannot place it. Why do you ask?"

"I don't know, and I'm not sure. Perhaps curiosity, that's all."

"Be careful, curiosity got you into this predicament."

"Yates also believes Constable Hastings is part of an Oriental gang called a tong."

"Hastings part of an Oriental gang? Interesting perspective. And yes, I'm aware of tongs in Wellington."

"He also said he believes money is behind it all."

Mr Pembroke actually laughed. "Constable Yates is an astute young man. Very possible indeed, very possible."

Mrs Pembroke sat quietly knitting, the rhythmic click of the needles reminded Leonard of his own mother.

"Mr Pembroke, tomorrow I want to find out all I can about Henrick Mueller. Mr Beaumont suggests going to the Wellington Council offices and going through their rate books. What do you think?"

Mrs Pembroke looked up from her knitting.

Mr Pembroke was quiet for a few seconds. "Yes, of course… and I'm curious if he owns other property, and if he does, he'll be paying taxes like the rest of us good citizens, and it will be listed."

Leonard nodded enthusiastically. "He also mentioned something about the wharves."

"Did he? Do you have a good relationship with the people at the wharves where you get all the shipping information?"

"I think so." He actually didn't, but he wasn't going to share that with him.

"I'm not sure, Leonard, it's a dangerous place to be wandering around, but if you must. I'm sure it will do no harm to ask them down there about Henrick Mueller. And what about any advertisers who you have dealings with? Are you on friendly terms with any of them?"

"There might be one or two, but other than that, not really, sir."

"Who might they be?"

"Mr Bailey from Bailey & Sons, Grain and Seed Merchants, and perhaps Mr Welford, the proprietor of the General Store."

"Pay them a visit and ask them if they have heard the name. And while you're there, see if their advertising needs have been met. May as well try to bring in a little income for the paper, eh? Keep Mr Beaumont happy."

"Would it not be a good idea to ask the police? I could ask Constable Yates about Henrick Mueller."

Mr Pembroke thought a moment. "I'm not sure. If Mueller is mixed up in this affair, and he's broken the law, then the police will nab him before we've had a chance to chat with the man." He came to a decision. "Very well, just don't tell the bloody constable why."

"Freddy, please," admonished Mrs Pembroke.

"Yes, sir, I'll do that," Leonard replied.

The sound of knitting stopped. "I've been thinking," said Mrs Pembroke.

Both men looked turned to look at her simultaneously.

"Why can't someone go to that Dr Schrader and apply some pressure for him to release Mrs Leyton."

"Are you suggesting strong-arm tactics, Louise?" smiled her husband.

"No, of course not, but if the man is as despicable as you say, then he may respond favourably to some pressure."

"You surprise me, m'dear."

She blushed and returned to her knitting.

"But not a bad idea at all," said her husband.

She tilted her head slightly and gave Leonard a surreptitious wink.

Leonard couldn't help himself and was smiling.

"Something amuses you, Mr Hardy?"

"No, sir."

Leonard took pleasure in how Mr and Mrs Pembroke interacted with each other; it was fresh and untypical of a couple married for so long. It kind of explained Mr Pembroke's penchant for making his wife appear uncaring and mean-spirited. It was his dry way of expressing his admiration and love for her.

"How long have you been married?" Leonard asked Mrs Pembroke.

She put her knitting down and thought briefly. "It's been, what, forty-eight years this year." She smiled and gave her husband a private look. He coughed.

"I understand you were married once, Leonard," she asked.

"Yes, my wife passed away a year and a half ago."

"I'm sorry if my questions upset you."

"No, they don't, not anymore. I'm learning to adjust. I actually like talking about her."

She looked at him kindly. "Were you happy?"

"Yes, we were. But we did have challenges."

"Oh, why was that?"

"Mae was Chinese, we grew up differently, and of course, we had to learn to adapt to each other's culture."

"And love conquered all."

Leonard hadn't thought of it in that way; there was an element of profoundness in her statement. "Yes, you are correct. Perhaps if we hadn't loved each other, it would have made the relationship very difficult."

Mrs Pembroke nodded. "Did you meet her in China and bring her here?"

"No, we met here."

"So she came here with family when she was young?"

"She never really liked talking about it, she found it distressing. But from the fragments she told me, her family died due to an accident in China, so she was sent here to be with an Uncle."

"Here in Wellington?" she asked.

"Yes, Uncle Jun has a Chinese herbal medicine shop on Frederick Street. It's really an apothecary of sorts."

"Yes, I know of it." Mrs Pembroke looked thoughtful for a moment. "And she must have been young when her family passed away?"

Leonard nodded. *Too young*, he thought. "I still find the circumstances around her death upsetting."

Mrs Pembroke remained silent and allowed him to talk.

He took a breath. "She was walking on Tory Street when a Hansom cab careened around a corner at full speed. The police were meticulous in their investigation and were very forthcoming and helpful. Witnesses reported that she must have tripped and fallen under the cab when she tried to move out of its path, but no one actually saw that. Everyone was focused on the erratic cab and said it was highly probable that the driver was intoxicated."

She raised a hand to her mouth. "Leonard, that is tragic. Was the cab driver brought to justice?"

Leonard spoke just beyond a whisper. "No, they were never able to identify the cab driver with certainty."

"Just like Dr Leyton," interjected Mr Pembroke.

"Those cabbies do have a reputation. Is a wonder more people aren't killed or maimed by their irresponsible driving," she said.

Leonard was momentarily distracted.

Mr Pembroke was studying Leonard very carefully. He kept quiet and allowed his wife to keep talking.

She shook her head in pity. "I'm so sorry, dear." She leaned sideways and patted his shoulder in sympathy.

Leonard looked at her, "Thank you, Mrs Pembroke." He took another big breath; the effects of the coffee were wearing off, and he was fatigued. "I think it's time I was going home." He stood and stretched.

"Thank you very much for keeping us informed, Leonard. I'm sorry you were unable to have your friend released from hospital, and I do hope we can arrive at a solution to make that happen. We want to help in any way we can."

"Thank you very much, Mrs Pembroke. And your home, it's spectacular, so beautiful."

"That's lovely of you to say, thank you, Leonard. We've been very fortunate."

Mr Pembroke eased himself from his chair. "I'll look forward to chatting with you tomorrow afternoon, Leonard. Hopefully, you'll have discovered some items of interest, eh." He walked Leonard to the door and fetched his jacket that hung from a stand. "Get a good night's sleep, lad, and don't worry about Miss Worthington, she will turn up. You'll feel better in the morning." He patted him on the shoulder.

Leonard retraced his steps from earlier on in the evening and found himself on The Terrace. Even though he was tired, he decided to walk back to Bridgette and Mary's home.

Chapter Fifteen

Endless rows and columns of names and information, carefully and meticulously handwritten in a ledger, stared up at him. Page after page, row after row, they all began to look the same. Leonard yawned, turned another page, and scanned down the list of homeowners and the properties they paid taxes on. Wellington council allowed Leonard to review old records, but not new ones, and he sat in a corner at the council offices where he'd been for the last two hours and let his eyes follow his ink-smudged finger as it slid down the page.

He'd immediately found Henrick Mueller's name, but it revealed nothing new. What he sought now were other interests listed in his name that he didn't know about. His left hand propped up his head while his right hand, specifically his ink-stained index finger, moved steadily down the page. Seemingly of its own accord, the finger stopped and moved back up three lines before his brain fully engaged. His finger had identified a property owned by Lawrence and Lance Schrader. Now, this was fascinating. Presumably, he now had Dr Schrader's residential address, but also the fact there was a relative, most likely a father or brother, registered as a titled co-owner. Constable Yates was almost correct, there was indeed a Lance Schrader, and he couldn't wait to tell him of the discovery. Leonard smiled; the morning had not been a waste of time. He copied the Schrader information into his notebook and continued searching.

The additional half-hour he spent at the council offices was, in fact, wasted, and he found nothing new other than what Mrs Theodopoulous had paid on her property rates two years ago. He thanked the staff and gratefully left the building.

Leonard walked towards the wharves and the office of the Harbour Master, where he obtained much of the shipping information he needed to complete the 'Shipping Intelligence' reports the paper published. The people who worked there were always harried and grumpy and fielded endless complaints from shipping companies wanting faster service, expanded facilities, and better moorings and berths for their prized ships. Leonard disliked going to the office, and once he obtained his bi-weekly list of shipping arrivals and departures, he couldn't wait to leave. He wasn't part of their nautical conclave and was deemed an outsider, or as some had referred to him, an 'indweller'. They tolerated him at best and made little attempt to be outwardly friendly, even after all the years he'd been going down there.

He stood at the counter and waited to be attended. It wasn't like there was a shortage of clerks; they were all scurrying about and involved in a myriad of important tasks, and serving a lowly reporter from the *Evening Standard* was not on their list of priorities. Leonard waited patiently, whistled nonchalantly, and casually strode around the small room with his hands in his pockets until, finally, someone spoke to him.

"What do you need, Mr Hardy, quickly now, don't have all day to discuss pleasantries."

"Are you familiar –" began Leonard, only to be cut off.

"Tell the sod to wait his bleedin' turn, he'll get to 'im when he can!" interrupted the harbour master's office clerk as he yelled to a co-worker. "What was that, Mr Hardy?"

"Do you know –"

"The harbour master is doin' is best, damn it! Tell 'im to prepare for customs, they'll come aboard first." He turned away from his co-worker and looked at Leonard again in question.

"Henrick Mueller, do you know him?" persisted Leonard.

"Of course." The clerk turned back over his shoulder. "I don't care if 'is ship is bleedin' sinkin', he's gotta wait for the tide!"

"Then you do know Henrick Mueller?"

"I told ya, I did. One moment." The clerk stormed off.

Leonard took a few moments and a couple more after that. Finally, the clerk returned.

"Quickly, Mr Hardy, what you need?"

"Where can I locate Henrick Mueller?"

Someone yelled for the clerk again. "Look, I must go –"

"Just tell me where I can find Mr Mueller, please?" exclaimed Leonard in frustration.

The assistant was already walking away and looked back over his shoulder. "Two sheds down on Queens Wharf, that's where you'll find him."

Leonard exited the harbour master's office ecstatic.

Wellington's wharves were busy - actually chaotic was a better expression. Leonard had no comprehension of how it all worked, and as far as he understood the process, a ship berthed at a wharf, men on board the vessel raised the goods to the wharf with derricks or cranes, and local men loaded them onto wagons that magically appeared to haul them away. As Wellington was geographically central, the town acted as a distribution point, and goods and merchandise came from everywhere to be shipped to other ports or foreign destinations. Loading the ships, as far as Leonard could see, was fairly simple, it was just the reverse operation of unloading.

But dangerous it was. The activity was frenetic. Whether loaded or empty, wagon drivers were desperate to leave as quickly as possible, and booms swung precariously overhead with goods dangling high above workers' heads. Men shouted instructions, hurled obscenities, and rebuked with familiar ease; it was wise to walk carefully or risk being run over or crushed, neither of which appealed to Leonard. Wisely, he altered his course to walk as close to the sheds as possible, where it was less perilous. The hours were long for these men; they worked hard in dangerous conditions in all types of weather. Schedules had to be met; ships loaded and unloaded, and there was always the fear there would be no work tomorrow.

Up ahead was the building where the harbour master's clerk indicated he could find Henrick Mueller. It was used by the Amalgamated Steam-Ship Company, a large shipping enterprise based in Wellington. Should he just go in and confront the man? And to what purpose? A better alternative might be to study and learn more about him before risking an encounter that would no doubt have unpleasant consequences.

Leonard positioned himself at the corner of an adjacent shed where he could clearly see the doorway that led into the building. He tried not to look obvious, but his clothing identified him as not belonging; he didn't look like a labourer. Nonetheless, his observation point concealed him from many who passed by, which would have to suffice. The crates stacked three high against the shed effectively screened him, so he pulled his hat down lower, leaned against the wall, and waited.

Waiting gave him time to think, and immediately his thoughts turned to Mary. Where was she? Had she come to grief? Was she another victim in some elaborate scheme like his dear friend Alex? And poor Bridgette, all locked up in a lunatic asylum. If only he could find a way to have her released. Mrs Pembroke had suggested applying pressure on Dr Schrader, but what pressure?

Time passed slowly, and Leonard continued to wait. He became footsore from standing and tried moving around, but nothing seemed to ease the ache.

People came and went; some stopped to chat outside, but Mr Mueller made no appearance. Leonard was beginning to doubt the information from the harbour master's office clerk was accurate when three men approached the building from the direction of Queens Wharf. Leonard's heart began to beat faster, and he forgot the pain in his aching feet. The gentleman in the middle was Winston Crumb, or rather Henrick Mueller. He was unmistakable, stylish, and stood out from the others in an almost theatrical way; he even wore the same homburg hat at the same rakish angle. Leonard couldn't believe it; he had found him, and now that he had, what to do?

His first impulse was to stride from behind the safety of the shed and approach him. He even took a tentative step, but on second thought, he decided it was best to wait. He would talk to Mr Pembroke and seek his advice and then plan. He eased back beside the shed wall and remained out of sight, his heart was still pounding, and he was surprised to realise he was a little frightened.

He waited a few minutes, mainly to calm down and relax, before he left the wharf and returned to the *Evening Standard*. When he arrived, the bullpen was empty, everyone had gone. Leonard sat at his desk, opened his notebook and reviewed the information he had copied earlier. Staring up at him was the name Lance Schrader.

The *Evening Standard* had a card indexing system used to cross-check a person's name with any previously published uses of that name. A valuable tool when researching an individual. The cabinets that contained the cards were against the front wall, and Leonard immediately searched for the name Schrader. It took only moments, and he discovered there were two cards for the name Schrader, one for Lawrence and another for Lance. He extracted both cards; the information written on the card for Lawrence had a date, the title of the article that was written, and then the word 'Hold.' This meant the story had never been published and was on file. He replaced the card into the card drawer and looked at the other. The card for Lance contained only abbreviated information - it said 'Obit' and had a date- he checked the reverse side in case there were any additional notes and found none.

The card told him that Lance Schrader had died almost three years ago, and the *Evening Standard* had listed his death in the obituaries. He needed to find the actual published newspaper edition if he wanted more information. More recent earlier editions of the paper were kept in the bullpen; older editions were held in a library near the typesetters. Leonard quickly replaced the card and ran downstairs to find the old edition of the newspaper.

It took some time to sort through the orderly stacked piles of newspapers, but he eventually located it. He flicked through the pages and quickly found the obituary notice for Lance Schrader. Leonard thought it was unimaginative and poorly written, and it didn't detail the specific cause of death other than list a 'natural cause'. He was disappointed. A natural cause could be anything, and one could even argue that having a sack of flour dropped on your head could be deemed a 'natural cause.'

Leonard was pacing the floor in the bullpen, trying to think of how he could obtain more information on the death of Lance Schrader. *The police maintained records; perhaps Constable Yates could research that for him*, he thought.

He looked out the window and saw people going about their daily business, the hustle and bustle of a busy town. Within sight of the *Evening Standard* offices were the blackened remains of burned buildings; they were a stark reminder all was not well. There were so many loose ends and unanswered questions - it was almost unbearable. Uncle Jun and Ming were still missing, and Mary had not yet appeared. Where was she, and did she need help? Meredith had not responded to the note he'd left for her at the hospital, and he wondered if Jonathan was responsible for preventing her from contacting him. He hoped not.

Leonard admitted to himself that perhaps his feelings towards Mary were more than platonic, that she was more than just a friend. He felt a baleful sense of loss from her absence; it was a feeling he was very familiar with and left him with an aching sensation in the pit of his stomach. The thought of her death would be too much for him to bear, but perhaps he should prepare himself for the inevitable. Considering everything else that had recently happened, it was entirely possible she was already dead.

The realisation gave him a sense of purpose and energy, and he needed to find Constable Yates immediately. He hurriedly retrieved his jacket and headed towards the devastation that once was the Royal Oak Hotel.

Constable Yates was talking to some labourers, and judging from the nature of his discussion, it wasn't at all a happy chat. Leonard waited until the labourers skulked away and then approached the constable, who was diligently writing in his notepad.

"I caught the blighters red-handed, I did," said the constable, his anger still evident. "They were stealing silverware and dishes by hiding them in a pile of burned timber and ash, then loading them into a wagon. Cheeky bastards! Then they denied it, even after I caught 'em." He shook his head.

"Difficult day, Tim?" Leonard asked.

"Some worse than others."

"When you finishing here?"

"I was supposed to have already gone." He broke into a smile. "I have something very interesting you may be curious to know about."

"Oh, good or bad?"

"After our little incident at the hospital yesterday, I kept thinking back to the doctor and when I thought his name was Lance. Do you remember?"

Leonard nodded.

"So I checked on a couple of things, didn't I. Well, let me tell ya, Lance Schrader did exist and –"

"– he died three years ago due to natural causes." Leonard finished Tim's sentence and grinned. "I did some research too."

Tim laughed. "I knew I remembered the name."

"Tell me what you discovered about him," Leonard asked.

"Well, that is interesting, he died of natural causes alright, but it was the result of being pursued by a constable on foot. His heart stopped beating, it just gave up and quit on him when he did a runner. Just like that." He snapped his fingers to emphasise the point. "I read the findings on the post-mortem report by your friend Dr Leyton. He wrote that the deceased had previously suffered from rheumatic fever, which affected the heart valves, or something like that. Proved to be fatal for him in the end."

"How is Lance Schrader related to Dr Schrader?"

"From what I can gather, they're brothers."

"And what had he done to warrant being pursued by the ever-vigilant constabulary?"

Tim raised an eyebrow at Leonard's comment and smirked. "An assault charge was filed against him by an Oriental lady; he couldn't keep his hands off her, he struck her too, apparently."

"A penchant that runs in the family. Can you recall who it was?" asked Leonard.

"I wrote it down 'cause I knew you'd ask." Tim flicked his notebook open. "Here it is, a Miss Mae-Ling Chen."

Leonard felt the blood rush to his head. He knew he would faint, and his legs were about to give way beneath him. He leaned towards an empty wagon that was waiting to be loaded.

"Leonard, are you alright?" Tim rushed over to support him as he almost fell against the wagon's side.

The memory came back in a flood. His dear Mae.

"Leonard, what's the matter?"

"I, I was there. Mae… I married her, she was my wife."

"What!"

Leonard turned his back to the constable and dropped his arms over the side of the wagon. "When that man, Lance Schrader, first attacked Mae, I was there. We nearly brawled, but he eventually walked away. But then, on another day, he accosted her again, and I told her she needed to report the man to the police because he wasn't going to stop. It all makes sense now.

"What does?"

Leonard turned and faced the constable. "Don't you see? Dr Schrader must have known I married Mae. It wouldn't have been difficult to ask around and find out who was the man with the Chinese woman. Or even my friend, Alex, the medical practitioner who performed the post-mortem. He consulted with Dr Schrader and may have said something. When Mary and I visited Schrader over Alex's death, he must have immediately realised who I was. Even Mary commented on that after our visit, Schrader paid her more attention and had attempted to touch her more than he normally did." Leonard shuddered. "Obviously, he holds me responsible for his brother's death."

Yates looked puzzled.

"Yesterday I said, what reason could Dr Schrader have to be so cruel to Bridgette, and you replied, maybe it's not her, it could be you. Do you remember?"

Constable Yates nodded.

"Dr Schrader doesn't care about Bridgette one way or another. He's seeking vengeance and doing all this to get his sixpence worth of revenge out of me."

"So you think he's behind the disappearance of your friend Mary, too?"

"I was going to ask you about that because I think he is behind it." Leonard took a big breath and prepared himself. "Have any unidentified female bodies been discovered in the last few days?"

Constable Yates thought a moment and slowly shook his head. "No, I don't believe so, but I will find out."

Leonard was relieved and overwhelmed. This was turning into quite a day, and he was struggling not to break down. He needed to focus. "Tim, can we link Dr Schrader to Constable Hastings?"

"Perhaps you're jumping to conclusions, Leonard. Why would you think they have an association?"

"It's a gut feeling, but I cannot prove it, and neither can I prove Dr Schrader is behind Mary's disappearance. And to make it worse, I don't believe Schrader has committed any crime by sending Bridgette to the lunatic asylum."

Now it was the constable's turn to look thoughtful. "So, what are you planning to do about Dr Schrader?"

"What can I do? Nothing," Leonard said in frustration, "absolutely nothing."

Constable Yates looked at Leonard. "Then explain to me about this Oriental woman Mae-Ling; you married her after the assault by Lance Schrader?"

"Yes, about a year later. But then she was killed by an unidentified wagon on Tory Street about a year and a half ago."

"My sympathies Leonard, I'm sorry. You've had it rough lately, haven't you?"

Leonard looked at the constable and remained silent, but his expression said it all.

A ringing bell announced the arrival of the southward-bound tram.

"I want to visit Bridgette."

"As we're goin' in the same direction, I'll keep you company.

I need to go to the depot. And in your state, I don't know I should leave you alone."

The Mount View Lunatic Asylum was on the east side of the Basin Reserve, and the Constabulary Depot was on the west side. Needless to say, both men hopped off the tram at the same location and went their separate ways after making an arrangement to meet the following day after the conclusion of their work.

The brief walk up the carriageway to the asylum was enjoyable; the grounds were splendid, birds chirped excitedly and enjoyed their freedom while residents inside the buildings did not. The main entrance to Mount View was in a three-storied building that sat slightly apart from the wings where patients were housed. Leonard was pleased; he was visiting at an earlier time as was recommended.

"Good afternoon, sir. How may we assist you?" inquired the young woman behind a large counter.

"I'm here to see a friend. She is a patient here, and her name is Mrs Bridgette Leyton." Leonard smiled.

"Of course, sir. One moment."

. The young woman referred to a chart on the wall and then walked out of sight into the office space behind the counter. Leonard waited and read some of the items posted on the wall. He saw that Mount View employees were invited to a staff picnic Sunday week, and an authority on multiple personality disorders would be giving a luncheon talk on Friday.

Leonard turned to the sound of footsteps and saw the young woman returning with a smallish man in a dark suit trailing behind. *Obviously, a clerk of some kind,* he thought. The woman stopped and allowed the man to approach the counter. He carried a piece of paper and wielded it with unquestioned authority. It didn't look good. He was more than a clerk.

"Afternoon, sir. I understand you wish to visit Mrs Leyton?" said the clerk squinting through smallish spectacles.

"That's correct."

"May I have your name, please?"

"Leonard Hardy."

"Yes, I was afraid of that," said the clerk as he rubbed his chin thoughtfully.

"Afraid of what? People generally aren't afraid of me and generally find me quite agreeable."

The clerk ignored Leonard's comment and then assumed a sombre look more befitting of an undertaker. "Mrs Leyton's physician at Wellington Hospital indicated that one of the contributing causes of her illness is related to your presence, sir." He gave an apologetic look and held up the document. "There's a comment here that's, well … of some concernment to this medical facility." The clerk held the paper up to his face and began to read. "…and further, an acquaintance, namely a Mr Leonard Hardy, has consistently provoked and upset Mrs Leyton to a degree I find disturbing. To assist with her recovery, I recommend that Mr Hardy be denied access to Mrs Leyton."

Leonard was quietly seething and forced himself to remain calm. "Who was the doctor that made this recommendation?"

"Ah, that is Dr Schrader, sir."

"Perhaps if you asked Mrs Leyton, she might provide a different account and may wish to see me."

"Mrs Leyton is in the care of this medical facility because she is unable to manage her affairs. Due to the nature of her state of mind, it would be irresponsible for us to take anything she said with any seriousness. I'm sure you understand, sir."

Leonard glared at the man, who stared defiantly back. "Are there others who have also been denied access to Mrs Leyton?"

"That information is confidential, and I'm not at liberty to say." The clerk continued to stare.

Leonard assessed the height and width of the counter in preparation to leap over it but quickly determined his current state of fitness would likely leave him stranded midway. The temptation to unleash his anger and frustrations was overwhelming, and if he did, he knew, it would only support Dr Schrader's view that he was volatile. He pulled himself together with considerable effort.

"You've been most helpful. I'm sure we can clear up this misunderstanding. Have a pleasant evening." Leonard turned to walk away.

"There's no misunderstanding; the doctor's notes are quite explicit."

Leonard paused momentarily, then continued out the door.

Down at the street, and once he'd unclenched his hands, Leonard considered his next option. Dr Schrader had with alacrity certainly outmanoeuvred him, and he'd give the doctor credit for that. If he applied himself in the same lecherous way with women, Leonard imagined he'd have a very high success rate, which made the man exceedingly dangerous.

But neither was the doctor a fool, Leonard reasoned, and while Dr Schrader had set the bar, then he would also act with cunning and guile and show he was not a person to be taken lightly or trifled with. He waved at a passing cab and, without sparing the cabbie any attention, gave him the address to Wellington Hospital.

Chapter Sixteen

"My wife, my wife, she's having a baby, where is she, please?" cried Leonard as he entered the casualty entrance to Wellington Hospital. He knew the staff at the front entrance recognised him, but perhaps not the medical staff at the hospital's side entrance.

A nurse pointed down the hallway. "Follow the sign, sir."

As was customary, women generally delivered their babies at home, nevertheless, in the event of complications, they were often admitted to the hospital when they needed expert medical attention. He knew Meredith's shift was almost over, but he was still taking a risk by assuming she was not attending to a patient either at their home or here at the hospital.

Leonard ran down the hallway and directly ahead saw the sign the nurse had indicated; it pointed to a nondescript door. He entered cautiously and saw a couple of worried-looking expectant fathers accompanied by relatives, waiting nervously for the news of childbirth. Judging by their dishevelled appearances, the men had been waiting a while. As he anticipated, no one paid undue attention to him, and he approached the nurse's desk.

"Excuse me, I'm looking for Midwife Rosewarne. It's important," he appealed.

Without a word, the nurse walked off. Leonard tried to calm his nerves and appear relaxed, but his heart was beating furiously. He sat on a chair, picked up a well-thumbed copy of the *Evening Standard,* and flicked through the pages.

"Leonard," loudly whispered Meredith, "what are you doing

here? You know you aren't allowed in the maternity area."

"Meredith, can we talk somewhere? It's very urgent."

She thought a moment and then grabbed his arm and led him to an empty room with a bed and two chairs. "You know you shouldn't be here. What's the matter?"

"Did you receive the message I left for you at reception?"

She looked at him quizzically, "No, what message?"

"I left a message for you at reception two days ago."

"I never received it."

"You didn't?" Leonard scratched his head. "Never mind, Meredith, have you heard from or seen Mary? She's gone missing!"

"I know the hospital has been looking for her, but I don't know where she is, and as far as I'm aware, the hospital still doesn't know her whereabouts. Is she alright? Has something happened?"

Leonard shrugged and looked down. "I don't know and am at a wit's end." He shook his head to clear his thoughts. "Meredith, are you aware Bridgette was admitted to the hospital for melancholia?"

"Yes, I visited her and was told earlier she's been discharged. How is she doing? You realise Jonathan doesn't want any contact with you or her and has forbidden me as well."

Leonard reached for both her hands and lowered his head to look at her closely. "She actually wasn't discharged; she was transferred to Mount View."

She pulled her hands away, and they flew to her mouth. "Oh! Poor Bridgette."

"But listen, Dr Schrader is behind it, and he has instructed Mount View not to allow me to visit or see her."

"But why?"

"It's a long story, and I can't explain it now. You need to go to

Bridgette, see how she is doing, and we need to find a way to get her out."

"That will require a doctor."

"Yes, it will, but Jonathan, you and I need to help Bridgette. Together we need to find a way to have her released. Please come to my home tomorrow evening as we need to discuss this. Can you do this, Meredith?"

"I will try."

"No, Meredith, I need your promise. If Jonathan refuses, then you come alone. Bridgette needs us, she's our friend, remember that."

Meredith looked at him and thought a moment in indecision. She nodded. "I understand, Leonard, and I will go to Mount View soon as I have finished here at six o'clock."

"Thank you, Meredith." He leaned forward and kissed her on the cheek.

"You had better leave before someone discovers you."

Leonard walked back down the corridor towards the side exit, lost in thought.

"Did you find your wife, and did she have the baby?" asked the same nurse surprising him.

"Yes, thank you, but the baby wasn't mine."

The nurse stood mutely still in the corridor as Leonard left the building and made his way home.

Constable Tim Yates was waiting at the bottom of Marjoribanks Street as Leonard approached. "I can see your afternoon hasn't gone well."

Leonard responded with a look that spoke more than words ever could.

"Oh, like that. Is it?"

"Tea, coffee or whiskey? What will it be, constable?" Leonard asked.

"Seeing as I'm off duty, then whiskey it is."

They walked up the street, and Leonard explained what happened at Mount View when he tried to visit Bridgette. There was little the constable could do but listen. They neared Leonard's home when Yates finally spoke.

"Perhaps this ain't the best time to tell you, but you asked me to enquire about any bodies that have been recently discovered."

Leonard stopped immediately and slowly turned to the constable, his face had gone deathly pale.

Seeing Leonard's reaction Yates quickly added, "A body was discovered in Evans Bay. It washed ashore two days ago. It was a man."

"It's William, isn't it?" Leonard asked, somewhat relieved.

Yates looked uncomfortable, "Apparently, identifying the body was difficult, it had begun to decompose, and fish had been... well, you know."

Leonard looked at Yates, who returned his gaze.

"He had a tattoo, and... and his family could identify enough of him to know that it was William."

"And the cause of death?"

Yates hesitated. "Leonard, he had his throat slashed."

Leonard closed his eyes and lowered his head. "I liked him, and he was a pleasant, young chap. It's so tragic."

No one spoke for a heartbeat or two.

"Let's go and find that bottle, shall we?"

Leonard unlocked the door, and both men entered. Constable Yates looked around while Leonard found the whiskey and two glasses.

"You got a nice place here," offered Yates as he walked into the kitchen. He saw the sack with walnuts stamped on the side. "You like walnuts, do ya?"

"The bag contains coffee beans," replied Leonard without thinking.

"Oh, I see... Where did ya get them from?"

Leonard walked from the kitchen into the living room with the constable following close behind - he ignored the question.

"That's two deaths, one person admitted to a lunatic asylum, two elderly Chinese immigrants missing, and one young woman still unaccounted for," said Leonard angrily.

He poured a healthy dollop of whisky into each glass, offered one to Tim, and raised his own. "Chin-chin," he downed the contents with a grimace. He refilled his and waited for Tim to finish before he topped up his glass.

"I can see the residue of languor, a foul, disagreeable actuality that lies within the pores of the inactive and slothful." Mr Pembroke brushed his fingers across his desktop and then looked at them closely as he rubbed them together. "But not here, not at my desk."

All the reporters in the bullpen had their heads down and appeared hard at work; they were trying their hardest not to laugh at Mr Pembroke's morning theatrics. As no one had been tardy, Mr Pembroke could not single out any individuals for rebuke. It lightened the atmosphere considerably.

"See to it that you remain productive," instructed Mr Pembroke.

Leonard had arrived at work early and was determined to finish his assignments to the high standard he set for himself. The obituary deadline was at three o'clock; he would have them completed ahead of schedule and approved by ten. He had some advertising copy to write, which would take him another couple of hours and hopefully, his superiors would notice his efforts.

The sound of Mr Pembroke removing his jacket and arranging his trusty pillow was familiar; everyone knew his morning routine by heart, and then they waited for the big sigh that signalled he was finally seated and ready to begin his day. Inside the bullpen, all was as it should be as the focus slowly returned to the individual tasks at hand.

There was only one entrance into the bullpen. It was through a door, a varnished door that had darkened a little with age and more so by repetitive touching of ink-smudged fingers. The lower two-thirds of the door was made of panelled wood, and the upper third housed a frosted glass window. It wasn't really a window, as it was impossible to see through, however, it allowed filtered light to pass. The architects who'd designed the building had deemed this suitable, if not slightly extravagant, when they initially conceded the expensive request from their client to replace the clear window with frosted glass.

The door handle, precisely positioned immediately below the glass, wasn't really a handle at all, it was a circular knob. Over time, the latching mechanism had loosened and now had excessive play due to wear. Not enough to affect the performance of the latching apparatus, but certainly, its movement created significant noise when rotated. For the employees of the *Evening Standard* who spent their productive time in the bullpen, this noise allowed them about a single second of advance warning that someone was about to enter the room. A second was plenty of time for an employee with keen hearing to adjust and almost instantly transform himself from absolute inactivity to assiduousness. To the employees, it was a boon.

But frequently, that same warning sound would work in reverse and cause a distraction. When everyone was legitimately busy, they lifted their heads and turned to see who the unexpected visitor was. They could be forgiven, as being reporters, they were naturally curious folk. However, from the perspective of a visitor entering the room, he or she would often be greeted by the sight of a roomful of sorrowful and pathetic-looking reporters staring unashamed and frequently with their mouths agape. For any sane person, this wasn't a delightful sight.

And so, when the sound of the rotating doorknob broke the concentration of the hardworking reporters in the bullpen, everyone stopped what they were doing, including Mr Pembroke, and as one, they turned. With almost a full second of suspenseful anticipation, they waited and were rewarded by the sight of a well-groomed gentleman wearing a stylish homburg hat, who strode confidently into the room. Only two people in the bullpen knew the identity of the unexpected caller, and both, in bewilderment, were temporarily unable to speak.

Leonard pushed his chair back and slowly rose. The caller had politely closed the door behind him and surveyed the room and its occupants.

"Forgive my intrusion."

Mr Pembroke coughed once. It was a polite cough and intended purely as a reminder that he ruled the bullpen, it was his domain, and nothing happened in it without his tacit approval. The stranger, now standing six feet away from Mr Pembroke's desk, had no consent or permission to enter, had not acknowledged the ruler, albeit the king, and if he wanted to establish good terms with the ruler, then following protocol was crucial. He wasn't faring at all well.

The visitor turned and saw Mr Pembroke, who was about to stand. "Good day to you, sir, my name is Winston Crumb...."

With their heads still turned, the first indication that the astonished reporters knew something was amiss was the expression on Mr Pembroke's normally imperturbable face; this prompted them to turn back to their work and pretend they weren't listening. Mr Pembroke's façade crumpled and he was unusually furious.

"Mr Hardy, if you will, please ask Mr Beaumont if he would care to join us in the meeting room." He rose from his chair and stepped toward the visitor. "This way, sir." Mr Pembroke indicated that the visitor should follow.

Leonard trailed them from the bullpen, then turned away hurriedly to find Mr Beaumont as instructed. It was evident that Mr Pembroke knew it was Henrick Mueller who had entered, but he was not aware of the outcome of Leonard's research yesterday and that he had been observing Mueller at the docks. But what was the man doing here?

He knocked urgently on the publisher's door and entered when commanded. Mr Beaumont sat with one of the newspaper's accountants, a tiny and nervous little man who habitually wore a peak and sleeve protectors. Both men looked curiously up at

Leonard as he entered.

Thankfully Leonard's voice was again functioning. "I apologise for interrupting, sir, but Mr Pembroke requests your presence in the meeting room." Leonard wanted to say more but decided it best to remain tight-lipped in front of the accountant.

Mr Beaumont was a perceptive man and understood the urgency of Leonard's request. Notwithstanding that, Leonard was hopping from one foot to another.

"We'll complete this later, Mr Simms."

The accountant gathered his ledger and gave Leonard a stern look as he departed the room. Mr Beaumont stood from behind his desk.

"What's the problem, Leonard?"

"It's Winston Crumb, I mean Henrick Mueller, he's here, sir. Just walked into the bullpen like he owned it."

Beaumont rubbed his chin thoughtfully.

"Yesterday, I discovered where he works; it's in the Amalgamated Steam Ship Company near Queens Wharf. I was nearby and saw him," explained Leonard hurriedly.

"What does he want?"

"I don't know, sir."

"Let's go and find out, shall we?"

They encountered Mr Pembroke in the hallway; he had returned to the bullpen to retrieve his notebook and spectacles. Leonard quickly explained to him what he had just told Mr Beaumont.

Pembroke nodded, then turned to Mr Beaumont. "He's alone in the meeting room."

In order of seniority, the three men entered the meeting room. Leonard closed the door and found a seat furthest away from the visitor, who stood at the window looking out with his hat in his hand. Mr Pembroke sat and placed his notebook on the table while Mr Beaumont remained standing.

"Is lamentable that our fair city is marred by the ravages of fire. Certainly, the irresponsible action of a single individual can affect the lives of so many, isn't that right, Mr Hardy?"

Leonard chose to remain silent.

"Mr Mueller, we are a busy newspaper, we have much to do today, and your unannounced visit is untimely and inconvenient. Is there something we can assist you with?" asked Mr Beaumont.

Henrick Mueller was caught entirely off guard. The discovery and use of his name was not what he expected, and his composure faltered. The smile that played on his lips froze and then just as quickly vanished. His eyes shifted from Mr Beaumont to Mr Pembroke and hardened. If Mueller had prepared theatrical dialogue for this encounter, then his plan was thwarted. The three newspapermen watching could see him furiously rethinking his strategy.

"I am unaccustomed to being stalked, Mr Beaumont. Yes, I know your name, and I resent having questions asked about me that infer I am up to mischief. As one gentleman to another, I ask you politely that you enforce your will as employer and cease this folly. Bring it to an end."

Leonard wanted to speak, but Mr Pembroke had carefully positioned himself so he could see Leonard and Mr Mueller easily, he shook his head imperceptibly.

"And yet you find it acceptable to stalk a valuable member of my staff, Mr Mueller. You've followed him, accosted him and threatened him. What say you in defence of your actions?"

Henrick Mueller laughed. "You have no perception of what is happening in your own city, do you? We never intended to cause Mr Hardy harm, far from it. We've been trying to protect him, keep him safe."

"Why would you or your organisation…." Mr Beaumont raised a hand to his chin and looked up at the ceiling as he tried to recall the name. "Ah yes, Patrons of New Zealand, feel the need to protect Mr Hardy? He's not committed any crime or run afoul of the law, yet you feel compelled to intrude on his life and assert yourself in a way that suggests to me that *you* are worthy of investigation and perhaps reprimand."

Leonard was impressed. He was surprised that Mr Beaumont had remembered details from past conversations they'd had.

Henrick Mueller was considering his response when Mr Beaumont continued. "As I said, Mr Mueller, we are busy and have no time for your games or pantomime." Mr Beaumont walked to the door and opened it. "You can choose to explain what is going on earnestly or leave. I'm sure you do not doubt our ability to uncover truths and report them, which is what we shall do, it's our job. The decision is entirely yours, sir."

Leonard held his breath and saw Mr Pembroke was equally captivated, while Henrick Mueller looked decidedly uncomfortable. He had come to the *Evening Standard* to intimidate, and his plan had gone totally awry. If Mueller exited the room, the newspaper would continue to research and investigate with the goal of publishing a newsworthy story. Such publicity may not be in the best interests of Mr Mueller and his organisation, and he hoped Mueller was quick-witted enough to understand. Mueller's other option was to explain in detail as Mr Beaumont asked and hope for a favourable outcome.

Mr Mueller made his mind up. "Have a pleasant day, gentlemen. I will not encroach on your valuable time again." He replaced his hat and exited through the door.

Mr Beaumont was aghast, as was Leonard; both men were sure Mueller would stay. Mr Beaumont turned to them and raised his eyebrows as if in apology.

Leonard quickly stood. He couldn't help himself. It was almost like a repeat of the incident at the Royal Oak Hotel with Constable Hastings, and he yelled at the departing Mr Mueller. "You're a Unionist, aren't you?"

Leonard heard an uncharacteristic sharp intake of breath from Mr Pembroke, and along with Mr Beaumont, both men turned to him, each with their mouth open.

Mr Pembroke recovered first. "What did you just say?"

Mr Beaumont shook his head with incredulity.

Leonard didn't know what to say. Again, and without a moment's thought, he'd spoken without thinking. He looked towards his feet for answers, but they didn't provide him with any inspiration to assist him with an excuse for his outburst. Help came from an unexpected source.

A homburg hat was thrown onto the table, and Henrick Mueller sat on a chair. "I take my hat off to you, Mr Hardy.

Chapter Seventeen

It was obvious to Leonard that Major Hutton was correct; Henrick Mueller had been acting the role of a character in a minor theatrical production. The pretence had vanished; the man who sat at the table was no longer Winston Crumb. Gone was the air of arrogant self-assuredness that was Winston Crumb. The man before him was Henrick Mueller, and judging from his deflated demeanour, he appeared ready to talk, albeit somewhat reluctantly.

A small smile played across the face of John Beaumont, the *Evening Standard's* publisher. He looked at Leonard and shook his head in wonder. He shut the door, returned to the table, and sat. Leonard quickly glanced at Mr Pembroke and wondered if he'd only imagined his brief lapse in self-control. Now composed, Mr Pembroke sat calmly at the table, vigorously rubbed the lenses on his spectacles, and appeared calm and unflappable as he always did. Leonard could feel the colour of his face returning to normal, and the thumping of his heart was beginning to settle down to a more acceptable rate.

Mr Mueller kept his gaze squarely on Leonard. "There's not a man in New Zealand, except my personal acquaintants, of course, that would stand up and accuse me of being a Unionist. Why do you accuse me, Mr Hardy, how did you know?"

All eyes were turned on Leonard, and it made him feel uncomfortable.

The three employees of the *Evening Standard* were well aware of news reports from England that spoke about 'New Unionism.' Miners, cotton mills, iron and steel workers, and those who worked at the docks were recruited to join the Union movement. In ever-increasing numbers, disaffected workers, including women, were being organized to protest against unfair and unsafe working conditions - rumours were rife of impending strike action. The impact of Union action could cripple employers and a fragile economy, and now it appeared the Unions were gaining a foothold in New Zealand; for many, this was cause for alarm.

"I wasn't sure. But I had an inkling after being at the docks for hours yesterday." Leonard looked around the room and saw all three men watching him. He licked his lips nervously. "When you first approached me, Mr Mueller, you said you represented an organization called Patrons of New Zealand. My friend, Mr McGready, told me he had worked on a case where a conversation was overheard that stated the Patrons of New Zealand were xenophobic."

Mueller shook his head, "That's not entirely accurate, but please continue."

"That is why I wanted to attend the White New Zealand League meeting at the Thistle Inn. I believed they probably shared similar values, or at least enough to provide me with some understanding of the nature of the organizations and those who supported them."

"And what did you deduce?" asked Mr Pembroke, leaning forward with his elbows on the table.

"That they didn't like me." Leonard didn't smile and kept his expression neutral. He recalled Mr Pembroke had been at the Thistle Inn, so he was aware of what was said there and witnessed his humiliating eviction. "Nearly all the men in attendance were unskilled labourers. Above all, they hold their jobs dear and fear losing them. They worry that Orientals are taking work away, and some form of organized effort was being made to petition the government to restrict Chinese workers from entering New Zealand."

"That is a fair assumption, but not a secret," Henrick Mueller stated. "And the Patrons of New Zealand are behind that petition; we urged the White New Zealand League to pursue that course of action."

"Then yesterday, while at the wharf, I watched honest men working, no, slaving away, being yelled at, screamed at, and told to work harder and faster. They risked injuring themselves to satisfy the unfair demands of their employer. I'm surprised more people aren't killed, yet no one spoke up for the bad treatment they received; these men had no collective voice." He paused a moment to think.

"Continue, Leonard," Mr Beaumont encouraged.

"It was then that I considered that if someone wanted to bring these men together where they could speak as one, then what better way than through an organization like the White New Zealand League where they already share a common interest – the fear of losing their jobs."

Mr Pembroke nodded in agreement; there was even a hint of a smile.

"If another organization such as Patrons of New Zealand, who by your admission," Leonard pointed to Mr Mueller, "assumed a behind-the-scenes governance role, they could manipulate and control those smaller fragmented and public brotherhoods such as the White New Zealand League or the Anti-Asian Society to do their bidding. From a logical perspective, I thought it would make the perfect foundation to begin a trade union movement."

The room was quiet as everyone considered Leonard's conclusion.

"Well?" asked Mr Beaumont as he turned to Henrick Mueller.

"I cannot fault his reasoning; however, some assumptions are incorrect."

Mueller shifted to a more comfortable position in his seat. "Despite what you may have heard or deduced, Patrons of New Zealand is not really xenophobic. Our concerns extend only to protect the jobs of good, hard-working men and women of New Zealand. We do not wish to see our jobs taken by foreign nationals from any country regardless of race; it just so happens that Orientals have been arriving on these shores in increasing numbers and threaten the livelihood of many. That is why Orientals were targeted, not because we have racist or elitist views. Do you understand?"

Leonard nodded.

"I may add, though, you arrived at a remarkable deduction, quite fortunate, really."

"No, not really," Mr Beaumont spoke up. "If the Patrons of New Zealand were truly a philanthropic organization or similar, they wouldn't be clouded in secrecy. I see the thread of Mr Hardy's reasoning."

"But perhaps there are men who wish to right injustices, and through their influence and social position, they can affect positive outcomes and remain in the background. The Patrons of New Zealand then becomes a useful, if not a clandestine tool, to achieve this," Mr Pembroke uncharacteristically added, much to Leonard and Mr Beaumont's surprise.

Henrick Mueller remained quiet as Leonard watched Mr

Pembroke. Although he privately disagreed with him. He shifted his gaze back to Mueller. "What I cannot determine is the relationship between the body murdered outside my home and you, Mr Mueller." Leonard's voice had taken on a pronounced hard edge, and he looked at Mueller intensely.

Mueller sighed. "Very unfortunate, I'm afraid. Trent Halpern worked for us, he was a lovely fellow and had a beautiful young family ... we believe orders were given to someone you know quite well to have him killed. We are unable to prove this, of course."

"Constable Hastings," stated Leonard.

Mueller nodded. "Not a pleasant chap at all."

"Why? What had Mr Halpern done?"

"He had information about the illegal immigration of Chinese workers."

"What is this?" Mr Beaumont exclaimed.

"There's a powerful Chinese underworld element that profits from bringing Chinese into the country; they've been operating unchallenged for some years now, and we have been trying our hardest to put an end to it. Mr Halpern had information that we could take to the authorities."

"And these men also threaten New Zealand jobs, is that correct?" Beaumont asked.

"Not just men, Mr Beaumont, it includes women and children as well, and some even sold into slavery. Is a sorry and immoral affair and one we would be happy to see an end to."

"Slavery?" Beaumont said disbelievingly.

"Chinese men come into New Zealand without women, and so Chinese women become a commodity, not just to them, but many European men seek them also," Mueller added.

Mr Pembroke stared at Mueller but said nothing.

This was worse than Leonard had even expected. No wonder there had been killings. There was much at stake for these people, and he wondered if they'd also killed Mary and Uncle Jun. There were many questions to ask, and he didn't know where to begin. "What do you know of the disappearance of Mary Worthington? Is she also involved in this somehow?"

Henrick Mueller looked puzzled, "I'm not familiar with her."

"She is a nurse at Wellington Hospital and went missing almost a week ago," offered Mr Pembroke, finally speaking up.

Mueller shrugged. "I'm unable to help you there."

"Then are you acquainted with Dr Lawrence Schrader?" asked Leonard.

"He's a deplorable individual and has a lot to answer for. We are very familiar with his antics and have been looking at ways to apply pressure, to remove him from his position and eventually face criminal charges. We know he's involved somehow with these Chinese women."

"Is he linked to the murder of Dr Alex Leyton and his assistant?" asked Leonard.

Mr Beaumont looked to Mueller with curiosity, while Mr Pembroke looked almost uncomfortable.

"Mr Hardy, I can't begin to speculate. I really don't know."

Leonard's mind was racing. All sorts of questions were coming to mind, but he needed to digest what he'd learned this morning. It was all becoming confusing, and sadly he was becoming overwhelmed.

"Mr Mueller, are you familiar with Mr Chen Jun Qiang and his wife, Ming? They are proprietors of a small Chinese herbal apothecary on Frederick Street."

Mueller shook his head again, "No, is it relevant?"

"Yes, indeed it is, they are also missing."

Leonard scratched his head. Something was wrong; while Mueller's answers and explanations appeared forthcoming, he didn't feel like he was being entirely truthful. "Mr Mueller, if I can impose on you one last time," Leonard smiled, "Why did you feel the need to protect me?"

Mueller's eyes immediately flicked around the room, and Leonard could see the question was causing him some difficulty in answering. Mueller paused a moment as he formulated his reply.

"Because you are an innocent party in this, a victim caught up in something much greater than you realize. We don't want to see innocent people hurt, Mr Hardy."

He was lying, and Leonard knew it with certainty. Henrick Mueller had suddenly become a thespian and was acting the role of Winston Crumb again. It was obvious. Slight and subtle changes in his mannerisms were now evident where before there were none. *You bastard*, he thought. "Thank you, Mr Mueller, I appreciate your candidness and honesty," he said with a hint of sarcasm and smiled again.

"Mr Hardy, perhaps you should return to your work. As I understand, you have a deadline to meet and copy to write," Mr Pembroke said suddenly, catching Leonard by surprise.

"Yes, of course, sir," Leonard acknowledged after a slight pause. He exited the room with his head spinning.

He could overhear Henrick Mueller asking Mr Beaumont not to publish any story that mentioned the Patrons of New Zealand. Leonard didn't care; he wasn't impressed with Henrick Mueller or his Patrons of New Zealand group.

When he entered the bullpen, he was peppered with questions about the drama around the gentleman visitor. Leonard casually explained the man had come to the *Evening Standard* because he wanted to lodge a complaint. That seemed to satisfy the inquisitive, and things almost returned to normal.

Leonard sat at his desk and stared at the front wall. He was angry and disappointed and hoped Mr Mueller could provide answers. Instead, the man had cleverly deflected his questions and admitted only to wanting to create a Trade Union movement, which in itself had a significant social impact and was worthy of news, but not in the area he was interested in. Mueller knew more than he admitted, and many of his answers were untrue; the man had been lying. Even Mr Pembroke, normally quick of mind, was content to sit back and, for the most part, not really involve himself.

He continued to look at the wall, at the calendar, the crude comments written on drawings, and the company memorandums, old and new. His mind was in turmoil, and he felt helpless and alone. Bridgette was still locked up, and there was nothing he could do to have her released. His eyes wandered across the wall, settled on the card index file cabinet, and froze. The card indexing system, of course. He sat straighter in his chair as an idea came to mind. The words of Louise Pembroke echoed in his head.

He looked behind him. Some reporters were deep in conversation; others were writing and paid him no attention. He reached for the obituary notices he'd completed earlier, rose from his chair and walked to the indexing file cabinet as if he was going to cross reference some names. He opened the drawer for 'S' and fingered through the cards until he found 'Schrader, Lawrence' and pulled the index card. He memorized the few details that it contained, quickly replaced it, and returned to his desk.

Mr Pembroke had still not reappeared, and Leonard wondered if he should take a risk and search for the article now or wait? He had no illusions that what he was about to do was wrong, and if he were caught, he would have to do some serious explaining.

There were large ring binders at the rear of the room near Mr Pembroke's desk that held articles that had never been published, and one of the binders contained what he needed. He calculated it would only take a few seconds to complete the task. He looked at the door one last time and took the chance. He slid his chair back, grabbed the obituaries and walked to the rear of the room. If asked, he would again offer the excuse he was checking on a name.

He pulled the applicable binder from the shelf, flicked through pages until he found the date range he sought and turned each page in quick succession until the article title leapt out at him - 'Derriere Doctor Shames Hospital'.

This was the story Mr Pembroke had told him the *Evening Standard* was going to publish on Dr Schrader, but on Mr Beaumont's suggestion, they had decided against it. No women were prepared to step forward and publicly denounce the doctor - but Schrader didn't know that.

He casually looked over his shoulder, but no one was paying him any attention, and without hesitation, he clicked open the binder, removed the article and replaced the binder on the shelf. For the second time that morning, his heart was beating furiously. He returned to his desk and casually put the article in his valise as the unmistakable sound of the doorknob warned someone was about to enter the bullpen. Leonard had a full second, plenty of time to appear busy as Mr Pembroke shuffled in. To all outward appearances, Leonard had his head down and was hard at work as the grizzled veteran reporter entered. He closed his eyes and sighed with relief.

The remainder of the day was business as usual. Mr Pembroke seemed preoccupied and did not mention the meeting with Henrick Mueller, and Leonard did not see Mr Beaumont.

Leonard finished work around four-thirty in the afternoon and walked unhurriedly towards home. His route would take him past the remains of the Royal Oak Hotel and Constable Yates, who he presumed was still assigned to watch over the area. He walked along Manners Street and approached the charred remains of businesses, then slowed when he saw Constable Yates in the distance. After a moment's thought, he stopped, tucked himself in a shadowed doorway, and observed him for a few minutes. He had no specific reason for watching Yates, but he wasn't entirely convinced he could trust the constable. Perhaps watching for a while would ease his concerns, so he pulled his hat lower and repositioned himself so that his head was all that was visible.

It was a good opportunity to do some thinking, and after today's surprise with the appearance of Henrick Mueller, Leonard realized that there was no one to whom he could turn for help. For want of a better term, Jonathan had recused himself from their friendship and insisted Meredith do the same. Mary had disappeared, Bridgette was being held in a lunatic asylum and probably diagnosed insane, and understandably Mr Beaumont held the interests of the *Evening Standard* as being more important than the plight of a junior employee. While Mr Pembroke seemed willing to offer support and assistance, Leonard wasn't completely certain his help was anything more than satisfying a tepid obligation and politeness.

On the other hand, Constable Yates had conveniently appeared at the right time and demonstrated an eager willingness to help him. Leonard was grateful, of that there was no doubt, but was the constable sincere?

He continued to observe the constable meandering around the affected area. He walked up Cuba Street, then back down and turned right onto Manners and then made his way east for a short distance before returning. Leonard could see he was observant, his head was always moving, and he appeared attentive to his surroundings. He doffed his hat at passing ladies, greeted passers-by politely and had a kind word to offer anyone. The labourers on site kept their distance, which came as no surprise, but as Leonard noticed, Yates also kept a wary eye on them.

Leonard had seen enough; he picked up his valise and strode towards the constable who was approaching the corner of Cuba and Manners Streets.

"Good afternoon, Constable."

"And to you too, Mr Hardy," Constable Yates said good-naturedly.

Both men respectfully doffed their hats as two ladies walked by.

"Any news of interest?" asked Leonard.

Yates shook his head. "Nothing."

"I see." Leonard looked thoughtful. "I was wondering, Tim, if you'd be agreeable to help me with a little plan I've concocted to liberate Bridgette from Mount View?"

Constable Yates raised a single eyebrow in question. "Does this involve criminal activity?"

"Oh no. Perhaps there may be some ethical and moral challenges to my plan, but that burden I shoulder alone," Leonard grinned. "Can you come to my home after you've finished work tomorrow, and then we shall make our way to John Street in Newtown a little later?"

A labourer walked by and deliberately avoided looking at the constable. "I don't trust that bugger," said Yates. "He's always up to something." The constable watched the labourer disappear and then faced Leonard, "Tell you what, you can explain what you're up to tomorrow night, and I'll decide then, suit you?"

"Wonderful, thank you, Tim." Leonard patted him on the shoulder and began to walk away. "Tomorrow!" he yelled over his shoulder.

He was running a little behind schedule. Meredith and perhaps Jonathan would be visiting him this evening, and he needed to clean the house and prepare. There was a lot to do.

Having completed all his tasks, Leonard finally sat at his bureau and stared guiltily at Frederick Pembroke's article, 'Derriere Doctor Shames Hospital'. The story wasn't a literary masterpiece, but it clearly highlighted the sordid activities of Dr Lawrence Schrader, and in no uncertain terms, the story brought ill repute to hospital management for failing to take action against one of their own.

The plan was simple, Leonard reasoned. He would copy the article in his own handwriting and change only two things, the date and the by-line, and then return the original document back to its binder in the morning. He began to copy the article word for word and was surprised when he heard a knock at the door. He'd completely lost track of time.

"Meredith, I'm pleased you came, where is Jonathan?"

"Leonard, he forbade me from coming here this evening, but I chose to come anyway."

"It's not like the two of you are married, and he has the right to place unreasonable demands on you," he grinned, "that would be unseemly, wouldn't it?" Leonard raised a welcoming arm. "Please, Meredith, come in." He leaned over and kissed her cheek.

Once seated and unable to contain himself, Leonard asked after Bridgette. As promised, Meredith had visited her and reported she was miserable and very disconsolate. The reason for her melancholia was obvious, Bridgette had said, but being held against her will at Mount View only added to her current emotional state.

Her initial breakdown, as Leonard and Meredith both knew, was a result of accumulated events that she couldn't cope with at the time.

Leonard sipped his tea as Meredith finished. "How do you think she is? Can the doctors truly justify having her admitted?" he asked.

"Leonard, Bridgette's husband died tragically; she loved him. Her reaction to his death is normal and is how I'd expect any sane woman would react. The fire at the Royal Oak Hotel and the discovery that her husband may have been murdered was too much for her to cope with at the time, but she's doing much better now, thank goodness."

"Is there any suggestion she will be released soon?"

"No, according to Bridgette, they keep telling her how unwell she is and that she needs constant care and attention."

Leonard placed his teacup on the table and began pacing the

room in indecision. He wasn't sure how much he should share with Meredith because he didn't want Jonathan to know.

"Leonard, what's the matter?"

He made his mind up and stopped pacing. He returned to his chair and leaned forward. "Meredith, I have a plan that I think will see Bridgette discharged."

"How? You need a doctor to authorize her release."

He nodded, "I know." He reached toward his bureau and retrieved the original copy of Mr Pembroke's article. He handed it to her to read.

Within moments Meredith's eyes opened wide in outrage. "Is this true?" She looked at him for confirmation.

"There's no reason to doubt it."

She continued to read the article and handed it back to him when finished. "That man is disgusting. I'd heard rumours but never paid them any mind. There's always talk and gossip in a hospital, but... that," she wrinkled her nose, "is abhorrent."

"He's worse in person."

"I agree," she replied, nodding in agreement. "I've never warmed to the man. What will you do with it? Is the *Evening Standard* going to print this?"

"No, the *Standard* isn't; they're unable to publish it, as none of the nurses who've been fondled and molested are prepared to come forward in fear of recrimination or punishment by the hospital." Leonard waved the document in the air. "I didn't write this, it's not mine. I took it from work and copied it." He reached over and held the copy for Meredith to see. "I've changed the date and the by-line, and it now appears as if I authored the story."

"But what can you do with it?"

"I'm going to pay Dr Schrader a visit tomorrow evening and show him my copy. He will believe that I've written the article and that I'll hand it in to be printed, and I dare say he won't be amused. However, I will offer him an alternative. Either he affects the immediate discharge of Bridgette from Mount View, or the story will be printed.

"Do you think he will?"

"Firstly, Meredith dear, he doesn't know the story will never be published, and he has much to fear in the belief it will." He leaned back in his chair and looked happy with himself.

"But surely the paper may find out. What you've done is wrong, Leonard."

"I will return the original document in the morning, and how will the *Evening Standard* ever find out? They won't."

"Will you'll be in danger from Dr Schrader? Can he harm you?"

"I'm bringing a constable with me; he can wait down the street out of sight until I've concluded business with Schrader. If things turn unpleasant, then I can hail him and have him at my side in moments. I've thought this through carefully, Meredith, and I believe it will work."

"I hope so, for Bridgette's sake," she replied.

"Now that brings me to the next part." Leonard scooted closer. "When Bridgette is discharged, can you stay with her for a while? She should have a friend and needs a woman with her as much as possible. You realize Mary still hasn't appeared?"

"Yes, I know, and I'm worried about her too, Leonard." Meredith began fidgeting with her nails as she was apt to do when faced with a difficult decision. "I told you earlier that Jonathan insisted that I not come here tonight; he said it could jeopardize his position with his law firm. I can't imagine he'll be overjoyed to know that I will stay with Bridgette for a few days." She looked a little despondent and then managed a smile. "But my friends need me, and I want to help Bridgette."

"Thank you, Meredith. I think that is a wise choice you've made. If Jonathan believes that by helping Bridgette that constitutes a conflict of interest for him, then don't talk to him for a few days until Bridgette is better or Mary returns."

Meredith laughed.

"Now, I have another question. When do the doctors finish seeing their patients for the day?"

"It varies, Leonard, as most doctors have their own practice and are not employed by the hospital. They come and go at all times, but mostly they tend to leave at the beginning of visiting hours."

"I think that will work nicely," Leonard sat back in his chair and thought of his surprise visit to the home of Dr Lawrence Schrader.

It was an easy day at work for Leonard, and he returned the article to the ring binder without anyone seeing him, and no one was any wiser. He completed all his regular duties and submitted them for approval and was now working on assembling the final results and awards on the recent Horticulture Show hosted by the Wellington Horticultural and Botanical Society. It was always a popular event and well-supported. Another reporter had actually been at the event, but Leonard's responsibility as a junior was to sort through the names and different competitions and create the final results lists.

So it was with interest that he stumbled upon Mrs L. Pembroke's name; she had been listed as a judge on the cucumber competition.

He wasn't surprised and could easily imagine her being an authority on cucumbers. He was going to mention it to Mr Pembroke, as he was in a rather churlish mood today. Experience told Leonard that it was best to leave him alone when in such a frame of mind. Thankfully, Mr Pembroke had a council meeting to report on and left the building soon after.

It was tedious work, and as always, Leonard's mind drifted to various topics and abstract thoughts, and it occurred to him how people's names frequently appeared on published lists from different organizations and clubs. It had never occurred to him to look at these lists when he was searching for information on Winston Crumb or Henrick Mueller and the secretive Patrons of New Zealand, or even Lawrence Schrader for that matter.

What bothered Leonard the most about Patrons of New Zealand was the fact that they were influencing people covertly, and in his opinion, people had a right to know. What other matters were the organization involved in, and who were the people behind it who wanted to remain secret? Were the activities of the organization unethical or illegal? Perhaps those activities represented a conflict of interest, which could explain why people didn't want their names made public. He thought about his success in finding the article on Dr Schrader's antics by using the card indexing system and wondered if the cards could further help him. It gave him an idea.

He tried to recollect any well-known clubs or organizations that featured prominently in stories written by the *Evening Standard*; a few came to mind, and he decided to try his luck.

Leonard turned to the indexing system and found a reference to a few recent articles on the 'Wellington Racing Club.' He found the printed editions easily and read the articles to see if they mentioned any names of interest. There were none.

He tried again and searched for any articles on the 'Star Boating Club,' one of Wellington's original boating organizations. There were a few references to events and competitions, and the first few articles were unhelpful. A later story detailed an ongoing argument by the club's directors over moving the club building to a new location. Some directors were in favour of the move, others against it. Director Mr F. Pembroke vehemently opposed the idea, and many club members supported him. The article listed the names of his advocates, including one of the club's rowing coaches, a Mr H. Mueller. Leonard almost dropped the newspaper on the floor. Was this merely a coincidence? No, he thought, it can't possibly be. The article suggested that Mueller supported Mr Pembroke's opposition to the building's relocation at the meeting. Therefore, Mr Pembroke and Mr Mueller were together in attendance at that meeting and, as club members, must be acquainted. Why did either of them not reveal this? Leonard shook his head in amazement.

According to Leonard's logic, was Mr Pembroke also a member of the Patrons of New Zealand? This would account for Mr Pembroke's peculiar behaviour yesterday that seemed so out of character.

Emboldened, Leonard searched for any articles on the newly formed 'Port Nicholson Yacht Club.' Being nautical and prestigious, he hoped this would also be attractive to Messers Mueller and Pembroke. There were quite a few recent articles about the formation of the new yacht club and some of the difficulties they encountered. Almost immediately, he found a reference to Mr F. Pembroke; his name had been submitted as a candidate as the club's first commodore. Leonard found no further listings of Mueller's name or anyone else he knew.

Leonard returned to his desk and mulled over the implications. If Mr Pembroke was a member of the Patrons of New Zealand, then what did that mean? Had Mr Pembroke said anything yesterday to protect Mueller?

But he had. When Leonard had asked Mueller why he was being protected, Mueller was uncomfortable and lied. Mr Pembroke immediately ordered Leonard back to the bullpen to work and eliminated any possibility that he may ask Mueller more awkward questions. Mr Pembroke had also unwittingly come to the defence of the Patrons when he had offered a possible reason why men joined the organization. It seemed far-fetched to assume that Mr Pembroke was, in fact, a member of the Patrons of New Zealand, but then he couldn't discount it either. What did this mean? Were the Patrons involved in illegal or immoral activities, and what should he do about it? Was Mr Beaumont aware of the relationship between Mueller and Pembroke, and should he bring it to his attention?

Leonard knew trade unions in England were becoming quite popular. Although craft guilds had existed for many a year, they tended to cater to skilled workers. Trade unions had solicited support largely from unskilled workers, creating considerable anxiety for employers. Perhaps Mr Pembroke didn't want to incur the wrath of employers by siding publicly and openly supporting a trade union movement.

He thought about his visit to the Pembrokes' and wondered if he'd misplaced his trust in them. He turned to face the room's rear, and his eyes fell on the row of dictionaries. Without a moment's thought, he rose from his chair and walked to the rear of the bullpen and extracted Cassell's Latin Dictionary from the shelf. He flicked through the pages and found what he sought. *Venenum* translated to 'poison or drug'. Mrs Pembroke's book, *Venenum Hortus, A Poison Garden.*

This was just more for him to think about, and as if he didn't have enough already. He looked at the clock and decided it was time to leave for his afternoon meetings with a few advertisers.

Chapter Eighteen

Leonard was pacing backwards and forwards in his living room, rehearsing what he'd say to Dr Schrader. The aggressive, I've got you over a barrel, approach wasn't working, and the conceited, I'm more intelligent than you, attitude didn't seem a good idea either. As he held the upper hand, then perhaps he should just be himself and talk to the doctor in a reasonable manner that may achieve better results. His preparations were interrupted by a knock on the door - Constable Yates had arrived.

It took only a few minutes to explain the basic plan to the constable, and he wasn't at all enthusiastic about it. "Blackmail is a crime, Leonard, and I cannot be a party to it," he explained whilst shaking his head.

"But the man is doing something wrong by not discharging Bridgette; he is holding her against her will."

"As much as I agree with you, the facts are simple: he is a doctor, Mrs Leyton suffers from melancholia, and that type of illness *is* treated in that torrid, awful asylum. He ain't breaking the law."

In frustration, Leonard began pacing again. "Yes, yes, you are correct, but Bridgette's condition isn't bad enough to warrant being there, don't you see? The only reason she was admitted in the first place is that the doctor has a personal vendetta against me," pleaded Leonard as he poked himself in the chest.

"And what you propose is blackmail, which is a crime, even if the man makes your gorge rise."

Leonard paced backwards and forwards in his small living room while the constable sat patiently and watched. Eventually, Leonard appealed to Tim from a different perspective. "Without question, Dr Schrader has been misusing his position as a doctor to engage inappropriately with hospital staff. All I'm proposing is to make that information public if he doesn't authorise Mrs Leyton's discharge."

Tim laughed. "Leonard, you ain't got evidence or proof, no one is prepared to come forward and accuse the man. Legally, it's only *your* opinion," he sighed. "Leonard, if I could help you, I would, but I can't be a party to your scheme."

"I do have evidence and can prove it," Leonard lied.

"Who?" Tim asked. "It's Miss Worthington and Mrs Leyton, isn't it?"

Leonard said nothing. Both Mary and Bridgette had never agreed to complain publicly about Schrader's unethical behaviour, but Tim didn't know that.

"And so, at the moment, you can't do anything about it, can you?"

Somewhat deflated, Leonard sat and leaned back in his chair. "Perhaps you are right, Tim. It is wrong to involve you in any plan that compromises your employment and the trust placed in you. I wasn't thinking, I apologise."

The constable shrugged and smiled.

"How is Inspector Gibbard coming along with his inquiries, any developments?" asked Leonard wanting to change the subject.

"He doesn't keep me informed of his progress, and I ain't heard much in the way of rumours. What I can tell you, though, Mr Hastings ain't welcome back as a constable, is all over for him."

"Is he likely to be seeking me out? I mean, should I be worried?"

"He was told that additional charges will be made against him if he steps out of line during the investigation, so I don't think you need be concerned."

"But the investigation was centred on the fire, and I thought he would only be charged with negligence. What else is he being investigated for?"

"Corruption and other charges, oh yes, assault too, I believe."

"Assault?"

"You weren't the only person to get on the wrong side of him; apparently, he seriously assaulted a man. The poor chap was too scared to report it to the police in fear Hastings would come back and give him another thrashing."

"I'm sure Hastings has more to worry about than me, so I can rest a little easier."

Constable Yates stood and stretched, "I must be leaving, time to go home. Sorry I couldn't be of more help, Leonard."

Leonard walked Constable Yates to the door, said goodnight and then watched him as he made his way down Marjoribanks Street towards home.

Leonard returned to his living room and sat at his bureau. Mae's picture stared back at him. The feeling of loss had not diminished, and her picture, a moment frozen in time, was a constant reminder of what once was. Would she approve of what he was going to do? It was a question that didn't need to be asked, he knew the answer.

He picked up his written copy of the *Derriere Doctor* article and looked at it thoughtfully. He stared into the yellow flame of his lamp, considered his next move, and after a heartbeat or two, he leaned forward and extinguished the light. He was going to pay Dr Schrader a visit.

A Hansom cab dropped him at the bottom of John Street in Newtown and then trotted away, leaving him alone as the sun slowly descended over the western hills. It was going to be another warm evening. *A pleasant night to be out for a stroll*, thought Leonard. The city council Rate book had provided him with Dr Schrader's address, the copy of the article was secure inside his jacket, and as prepared as he could be, he began walking.

The doctor's house was located a considerable way up John Street and was set back from the road on a large sloping property. It was another grand estate, and Leonard questioned where the money came from to purchase such a large home. Mr Pembroke's house was also large and impressive, while the doctor's house was equally as grand if not bigger, although the grounds looked neglected and overgrown. Obviously, Dr Schrader had no love for gardening, which accounted for his absence from the Wellington Horticultural and Botanical Society's recent show and competition. Leonard tried to picture the corpulent little man standing proudly with his Brussels sprouts as he received an award - and failed. To Leonard's thinking, Dr Schrader enjoyed more lurid hobbies.

At first, he walked briskly past the house and casually turned to look as any curious passer-by would. He couldn't see any lights burning, and so, on the return, he sauntered at a more measured pace, like a gentleman enjoying a leisurely evening stroll.

The bravado he felt at home was quickly disappearing and replaced by considerable anxiety and fear. The feeling was compounded by an inkling, an impression that he was being observed – that someone was watching him. He paused and glanced around, but he seemed to be alone; John Street was deserted, and he saw no one. He put it down to nervousness and shrugged off the feeling. He peeked through the trees and continued a more thorough examination of the house from the safety of the street – no lights burned inside, it was dark and looked forbidding. It seemed that no one was home. He crossed the street and paid more attention to the neighbours and which of them had an unobstructed view of Schrader's door. As far as he could determine, trees and plants obscured much of the house from the road.

At first, Leonard was disappointed Schrader wasn't at home. Still, after some careful consideration, he was pleased he had the opportunity to perform a reconnaissance of sorts. As he imagined, similar to a soldier before going into battle. With a sigh, he retraced his steps and now knew what to expect on his return visit.

Fridays were always hectic at the *Evening Standard*. Reporters were given schedules and assignments for the events they were to attend over the weekend, deadlines were met, and new ones were created. The routine was always the same for Leonard, who preferred it that way. So it came as some surprise when Mr Pembroke called him over to his desk and told him that Mr Bailey, from Bailey & Sons, Grain and Seed Merchants, had requested that Leonard pay him a visit to discuss altering the long-running advertisement he had placed with the paper. That in itself wasn't unusual; it was when Mr Pembroke added that Mr Bailey would only be available after the close of normal business hours and was expecting Leonard at around seven later this evening that he raised an eyebrow.

"You have another engagement, Mr Hardy?" asked Mr Pembroke without looking up.

"No, sir. It just comes as a surprise that he is working late. He normally leaves for an ale mid-afternoon on a Friday."

"Then I'm sure you'll take care of his needs and keep the man happy."

"Yes, sir."

"That will be all."

Leonard returned to his desk and ignored Mr Pembroke's brusqueness. He calculated he could attend to Bailey's business, then leave from the grain warehouse and go directly to Schrader's home, which suited him perfectly.

Once he'd completed his most immediate duties, Leonard devoted some time to thinking about Mr Pembroke. Since the surprise meeting with Henrick Mueller, Mr Pembroke had been out of sorts and more grumpy than usual. He wondered how much of his current disposition was related to Mueller. If Leonard was correct, and he was a member of the Patrons of New Zealand, then Mueller's unannounced visit to the *Evening Standard* might not have been well thought out. The outcome was not what Mueller had expected, and it may have ruffled a few of Mr Pembroke's feathers.

The challenge for Leonard, amongst all the others he had taken on recently, was to find a way to confirm his theory about Mr Pembroke being a member of Patrons of New Zealand. Undoubtedly, Mueller and Pembroke knew each other, and there was no crime in that. However, in light of the personal attacks made on him, and the warnings he'd received, either of the two men should have admitted they knew each other, but they hadn't. They pretended to be strangers. According to Leonard's logic, if neither man had acknowledged the other, then it must have been deliberate. If it was deliberate, then it was planned, which raises the question of the integrity of both men.

Should he tell Mr Beaumont?

If he were in Beaumont's shoes, then yes, he'd want to know, but would informing Beaumont jeopardise his own position within the company? It may be prudent to not involve with senior management problems and thus ensure he remained gainfully employed. This becomes an ethical problem and one he'd rather not agonise over. He had more than enough to concern himself with. One of those concerns was finding information on the Chinese tongs.

"Have you lost something, Mr Hardy?" bellowed Mr Pembroke from the far side of the room. His tone of voice suggested he was not asking out of concern.

"No, sir, I was just thinking about my visit to Mr Bailey."

"Then think as you do your work!"

"Of course, Mr Pembroke." In response, Leonard dipped his head and tried to focus on his tasks, but he struggled.

"What's got into him, then," whispered Mr Keegan, who sat behind Leonard.

"Old age and senility," hissed Leonard in reply.

The clock in the room seemed to have frozen; the hands had barely moved, and the remainder of the afternoon was spent trying desperately to avoid the wrath of Mr Pembroke, while others were not so lucky.

The mechanical sound of the door handle turning gave fair warning that someone was about to enter the bullpen. All reporters, including Mr Pembroke, turned their heads and waited almost an entire second to discover who was about to enter. A collective sigh of disappointment greeted Mr Armitage as he strode into the room.

"You're late," welcomed Mr Pembroke.

"Yes, sir. I was held up at the depot."

"Then it must have been quite a drama to have kept you from the important work that awaits you here?"

"Actually, not really but I wasn't to know that until after I waited to be briefed, sir," Mr Armitage offered. The other reporters had their heads down and, without exception, pretended to be hard at work as they listened.

"I see, and what were you briefed on, Mr Armitage?"

"Apparently, the police are investigating the theft of a crate of Arabica coffee beans, sir."

Leonard almost choked.

The bullpen was deathly quiet.

"Coffee beans?" repeated Mr Pembroke with slowness.

"A consignment for the governor, apparently."

Mr Pembroke gave the matter a second or two of thought. "Continue with your work, Mr Armitage."

"Yes, sir."

Leonard couldn't sit any lower or drop his head more than it already was. His forehead almost touched his desk, and he hardly dared breathe, fearing it would draw attention to him. The seconds ticked by, and he was beginning to relax a little.

"You wouldn't happen to know anything about who may have absconded with a crate of Arabica coffee beans, would you... Mr Hardy?"

With his face portraying the innocence of the Blessed Virgin Mary, Leonard slowly turned to Mr Pembroke. "I beg your pardon, sir, I was concentrating. Could you repeat that?"

"A pallet of Arabica coffee beans has been purloined; I'm presuming you know nothing about that."

Leonard swallowed. "That's correct, sir."

"Sounds like trouble is brewing," whispered someone behind Leonard.

"Do you have something to add, Mr Keegan?" asked Mr Pembroke without pause.

"No, sir," replied Mr Keegan.

Leonard wasn't sure, but he thought Mr Pembroke's mouth might have twitched upwards very briefly.

The clock ticked, and Leonard maintained his facade of sanctity.

"Back to work, everyone."

Leonard breathed out slowly.

It was finally time to go home, and as proper etiquette dictated, no one made a move until Mr Pembroke left the building. Once he'd safely departed, it was like a stampede, and the room drained as if someone had declared an emergency. Leonard found himself outside in the fresh air, feeling pleased he was finally free from the bullpen's constraints.

He detoured from his regular route home and headed to the markets at the bottom of Tory Street. Once there, he intended to converse with some of the Chinese growers who had a stall and regularly sold fresh produce. Mae had originally made the introductions to him, and since then, Leonard delighted in practising the little Chinese he'd been taught when he came to buy vegetables.

As expected, the Chinese market gardeners sat communally together and smiled broadly when they recognised him. Many spoke no English, a few some, and one or two, only just. It required patience, much head nodding and laughter to communicate.

Leonard selected a few potatoes, a cabbage and some carrots, but as usual, they wouldn't accept his money. He left payment for them regardless, which he knew they appreciated, and when invited, he sat down on a rickety stool, smiled warmly and chatted clumsily. After a few minutes, they handed him a cup of tea, and during a break in their conversation, he asked them about the secretive Chinese organisations called Tongs that he knew operated in Wellington. Instantly the mood changed, and a few men looked nervously around while Leonard curiously waited for an answer.

After some rapid discussion that Leonard could not understand, one man named Ben, who spoke the best English, had something to say.

"Why you want to know this, Leo?"

"It is very important to me to know a little about the Tong in Wellington. It is a long story, and I cannot tell you about it now."

More quick discussion ensued as Ben made the translation, and worried faces stared back. "We cannot speak of this," Ben shook his head. "We are simple farmers."

Leonard looked at the craggy and tired faces of the men; they appeared frightened, and he did not want to put them in a difficult position or endanger them. He nodded and smiled, "I understand, Ben. Thank you."

He finished his tea and shortly after said farewell, nodded his head a few times in gratitude, gathered his vegetables, and left them with a promise to visit again soon. He unhurriedly walked toward home as he considered the power of the Tongs and the ability to frighten men so easily. They obviously had significant influence amongst the Chinese community and a far reach. Mae had never been willing to discuss the Tongs and admonished him for mentioning them.

"Mr Leo, Mr Leo!"

Leonard stopped and turned at the sound of his name being called. A young Oriental man was running to catch up with him. Immediately he checked to see if he'd forgotten anything from the market, but he had everything with him, so he curiously waited as the young man approached.

"Mr Leo, thank you for stopping," he exclaimed in surprisingly good English.

He was neither a youth nor an adult but somewhere in between. Perhaps he was the son of one of the men he had just visited. He smiled and waited for the fellow to explain himself.

"After you left, the men were talking, they are very frighten and do not wish to cause anger to our community leader."

"Yes, I understand the fear they feel," replied Leonard, intrigued by the nature of the discussion.

"But I can help you a little, what do you want to know?"

"Did Ben send you to me?"

The young man nodded, "Yes, Mr Leo."

"Let's stroll and talk, shall we?" Leonard glanced around; there was no one near them who could overhear, and they began to walk. "I would like to learn more about the Tong here in Wellington. What can you tell me about them?"

"There is more than one Tong here in Wellington - some are good, other not so good."

"The bad Tong, what bad things do they do?"

"Opium, they bring opium here and also gambling."

"And what of bringing people to New Zealand? Slaves? Do you know of this?"

The young man's expression changed, and he looked sad. "Yes, mostly young girl from China, they sell girl, Mr Leo. Not good."

"To whom? Who buys these girls?"

"If you have money, you can buy."

Leonard thought carefully. "Do you know who these men are?"

The young man shook his head.

"Where do these bad men work or live, do you know?"

"Everywhere, here, Chinatown." He waved his arms around.

They stopped walking, and Leonard leant forward slightly to face the young man. "What is this Tong called, do you have a name?

"*Tiandihui*," he whispered.

"Tian-dih-ui?" slowly repeated Leonard.

"Yes, Hongmen, that is what we call them."

Leonard thought, walked on a few steps, and then stopped again. "Are there European men mixed up with these Hongmen?"

The young man looked puzzled.

Leonard rephrased the question. "Western men, are they part of the bad Tong?"

Again the young man nodded.

"Do you know who these western men are?"

The young man looked around as he thought. "Maybe one man, with big nose. Bad man."

Leonard wasn't surprised, "Is the man with the big nose a constable, a policeman?"

"Yes, Mr Leo."

"What about a short, fat man, a man called Dr Schrader, is he part of the Tong?"

The young man looked at Leonard but could offer nothing.

"What is your name?"

"You call me Chang."

"Thank you, Chang, you've been very helpful to me. Do you work at the market?"

"Only late in day, in morning, I work in garden. I go now, Mr Leo."

Then he was gone. Chang ran off back towards Tory Street.

Leonard recalled the evening at the Royal Oak Hotel, the night it burned, and the two Oriental men he had seen at the St George Hotel. The same men had dragged Constable Hastings down the stairs after the fire began. Obviously, they had been watching him and were there to protect Hastings. He recalled the morning he visited Uncle Jun and the young men who had accosted him; they had been set upon by two Oriental men, which didn't make sense. There were still so many unanswered questions.

He arrived home, put away his vegetables and prepared for his visit with Bailey. It was, in his opinion, a rather peculiar time to conduct business, but perhaps Bailey was busy, and this was the only time he had.

It took Leonard about fifteen minutes to walk to Bailey & Sons warehouse on Taranaki Street. As he approached, he saw the large doors were closed, and through a window, light filtered through pulled shades. He walked to a small door inset into the larger sliding main door, thumped it several times, and stepped back. Within moments he heard a bolt being slid back, and the small door squeaked open. Bailey stood in the shadows with a big smile as Leonard crouched to enter the warehouse through the low entrance.

"Leo, is good to see you," said Mr Bailey once Leonard had stepped through and straightened. He reached out with a big hand and gave Leonard's hand, arm and upper body a vigorous welcoming

301

shake. "Oh my, you keep losing weight, look at you." The big man stood back, grinning.

"It's always a treat to see you, Bailey. Are you well?"

He carefully ensured the small door was again bolted. "I'd be better if I could only get my lazy sons to work ... the younger ones these days, they don't know what hard graft is. Not like you, though, eh? Come and work for me, Leo, you'd love it," jibed Mr Bailey in typically good spirits.

He draped an arm over Leonard's shoulder and led him towards his office - which wasn't really an office at all. It was a shed with temporary windows hastily erected in the front corner of the warehouse, which had now become more or less permanent. He opened the office door and politely allowed Leonard to enter first.

The first thing Leonard saw was a man seated with his back to the door. As he entered the office, the man rose from his seat and turned around. Leonard nearly fainted; it was Uncle Jun.

Without a moment's thought, Leonard rushed toward the frail old man and enveloped him in a warm embrace.

"Better let him go, Leo, or you'll squash the old bugger," laughed Bailey.

"Where have you been? What is going on here?" Leonard gushed. He turned from Uncle Jun to Bailey in question. "How did you... I mean, I didn't know you were acquainted?"

Uncle Jun was beaming and was delighted to see Leonard.

"If it wasn't for Jun, I doubt I'd still be in business; he's been buying from me for years. But sit down, Leo. Jun has a few things to tell you, and it isn't good." Bailey's appearance was serious, an expression Leonard had seldom seen on the big man.

Uncle Jun sat in the chair and clutched his cloth cap that he held in his lap, Leonard sat opposite him, and Bailey sat beside a worktop bench nailed to the wall that was likely used as an office desk.

As the joy and surprise of seeing Uncle Jun began to wear off, Leonard was puzzled and looked to both men in question.

"Remember when you ask me for name of man who dead?" began Uncle Jun.

Leonard nodded, "Yes, I now know his name."

"When I ask people to give me name, it make some man very angry. He not want me to ask question. He come to see me and tell me not to help you."

"What men?" Leonard asked.

Bailey held up a hand, signalling him to wait.

Uncle Jun continued. "If I help you, then he tell me you die too. Leo, these are bad man, not good." Uncle Jun shook his head. "When you come to shop, I must go upstair and wait for you to go. But I know you in danger. We have some good man keep watch on you, but you, silly boy, you not stop asking question. Make bad man very angry. You nearly die many time, Leo, and we protect you. Why you keep ask question?"

The small office was quiet; Uncle Jun fidgeted with his hat while Bailey watched. Leonard was deep in thought as he took in what he'd learned.

"Who are these bad men, Uncle Jun, are these the Hongmen, the *Tiandihui* Tong?"

Uncle Jun glanced at Bailey. Leonard could see there was more they had not told him.

Bailey leaned forward. "Leonard, you speak of the triad. These men are part of some underworld crime gang and are ruthless; if you get in their way, death means nothing to them. These people control

303

the opium and gambling and…."

"The women slaves, yes, I know about that," interrupted Leonard. "But how could Uncle Jun protect me if this criminal gang are so powerful?"

"There are many man from China who are good man, they not want problem with Hongmen, they called, Chee Kung Tong Society, you know this?" asked Uncle Jun.

Leonard shook his head; he had never heard of them.

"They are like Free Masons, organised, with many members, good men," added Bailey. "Some call them a Tong as well, but Tong isn't a bad word, it translates to 'family meeting in hall.'"

Leonard turned back to Uncle Jun, who nodded in agreement.

"We make sure you are safe, and we follow you."

"How come you're involved with this and so well informed, Bailey?"

Bailey unfolded his arms and placed his massive hands on his thighs; he looked at Jun and grinned. "The land Mr Chen now owns and the building he lives in used to belong to me; that was where Bailey & Sons first began." We outgrew it, and I sold it to a wonderful man who had newly arrived in Wellington with his young family. The sale of that building allowed me to buy this warehouse. We became good friends and have remained so for many years."

Leonard looked in confusion at both men. "But why did neither of you tell me you knew each other."

"We quickly realised that we could benefit more if we kept our friendship private, although it was never really a secret. In this business, I must be careful of unscrupulous men who try to control the transportation of my goods from the wharves. I turned to Jun for advice as the triad gangs wanted to control who delivered my goods from the docks. With his help and the assistance of Chee Kung Tong Society, we kept the gangs away. In turn, I recommended customers and arranged cheaper shipping costs for goods Jun and other members of the Chee Kung Tong brought into the country. We help each other." Bailey leaned back in the protesting chair that threatened to collapse. "Had you asked either of us, we would have told you we knew each other, but you never did. So no, our friendship wasn't a secret, just guarded."

Leonard scratched the back of his head. It was true; he had never asked Bailey and Uncle Jun if they knew each other. He couldn't think of a reason why he would have asked that question.

"I'd been so worried about you and was convinced you'd been killed like the others," Leonard said to Uncle Jun.

"And you stupid boy, you no listen when you told, no more question. But you keep doing," Uncle Jun shook his head.

"Have either of you any information on Patrons of New Zealand or a gentleman called Henrick Mueller?"

Both men nodded.

Bailey spoke first. "I've encountered them a few times, mostly through Jun and his Chee Kung Tong organisation. From what I can glean, they don't want foreigners coming to New Zealand, and just like the triads, they want to control the wharves and what arrives and leaves. They've been at each other for years, but neither has managed a strong foothold. That Mueller fellow is a piece of work, I tell you."

"No like man, not good, he dishonest," Uncle Jun spoke. "He want much money to allow me to ship goods here."

Leonard turned to Bailey.

"What he says is accurate," Bailey added, "They want the

receivers of goods to pay extra to ensure safe delivery. If you don't pay, then your goods may not arrive, or if they do, they may be damaged."

"But not for you?" Leonard asked.

Bailey laughed. "No, because I use my own wagons and drivers, and I get the goods off the ships fast, so the shipping companies like me. And I had a little chat with Mr Mueller one day behind a wharf building."

Leonard raised his eyebrows in surprise, although he shouldn't have, he knew what Bailey was capable of. "And you don't fear reprisal?"

"No, Leo, because where do you think all those dockworkers get a lot of their household goods from, and at a price cheaper than anywhere else? I take good care of them. No one would lift a finger against my lads or me, and Mueller knows it."

It was so much information for Leonard to digest.

"Do either of you know of a Dr Schrader?"

Bailey and Uncle Jun both shook their heads.

"What about a large man with a big nose named Hastings? Until recently, he was a constable."

"No like him, very bad man, he a Hongman," answered Uncle Jun.

"I've seen him around, but he keeps his distance from me," replied Bailey

"Yes, I see," answered Leonard. "But tell me, why did you decide to come forward and share with me all this information now?"

"Because they want to kill you!"

Leonard felt a chill. His first response was to quickly look around the room, the second to place his head in his hands. He felt frightened.

The room was silent.

"Who wants to kill me?" he managed to eventually ask, it sounded like a squeak.

"*Tiandihui,*" replied Uncle Jun. "Triad. And boss-man very bad man, he is call four-eight-nine."

"A number?"

"Yes, it mean, Mountain Master. He leader," explained Jun.

It was all too much for Leonard to take in. "Do you know why? What have I done to him that I deserve to die?"

"Because you know too much, Leo," said Uncle Jun, quickly wishing the topic would change. Leonard understood he was no hero; he didn't want to die just because someone believed he knew too much. He prided himself on knowing a lot about many things, so what things did he know that frightened people enough to want to see him dead? He removed his hands from his face. "But how does this triad know I know too much? That's ridiculous!"

"You must have told someone and kept them up to date on what you've been learning, and they've told the triad," suggested Bailey.

"And Uncle Jun, how do you know they wish to see me dead?"

"A man tell me, he know Hongmen, and he say you make Hongmen very unhappy and talk too much. Mr Hardy have big mouth, he say."

Would they send Hastings to kill him; would the big man put his hands around his throat and squeeze, or make it fast with a gunshot? Or would he die like his friend and be tossed casually under a wagon on a busy street? Neither idea appealed to him. "Oh dear, that's given me something to think about, hasn't it?" He took a deep breath. "And what do I do now, go into hiding?"

"Who you tell with big mouth, Leo?"

"Perhaps, Leonard, you should explain all that has happened; let's piece this together." Bailey reached under his worktop and pulled a bottle of whiskey, rummaged for some glasses, wiped them with his shirt and poured a healthy measure into three glasses. He settled back as Leonard told all he knew.

Uncle Jun wanted a refill, and Leonard was quiet and thinking. If Bailey was correct, someone he'd been talking to had informed the triad.

"That's quite a story, Leo. If I understand all you've told me, the people who know everything that has happened are your employer, Mr Beaumont, that crusty old man Mr Pembroke, Constable Yates, and Miss Rosewarne. Now, what about her suitor, Jonathan McGready?"

"The only way Jonathan would know anything is if Meredith told him," replied Leonard.

"But if he is already communicating with Hastings, then he seems to be the likely suspect, doesn't he?"

"I no trust him, your friend Jonathan, he talk, he the one," volunteered Uncle Jun.

"You don't think it's Mr Pembroke?"

"No, no, he is Patron of New Zealand, he not talk to Chinaman. Not him."

"I agree with Jun, unlikely to be Pembroke. What do you make of Constable Yates?"

"I like him; he knows everything that's going on, but he seems very honest."

"I don't trust your employer, Mr Beaumont; he's a shifty one, I never thought much of him. That's why I insist I only talk to you if I have business with the newspaper. So, it could also be him." Bailey looked contemplative for a moment. His demeanour changed; the affable grain merchant was gone, and replaced by a shrewd, intelligent, astute businessman. "Leonard, you must be aware that your employer, as agreeable as he appears to you, serves his own interests and that of the *Evening Standard*. He needs to provide stories, articles and reports of community appeal to his readers and, above all, sell advertising. You represent such a story to his beloved paper, and any perceived kindness is motivated by the grandeur of that story and does not rise alone from the goodness of his heart."

"You listen, Leo, he speak wise word," Uncle Jun added.

Leonard gave the matter some thought. "Yes, you are both correct; I must keep things in perspective."

Bailey nodded, "Continue, Leo."

"And then there's Jonathan." He took a big breath and exhaled. "Of all of them, Jonathan McGready communicates with Hastings, and he's a clever fellow; he could easily get information from Meredith," Leonard said, but quietly hoping it wasn't his friend who was betraying him.

Uncle Jun had emptied his glass again, and Leonard turned to him. "And you are sure; your friend told you the triad wants to kill me? It's not a mistake?"

"No mistake, Leo. Hongmen no like you very much."

"I hope the triad doesn't find out you've been helping me, I would hate to see you get into any trouble."

"Only if you open big mouth, Leo. Good idea to keep close, eh."

"Am I in danger from now, when I leave here tonight?"

Uncle Jun shook his head. "No, not tonight, triad have meeting to discuss next week, then they decide what to do."

"I have some thinking to do and find a way to protect myself."

"And find out who is talking to the triad." reminded Bailey.

It was turning into some evening. His head spun with all he'd learned. So far, he had not talked much about Dr Schrader and the details around getting Bridgette discharged. He wondered if he should say something or keep quiet. Uncle Jun made his mind up for him.

"How you get your friend from asylum?" asked Jun as if he was reading his mind.

Again, Leonard explained everything about Schrader, his brother and what he'd learned about the man.

Uncle Jun was shaking his head and unusually said nothing and kept quiet.

"You are convinced this is a personal vendetta against you?" Bailey asked. "What you suggest about getting your friend out of the asylum might work, Leonard, but it is chancy. Seems that Schrader may not be a Hongman, but he is probably a customer of the triad. If he's a good customer, then the triad will protect him. And you will further rile the triad if he reports to them what you've done."

"And what can the triad do, Bailey, kill me again? I have to do something to get Bridgette released. Sitting back and doing nothing when the only reason she's in that place is because that doctor hates me... I have a moral obligation to do something."

"And are you convinced the doctor is holding your other friend Miss Worthington?"

"No, I don't know. It's just that she has disappeared, and the logical conclusion is either the triad or Schrader have her or have done something to her."

"I ask my friend for you, Leo. He will tell me, no worry," offered Uncle Jun.

"When will you see the doctor and tell him about the article the paper wants to print?" Bailey asked.

"When I leave here, if it's not too late."

"What you want to do is dangerous, Leo. You could get hurt."

"Dr Schrader is a small, obese little man; he couldn't hurt me unless he fell and rolled on top of me. I'm in no danger from him. I've already seen where he lives. I'll knock on the door, and when he answers, I'll show him the copy I made and give him a choice. How can I possibly hurt myself?"

"It's the unexpected. That's what worries me, Leo." Bailey rubbed his chin in thought.

"Leo, you must be careful," said Uncle Jun, "I worry for you."

"Come by here on Sunday evening, same time," requested Bailey.

"And what of the advertisement?"

"Ah, yes. Uh, I want you to add flour to it."

"Just the word flour, no other changes?"

"That's right."

Leonard nodded and stood.

"And are you going to the doctor's house now?"

"Yes, I will."

Bailey could see Leonard was serious about approaching the doctor this evening. All three men slowly walked out of the office into the warehouse.

"Thank you both for all you've done. I am so relieved you have not been harmed, Uncle Jun. And Bailey, you truly are a good friend."

Bailey unbolted the door, opened it, stuck his head through it, and whistled. The door remained open, and within seconds Leonard heard footsteps quickly approaching, and one of Bailey's workers entered the warehouse.

"Have you met Rangi?" asked Bailey with a smile. "He was keeping an eye on the place while we talked."

Leonard looked at the young man and shook his head.

Bailey laughed, "He's been following you off and on for the last couple of weeks."

Leonard looked shocked, "He has? I haven't seen him before." He reached out and offered his hand to the young Māori.

"You weren't supposed to," Bailey laughed. "Rangi, I want you to keep an eye on Leonard as he goes to John Street and make sure he doesn't get into trouble."

Rangi nodded and looked at Leonard, and grinned.

"Leo, remember, keep mouth closed. No come to shop!" reminded Uncle Jun.

Chapter Nineteen

It was a little later than Leonard had hoped. His meeting with Mr Bailey and Uncle Jun had taken considerably longer than expected. He was still shaken by what he had learned, and the knowledge he was to be targeted for execution was overwhelming - actually, it was unbelievable. The good news was that Uncle Jun had not been killed and, by disassociation, had kept him safe. He didn't blame the man for not keeping in contact, Leonard mused, in the same circumstance, he would do the same to protect a friend.

Perhaps equally disturbing was the revelation that a trusted friend had abused their relationship and was sharing information with a Chinese triad. It was disheartening and highlighted to Leonard the value of true friends. A friend wouldn't do that to a friend. He spared a thought for Jonathan and hoped it wasn't him. And if it wasn't him, then it must be someone else – then who?

He stood near the bottom of John Street and looked up at the dark street as a gust of wind rattled some sheet iron against a nearby building. Trees disturbed by the errant wind rustled, and a dog barked obsessively at something unseen. He secured his hat and strode up the street. Somewhere lurking behind him, Rangi, the young Māori, followed, and he felt a little more secure.

His anger had provided him with resolve and perhaps even a little courage. His step was determined, his stride purposeful, and he walked to Dr Schrader's residence with little patience for the detestable little man. As he walked up the hill, he saw the partial outline of the large house silhouetted against the night sky. A yellow glow seeped from a ground-floor window - someone was home.

On the opposite side of the street, he saw a curtain move. Backlit from the glow of a candlestick, he saw the darkened figure of a woman peek from behind drapes. Leonard smiled with the revelation every neighbourhood had a Mrs Theodopoulous. Ahead and to the left was Schrader's home. The large property had two entrances: one for a wagon and presumably a horse that could graze inside the expansive and enclosed grounds, and the other for people. He swallowed; his mouth was dry, and he still had the lingering aftertaste of the coarse whiskey Bailey had given him. He took a big breath and lifted the latch. The gate screeched ominously as it opened and again as it closed. Overgrown shrubs and thin reedy trees lined the path that curved around to the front of the house leading to a large door - the crunch of gravel beneath his feet seemed very loud.

A set of two wide steps was all Leonard needed to climb when the door opened with a rattle. With an oil lamp in hand and filling the entranceway stood Dr Lawrence Schrader.

"Who is there?" queried the doctor, squinting into the darkness.

Leonard ignored him and slowly climbed each step with deliberate slowness. He wanted Schrader to experience some fear.

"You! What do you want here?" yelled Schrader. He took a small half-step backwards as he recognised his caller.

"I have something of interest for you," replied Leonard as he reached into his jacket and extracted the *Derriere Doctor* story. He held the folded document into the light for the doctor to see.

"What is the meaning of this intrusion? Be gone with you!"

"Do you not care to know what this document contains? After

all, your future hinges on this." Leonard waved it again, only closer to the doctor's face.

"What is it? Speak up, man, it's late, and I haven't all evening."

Leonard unfolded the paper and held it close for Schrader to examine. The doctor leaned forward, raised the lamp and began to read. After twenty seconds or so, Leonard removed the article.

"Do you know what this is?"

Schrader's mouth was open, and his jowls rippled as he shook his head.

"This is a story I've written for the *Evening Standard* newspaper. Did you read the title? It says "Derriere Doctor Shames Hospital." It's a wonderful title, don't you think?"

Dr Schrader's eyes narrowed as he tried to compose himself. "Your accusations are baseless, and there is no foundation. What you've written are pure lies. It's meaningless."

"But not when the claims made in this article are supported by eyewitness accounts and victims of your lewd acts."

Schrader licked his lips; his small tongue darted from his mouth like a snake. He said nothing.

"Your career will be over, you've abused the trust placed in you, and you'll never practice medicine again. You'll be humiliated." Leonard placed his hands and the document in his pocket, hoping the doctor wouldn't see them trembling.

Leonard could see Schrader's mind working as he weighed up his options. He heard a footfall inside the house, and he risked a look behind Schrader but couldn't see past the man.

"What do you want, Mr Hardy, is it money, women? I know your type, and certainly, I know your fondness for the Oriental beauties, hmmm. Come inside, your pleasures await," Schrader smirked, his self-confidence returning.

If ever there was a time where Leonard felt the need to lash out and strike a man, this was it. It took all his self-control to remain level-headed and calm. "What I want, Mr Schrader, are two things. Firstly, you will authorise the immediate discharge of Mrs Leyton from Mount View Lunatic Asylum."

Schrader laughed. It was more like a shriek as his voice pitched up an octave. Leonard waited until he was finished.

"And the second, you will release Miss Mary Worthington."

This time Schrader didn't laugh. But his eyes betrayed him, and Leonard saw a brief look of uncertainty. Schrader wiped his brow with the sleeve of his jacket, his mind working furiously as he stalled for time to think.

"Ward Sister Worthington, eh." He snickered and took a step closer to Leonard. "She is my insurance. Let me tell you what I will do. You give me that document, and tomorrow I will see your friend released from Mount View. You have my word." He gave Leonard a sneer. "But for the time being, I will continue safeguarding the virtuous Miss Worthington." He held out a fleshy hand, an indication he wanted the document.

Leonard laughed and pulled the paper away and out of Schrader's reach, then leaned forward, causing him to take a step backwards. "You will do exactly as I tell you," he hissed.

From the yellow glow of the lamp, Leonard could see Schrader's eyes darting everywhere. His shifty eyes wouldn't meet his gaze.

Leonard's mind worked furiously as he considered his options. At least Schrader admitted to having Mary but wouldn't guarantee when he would release her. This was a problem.

"Nurse Worthington is not here, she's being held somewhere

else," Schrader quickly offered, "and don't worry, she's come to no misfortune."

"I want an assurance she is unharmed and well.

"Why Mr Hardy, I'm a physician, I have sworn a Hippocratic Oath. You have no reason to suspect I would cause her harm or duress. You'll have to trust me."

"I have every reason to suspect you'll do that, which is why I will go to the police."

Schrader squealed in delight, his confidence returning. "Do you take me for a fool? She's not here, and the police will find nothing. Anyway, it will take me some time to have word sent to expedite her release. Meanwhile, my friends may still have the opportunity to enjoy her." His expression hardened. "Hand it over." He curled his fingers on his outstretched hand repeatedly.

Leonard fought his composure. He clamped his jaw tightly together to refrain from screaming at the horrible little man.

He couldn't allow Dr Schrader to read the entire document; he would see there were no names of victims or witnesses. He pulled the article from his pocket and folded it until it was narrow and thin, almost like a taper, he leaned forward and placed the end into the top portion of the lamp that Schrader held. It caught fire, the flames quickly racing up the length of the paper. "If you are lying to me, I can always write another," he stated with teeth clenched. Before the flames reached his fingers, he dropped the burning document to the porch and watched it turn to blackened ash.

"How will I know you don't have a copy and publish it anyway?"

"Because I gave you my word. I will expect Mrs Leyton to be discharged at midday, and I expect Mary Worthington to be released by tomorrow evening or sooner. He turned abruptly and walked away. His anger threatened to subjugate common sense and reason.

Behind him, he heard Schrader speak; his voice cut through the night like a knife. "Everything is better with a smile," he taunted.

Leonard stopped, closed his eyes and sought strength, he willed his body not to turn and rush the fat little man but instead to walk on and walk away. The words Schrader used were Mary's words. 'Everything is better with a smile,' she always said.

He could hear Schrader's high-pitched laugh as he strode down John Street.

He intended to walk down John Street and find a Hansom cab to take him home, but he was so distraught and angry that he couldn't focus and just continued walking. *Poor Mary, what must she be going through?* The thought of Schrader fondling and touching her made him sick to his stomach.

Leonard didn't greet people he passed; he acknowledged no one and walked only with rage for company. He passed Wellington Hospital on his right and gave it a cursory glance that only evoked his anger even more. He reached the end of Riddiford Street and continued down Adelaide Road. By the time he reached the Basin Reserve, he had cursed Lawrence Schrader in every imaginable way and was still thinking of more disparaging admonitions when he paused outside Mount View Lunatic Asylum. He allowed himself a little respite from his invectives and thought of what he had achieved this evening. All going well, and if Schrader could be trusted, Bridgette would be discharged at midday tomorrow. Certainly, that was some consolation, but what Leonard feared was Mary's condition. Schrader had suggested others were holding her, and for what possible reason? It didn't make sense.

On his left, up Buckle Street, was the Mount Cook Depot. He could go to the police, but what did he have? He had nothing to support his claim that Mary had been abducted. Yes, he could prove she was missing, but he had no evidence to link Schrader to her disappearance. Again, he was fuming. *Why does the law have to be so damn literal*, he wondered?

He arrived home tired and emotionally drained. His thoughts returned to the triad that wanted to see him killed. It was a preposterous notion to be killed because he knew too much. What did he know that posed such an extreme threat to them? He began heating water on the stove so he could bathe, and as he waited, he returned to disseminating what he'd learned - fact by fact. He didn't achieve much as a knock on the door inconveniently disturbed his concentration. He walked to the door and cautiously opened it.

"Good evening Leonard," greeted Constable Yates with a smile. "I happened to be nearby and thought I would pay you a little visit as I did not see you earlier today."

"Hello, Tim. Please come in."

Leonard showed Tim to the living room while he checked on the water heating on the stove.

He returned to the living room. "Any news?" Tim asked.

Leonard was about to tell him of the outcome of his visit with Schrader, then decided against it. Uncle Jun's words resonated clearly. "No, I had some late work to do."

"I hope you ain't angry with me for not wanting to go with you to see the doctor, but you know how it goes, occupational hazard." Tim laughed. "I have to be careful not to put myself in a compromising situation."

"No, not at all, I completely understand, think nothing of it."

"So you didn't go to see him then?"

"No, I took your advice; I can't involve myself in criminal activities, and I just got carried away a little."

"That's good; I'm relieved you saw sense."

The thought of a trusted friend betraying him was unthinkable. If Constable Yates was indeed sharing information with the triads, then some false information may prove interesting.

"What do you know about the triads, the Chinese gangs that operate in Wellington?" Leonard asked, quickly changing the subject.

Tim leaned back and crossed his legs. "Not a lot, really; they're involved in the normal things you'd expect. But we seldom can prosecute them. Why do you want to know?"

"Those things they are involved in, does that include the buying and selling of women?"

"I've heard rumours, is all, but possible, I'd say."

"And where would they keep them if they had them?"

"I can't help ya, Leo. Why do you ask?" Constable Yates pressed the point.

"It was something I'd overheard when I was at the wharf the other day," Leonard lied again.

"What did you hear?" The constable leaned forward.

"It was at the office of the harbour master. It was nothing, as I only heard part of the conversation, a snippet about raiding a building on Frederick Street and enslaved women. That's why I'm asking if you knew anything about it."

Constable Yates sat back, he looked puzzled. "No, I haven't heard a thing. But why would they be talking about that at the harbour master's office?"

"Someone was asking questions about ships bringing them in. Was probably nothing," said Leonard as he went back to check on his water.

"Were the police there?" Yates shouted.

"No, not at all. It was the clerks who were talking."

Constable Yates was silent for a few moments and walked into the kitchen, "I'll let you take your bath, Leonard. I'm going home, I'll see myself out. Good night."

"Good night, Tim."

Leonard heard the constable walk down the hallway and leave through the door. It was bath time.

The sound of birds woke Leonard early on a beautiful Saturday morning. He lay in bed listening to their different voices. The twitters and tweets, the whistles, squawks and chirps, it was like a dawn cry, a greeting to the world. He liked the sound; it made him feel happy, despite his impending execution and the challenges he still faced.

He crawled out of bed, opened the curtains and sat on the edge of the bed, thinking about the day he had planned. A little later this morning, he would have brunch in Oriental Quay at a popular tea room with Meredith, and then he would go to Mount View just before midday and wait for Bridgette. He hoped Meredith would agree to come with him. Part of him doubted Schrader would honour his word, and Bridgette would forever remain constrained inside the oppressive facility. 'Hope is eternal,' as Mae had frequently reminded him. But her favourite quote was the most relevant, 'After rain comes sunshine.' And so motivated, Leonard padded into the kitchen and lit the fire, put water on the stove and looked forward to his morning coffee.

An hour and a half later, Leonard ambled down Oriental Quay and looked out across the harbour and the spectacle of ships at anchor. Some had colourful flags and pennants hoisted that flapped enthusiastically in the light breeze, while others had tenders and small boats plying to and fro, ferrying people from ship to shore. Oriental Quay didn't have a typical sandy beach where children could build sand castles and dig for treasure; instead, under the watchful eye of parents, they gingerly stepped over rocks and played with childish glee at the water's edge. Small wavelets lapped ashore while seagulls patrolled backwards and forwards, selfishly looking for scraps and hand-outs. Along the parade, a few couples strolled, enjoying the morning sunshine, while a wagon loaded with pigs made its way from one of the farms that overlooked Evans Bay and headed into town. Leonard leaned against a tree and watched Meredith arrive alone in a cab.

They weren't typical tea rooms as one would expect in the conventional sense, nor were the amenities even refined. The tea rooms were, in fact, a 'lean-to', where a local farmer and his wife offered a limited selection of home-cooked snacks, tea, and scones under a temporary shelter. Some potted plants, a hedge and a few mismatched tables and chairs provided comfort and protection from the elements, and while the tea was acceptable, the scones, cream, and jam were exceptional. For a modest amount, one could enjoy the refreshments and the panoramic view of the seashore, the harbour and the green Tinakori hills beyond.

Leonard was licking cream from his fingers as Meredith watched, unimpressed.

"That isn't normal morning fare, Leonard." Meredith shook her head. "And look at you; you're making a real hash of it."

"It isn't possible to enjoy the scones and not end up with cream and jam on your hand," said Leonard once he'd determined his fingers were clean.

"It is possible if you don't heap cream and jam in such huge quantities on top. It isn't a feast, Leonard, it's brunch. For most civilised people, it's an occasion to enjoy a light, late morning refreshment with some delicate treats. You've turned it into a banquet for the entire Hardy clan."

Leonard ignored her and wiped his mouth with a serviette, and grinned. "Now, m'dear, tell me about Jonathan. How's he doing with this Hastings legal case that will define his career?"

"He scolded me, you know. He was quite agitated that I went to your home unescorted after he forbade me."

"That's Jonathan; he isn't happy unless he's quibbling. You're both similar in that regard," he laughed, enjoying the opportunity to torment her. Meredith tossed her serviette at him. She couldn't help but smile.

After a moment's pause, Meredith's expression changed. "Leonard, do you think Bridgette really will be discharged today?"

"I'd like to think so. We'll know soon enough, won't we?"

"And Mary?"

Leonard shook his head, "I'm unsure. I wish I knew. We'll have to wait and see."

"This is just horrid. I can't believe all these things are happening to us all. Our lives have been completely turned around, and poor Bridgette lost her husband, and we lost a friend." She looked sad.

Leonard reached over and gave her hand a reassuring pat. Meredith was a widow and had lost a husband unexpectedly; she understood what Bridgette was going through.

"How will Jonathan respond to you sleeping at Bridgette's and looking after her?"

"He isn't going to be thrilled about it when I tell him."

Leonard looked thoughtful. "Meredith, please be circumspect about what you tell him. Yes, he is a dear friend, but I don't know with certainty if anything you tell him is being passed on to others and then getting back to Hastings. Please be careful what you say."

"Oh, Leonard, you're overreacting. Jonathan's no fool; he wouldn't pass on any information that could hurt you."

"You do not know that with certainty, Meredith. I implore you to be careful what you say to him about this mess," Leonard pleaded.

"You are such a worry-wart sometimes." She shook her head.

"It's time to go to Mount View. Will you come with me?"

"Yes, and then if Bridgette is discharged, I will go home, pack some things, and meet you at Bridgette's a little later.

They walked along Oriental Parade towards downtown and waited for a tram at Courtenay Place that would take them to Mount View. Leonard was apprehensive; he had little faith in Schrader and doubted honour played any part in the man's sordid life. It was nearing midday, and before long, they'd know one way or another if Bridgette would be discharged.

They hopped off the tram, walked back towards the Basin

Reserve, and stood at the bottom of the carriageway that swept up into the expansive grounds of the asylum.

"They don't have a particular fondness for me up there. Apparently, Schrader poisoned them against me. I'm wondering if it's best I wait here, and you go up and meet Bridgette," Leonard suggested.

"What do I tell them?"

"Just say that you are here to receive Mrs Leyton who is being discharged at the request of Dr Schrader."

Meredith looked tentative. "I hope that works, Leonard."

Leonard smiled, "Of course, it will," he said with more conviction than he felt.

She turned and, with an air of determination, walked up the carriageway and disappeared. Leonard began pacing; he walked past the gated entrance towards Adelaide Road, returned, looked up the carriageway, and then continued towards Ellis Street and back again. Each time he passed the entrance, he looked up expectantly, hoping to see them both walking down.

It was on his fourth lap when he saw her. He just stopped and stared; he couldn't believe it. Meredith's joyous yell shocked him into action, and he immediately ran up the carriageway to meet them. As he drew closer, he could see Bridgette weeping and smiling simultaneously, and by the time he arrived, she was crying uncontrollably and launched herself into his arms. She held him tightly as if her life depended on him, and he could feel her entire body trembling with pent-up emotion. He let her cry and consoled her with soothing words and reminded her that the ordeal was finally over, and slowly he could feel her begin to relax as her breathing returned to normal. Meredith, also in tears, decided to join in, and Leonard embraced them both. A speck of dust caused him to quickly wipe his eyes when they weren't looking.

Bridgette's impassioned reaction was more than just being discharged from the asylum; it was an outpouring of grief. It was knowing she had friends that cared for her enough and sought her release, and it was relief at being free and no longer being held against her will. Comforted by her two friends, Bridgette soon calmed down and dabbed her eyes with a borrowed handkerchief from Leonard when she could finally talk.

"Leo, how did you manage it?" Bridgette asked.

"It's a long story, Bridgette. Let me get you home first, and we can explain it all to you," he offered. He picked up Bridgette's suitcase and couldn't stop grinning.

Bridgette immediately ordered Leonard to open the windows and allow fresh air into the house, and now she was fussing and cleaning and wouldn't take a moment to sit and rest. Leonard observed her and could see much of her spirit had returned. He explained how he'd convinced Schrader to authorise her discharge but left out other details, preferring to protect her emotionally from further worry. He couldn't avoid explaining to her about Mary's disappearance, and he hoped she could provide some insights or clues as to how Schrader had managed to abduct her. Bridgette had stated empathically it was a kidnapping but could not offer any helpful information. As Schrader had surprisingly honoured his word and arranged for Bridgette's discharge, Leonard fully expected Mary to be released later today. He hoped Schrader was telling the truth about releasing Mary and that she was also safe.

Bridgette told Leonard he must leave once Meredith arrived.

She'd waved a finger and told him she intended to have a bath and it wouldn't be decent for him to tarry around her home while she attended to personal matters. Leonard required no further prompting as he had plenty to do and think about; his only request was to send word to him when Mary returned.

Leonard was looking out the open window, enjoying the cooling breeze when he felt the presence of Bridgette standing beside him.

"Leo?"

He turned to face her.

"What will I do about my work at the hospital? I don't know how I can perform my duties and interact with that appalling, vulgar man."

Leonard had already anticipated Bridgette's reticence to return to work and had given the matter some thought. "I think the best approach will be to speak to the hospital superintendent and detail Dr Schrader's continued inappropriate behaviour towards nurses. I think you will find his view on the matter may differ from his past conclusions."

"I have no flair for discussing those matters with the superintendent, and I will likely make a real muddle of it," Bridgette stated with a worried frown.

"I will speak for you and Mary, so you do not have to concern yourself with it. My goal is to see Dr Schrader removed from his responsibilities, and I'll take steps to ensure he does not practice medicine again."

"You're serious about this?"

"Yes, Bridgette, very serious."

They could both hear the clatter of a suitcase banging against the wall as Meredith struggled with its weight.

"I think I should offer some assistance before she destroys the house," offered Leonard as he went to lend a gentlemanly hand.

Chapter Twenty

The sun and warmth of the afternoon reluctantly gave way to a cooling southerly breeze. Dark oppressive clouds rolled in during the late afternoon and now, as evening fell, obscured all celestial bodies that normally shone so bright. While Leonard hoped for help from all sources to free Mary, he doubted he'd receive divine guidance from above on this dark and cold night.

If there was anything positive he could take from chill and clouds – they would likely bring rain. *That will make the city fathers happy*, he thought. Wellington was prone to water shortages, and rain to replenish supplies was always welcomed.

He locked his door, turned up the collar on his coat, and pulled his hat lower on his head. Then set off down Marjoribanks Street towards Courtenay Place to enjoy a delicious meal at Mummy Thomas's Dinner and Desserts.

Unlike the name suggested, there was no 'Mummy Thomas' or even a 'Mummy' for that matter. A burly and excessively hairy gentleman known simply as Willy was the proprietor of the popular dining establishment, and once upon a time, there may have been a Mummy or a Thomas, but if there were, then they had long been forgotten. The menu was non-existent, and Willy cooked only one type of dinner; tonight, it was pork chops with potatoes, beans, carrots and gravy. Locals affectionately called the place *Yummy Mummy's*. Willy's meals were superb and far outweighed his skills at human interaction, as the poor gentleman who had just received his meal could testify. Leonard stood behind the man at the counter as he complained bitterly he didn't want gravy.

Willy sighed, looked up at the man and spoke as if talking to a child, "If you don't want gravy, then scrape it off the plate."

It was difficult not to laugh; Leonard had heard it all before, and unsuspecting customers always fell victim to Willy's caustic retorts. Motivated by his appetite more than indignation, the customer quickly took the plate and sat at a table to eat.

Willy dished a plate for Leonard without saying a word and looked questioningly at him.

"Apple pie," said Leonard keeping words to a minimum, just as Willy preferred.

"No, you won't, you'll have peach pie," Willy stated gruffly.

Leonard was disappointed, he wanted apple pie.

"Serves you right, shoulda been here earlier, is all gone," informed Willy after seeing Leonard's expression. He must have felt a modicum of pity for his customer as an extra large dollop of cream was added to the pie, but no other words were exchanged. Leonard handed over the money, took both plates and sat at his customary place near the window.

It wasn't until he'd finished his dinner that he devoted time to glancing outside. With his appetite largely satiated, he took his time with dessert and people-watched as he placed another generous spoonful of peach pie into his mouth.

While Wellington was labelled a city, its European population didn't exceed twenty thousand people. It was relatively small. As a result, it wasn't uncommon to see the same faces time and time again, even though you'd never actually been introduced. Some would nod a friendly greeting in respectful recognition when you encountered them; others would just look away. So it wasn't abnormal to happen upon friends or acquaintances when out. At first, Leonard wasn't surprised when a cab stopped next door to Mummy Thomas's Dinner and Desserts and Mr Beaumont climbed down. He'd seen his employer in and around Wellington on occasion, so with mild curiosity, he watched him straighten his coat, reposition his hat and disappear into the premises of the adjoining building.

Leonard's attention returned to his peach pie, and with surprising patience, he bided his time with measured spoonfuls. Once absolutely positive no cream remained in the bowl, determined with the expert and well-practised use of his finger, he returned the dishes to the counter as a courtesy to Willy. He turned up the collar on his coat, pulled his hat down securely and stepped out into the fresh night-time air He prepared himself to visit Bridgette and hopefully see Mary. He began to walk towards the tram, then stopped, turned around and retraced his steps.

A weathered sign that advertised 'Woodcarving & Furniture' identified the premises immediately adjacent to Mummy's that Mr Beaumont had disappeared into. Leonard knew of the company; they were a frequent advertiser with the *Evening Standard,* and presumably, Mr Beaumont was discussing business early on a Saturday evening. What surprised Leonard was the presence of a large muscular Oriental man standing in the darkened recesses of the doorway. When Leonard stopped to read the sign, he inadvertently stood directly facing the man. The big man didn't look delighted that Leonard was taking an unusual interest in him and the enterprise of Woodcarving and Furniture while the shop was closed for business.

"That's my employer in there," Leonard attempted to appease the Oriental monster by offering a friendly smile to reinforce his harmless intentions. "I work for the *Evening Standard*."

The man took a lumbering step forward, then another, which coincidently was when Leonard remembered he needed to catch a tram to Bridgette's.

Safely on the tram, Leonard considered the minder who stood guard outside the furniture shop. That in itself was peculiar. Obviously, he was there to safeguard someone, and it was very unlikely to be Mr Beaumont, as he had arrived unaccompanied only ten minutes earlier. Therefore the man was protecting someone with whom Mr Beaumont was visiting. A furniture and woodcarving shop required a minder? This was a curious development, and Mr Bailey's words and warnings permeated his thoughts.

Bridgette answered the door and looked to be in remarkable spirits; the bath had done wonders, and she appeared to be back to her usual self. After a peck on both cheeks, she quickly told him Mary had not shown.

Leonard paused in the doorway, his mind working furiously.

"Come inside, Leonard, it's cold," suggested Bridgette, seeing the worry on his face.

Once inside, she took his hat and coat, and he greeted Meredith. She, too, looked apprehensive.

"What should we do, Leonard?"

Leonard sat and thought of the possibilities. After a minute or two, he leaned forward. "Mary may still turn up; the night isn't over yet. But I believe if she hasn't arrived by now, then she is unlikely to."

Bridgette had joined them and sat beside Meredith on the settee.

"I think I will pay Dr Schrader another visit. That's the only way to resolve this."

"Will you go tonight? Meredith asked.

"No, tomorrow."

"I don't think that's a good idea, Leonard," Bridgette said.

"I wish there was another way." Leonard stood. "I think it is time to go home, and if Mary does show, please notify me."

Leonard spent the following day at home working on various tasks that needed his attention, but his thoughts were never far from Mary and the ordeal she must have endured. No message came, and he assumed she had still not been released. One thing became evident; he would visit Schrader this evening and wouldn't leave the man's home until he knew Mary was safe. He'd had enough of Schrader and the games he played.

He stomped around the house in anger. His feelings towards Dr Schrader were less than gracious, and there were times when he'd considered dropping what he was doing and just confronting the man. However, common sense prevailed, and he waited impatiently for the time when he was to meet with Bailey and Uncle Jun in the early evening.

Leonard stood outside Bailey's warehouse, and as before, he could see a light burning behind the shades pulled across the windows. He looked around, wondering if Bailey's worker, Rangi, was watching. All appeared quiet, and Leonard banged on the door with his fist, stood back and waited.

Within moments, he heard the bolt being slid back, and Bailey beckoned him with a meaty arm.

"Welcome, Leonard," Bailey greeted once they were inside the warehouse. "Jun is in the office."

Leonard nodded and followed Bailey.

"Uncle Jun," beamed Leonard when he saw the tiny man.

"Leo, is good to see you, sit, sit."

The three men all sat in the same place as their previous meeting.

After the pleasantries were dispensed with, Leonard immediately told them of Bridgette's release from Mount View.

"But your friend Miss Worthington hasn't shown up yet?" Bailey asked.

"No," Leonard shook his head. "I'm going to visit Schrader again when I leave here." His anger was evident.

Bailey's eyes flicked to Jun's in unspoken concern.

"Leo, I ask friend, he say, no white lady at doctor home. Only many young Chinese girl.

"Yes, that doesn't surprise me. Schrader said she wasn't there, but he knows where she is, though."

They remained silent for a few heartbeats.

Bailey finally looked up. "What have you discovered about who is talking about you to the triad?"

"Ah yes, the traitor. I can rule out Meredith Rosewarne."

"Oh, why?"

"Because I told her about my plan about the *Derriere Doctor* article. If she had talked of it to Jonathan McGready and he, in turn, told Hastings, he presumably would have informed Schrader."

It was a convincing argument, reasoned Bailey and Jun.

"And now we can eliminate Miss Rosewarne and the nasty fellow Pembroke from the list. So that leaves your employer,

Beaumont and the constable."

Leonard turned to Uncle Jun, "Are you aware of the Wood Carving and Furniture business beside Mummy Thomas's?"

Uncle Jun nodded while Bailey shook his head. "He a Hongmen and he own business, he own many business here," informed Jun. "Why you need to know?"

Leonard explained how he witnessed Mr Beaumont entering the building on Saturday evening and the huge man standing guard outside.

"Then it appears Beaumont is your traitor," suggested Bailey.

"I'm not sure. The *Evening Standard* has many customers; some are difficult to deal with and require personal visits. Just like how I visit with you, Bailey. Mr Beaumont may only have been conducting business. However, I fed some misinformation to Constable Yates on Friday, so it will be interesting if my comment to him created a reaction."

"And what did you tell him?" queried Bailey.

"I told him that I overheard at the office of the Harbour Master how the police were investigating Chinese slaves and intended to visit some Frederick Street establishments on Saturday searching for girls."

Bailey looked puzzled. "As a constable, wouldn't Yates know that?"

Leonard shook his head. "Not necessarily."

Uncle Jun looked up. "On Saturday, many Chinese girl taken away from Frederick Street. You know who I saw?" Without waiting, Jun continued. "I saw big nose man, Hasting."

"It's Yates, it has to be!" exclaimed Leonard. "He's been telling people about me."

Bailey stood from his chair and, with his huge hand, rubbed his chin. "I wonder if Inspector Gibbard is aware."

Leonard was seething. Constable Yates had, under the guise of friendship and a willingness to help, deceived him. "What can I do about Yates?"

"Again, Leo, you don't really have proof. Of course, you could whisper in the ear of Inspector Gibbard, but whether he believes you and acts on it is another matter."

Uncle Jun listened to both men banter. "What about your friend Mary? Does constable know what you do, Leo? Or is big mouth closed?"

"I have told him nothing."

"And you go to doctor house?"

"Yes, when I leave here."

Uncle Jun shook his head. "Not good idea Leo."

"I agree with Jun, you should reconsider. Go and talk to Inspector Gibbard first, see what he has to say."

"But that won't be until tomorrow after I finish work; that will be another night for her. And then what, wait while he decides what to do? If he doesn't believe me and chooses to do nothing, then I'm back where I started." Leonard shook his head, "And don't forget my impending execution, so there's no option, it has to be tonight."

"I no trust police, who you go to tell? Hastings and Yates no good, and inspector?" Jun raised his hands. "I no trust."

Bailey returned to his seat and leaned forward. "Leo, listen to me. Schrader is obviously involved with that triad or some type of illegal activity. These people will protect him, and if you go to his home, you put yourself at risk."

"If I go to Schrader's home and can somehow find out where

Mary is, and ask him to release her, then we have proof, a witness to testify against the doctor."

"You think Hongmen will let your friend go? I no think so, Leo."

"But Schrader did authorise Bridgette's discharge, so why can't he release Mary?" reasoned Leonard.

"Because the triad didn't have Mrs Leyton, but according to Schrader, they have Mary," Bailey offered.

Leonard sat back in his chair and looked at the dusty beams above him. He realised what both his friends said was very true. They wouldn't risk letting Mary go, which put her in even more peril if she wasn't already dead. He thought of Uncle Jun's words again, and that gave him all the incentive he needed to go to Schrader's home; he had to find out. His mind was made up, and he sat forward. "How well do you know Inspector Gibbard, Bailey?"

"I take care of him from time to time, and he comes here when he needs something. I wouldn't say we are close friends but certainly acquainted. I could send a message to him and have him come here after you've finished work tomorrow. What do you say, eh?"

"Yes, let's do that."

Uncle Jun shook his head. "No trust, bad idea."

Arrangements were made, and Leonard left the building and walked down Taranaki Street towards home. Once he reached Courtenay Place, he turned right and looked for a cab.

Leonard climbed down from the cab at the intersection of John and Riddiford Streets in Newtown, or as the locals referred to it as 'Howell's Corner,' the same place where he asked the cab to stop when he went to Schrader's home two nights ago.

The streets were eerily deserted; he could hear a baby crying from a nearby house, and the same metal siding still clanged. He thought its erratic cadence was surely an irritant to anyone living in proximity. A steady breeze blew off the southern hills and raced down Riddiford Street, leaving a chill in its wake, a stark reminder summer was at an end, and colder weather would soon follow.

As before, the stars and moon provided almost no light, and street gas lamps didn't extend this far south, so it was dark, forbidding, and Leonard felt very much alone and vulnerable. Truth be told, he *was* frightened and would derive no pleasure in confronting Dr Schrader again, but a sense of moral duty gave him strength. While he had difficulty admitting it, he had affections for Mary that extended far beyond a casual acquaintanceship that further motivated him.

Leonard didn't think for a moment that Bailey and Uncle Jun believed he'd returned home. They knew he'd go to Schrader's, and he wondered if Rangi had been given instructions to follow. He looked around, but it was too dark to see anything; the night was black. With his hands buried deep in his coat pockets, he began to walk nervously up John Street.

Here the properties were more prominent, and many sections were still vacant. Mature trees were plentiful on the spacious one-acre lots, and the wind whistled eerily through them. Branches rubbed together and created strange creaking sounds and eliminated the intimation of human habitation. Many homes he passed were already dark; a few had lamps burning from upper rooms, and Leonard wondered if the doctor had retired for the evening. It wasn't that late, but on a cold Sunday evening, people probably preferred the warmth of bed.

Schrader's home was just ahead on the left, and Leonard stopped, wanting to observe the house for a moment or two before he continued. He quickly looked around to ensure no one was watching and then moved across to a tree that stood on an adjacent empty property and peeked out from behind its trunk at the large house. Lamps were burning in multiple rooms, but he couldn't see inside as all the curtains were drawn. With all the lights burning, he assumed Schrader was home and may even have guests. His first thought was to turn back and go home, but on reflection, he decided if Schrader was entertaining, he might be more willing and agreeable to see reason rather than risk embarrassment in front of his friends. He watched for a minute or two longer, then stepped out and slowly walked towards the noisy gate. Thankfully it was already open and wouldn't screech as it did two nights ago. Leonard entered and moved onto the gravel path that curved around to the front door of the large house. His heart began beating furiously, and he paused to gather his wits. His mouth was suddenly dry, and he needed to urinate badly.

Being here didn't seem like such a good idea now, and he wished he had someone else with him like Constable Yates. Then he recalled with disappointment that Yates wasn't a friend at all. A sudden noise startled him and made him jump as a cat ran through the garden onto the porch and around the side of the house. He tried to control his breathing, but it was difficult. He stood still and gathered his willpower, his resolve, and with determination, took another step only to have a hand firmly clamp down onto his shoulder from behind.

He would have leapt, but the hand held him securely. His heart that had only just begun to settle down now pounded again; he'd never felt more terrified in his life.

"Look what we have here, then," said William Hastings. He gave Leonard a shove, then grasped him by the collar propelling him forward. "Out for an evening stroll, are we?"

Leonard stumbled, but Hasting's tight grip kept him upright. "Take your hands off me!" He managed to say with bluster. He tried unsuccessfully to shrug off the hand that held him securely.

Hastings laughed and once more propelled him towards the porch and steps. Leonard had no option but to comply; the ex-constable was much larger and stronger and enforced his will with physical strength Leonard couldn't equal. Hastings, without bothering to knock, opened the door and pushed Leonard inside Dr Schrader's home.

Leonard stood blinking in the light, and standing before him in the hallway was Dr Schrader, wearing a puzzled expression.

"I found him outside, snooping he was."

The doctor's expression slowly changed from puzzlement to a sneer. "Bring him in."

Hastings manhandled Leonard down the hallway into a large, lavishly decorated living room. On entering, he saw two young Chinese girls sitting on a settee; they were clothed in expensive dresses, but it did little to hide their apprehension.

"Where is Miss Worthington? You promised to let her go, and you haven't done so," Leonard said with as much pretence as he could muster.

Hastings laughed.

Schrader slowly made his way around the room and picked up a glass tumbler from a low table, held it to his lips and downed its contents. He held out the empty glass for one of the girls to take and turned back to face Leonard. "I told you, I don't have her." He snapped his fingers impatiently, and one of the girls obediently refilled his glass from a decanter and handed it back to him. "It's you I am more concerned with." He looked at Hastings. "Was anyone with him?"

Hastings shook his head.

"Are you sure?"

"Yes, I waited and watched to see if he was being followed, I saw nothing."

"Even better that you came here alone. What for? Just to ask about your friend who I don't have? She must mean something to you?"

"You told me you had her and would release her last night after you authorised Mrs Leyton's release."

"I lied. I wanted to give you false hope."

"What shall we do with him? Want me to toss him outside back onto the street?" asked Hastings.

Schrader looked thoughtful for a moment. "No, put him in the room with the others."

"Doctor, I don't think that's a good idea..."

"William, he knows too much, we can't release him. Anyway, now that we have him, uh, four-eight-nine has expressed his desire to meet with Mr Hardy. Then you can throw him in Evans Bay."

"I'm not sure 'bout killing him, doctor. There's been enough of that lately, which only draws more attention to us and me, which I don't need. I have enough problems without adding to them."

"I don't care how you do it, just make sure you do. But not until after four-eight-nine has had a word or two with him, and that won't be until after he returns tomorrow."

Leonard was shocked. His mouth was open, but he couldn't speak; he was dumbfounded. He looked from Schrader and then turned to Hastings. "Let me go, I insist!" he finally managed to yell. He was near panic.

Hastings gave him another violent shove towards the hallway. Leonard had twisted his body to look behind at Hastings and was off balance and fell heavily. He put his left arm out to break his fall and landed awkwardly on the hard wooden floor. He immediately felt a sharp stab in his shoulder and resisted the urge to scream. It was almost unbearable, and he lay on the floor with his eyes tightly closed, hoping the searing pain would dissipate.

"C'mon, up ya get." Hastings grabbed him by the collar and his good arm and hauled him upright.

This time Leonard did yell, the movement causing him unbearable agony. Once standing, he cradled his left arm with his right; it seemed to offer some relief, but the pain was still excruciating. Schrader did not comment and watched with an amused expression. His focus returned to the girls and the late-night guests he was about to receive.

"I've hurt myself, please let me go," gasped Leonard between quick ragged breaths.

Hastings ignored Leonard's pleas and pushed him down the long hallway towards the rear of the house. He opened a door and stepped back. The stink of unwashed bodies, sweat and fear, oozed out. A lamp hanging from the wall illuminated the space, and Leonard was pushed in – he froze in horror. Devoid of any furnishings, the room was all but empty except for two young Chinese women who sat cowering on grimy pillows with dirty blankets wrapped tightly around them. They crouched silently, their eyes cast down in submissive fear.

"Sit," ordered Hastings.

Leonard had no option but to obey, and as he stepped closer to the girls, he could see they were tied to each other and then chained to an iron bar firmly affixed to the floor. They were captives, prisoners – slaves. He shook his head in pity and disbelief. He turned to Hastings, his own pain temporarily forgotten and spoke slowly, "What have you done?"

Hastings didn't reply. With practised ease, he clamped a metal band with a crude locking mechanism around Leonard's ankle. A sturdy chain restricted his movements to only a few steps - he was now a prisoner. Satisfied Leonard wasn't going anywhere, Hastings stood and peered down his nose at him. He sneered and, with perverse pleasure, launched a brutal kick at Leonard's chest. Pain and then blackness enveloped him.

Chapter Twenty-One

Leonard awoke in unbearable agony, and his shoulder hurt in a way he couldn't believe possible. He kept his eyes tightly closed and realised he was breathing in fast, shallow breaths. He forced his mind to relax, and slowly his breathing returned more or less to normal. Without moving, he opened his eyes and took in his surroundings. He was lying on the floor and on his side and was still in the filthy room with the two girls in Dr Schrader's house.

It was a medium-sized room about ten feet by fifteen feet. On one side was a narrow window near the top of the wall, and an opening on the floor in the corner, presumably for human waste. Understandably, the girls lay as far away as possible from it. A metal bucket with water and a tin cup sat in the corner, and two empty food bowls lay discarded near the door. The lamp was still burning, and he assumed he had not been unconscious for long.

He tried to sit up, and a groan escaped his lips; it hurt too much to move, and he almost passed out again. Seeing him struggle, the girls slid over to help him sit. One girl went to hold him around his shoulders, and he involuntary cried out in pain. It startled her, and she retreated to the corner.

"Do you speak English?" he asked between gasps.

Both girls answered with blank stares, and he didn't know enough Chinese to be able to communicate with them. While still lying on his side, he pointed to his injured shoulder and mimicked a wince. With his free hand, he indicated for them to try again.

They seemed to understand, and one girl moved near his head

and placed her hand under his good shoulder; he tried to move a little to help. The other girl slid over and put her hands under his chest. Leonard braced himself for the pain that would follow.

Very slowly, he began to move. The girls pushed and lifted together, and with the support of his good arm, he managed to sit upright. The aching was unbearable, and he felt lightheaded; despite the cool evening air, he broke out in a sweat and was sure he would pass out again. One girl thoughtfully placed a pillow behind him, and Leonard gingerly eased back into it and leaned against the wall at an angle that protected his injured shoulder. Sitting helped, and his shoulder didn't hurt quite much in this position. He cradled his arm with his good hand across the front of his body and forced himself to breathe deeply. He shut his eyes and thanked them in Chinese.

One of the girls, who looked to be the older of the two, was studying Leonard carefully. She spoke to her friend at length. She grabbed a pillow, removed the dirty pillowcase and tried to rip it, but it was too difficult. Both girls attempted together, each pulling the opening in a different direction, and finally, it tore down its entire length. Leonard was wondering what it was they were doing. Now the pillowcase was twice as long, and they stopped pulling before they tore it completely in two.

The older of the two girls sat in front of Leonard and, with the help of the other, placed her arm in the pillowcase, keeping her arm in the same position as his. The other girl passed the newly torn portion of linen around her neck and under her arm and pretended to tie the ends together. Leonard saw what they were doing; they were demonstrating their idea to him. He knew it would hurt, but the sling would keep his arm and shoulder from moving. He forced himself to smile at them and gave a simple nod for them to continue.

He still wore his coat and wanted to take it off before putting the sling on. He pointed to his coat, and they nodded, they both understood. It took a while, and after gently sliding his coat from his good arm, he moved and leaned forward so they could move it away from his back. Then came the hard part, sliding the sleeve over his bad arm and shoulder.

He put his faith in them, shut his eyes, and leaned forward slightly. One girl eased his good arm back and out of the way and then slowly pulled the sleeve over his bad shoulder and arm. The coat's smooth inner lining and their patience helped; the sleeve slid off easily, and the pain was just tolerable. It worked, and he was unencumbered.

After a few deep breaths, he shut his eyes again and prepared himself for the next step. He had no option but to allow the girls to put his arm in the sling; he knew he had to immobilise his arm and shoulder, and he couldn't do it alone. Moving his arm to put in the sling would move his shoulder, which was where the pain was. They cautiously began, and he screamed - the blackness was welcoming.

"What the hell is goin' on in here?" Hastings yelled. He looked down at Leonard, who was blinking back to consciousness. "Oh, is you." He laughed and closed the door leaving the three of them alone again.

Leonard swallowed dryly. Beads of sweat had formed on his face, and one of the girls softly wiped his brow. The other brought him a cup of water to drink. His arm was in the sling the girls had created. He felt some relief and could begin to breathe easier and relax a little. He thanked them again. In response, they draped his coat over his good shoulder and chest to ward off the evening cold.

The girls were young; Leonard thought maybe about fifteen or sixteen years old. They were beautiful in the classic Chinese sense. They each wore a shapeless tunic made from a coarse material; it almost looked like hemp. While it was obvious they were held prisoner, they did not look unhealthy or poorly. If these girls were brought to New Zealand to be sold, then they needed to look good. It didn't make sense to neglect or abuse them. That was the only thing in their favour.

They all heard the approaching footsteps, and then the door clattered open, and Hastings re-entered the room. He looked at Leonard and grinned. "Feelin' a little poorly, are we, Mr Hardy?"

"My friends know I'm here. And with certainty, they'll report my absence to the police. It would behove you to release these girls and me before you make it worse," Leonard appealed.

Hastings wasn't listening; he was unshackling the girls from the metal bar. He spoke to them harshly in fluent Chinese. Both girls were still chained to each other, and he led them out of the room. One began to weep and looked back over her shoulder at Leonard.

"If I was in your shoes, I'd be worryin' about meself, I would," laughed Hastings as he closed the door.

He was alone. He could hear the distant muffled sounds of voices and laughter coming from another part of the house. Perhaps the doctor had guests, he thought. Leonard was exhausted, suffering and frightened; he closed his eyes and drifted into a troubled, shallow sleep.

The sound of the door opening woke him with a start. Hastings had returned and brought back the youngest girl without her friend.

"Where is she, what have you done with her?" he asked.

"We've found her a lovely home. But you needn't worry about her," Hastings replied as he chained the girl back to the metal bar.

"I require medical attention... I'm in great pain."

"Well, fancy that, and isn't it a coincidence that a doctor lives here." Hastings stood with the girl securely re-attached to the bar and looked down at Leonard. "Is it your left shoulder?" he asked in mock sympathy. He lifted his left foot, pulled back slowly and drove it forward with force, this time to Leonard's right shoulder.

Leonard couldn't move out of the way. He jerked in reaction, causing his bad shoulder to move, and he screamed.

The girl screamed.

Hastings laughed. "That's for the Royal Oak Hotel, you whoreson!" He stormed from the room, slamming the door.

Leonard was gasping for air. The kick had hurt, and his arm had taken the brunt. It felt a little numb, and he hoped it hadn't done any more than cause a bruise.

He looked at the frightened girl and managed a weak smile. He wondered what had happened to the other girl. Perhaps the guests were here to purchase them, which would explain why they led them out. Presumably to parade and show them off.

Now he understood why Dr Schrader took such an interest in the Chinese girls. He oversaw all their needs when they needed medical attention. Even once they were sold, he would continue to treat them through his private practice and the serious cases he would admit to the hospital, including the ones who were experiencing difficulties during childbirth. It all made logical sense. It was an elaborate scheme and begged the question of how many girls were there and how long had Schrader been doing this?

He looked over at the young girl with compassion and sadness. "I am Leo," he pointed to himself. "Leo," he repeated. He pointed to her and inclined his head in question.

"Ping," she replied and offered a hint of a smile.

He offered her a formal Chinese greeting that Mae had taught him, which made her laugh. No doubt in response to his poor pronunciation, he presumed. He wanted to do something to help the poor girl, but there was little he could do. She looked cold, and he indicated she should come and sit beside him and share body heat. She arranged the chain to allow easier movement and dragged a pillow and blanket with her. She sat down on his right side and leaned into him very gently so as not to cause any more hurt.

They both sat that way for a while; she had been crying and he could feel her body heaving from time to time. The house had quieted down. The voices he'd heard earlier had gone, and he wondered if Schrader had gone to bed when he heard footsteps approaching the room. They weren't the heavy footfalls of Hasting's large stride; these were different.

The door opened, and Lawrence Schrader walked in. His round body looked like it would burst through his clothes. His nose wrinkled at the odour as he glanced around the room, eventually settling on Ping.

"Where is Miss Worthington?" Leonard asked quietly.

Schrader reluctantly tore his eyes away from her and stared at Leonard. "I told you I don't have her."

"You quoted something she always says, and you wouldn't know that if you didn't have her."

Schrader looked puzzled.

"Everything is better with a smile," Leonard reminded him.

The doctor laughed.

"Oh yes, Miss Worthington, or can I address her as Mary? The lovely Mary...."

"No, you may not," interrupted Leonard, "you will not defile her by the familiar use of her name!"

Schrader ignored the outburst and continued. "She has exquisite skin, remarkably soft. In fact, she is quite a beautiful woman, good breeding, I'd say. Her neck is delightfully slender, long and perfectly proportioned to match her flawless cheekbones. And those eyes...." He sighed and looked upwards as if remembering her. "And her form, yes, classic in the true sense, wouldn't you agree, Mr Hardy? But it is unlikely you'll ever see her again."

"What have you done with her?" Leonard's frustration was building, and he desperately wanted to lash out at the man, but he was helpless and injured. All he could do was listen, and even that was proving to be painful.

"I told you, I do not have her, although I do know where she is," he taunted.

"Where then, tell me, has she come to harm?"

"Oh, I wouldn't say she's come to harm." Dr Schrader's expression hardened, and his eyes became slits as he stared at Leonard. "She's not in Wellington, and I believe she had to rush off to see her poorly aunt."

Leonard's mouth opened.

"According to her messages, Miss Worthington stated her aunt had influenza. And for you layman, that's inflammation of the lungs ... quite a serious malady, and potentially fatal if not properly treated. But you needn't concern yourself about the condition of Mary's aunt, she's been in good hands, and I expect Mary will be making plans to return to Wellington any day now. A shame you will not be here to greet her."

Leonard was stupefied, "What messages? No one received any messages!"

"Dear me, I apologise, I've been remiss. Ward Sister Worthington did leave some messages at Wellington Hospital reception, and I took charge of them and volunteered to ensure prompt delivery, and that responsibility completely slipped my mind. Age must be creeping up on me." Schrader smiled, but his eyes showed no warmth.

"You are a demented and sick man!" Leonard yelled.

Schrader had already turned and exited the room. The door closing was an emphatic statement that he held the power, and Leonard's life was in his hands.

He was totally at the mercy of that nasty, little man.

Mary had left messages, but no one had ever received them. Schrader had kept them. And, of course, the message he'd left for Meredith that she never received. Schrader must have taken that one as well. The woman at reception, the severe unfriendly one, was no doubt complicit and part of Schrader's little circle of colluders. Who else, he wondered? How many people were involved with Schrader and Hastings? And the people who purchased the girls, were they European or Chinese and how many were there? It saddened him to think of these young girls being bought and sold like mere chattels.

Leonard leaned against the wall in despair. Ping lay against him with her filthy blanket pulled to her chin, and he looked down at the top of her head and her long black silky hair. Unusually his thoughts turned to Mary, and not Mae, and the immense relief he felt at knowing she was safe and not in the hands of Schrader or his accomplices.

More footsteps sounded in the hallway, and Leonard looked up expectantly, hoping it was a friend coming to rescue him. The door opened, and a tiny middle-aged Chinese woman entered. She glanced at the bucket and, made sure it still contained water, removed the two empty bowls and the lamp before she left the room, leaving it in total darkness. Now, more than ever, even though Ping was with him, he felt truly alone and terrified.

The gift of sleep never came, and unable to find any position that offered comfort, he spent a disagreeable night in abject misery. He spent countless hours tormented by thoughts of Schrader, death and despair. He concocted plans of revenge and imagined being able to retaliate and see Schrader and Hastings beg him for forgiveness. He thought of what he wanted to share with Mary and if he dared to whisper to her his feelings. The self-acknowledgement that he loved her, without guilt, came as a surprise. He imagined the last meal he enjoyed and the peach pie with all that heaped cream...

With no freedom of movement, Leonard tried everything he could to find physical relief and eventually settled on a rotation of three positions that provided only minutes of respite. He must have dozed from time to time as when he opened his eyes, he saw the beginning of daybreak as grey light filtered in from the narrow window above them.

Ping lay curled up on the floor beside him. She slept solidly with an occasional whimper, but her breathing was regular and constant, and she slept without interruption throughout the night. He moved into position number two, closed his eyes and prayed for sleep.

The sound of Ping stirring woke him, and he opened his eyes and watched her as she stood and stretched. He must have fallen asleep, as the sun now streamed through the north-facing window, but any sleep he'd had did little to help. He wanted desperately to stand and ease his cramped muscles. His entire body ached. He could feel a severe bruise on his right arm where Hastings had kicked him while his left shoulder throbbed intolerably.

Carefully he twisted his body and rocked onto his knees, and then with his free hand on the wall for support and balance, he slowly raised himself. Seeing what he was doing, Ping lent a willing hand and helped. Seconds later, he was standing.

Ping looked at the hole in the floor in the far corner, then at Leonard. She needed to relieve herself, and this posed a problem. He considered his few options and then pointed to his coat that lay discarded on the floor, Ping retrieved it for him, and he pulled it over his head and faced the wall away from the hole. It was all he could think to do to preserve her dignity.

Within moments, he could hear her tinkling, which immediately triggered his need to go. It would be challenging to say the least. He felt her movement beside him, and he removed the coat, pointed to the hole, and then himself. She took the coat, copied his actions, and placed it over her head. Modesty be damned, he needed to go. He kicked the chain closer to the hole with his foot and, with one hand, managed the delicate task.

It was Monday morning; Mr Pembroke would be beside himself at his failure to arrive at work on time. Would he initiate any action to find out why Leonard had not arrived? And if he did, what would he do? Mr Pembroke did not know where Schrader lived or the fact that he'd even gone to see the man. That left Bailey and Uncle Jun. Did they suspect he was now chained to an iron bar in a house on John Street with an injured shoulder? Bridgette and Meredith knew he was going to Schrader's home, but it would be days before they realised he was missing. Leonard felt hopelessness set in, but the reality of his situation was a fact he needed to face.

Soft footfalls came from outside in the hall. The door opened, and the Chinese woman entered carrying two rice bowls. She wrinkled her nose at the smell and quickly placed both bowls and two pairs of chopsticks on the floor. She spoke harshly to Ping, who answered with a single word, then exited the room and hurriedly shut the door.

Ping was evidently thinking more clearly, and quickly realised Leonard couldn't feed himself. It wasn't possible for him to hold the bowl and chopsticks at the same time. She indicated if he preferred to sit. Leonard shook his head, he wanted to remain standing. Against his protestations, Ping held the bowl close to his face and insisted that he eat first. Realising the futility of saying no, he began to eat the bland meal. She expressed surprise when she saw him expertly use the chopsticks.

After eating, Leonard remained standing and leaned against the wall. He spared some thought to his conversation with Schrader the previous evening. He was curious as to who was the person that wanted to meet him and the number four-eight-nine the doctor referred to.

Mae had begun teaching him the Chinese language and only some elementary basics, but he knew his numbers. He turned to Ping and said, "*Si – Ba – Jiu.*"

Her response was immediate; she looked around the room

fearfully, placed her finger to her lips as a warning, and then rattled off a complex explanation he couldn't understand. His expression must have conveyed his incomprehension. She tried a more straightforward version and spoke slowly, "*Huainanren*."

She had said something about a man, a bad man? Ping feared four-eight-nine, so he must be the person Uncle Jun spoke of. He had also said his Hongmen friend had told him a decision would be made at a meeting during the week if Leonard were to be killed. Schrader had said they were having a meeting on Monday evening with four-eight-nine. That was tonight!

Leonard thought it preposterous. Why would anyone want to see him killed? He'd done nothing and learned nothing that wasn't readily available to anyone. It was fantasy, yet here he was chained to a bar in a house with the threat of death looming over him. There was more to this. Of that, he was sure.

Dr Schrader did not attempt to enter their prison, and Leonard guessed he'd departed for work. If anyone was going to rescue him, then this would be the time to do it, as it seemed only the older Chinese housekeeper was home.

Ping had been busy and gathered all the pillows and blankets, except one, keeping that for herself. She positioned them in a way that would offer more comfort to Leonard when he sat. She helped him as he eased into the soft pillows, and within moments his eyelids grew heavy. The incessant throbbing of his shoulder was only just tolerable if he didn't move.

The day was spent in a state of half-sleep and suffering. He wasn't conscious of the minutes turning into hours and the hours dissolving into evening. The slightest movement brought immediate sharp, stabbing pains, and he began quick, shallow breaths until the torment subsided into a barely manageable ache. At times, Ping tended to him and brought him water, repositioned an errant pillow and did what she could for him, but there was little else to be done.

It had not long grown dark when the door opened, and Schrader's dour housekeeper entered the room. She brought their evening meal and hung the lamp from the hook. It was the same as the morning meal, consisting of rice and a few vegetables, and it was bland and tasteless. He didn't feel like eating, but Ping insisted with stern words he didn't understand and ended up feeding him herself.

It dawned on him that the mystery man, Trent Halpern, who was part of the Patrons of New Zealand organisation, had been here. Schrader had held him captive too. Of course. That explained the mark on his ankle and the rice in his stomach. Leonard reasoned that when they found his body, the medical practitioner would find exactly the same things. As Alex was dead and his notes had been taken, no one would see the similarities. But Trent Halpern had escaped from here or while being transported before being killed, so there was still a sliver of hope.

As Leonard mentally prepared for his second night chained inside Schrader's house, he began to lose faith that he would be rescued. He reasoned that they should have come for him by now; someone must have realised he was missing. He turned his thoughts towards escape.

Chapter Twenty-Two

The clump of heavy footsteps from the hall frightened him; he blinked open his eyes, tried to stand, and failed. Ping helped, and with some difficulty, he was almost upright when the door burst open, and Hastings strode arrogantly in. He glanced around the room to ensure everything was in order, and finally, his eyes settled on Leonard. Ping separated herself and edged deep into the corner.

"Look at you. Have you no pride, Mr Hardy? What a sorry state you are in." He shook his head in mock pity. "I suggest you pull yourself together; someone wants to meet you, he does." Hastings approached Leonard, crouched down and fumbled with the manacle, eventually releasing him from the chain. He grabbed Leonard by the collar, causing a sharp intake of breath, and pushed him roughly out into the hall and down towards the living room.

Schrader sat smugly on a settee with a Chinese girl sitting on either side. On another settee, opposite Schrader, sat an older distinguished Oriental man. He was impeccably dressed and, with self-assuredness, exuded authority, a man used to issuing commands and expecting them to be obeyed. He regarded Leonard with cold, lifeless eyes. Behind him, and alert in the shadows, stood another Oriental man; he was neither large nor small and appeared indifferent. Leonard assumed he was a bodyguard.

"Where is Yates?" asked Schrader.

"He'd be outside, having a wander round, I expect," replied Hastings.

Schrader nodded. "Looks to me as if you have a fractured

clavicle, Mr Hardy. Your shoulder is drooping, and I understand such an injury can be quite painful," he said without an offer of medical help.

Leonard was too exhausted to play games with him and chose to remain silent. He wasn't offered a seat.

Schrader picked up a tumbler from the table, took a sip and leaned forward as much as his stomach would allow. "This is Fung Ti Chu, Mr Hardy. He's been interested in making your acquaintance for quite some time, and I'm pleased I can facilitate the introduction." Leonard turned to face the gentleman who had yet to speak a word. The stranger leaned forward and looked intently at him. Leonard met his gaze and held it - at this point, he didn't care if his own curious gaze offended the man. Could this man be four-eight-nine?

Fung Ti Chu was unfamiliar to Leonard; he'd never heard of his name or seen the man before; he was a total stranger. In a small city like Wellington, it was unusual not to encounter wealthy and influential people from time to time. On occasion, they liked to be socially active and involve themselves in civic and community affairs and enjoyed the public attention their status afforded. Mostly, they relished being seen to flaunt their wealth, but this man he'd never chanced upon before.

Mr Fung's eyes were unsympathetic, void of life, like the eyes of a dead person. It made Leonard uncomfortable to look at him; obviously, the man knew this, which was why he continued to stare and intimidate. Leonard was past caring. The man could look at him all night long if he wished.

"You've created quite a few challenges for me, Mr Hardy," Mr Fung finally said. He spoke excellent cultured English without any trace of a Chinese accent. "For the most part, you are an innocent party, or perhaps 'victim' might be a more apt noun. Sadly for you, your persistence has caused me considerable embarrassment." Fung's expression hardened. "I do not like to lose face, Mr Hardy; it affects my business, and I take it personally."

Mr Fung leaned back on the settee and extracted a leather case from his pocket. He opened it reverently, debated which cigar was worthy of selection, and then delicately removed a candidate. He sniffed it once, enjoying the pleasing aroma and held it up as his bodyguard leaned forward, cut the cap, and then held a flame from a match. He puffed a time or two until it was lit. He replaced the case back into his pocket, inspected the glowing end with regard, tilted his head back and blew a gentle stream of smoke upwards. He turned his attention back to Leonard.

In response, Leonard blankly returned the stare.

"I'm quite disappointed. I expected a more...." Mr Fung dramatically pretended to search for the appropriate words, "... worthy adversary."

"You are sadly mistaken, we are not adversaries. You are unfamiliar to me, and while we've never met, I sincerely doubt I would waste my energy and knowingly make the acquaintance of a simple criminal," Leonard stated with disdain. He heard Schrader's reaction to the insult directed at his honoured guest.

Hastings stomped from the living room door he guarded and drove his fist into Leonard's back.

Leonard screamed and fell to his knees, gasping for air. It was a savage and cruel blow, and Hastings knew precisely where to strike him to inflict damage. Leonard kept his eyes firmly closed as he tried to overcome the stabbing pain.

"You'll treat Mr Fung with respect," barked Hastings as he

resumed his position.

With effort, Leonard staggered to his feet.

Mr Fung ignored Leonard's insult. "Both you and your wife, Mae-Ling, have been a thorn in my side for some years. By the honour of a simple agreement, I was bound to overlook some wrongs and weather the financial loss, but you overstepped the parameters that kept you safe. This unpleasant situation you now find yourself in is your own doing, Mr Hardy."

"Again, you are mistaken. As I understand it, I'm in this predicament because of you, not because I choose to be," hissed Leonard.

Hastings stepped forward and delivered another vicious punch. This time Leonard was ready and swivelled at the waist, and his fist struck bone, directly on his hip. He heard Hastings gasp, yet the jarring impact still drove Leonard to his knees. With strength he didn't know he had, he struggled to his feet and regained his composure.

Mr Fung smiled.

Leonard's mind was struggling to make sense of what the villain talked about - he was confused. He risked a look around the room.

Schrader sat back on the settee with his beverage; both Chinese girls were uninvolved but fulfilled their duties by sitting as close as possible and feigning undying admiration and affection for him. *It just shows that* Leonard thought contemptuously that *it is possible to purchase love.* Hastings returned to the door and stared at him scornfully down the length of his nose while he held his injured hand. The bodyguard remained impassive.

"The incident at the Royal Oak Hotel was the last straw. Really, that little game you played cost me substantially." He gave a sideways glance at Hastings, who decided at that moment to look down his nose at the floor. "Appearances are everything. I cannot be perceived as weak and can no longer overlook all that has happened." Mr Fung leaned forward and rolled the cigar tip in the ashtray. "Over the years, you've humiliated me by flaunting your relationship with Mae-Ling when you had no right to do so. She was mine; I paid for her and belonged to me. That represented a significant and substantial financial loss." Fung's expression hardened. "It's about honour and respect. And if I can be quite frank, I've had enough, and to hell with any previous agreements. I now deem them null and void!"

Leonard shook his head slowly; what was he talking about? The man was deranged. It made no sense.

"Something you wish to add, Mr Hardy?"

Before he could reply, the living room door opened, and Hastings stood aside as Constable Yates entered.

Leonard looked behind him and immediately felt anger and betrayal. He clenched his jaw and glared at Yates.

Hastings moved to the other side of the room and took a seat as Yates took his position guarding the door.

"Hello, Leo," said Yates without any shame or guilt. He didn't wait for a response and turned to Schrader. "I've checked around the property; other than your men," he inclined his head respectfully at Fung Ti Chu, "there's no one around, and the street is empty."

Schrader nodded, and Fung didn't respond.

Leonard had never felt so consumed by rage; he detested all the men in this room except the bodyguard who had given him no cause, although he believed if he thought long and hard, he'd probably find a reason to dislike him too. He wanted to grab each one by the neck and throttle till they breathed no more. He closed his eyes, lowered his head, and sought strength to overcome the pain, and humiliation and challenge these deplorable men before him.

"I see you feel remorse for your actions," said Mr Fung, misreading Leonard's body language. "Perhaps you are wise after all," he laughed, but his outburst contained no mirth. "Mr Yates, would you please escort Mr Hardy back to his room? Now is a good time for us to discuss his future." He looked dismissively away and puffed on his cigar.

Constable Yates stepped forward and roughly grabbed Leonard's good arm, "This way Leo, time to go back."

Leonard fought his pent-up emotions and resisted the urge to lash out. He knew if he did, he'd forfeit his life in this room.

Yates opened the door and pushed him through. Once in the hallway, he closed the door and leaned close to Leonard's ear. "Trust me, Leonard, but please be quiet."

Leonard was dumbfounded; *what is this*? Now Yates is seeking forgiveness and wants me to trust him? The man nauseated him. Resigned to spending another night chained in the oppressive room, he stepped towards the prison down the hall only to be held back by Yates.

"This way." He still maintained a firm grip on Leonard's arm and pulled him in the other direction towards the front door. "Hurry," he breathed.

Silently Yates opened the door, and directly ahead through the opening, Leonard could see indistinct shadows moving in the darkness. They were people but indistinguishable. Was this the moment... the time when he would be killed and then tossed into the ocean like a sheep carcass, only to bloat and fester on wave tops like young William? He tried to resist and pull away from Yates, but he held him firmly.

"Leo, calm down," hissed Yates, "I'm here to help. Quickly, now." The constable tugged Leonard's arm.

Tentatively, Leonard allowed Yates to direct him outside; it was difficult to see as his eyes were still attuned to Dr Schrader's brightly lit living room. A shape materialised out of the gloom and quickly walked towards them; he immediately recognised the approaching figure of Inspector Gibbard.

Gibbard quickly looked at Leonard and saw the sling and his sorry and dishevelled appearance. "My God, what have they done to you?" He shook his head in anger. "This way, Mr Hardy, quickly now."

Leonard was puzzled. At first, he believed the inspector was part of Schrader's circle of accomplices, then the realisation hit him - these men were here to offer assistance and to rescue him! Another form appeared out of the darkness and dissolved into a person he easily recognised and trusted. It was Bailey!

"Go with him," urged Yates, who then spun and quickly returned to Inspector Gibbard, and they began pointing and talking urgently in hushed tones.

It was all too much for Leonard. As he stood outside the doctor's home, he knew Schrader and his accomplices were inside, callously deciding his fate. Decisions were being made about whether he should live or die. As if he was nothing more than a lifeless possession. He wanted to scream at them, to yell that they had no right.

"Come, Leonard, let's get you away from here and to the hospital," suggested Bailey in a calm, soothing voice.

Overcome, Leonard couldn't speak.

Men in uniform carrying firearms moved past them and headed for the house. Some went around back, others stood near the front door; Inspector Gibbard directed them all to their locations like a battlefield General preparing for his finest hour.

Leonard stopped and turned to Bailey. "Inside, down the hall, there's a young girl, her name is Ping...."

Bailey needed no further prompting. He ran to Inspector Gibbard, who nodded in understanding and quickly jogged back. "She'll be taken care of, Leo, don't worry, come." Bailey gently helped Leonard down the gravel path to the street. Once on the street, he spoke to Rangi, who quickly ran into the darkness.

Within a moment or two, a covered wagon waiting a short distance away revealed itself and pulled up outside the house. Leonard recognised it as a conveyance from the hospital used to transport patients. A lamp lit the interior, and Leonard saw the silhouette of a nurse inside. Men were all around, not police but civilians, and they stood in small groups, like spectators watching events unfold. One man stood near the house, slightly apart from everyone else and observed from a position of moderate safety. From the light spilling out from the window, Leonard identified a stylish homburg hat and a tan overcoat. In question, he turned to Bailey.

"Apparently, you have some powerful friends, Leo. I understand that crusty, ole bugger Pembroke had some influence with that man," Bailey pointed to Henrick Mueller, "and he organised some civilian support for the police."

Leonard must have looked surprised because Bailey laughed.

"Look the other way, up the street Leo."

Leonard shifted his gaze to the other direction. More men stood in groups waiting, there were men everywhere.

"Those men are Chinese and Jun's men from the Chee Kung Tong. He ensured that the Triad couldn't mount a rescue and retaliate, and between the group down one end of the street and Jun's men up the other, the Triad cannot come near this house. Consider it a community effort. I wouldn't have believed it if I hadn't seen it."

"Is Uncle Jun here?"

Bailey shook his head. "No, he says he's too old to be out this late and involving himself in young men's activities."

Leonard looked around, "The guards, where are they?"

"Oh, they were taken care of a short while ago."

This was all too much, Leonard turned back to Mueller, who remained in the same place. He doffed his homburg in salute.

Shouting and yelling signalled that Inspector Gibbard and his men had entered Schrader's home, and judging from the sound of glass breaking and heavy crashes, the constables were meeting with resistance. Everyone outside tensed, partially in anticipation that the intrusion could escalate and in some concern that more of Mr Fung's men were near. Bailey urged Leonard forward to the wagon. The sound of Lawrence Schrader shrieking gave him pause; he looked back over his shoulder and managed a weak smile.

"Oh, Leonard, what have you done?"

He turned back to the covered hospital wagon, and in the light of its lamp, he saw Mary. Affected by exhaustion, pain and the stress of the last twenty-four hours, he couldn't find any words to express himself. He just stared at her open-mouthed. He felt his eyes well up and looked away, ashamed. He'd been so frightened and convinced that he would die this evening, and now... all this, and there was his

Mary. He wiped his eyes, swallowed thickly, and turned back to her.

She quickly descended the wagon's steps and immediately rushed to him and, much to Bailey's astonishment, smothered Leonard with a long, passionate kiss.

Through Leonard's shimmering gaze, he could see the tears on her face. She stood back, tilted her head slightly and looked at him in a way that left no doubt about how she felt. "I was so scared for you, Leo," she whispered so no one could hear, "I came to realise how much you mean to me and how much I love you."

The look on her face said more to him than he could have ever wished for. She reached out, took his hand to her chest, looked up, and kissed him on the cheek. With the help of Bailey, who shook his head in bewilderment, led him carefully up the steps and into the wagon.

With a rattle, a police wagon rumbled up the street and pulled up behind them with the horse snorting in excitement, while in the background, he could still hear Schrader shrieking. Someone was calling for stretchers to carry people out; Leonard hoped one of them was for Hastings.

He was in a daze and nothing made sense. He wanted to ask questions …

"Here, Leo, take this, it will help with the pain." Mary administered some laudanum from a bottle, and almost immediately, the potent opiate took effect. He could barely register being eased back onto a mattress.

He was in an opium-induced torpor and was barely conscious of the short journey to the hospital. On arrival, he remembered hearing stern words as Mary admonished someone for their carelessness and thoughtlessness, but it mattered not, he was safe, and she'd come and whispered those magic words that she loved him. He was fussed over, laid back, sat up and moved. With the laudanum unable to completely mask his pain, an occasional cry escaped his lips, but Mary was always with him, hovering nearby and overseeing his care. He was cleaned, his shoulder and arm were securely bandaged, and he now lay in reasonable comfort in the men's ward of Wellington Hospital. He was physically and emotionally exhausted, and sleep came easily.

The opiate fostered strange dreams, and his sleep was disturbed. He woke periodically and cried out in pain as he tried to move. But every time he opened his eyes, there was Mary.

Chapter Twenty-Three

"It's visiting time, Leo, and you have a visitor who has patiently waited for an hour to see you," smiled Mary.

"Who is it?" He asked. He knew he'd receive many visitors and was curious who'd be first.

"It's Mr Chen," she replied, "what a dear man."

"That he is," smiled Leonard.

Mary asked a probationer nurse to fetch Mr Chen while she assisted Leonard to sit up.

Within a short time, the nurse escorted the elderly man into the ward. Leonard and Mary watched as Uncle Jun shuffled towards them and looked around the ward in wonder. His head swivelled from side to side at the modern and brand-new medical facility.

"I no like, place is noisy, too many people, best to be home," said Uncle Jun dryly as he approached, then stood with his cloth cap in hand at the foot of Leonard's bed and appraised the patient with a practised eye.

"I will leave you alone to talk," offered Mary. "Please take a seat, Mr Chen."

With a look of worry, she assisted the old man to the chair and walked to the far end of the ward to observe. She knew what Mr Chen would tell Leonard and was deeply concerned about how he would take the news.

"You silly boy," Uncle Jun finally spoke. "You do foolish thing, you could be dead."

"I know, but I did what I believed was the right thing to do,

Uncle Jun. I had no options, and what else could I have done?"

Uncle Jun looked down at his lap where he was toying with his hat. He remained quiet. Leonard knew him well enough to know that Uncle Jun was preparing to say something important. This was his way and gave him time to formulate his thoughts.

With a sigh, Uncle Jun reached into his pocket and extracted a bottle. "Here, you take. Make you feel good and help shoulder heal. Better than what they give you here." He put the bottle on the bed and scooted his chair closer to Leonard.

"What is it?" Leonard asked.

"No worry, you take, is good." Uncle Jun didn't smile and paused for a few heartbeats. "I have to tell you story, Leo. But you must know, I made promise not to ever tell you. Now is time, and I break promise."

"Who made you promise?"

"Mae-Ling."

"Mae?"

Jun nodded. "For long time, I know Fung Ti Chu, he bad man. He bring many Chinese girl here, he take girl from family in China, sometime poor family sell girl, and he buy. Other time he take girl." Uncle Jun was fidgeting with his hat again. "One time he take beautiful China girl from family, and family very angry. They try to take back beautiful daughter but Fung Ti Chu he mad, and he kill girl mother and father and take beautiful girl to New Zealand. He make her slave and tied to other slave girl, and he do many bad thing to her. But he like this beautiful girl very much and he not sell, he keep her for himself." Uncle Jun shook his head sadly as if recalling the memory. "But girl very, very unhappy. One day she escape and run from him, and he cannot find her and she go to me in shop. She tell Ming and me sad story and I tell girl, no problem, I keep you safe. But Fung Ti Chu he have many spy, and they tell him where beautiful girl now live. He come to see me, and I say, you cannot have girl back."

Uncle Jun reached over and helped himself to a sip of Leonard's water.

Leonard had never heard any of this before; in fear of what he was learning, his stomach tightened into knots.

"Fung Ti Chu say to me, 'give me girl or I make big trouble for you'. I say to him, 'I make big problem for you – no have girl!'"

A few visitors and patients lifted their heads at Jun's passionate outburst.

"How can you stand up to the Triad and resist them with all their men and money? You are but a shopkeeper," asked Leonard.

Uncle Jun nodded. "I belong to tong, called 'Chee Kung Tong.' Is big Tong and have many men. Chee Kung Tong is good Tong we help Chinese people. Fung Ti Chu belongs to bad Tong, but not as many men."

Leonard nodded in understanding. He risked a quick glance at Mary; she was still at the other end of the ward with her arms folded. He gave her a nervous smile.

"So Fung Ti Chu, he decide not to take girl, he leave her alone. But one-day beautiful girl go to market to buy vegetable for Ming. One of Fung Ti Chu men see girl."

Leonard's stomach tightened. He knew where this conversation was going, and he could feel himself begin to tremble. Uncle Jun looked up from his hat and turned to face him. Leonard saw tears glistening in the old man's eyes. Unable to continue, he reached for Leonard's water again.

Leonard felt lightheaded and struggled; the effects of the laudanum made it difficult for him to control rational thoughts and emotions. What Uncle Jun was revealing was both horrifying and heart-breaking. His mind was in a state of flux, an amalgam of half-finished ideas and incomplete assumptions – so confusing. Why did Mae keep this from him? Why could she not have told him? Leonard shook his head in bewilderment; he was shocked. His poor dear Mae. He instantly recalled that room at Schrader's home – that prison – and he imagined seeing Mae tied to Ping and laying on soiled blankets and filthy pillows in abject fear. He felt such an overwhelming feeling of despair for her. Perhaps if she had told of her ordeal when they first met, he might not have genuinely understood - but now he did.

Uncle Jun took another big breath and looked again down at his hat that he slowly rotated on his lap and attempted to continue. "The man who see beautiful girl at market was Dr Schrader brother, he fat man, very bad health. He was angry at seeing girl. He remember her, and he want to take girl back to Fung Ti Chu…."

Leonard clearly remembered that day; it was a turning point in their lives.

Uncle Jun was struggling and brought his hands to his face. Leonard could see the frail old man's back rising up and down as his emotions got the better of him. Leonard was in no better shape.

"I understand how you feel, Uncle Jun, I feel the same. We both miss her very much. You needn't continue, I know the rest of the story."

Jun shook his head. "No, you don't." He sniffed. "When you and Mae fell in love, I was very happy, so was Ming, we happy for you both. I see Mae with big smile every day, she love you, Leo, and she good for you and you good for her. Even though you silly boy." Jun looked up and gave Leonard a toothless grin. "When you buy house, life for both of you is perfect. Mae is like daughter to me, and want her to be happy. But Fung Ti Chu believe he lose face, and Dr Schrader he angry and blame you for brother death. The more happy you are, the angrier Schrader and Fung Ti Chu become. They decide to have accident to kill Mae."

Leonard turned away.

"They think they are clever, and so at night, they light fire to your neighbour house and think your house will burn."

Leonard remembered the night of the fire at the Welshman's home; it was only by good fortune that the fire was seen, and although it was too late for the Welshman, it was not too late to save his home. But a deliberate act of arson? That thought had never crossed his mind.

"I hear of what they did and I go to Fung Ti Chu and tell him no more, or I make big trouble for him, or his business suffer. He say no problem, and stop. But he lie to me." Uncle Jun paused and looked at Leonard, their eyes met. "He patient and wait then he have Hongmen push Mae under wagon. He... he... responsible, and he tell his man... to push her." Uncle Jun was distraught and unable to carry on. Despite the pain, Leonard leaned forward and held the old man with his good arm.

Mary couldn't hear what was being said, but she had spoken to Uncle Jun earlier as he waited, and he had told her briefly what he had kept from Leonard all this time. What Leonard didn't know was Uncle Jun held himself responsible for Mae's death and believed he might have been able to do more to protect her. She dabbed at her own eyes as she saw Leonard struggling so hard with his emotions at knowing what had happened to his wife.

Uncle Jun separated himself from Leonard and helped himself to the water, wiped his nose on the sleeve of his jacket and continued. "When you find body of man outside your house, it was just bad luck. That man was prisoner in Schrader's house, but I not know why. He escape, and Hastings find him and shoot him and leave body."

Leonard's mouth fell open.

"But Leo, when you begin ask question, Fung Ti Chu and Schrader get angry again."

"Why, Uncle Jun?"

"Because Hastings have big problem because you keep ask question and no stop. You bring attention to him. Police want to know what Hastings doing. When big fire happen, Fung Ti Chu lose many business and now Hastings in trouble. They see you, Leo, and decide to kill you."

Leonard nodded guiltily.

"You no understand - Fung Ti Chu lose face because Mae-Ling choose you and not him. He hate you, and Schrader and Hastings no like you, understand?"

"I think so."

"I send many men to follow you, and Fung Ti Chu nearly catch you many time, you silly boy. But we keep watching you and stop them from hurting you. In end, you help us to stop Fung Ti Chu just like I tell him. He in gaol now."

Both men remained quiet as they remembered the woman they both loved.

"For all this time, Mae kept her terrible secret from me," Leonard said reflectively. He truly wondered how he would have reacted had she told him about her ordeal and how it may have affected their relationship. If that body had never been dumped in front of his house, he would never have learned what Mae had endured at the hands of Mr Fung.

"Uncle Jun? What role did Dr Schrader play in Mr Fung's organisation?"

"Fung Ti Chu, he go to China many, many time to get many girl, but he need New Zealand man to help sell girl. Schrader and Hastings, both men, they help sell China girl and are partner. Hastings, he introduce Fung Ti Chu to Schrader. Because he doctor is good for Fung Ti Chu and for girl. Keep girl healthy and no problem."

"How did you come to learn of where I was, that I was held captive at Schrader's home?"

"Oh, you talk to Bailey, he come see you. He good man, Leo. Now I go, is late and Ming worry, she want to see you when better." Uncle Jun creaked up from his chair and looked at Leonard. "Your lady friend, Mary, she good girl, you bring to see Ming." He pointed to the bottle he gave Leonard. "You take Chinese medicine, is good."

He paused a moment, and Leonard could see he wanted to say more.

"I sorry for not telling you about Mae. I tell her, 'you silly girl, you tell Leo'. She say you no understand and is better if you not know."

"Thank you, and I appreciate all you have done. But before you go, what happened to the girl who was tied up with me?"

Uncle Jun smiled. "Ping come to us, Ming look after her, she good girl Leo."

Mary and a probationer nurse walked over and stood near the

bed.

Uncle Jun patted Leonard's leg and shuffled away with the nurse. Mary sat down, picked up the bottle Jun had left, and toyed with it absentmindedly. "You know Uncle Jun told me earlier what he was going to tell you... How are you coping?"

"I have learned so much, and to be candid, it comes as a surprise and a shock. It explains a lot. It's almost a relief like a great burden has been lifted." He reached for Mary's hand. "The old man likes you and wants me to bring you to his shop to meet Ming."

Leonard felt someone watching, and he looked up to see Constable Yates standing at the entrance to the ward. "Don't leave, Mary."

Yates clomped confidently through the ward and stopped at the bed.

"Constable Yates, this is Ward Sister Mary Worthington, whom you've heard so much about."

Yates nodded politely at Mary and remained motionless.

Mary quickly located another chair. "Please take a seat, constable."

"I have some explaining to do and apologies to make, Leonard. I intend to do both if you'll allow me."

"Thank you, I welcome the gesture," Leonard responded coolly.

Yates looked at the bandages bound over Leonard's shoulder and arm. "Looks painful," he said in a conciliatory tone.

"If you knew the half of it."

Constable Yates cleared his throat. "The constabulary has been aware of the illegal activities of Fung Ti Chu for some time. It's almost impossible to infiltrate the Tongs as they tend to be very secretive. Not to mention they are often family driven, and a good grasp of the Chinese language is needed. We could not make any headway until you came along and challenged William Hastings. We had suspected him of being involved in the Tong for several reasons, and Inspector Gibbard felt that if you continued to rile him, as you were successfully doing, then that might open the door for us to investigate him more closely, especially if he made a mistake."

"And he did, the fire at the Royal Oak Hotel," Leonard suggested.

"Yes, he appeared to have a more than a casual dislike for you that we could not fathom. After the interview at the *Evening Standard* office, Inspector Gibbard realised you were really over your head and had little or no understanding of what you may have been up against. If you had known, you wouldn't have baited Hastings to the extent you did."

Leonard acknowledged to himself the truth of that statement.

Yates gave himself some time to frame his words.

"It was about three months ago when Hastings first began talking to me and hinting that extra money could be earned if I did a few small errands for him. Dutifully, I informed Inspector Gibbard, who suggested I accept; this might be a way to get close to Hastings. At first, I appeared reluctant and refused, then agreed to do one favour, which led to another, and so on. Then after the Royal Oak fire, the inspector suggested that I also befriend you."

Leonard didn't look happy.

"He said you had an uncanny knack of finding information that could help but were also impetuous and tended to be somewhat reckless. Becoming your friend meant I had a valid reason to be near you and could protect you if needed and at the same time learn about what you were discovering."

"But you gave me information about Hastings," Leonard

queried.

"Yes, and that information would have been easily obtainable if you would have searched for it. I gave nothing away that was sensitive, and I recall telling you that at the time. Anyway, we knew you'd been taken and held against your will that same night. But we couldn't affect an immediate rescue, and we had neither the resources nor the manpower to defend ourselves or protect you if the Tong had many men guarding Schrader's home. It was Mr Chen, uh, Uncle Jun who said he could provide able-bodied men that we could use only in the event things didn't go to plan."

"But what about Mr Mueller? I saw him at Schrader's house."

"I'm getting to that, Leonard. It was Mr Bailey acting as an intermediary between us, Mr Chen and Mr Pembroke. Mr Bailey informed your employer what had happened to you. Mr Pembroke, much to everyone's surprise, said he would arrange for additional men to be conveniently near if the situation escalated and further assistance was required. As you'd accurately guessed, Mr Pembroke admitted to being involved with Patrons of New Zealand. Henrick Mueller was only too happy to help. In fact, he even stated that the willingness of his men to work alongside the men of Chee Kung Tong for a common cause was proof that they weren't racist."

Leonard wasn't surprised that Mueller had used the incident to make a public statement to support his ideals.

"What is interesting, though, is that the Patrons of New Zealand had been watching Fung Ti Chu for some time as they suspected he was actively involved in human trafficking and were looking for evidence to take to the police. The man who was shot outside your home was one of Mueller's men who had been caught looking for information. This is why Henrick Mueller first approached you. He sincerely wanted to ensure you wouldn't pursue the matter as he knew how dangerous Fung Ti Chu was. And of course, Mr Pembroke had considerable influence over Mr Mueller, and we didn't hesitate to assume Pembroke played a central part in making sure you also came to no harm."

This was all too much for Leonard. "I can't believe all this... it's unbelievable."

"Yes, from your perspective, it is. But do remember, and as far as we are aware, neither Patrons of New Zealand or the Che Kung Tong did anything illegal – at no time did they break any laws."

"Schrader, Hastings and his cohorts certainly did," said Leonard bitterly.

"We are hoping to charge Hastings, Fung Ti Chu, and Lawrence Schrader with multiple counts of homicide, debt slavery, and a handful of other laws they broke. Others may yet still be implicated as the net is being cast far and wide."

"And yesterday, how did you arrange to be at the house and know you'd be guarding me?" Leonard asked while stifling a yawn.

"Hastings told me they were going to have a meeting to discuss a number of important issues, and your future was one of them. As Hastings was a participant in the meeting, he asked me to be responsible for making sure everything was secure and keep you locked up. It was easy to play that part."

"You had me fooled, and you made a good rogue. Played your part with a touch more enthusiasm than was needed," Leonard grinned. "But you put your own life in danger; if your ruse would have been discovered, then I hate to think what they would have done to you."

"That's my job, Leo." Constable Yates returned the smile.

"Will those men be charged with the death of Dr Leyton?" asked Mary, speaking for the first time.

"Yes, most certainly," Yates replied.

"And is Leonard still in any danger?"

"Miss Worthington, I can assure you he is in no danger except from himself," Yates smiled.

Leonard looked sheepish.

"I would like to apologise for my deception, Leo, although it is important that you understand that our friendship was real. Sadly, my profession requires that I act in a way that is sometimes contrary to my beliefs. In this case, I believe it was necessary and may have saved your life. I hope you will forgive me and still consider me your friend."

Leonard looked thoughtful for a moment, his expression neutral. "I understand that you put your life in danger for me; without your help, my carcass could now be floating in Wellington Harbour. By your actions, you saved not just my life but also, I hope, put an end to the activities of those despicable men, and saved the dignity and lives of many young women. I sincerely thank you, Tim."

"As do I, constable," added Mary.

Leonard had trouble keeping his eyes open, his lids growing heavier by the second. Constable Yates and Mary watched as he finally succumbed to Morpheus. Leonard's chest rose and fell in the regular rhythm of an untroubled man at rest.

While a good opium-induced sleep worked wonders, Leonard felt emotionally drained. What he'd learned about Mae was a revelation that changed his entire belief about his marriage and his wife. Of course, he loved her, and if she had told him of her ordeal with Fung Ti Chu, he wouldn't have loved her any less. But because she hadn't told him, he felt a little empty and disappointed. Parts of their relationship weren't real, they were fabricated, and it was deception regardless of her motive. She had told Uncle Jun she thought he wouldn't have understood, and she might have been right, but if love prevailed, then shouldn't he have been allowed to work through with her those troubling experiences? Perhaps it didn't matter anymore, he reasoned, turning away from the past and what once was seemed a natural healthy progression. The future held promise and hope.

The effects of laudanum dulled the pain and enabled him to doze. When he wasn't sleeping, he was aware of the activity in the ward around him. He watched as nurses went about their duties, tended to patients who complained bitterly about this or that, changed soiled bed linen and administered concoctions and potions to alleviate all sorts of ailments. He marvelled at their patience and dedication. It gave him ample opportunity to think about Mary.

Late the next morning, Leonard received surprise callers. Led by Matron and the surgeon superintendent, Inspector Gibbard followed meekly behind the solemn procession as it made its way through the ward to Leonard's bed.

A formal apology was offered to Leonard for the hospital's inexcusable and reprehensible behaviour and how they had already taken steps to ensure it never happened again. The superintendent suggested, with a nod and wink, that the hospital was better suited to administering and making its own adjustments to correct minor nuances and staffing issues without public interference. A casual hint that the *Evening Standard* did not write an article on the hospital's shortcomings and failures.

Leonard nodded appropriately when required to do so and asked for clarification that Bridgette would be welcomed back after a brief sojourn. Matron and the superintendent were in vigorous agreement, and he responded by telling them he would speak to the *Evening Standard's* publisher on their behalf.

They departed somewhat appeased, leaving Inspector Gibbard standing awkwardly at Leonard's bed. It was nothing more than a polite courtesy call, and after checking on his well-being, the inspector had a few pertinent questions to ask and enquired if he was agreeable to be a witness for the Crown. The inspector left the hospital soon after.

Bridgette and Meredith arrived shortly before regular visiting hours and updated him on what had transpired in the few days since his injury. Notably, Jonathan's excitement that Hollister, Hollister and Davidson, in addition to defending William Hastings, would also be defending Fung Ti Chu and Lawrence Schrader against numerous criminal charges brought against them.

Meredith had pointed out to Jonathan that she was pleased for him, and if his career saw advancement as a result, then she wouldn't stand in his way. Leonard found it particularly amusing that Meredith had also informed Jonathan that to better aid his prospects for preferment, his free time would be better served attending to his clients and law firm than to her. She added that he was unwelcome to continue to call on her. Jonathan had voiced his opinion forcefully and stated quite clearly that he found her request entirely unreasonable, further supporting her belief that she had made the right decision.

Their cosy little chat was cut short by the appearance of an elderly woman who slowly made her way through the ward; she smiled warmly at the patients as she passed them by and walked uncertainly towards the bed where Leonard lay.

"That's Mrs Pembroke," he whispered to his friends.

Mary stood and politely greeted the older woman, then kindly offered her a seat.

"Thank you, dear, but if I am interrupting something, then I can come back," she suggested.

"We were just leaving and have taken enough of Leonard's time," replied Bridgette. "We'll leave the two of you to chat."

"Oh my, this new hospital is quite something, isn't it, Leonard?" said Mrs Pembroke, still looking around the room. "You know, back when I was nursing, it was all so different."

Leonard smiled.

"And you must be Mary. I've heard all about you, dear, and I'm pleased you've returned. Leonard was very concerned for you."

Mary smiled at Leonard. "Thank you, Mrs Pembroke. I shall allow you both some privacy as I have things to attend to. If you need me, just ask."

Mrs Pembroke turned her attention back to Leonard and smiled approvingly. "A lovely young woman, Leonard." She watched Mary walk away. "I must apologise for not bringing Frederick; he wasn't up to leaving the house. His knees, they hurt him quite a bit these days," she said.

"That's quite alright. I understand Mrs Pembroke, and it's very thoughtful of you to come all this way alone to see me."

"I was out anyway. I was on roster this afternoon."

"Oh, volunteer work?"

"Yes, three times a week. I like to do my civic duty, so it's not inconvenient."

"Thank you, I'm pleased you decided to visit anyway."

She nodded and looked apprehensive.

"Is there something wrong, Mrs Pembroke?" Leonard enquired, seeing the look on her face.

"Uh, no, dear... well, actually, yes, there is. It's the reason I've come here."

Leonard's curiosity was piqued. "Can I have a nurse bring you something?" he asked.

"No, no. It's just a little difficult for me, that's all." She took off her gloves and carefully folded and aligned them neatly on her lap. "Mr Hardy, Frederick and I have not been entirely honest with you."

He noticed her proper use of his name and wished he could easily sit up, but he couldn't.

"We had a daughter in England; she was a lovely little thing and grew into a beautiful young woman. Those were happy times for us. We were poor, but life was simple, we worked hard and had each other." She turned to Leonard and smiled at the memory. "Her name was Lilly, Lilly Margaret Pembroke. She met a man, he was a good man, a hard worker, and he would have provided well for her eventually. They married, and she had to work as a seamstress. It was hard work. Her fingers were always sore and frequently bled, and her employer was unforgiving and made her work tirelessly long hours."

Leonard was puzzled and wondering where all this was leading.

"She worked so hard she eventually became ill. It was

exhaustion. She was never the strongest of children, but her work was arduous. She complained to her employer, but they told her she could either leave her job or stay and work the hours demanded by them. She had little option; they needed the money."

Leonard had an inkling of where this was heading and remained quiet. He could see Mrs Pembroke was struggling to maintain her composure and allowed her to continue.

"She fell ill and collapsed on the street outside her work where she was taken to hospital and treated by a young doctor."

"Was his name Lawrence Schrader?" asked Leonard grimly.

She nodded despondently. "After a few days, her husband, Thomas, took her home from the hospital, and she confided in him that the doctor had done unspeakable things to her. She felt dirty and tainted and was worried that her husband would always look at her differently. She was ashamed, Leonard. I don't expect you to understand this from a woman's perspective, but for Lilly, it was too much to bear. Of course, Thomas told Frederick and me. We reported what the doctor had done but could prove nothing - it was the doctor's word against that of a lowly seamstress. Two days later she...." Mrs Pembroke cleared her throat. "Two days later, she took her own life."

Leonard reached out and clasped Mrs Pembroke's hand to offer some comfort. He was moved. What a tragic and sad story!

"Frederick and I decided we would do what we could to end Schrader's vile penchant for molesting women. We believed Lily wasn't the first and wouldn't be the last, and we didn't want other girls to endure what Lilly went through. We were lucky; an inheritance saw our financial position change, and we no longer needed to work again if we didn't wish to, so we eventually followed Schrader to

New Zealand. Do you understand, Leonard?"

"Yes, Mrs Pembroke, I'm so sorry for your loss. I saw the pictures of Lilly at your home, and I'm sure you loved her very much."

"Thank you," she smiled. "Two things happened as a result of Lilly's death. Frederick decided that workers should not be abused by their employers and began to involve himself in the new Trade Union Movement. He wanted workers to have rights, and the second thing was to find a way to terminate Dr Schrader's career and put an end to his disgusting activities by bringing him to justice. I think you can surmise the rest."

"Thank you for sharing with me. I'm saddened to learn of this." Leonard shook his head in horror at what Lawrence Schrader had done.

"Frederick couldn't come here today to tell you himself; he's a proud, principled man, and he finds it impossible to communicate such sensitive things. Truth be told, he wouldn't have been able to talk to you about this without becoming emotional, and we both beg of you, please respect our wishes and be circumspect. Please tell no one. Although I understand you may wish to discuss this with your friend Miss Worthington."

"Of course, Mrs Pembroke. Does he know you are here?"

She nodded in assent, "Yes, he does. We both felt in light of what you suffered through, it would only be fair, to be honest. We want to thank you for all you've done, and we do hope justice will finally be served."

"I hope so too."

"Perhaps once you are feeling a little better, you would bring your lovely friend, Miss Worthington, and have dinner with us.

Both Frederick and I would enjoy that."

Leonard was truly moved. Mrs Pembroke's confession explained much about Mr Pembroke's involvement with Patrons of New Zealand and his dislike for Schrader. It all made sense now, but the pain this couple had suffered over the years at the hands of that man was unimaginable.

Chapter Twenty-Four

Meredith immediately sat up at the sound of someone thumping on the door. "I'll go," she offered and rushed quickly down the hall. Bridgette and Mary exchanged a knowing smile.

"Care to illuminate me with what you find amusing?" Leonard asked.

Mary leaned in closer so her voice wouldn't be overheard. "We think Meredith has a fancy for Tim Yates."

Leonard looked to Bridgette, and she nodded in agreement. "That doesn't surprise me; he's been asking about her every time I see him."

The girls laughed.

"Has anyone seen or heard from Jonathan?"

"No, I haven't seen him in weeks," offered Bridgette.

They could hear laughing emanating from the hall, but Meredith and Tim had not moved from the door and, judging from the sound, were enjoying a private moment together.

"What parlour game have you chosen for us to play tonight?" Mary asked, changing the subject.

"I thought we could begin with 'Pigeon Flies.' We haven't played that for a long time," said Bridgette.

Meredith and Tim walked into the living room together, and Tim greeted everyone warmly in his usual affable way. Once settled, after Meredith had poured him a drink, he sat back with a grin.

"Care to tell us what you are smiling about?" asked Leonard taking the bait.

"Most certainly, but first, how's the shoulder?"

Leonard still wore a sling, but periodically he'd remove his arm from it so he could exercise. "Another few weeks or so, I can remove the sling and return to a more normal way of life."

"How long has it been?" Meredith asked.

"Four weeks now. Doesn't time fly?" Leonard replied. "Now, what is this news you are dying to tell us, Tim? Speak up or forever hold your tongue." He slid forward on the settee, keen for the news.

"Oh, yes. Do you remember? You asked me to check with Inspector Gibbard about your employer, Mr Beaumont?"

"I forgot about that, yes. What did the inspector say?"

"Apparently, the gentleman at the Woodcarving and Furniture shop pays his monthly bills in cash, and all creditors visit him monthly to receive payment. It appears Mr Beaumont was not involved in any mischief."

"But the minder, the big bodyguard at the door...."

"Only protecting the cash," said Tim.

"Oh... I suppose that is a relief," Leonard replied. "At least Mr Beaumont isn't involved in underworld activities," he laughed. "And the other news I can see is eating away at you?"

Constable Yates could barely contain himself. "There has been an unfortunate bout of food poisoning at the gaol."

"Food poisoning?" queried Leonard, "How does that constitute good news?"

"Actually, it was rather critical - it was fatal."

"Are you serious?" Bridgette asked. "How do they know it was food poisoning? People do not normally die from that."

"Some forms of food poisoning can be fatal - but to die within hours..." said Mary disbelievingly.

Leonard had been silent. "Who died?"

Tim's grin vanished, and he turned to Leonard. "There were three deaths; all three men were awaiting trial. A Chinaman named Fung Ti Chu, an ex-constable William Hastings, and a Dr Lawrence Schrader."

Mary and Bridgette gasped.

"Oh dear me," stated Meredith, covering her mouth with her hands.

Leonard hadn't moved or said a word, and all eyes turned to him.

"Are you unwell, Leonard?" asked Mary in shock herself.

Everyone was silent as they waited for Leonard to respond. He was visible stunned.

"And they know with certainty it was food poisoning?" he finally asked.

"Yes, a post-mortem was performed at the prison. There was no sign of injury or foul play, and all three men had eaten the same food. They died during the night, and the bodies were discovered yesterday morning. They were not kept together and housed apart, and the attending physician who performed the post-mortem examination announced the unusual deaths were a result of tainted food."

He couldn't believe it, or perhaps he should. "That's quite something. I'm sure a few people will be extremely happy," he said.

"Except Jonathan," laughed Meredith, and they all joined in.

Mary leaned over and whispered in his ear, saying only one word. "Jun?"

Leonard looked thoughtful for a moment and shook his head.

393

"No, it wasn't him; he wouldn't do such a thing."

"Then who?"

"I don't know."

Epilogue

"Is dinner to your liking, Leonard?" asked Mrs Pembroke.

"Yes, thank you, it's delicious," he replied with his fork midway to his mouth.

Mrs Pembroke smiled and turned to Mary.

"It's a wonderful meal, thank you so much for inviting us," Mary offered. "We seldom enjoy dining like this, and we always seem to be in such a hurry these days."

"Is good to see you're finally able to use your arm again; perhaps you'll be more productive at work," offered Mr Pembroke dryly.

"Freddy! Now isn't the time," admonished Mrs Pembroke. "And yes, dear. But we don't eat like this as much as we would like either."

"If you didn't spend so much time volunteering, we probably would," grizzled Mr Pembroke with a hint of a smile as he looked to his wife.

Leonard and Mary were dinner guests at the Pembroke's. Mrs Pembroke had insisted they come for dinner once his shoulder had healed sufficiently and urged he bring Mary.

Mary sat beside Leonard, and Mr Pembroke sat at the head of the large mahogany table, while Mrs Pembroke sat at the other end in their ornate dining room.

"Oh, what volunteering do you do?" Mary asked.

"That Woman's Group sees more of her than I do," lamented Mr Pembroke. "And probably eat better too."

That explained the lack of alcohol at the table, Leonard thought. He knew the Woman's Christian Temperance Union promoted abstinence from the use of alcohol, tobacco and other drugs.

Although Mrs Pembroke had failed to fully convert her husband, he still smoked his pipe and, as evidenced, secretly still drank alcohol.

"I do what I can to help those in need," she smiled warmly at Mary. "My civic duty."

Mary nodded in understanding.

"And my penance," grizzled Mr Pembroke.

"So you assist with meals?" asked Leonard, ignoring Mr Pembroke's jibe.

"The Woman's Christian Temperance Union's latest crusade is all about eating healthily and consuming pure food," stated Mr Pembroke. "Then, along with fine cuisine, you throw into the mix their objectives to see prisons reformed, and what do you get? Prisoners eating better than we do!"

"Oh, that's not true, Frederick, and you know it."

Mary laughed.

Leonard was cutting a piece of meat and froze. With slow deliberation, he turned to face Mrs Pembroke as the realisation dawned on him. All the details fell into place. The book in the living room titled *Venenum Hortus - A Poisonous Garden,* Mrs Pembroke's volunteer service helping prepare meals for the prisoners, and of course, she also had access to them. Above all - she had a motive.

"Leonard?" whispered Mary in concern as she saw the look on his face.

Mrs Pembroke turned away from her husband and met his gaze. She knew he'd discovered her secret. Her sparkling blue eyes were cold. Gone was the congenial ageing wife of a newspaper reporter. The hairs on Leonard's arms stood on end as he looked into her face.

The End

Author's Notes

This novel is a work of fiction; any similarity to persons living or dead is coincidental and unintentional.

Even New World countries like New Zealand, with a relatively short European history, have significant chronicled events that remain veiled in the shadows of social injustice. Notwithstanding past and ongoing disputes with New Zealand's native Māori, Chinese people suffered too.

No offence is intended or implied at the use of the word Oriental when referring to Asians. In context and during this period, the term Oriental was applied to describe people of Asian descent.

Initially brought to New Zealand to work in the gold fields, Chinese men were touted as being hard-working and law-abiding. By 1881, there were reportedly 4,995 Chinese men working in New Zealand and only 9 Chinese women. Needless to say, concerns were raised by The Woman's Christian Temperance Union, who felt women were in danger and could fall victim to the immoral conduct of men seeking more than friendly companionship.

As the demand for gold miners decreased, anti-Chinese sentiment grew, and some people even suggested that a conspiracy existed to overrun New Zealand with 'Coolie-Slaves.'

Organisations like the Anti-Chinese Association, the Anti-Chinese League, the Anti-Asiatic League and the White New Zealand League grew from fear and existed in opposition to Chinese immigration. These legitimate societies enjoyed public support from politicians, community leaders, respected statesmen and collectively wielded considerable influence. They applied pressure on the Government to effect change, and in response, the Government introduced the Chinese Immigrants Act of 1881.

In 1878, William Hutchinson MHR (Member of the House of Representatives) was quoted as saying at a meeting organised by Wellington's Mayor that Chinese workers were *'a debasing and demoralising influence'* and that *'any attempt to swamp the labour market with an inferior race should be resisted.'*

But these sentiments weren't just limited to a few. In 1879, ex-New Zealand Governor, Sir George Grey, presented a memo to Parliament on the subject of Chinese immigration. He saw New Zealand's role in the South Pacific as pivotal in maintaining racial purity. An extract from his memorandum reads in part: *'No possible chance should be allowed to arise of the European population being over-borne, or even to any extent interfered with, by a people of an inferior degree of civilisation."* And others shared a similar outlook. Opportunities for the public to voice their concerns were plentiful and anti-Chinese literature circulated. Except for the venue and time of the meeting, the leaflet handed to Leonard by the White New Zealand League was a word-for-word copy of an actual advertisement of that time.

While some opponents of Chinese immigration focused on 'Racial Purity' as William Hutchinson MHR and Governor Grey publicly detailed, I surmise that initially, those organisations were thus motivated and existed to protect the jobs of European workers in New Zealand, and felt this overlapped perfectly with the objectives of the Trade Union Movement.

Times were tough, and around the same time in England, the Trade Unionist Movement first began to raise awareness of the plight of unskilled general workers who suffered with little or no rights at the pleasure of their employer's demands. It seemed feasible that I could exercise my writer's prerogative and create a fictional secretive society that bridged the racist organisations with the fledgling New Zealand Trade Union movement; I called them 'Patrons of New Zealand.'

With all the negative pressure Chinese immigrants were receiving, it should be no surprise that they formed their own organisations, some secretive, others not.

'Chee Kung Tong,' translated to 'Hall of Universal Justice', is styled as Chinese Freemasonry, but that is where any similarity with its English counterpart ends. The Tong likely provided group political and religious assistance to single Chinese males and individual support when needed. Indeed, mystery surrounds these organisations, but in 'A Sinister Consequence', I've detailed Chee Kung Tong as a peaceful Chinese community organisation uninvolved in any criminal activity.

A century of gentrification has impacted Wellington's old 'Chinatown' area. When walking down present-day Haining or Frederick Streets, it is difficult to imagine the area dominated by Chinese culture as it was 140+ years ago. The opium dens, gambling halls and teashops have all disappeared; nothing remains of this once colourful area except multiple occupancy dwellings.

Wellington's great fire of 1879 was not caused by the reactive aggression of Constable Hastings at the Royal Oak Hotel, but instead, it was thought to have started in the dome, which was used for interior lighting, atop the neighbouring Imperial Opera House. The extent of the damage is, as I describe, and tragically destroyed 30 buildings covering an estimated 10 acres of land. Amazingly there was no reported loss of life.

At first, it was believed the Royal Oak Hotel would be spared, but after the adjoining Wesleyan Church and school house caught fire, the rain of sparks and flaming debris were too much, and the hotel was quickly alight and eventually razed to the ground. An estimated 13,000 Wellingtonians witnessed the spectacle that evening.

Constructed mainly by prisoners, Wellington's impressive new hospital was opened in 1881 and contained four wards. It is difficult to truly understand by today's standards what it was like to be a nurse during that time. Notwithstanding the role of the Surgeon Superintendent, the matron ruled supreme in a clearly defined hierarchical environment. She was responsible for all nursing staff, porters and attendants, domestic help, money, valuables and dispensing alcohol to patients. Hours were long, and senior nurses were graciously permitted to leave the hospital weekly on Sundays from 2:30 pm to 10:00 pm. Nurses were committed to an honourable and demanding profession and can only be admired.

Within the framework of this novel, I strayed from accuracy and altered the nurse's role to suit the context of the plot. However, when possible, I maintained historical authenticity with Wellington Hospital, especially in describing the wards. Yes, there was carpet on the floor.

The condition of 'depression' or 'melancholia' as it was referred to, was considered a mental disease that could lead to insanity, and it was normal practice to admit a patient with this condition to a lunatic asylum.

Mount View Lunatic Asylum was situated where 'Government House,' the official residence of New Zealand's Governor General, is now located, opposite the Basin Reserve in Wellington and approximately 1.4 km from Wellington Hospital. It seemed a natural and obvious choice for Bridgette to be admitted there.

Sexual abuse of women was prevalent then, as it is today and I find it abhorent when little is done to bring offenders to justice. Sweeping any form of sexuxual misconduct under the rug and pretending it doesnt exist only empowers the guilty - the victims suffer regardless.

Another Leonard Hardy novel, *A Questionable Virtue,* is on the way.

Thank you,
Paul W. Feenstra

Other books by
Paul W. Feenstra
Published by Mellester Press

Boundary

The Breath of God (Book 1 in Moana Rangitira series)

For Want of a Shilling (Book 2 in Moana Rangitira series)

Gunpowder Green

Into the Shade

Falls Ende short story eBooks
1. The Oath
2. Courser
3. The King

Falls Ende full length novels.
1. Falls Ende – Primus (eBooks 1,2 & 3)
2. Falls Ende – Secundus
3. Falls Ende – Tertium
4. Falls Ende – Quartus
5. Falls Ende – Quintus

Leonard Hardy Series
A Sinister Consequence
A Questionable Virtue - Coming soon.

Lightning Source UK Ltd.
Milton Keynes UK
UKHW041948311022
411431UK00012B/58/J